WEDDING NIGHT

It was quite late that night before Juliet was allowed to leave the wickiup. All smiles and giggles, the women came to escort her. The women fussed over her, straightened her clothing, slipped several beaded bracelets over each wrist, and poked at her hair. When her appearance finally satisfied them, they fastened a soft narrow piece of leather over her eyes as a blind-fold and led her outside amid a gale of laughter.

The delicious scent of roasting meat assaulted her nostrils. To her left, a fire crackled. As the women led her around it, she could feel its heat. People jostled her on every side. Finally, the little procession came to a standstill, and someone lifted Juliet's hand and held it out. Another hand—warm and strong—clasped hers; at the same moment, her blindfold was removed.

She found herself facing Noah—a clean-shaven, handsome Noah dressed as she was in a soft, buttery buckskin with elaborate fringe. His eyes twinkled as he gazed down at her. "I think we are being married," he said, grinning at her.

They stood looking at each other, unsure of what to do next, until the translator came pushing through the crowd. Like nearly everyone else, he was in a jovial mood. "This . . . ," he said, pointing to the wickiup in front of where they stood. "You wickiup. Belong Sha-man Woman and Red-Hair now."

KATHARINE KINCAID

PROMISE ME HEAVEN

ZEBRA BOOKS
KENSINGTON PUBLISHING CORP.

ZEBRA BOOKS are published by

Kensington Publishing Corp.
475 Park Avenue South
New York, NY 10016

First Printing: October, 1993

Printed in the United States of America

For Joyce, my sister-in-law and friend,
with thanks for sharing the treasures of the desert.
Wishing you and Tom romance always . . .

Prologue

Ancient Greece
401 B.C.

The white bull stood motionless among the silver-leafed trees of the olive grove. His mysterious, all-knowing eyes watched me intently, and I knew he was no ordinary animal used to pull a cart or breed stupid, dull creatures even a child could manage. . . . No, this was a magnificent beast whose power emanated from every sculpted muscle and faintly throbbing vein. His white skin shimmered with a silvery iridescence. His eyes glowed. Silent and majestic, he commanded the grove, compelling me to come to him.

Fear rippled down my spine. 'Twas said the gods assumed the shape of familiar creatures when they deigned to visit mortals, for it was forbidden to look directly upon a god or goddess. At best, a mortal might be blinded by the magnificence of the deity; at worst, the experience would result in death. . . . Could the white bull be a god descended from Mount Olympus? But which god? Surely, not Zeus! And what could he possibly want with me, a maiden of the lowest echelons of the aristocracy, one soon to wed a young man of only slightly less modest origins?

I wished the bull would go away—or that I had not needed to venture into the grove on this particular morning. I had come to fetch water from the sacred spring

7

on the other side of the twisted old trees, for as custom dictated, on this day before my wedding, I must bathe in the holy waters. I had also hoped to gather leaves and wildflowers to fashion a garland for the ceremony.

Carefully, I set down the loutrophorus, *the precious ceremonial vase used to carry the water. My mother would be furious if the vase were accidentally broken. Even now, at such a moment, her warnings drummed in my ears: "If you break the sacred vase, you will destroy all chance of future happiness. Do not disregard my words, Daughter, as you have disregarded so much else I have tried to teach you. If you rebel in this, you will regret it until your dying day."*

Yes, I was most careful of the loutrophorus. *In my heart, I had never really been rebellious. I had only been . . . determined. And I had won what I wanted most from life—the love of a man who cherished me for my mind as well as my body, a rare thing from all I had observed in those around me, most especially my own mother. Today of all days, everything must be perfect, performed precisely according to plan and tradition, unmarred by any unusual or evil occurrence. . . . Yet here stood this great white bull, blocking my path through the grove and watching me with his dark, compelling eyes.*

Come to me, *a voice suddenly said. Startled, I glanced about, searching for the source of the deep, reverberating command. An eerie silence had descended upon the grove and the grassy meadow in which it stood. Gone were the drone of honeybees and the birdsong that had gladdened the morning. Even the sigh of the sweet-smelling breeze as it rustled the silvery leaves had disappeared. I was abruptly conscious of the rich scent of the earth, tinged with something musky and sensual that tantalized and teased my nostrils, making me feel suddenly light-headed.*

Come to me, *the voice repeated, and I realized it was*

8

the bull who spoke, though his mouth had not opened, nor had he so much as swished his long, silver tail.

"Who are you?" I asked, my voice wavering, sounding absurdly loud in the ominous silence.

I am Zeus, the bull said, his awesome presence flowing over and through me, leaving no doubt he was who he claimed to be—Zeus, the emperor of the skies, the king of all the lesser gods, Zeus, the all-powerful, the ruler of the universe.

I trembled and shook like a vine buffeted by the wind. I wanted to flee, but there was nowhere to run, no place to hide. I had grown up hearing tales of Zeus's power— and his attraction for mortal women. According to legend, he occasionally took humans as lovers, appearing to them in various guises and even tricking them when they sought to resist him.

"What do you want with me?" I boldly inquired, unable to credit that he had come to me because I possessed any unusual appeal. In her zeal to mold me into the perfect daughter, the peerless future wife—what all Greece demanded a young maiden to be—my mother had taken pains to assure me that I was no dazzling beauty. I should therefore embrace conformity and cease challenging the way things were.

Only my betrothed had thus far found me beautiful, and his opinion hardly signified since we had befriended each other as children meeting secretly in my parents' vineyard. Jason, named after the famed Jason who stole the golden fleece, was wonderfully prejudiced in my favor, a fact that continued to amaze both my parents. They had finally accepted this wedding, but they were not happy about it. I had, after all, betrayed them by rejecting the young man they had chosen.

I have come to take you away, the bull answered. I will bear you to Crete upon my back, and there we will play together and be happy. There also will you bear my children who will then be immortal, part god and part human.

His words made me shiver with dread. Incredible as it seemed, I had caught the god's lustful eye, and he would force me to go away with him, lie with him, and bear his children. When he had tired of me, he would abandon me to the jealous rage of his wife and sister, the goddess, Hera . . . Hera of the beautiful white arms; Hera, sometimes called Hera the Cruel, because of the torments she devised for Zeus's lovers and the children borne of his unions with mortals.

"And what of Hera?" In my rising panic, I did not care if I angered him. "I know the tales. You once took a princess named Europa to Crete, and Hera saw to it she never returned. Another time, you fell in love with a woman named Io and turned her into a white cow to hide her from your wife. But Hera found out about her anyway. First, she sent Argus, her hundred-eyed servant to harass poor, tethered Io. Then she sent a gadfly to chase and sting her all the way to Egypt."

The god's voice boomed in my head. This time, she will not discover I have taken a lover. Come away with me, pretty child. You are innocent, beautiful, and spirited—a fit vessel for a god's passion. I will pleasure you as you have never known pleasure . . . and through our children, you will live forever.

"No," I whispered. Terror rose in my breast, threatening to overwhelm me. I fought it with a desperate resolve. I had not come this far and dared this much, to lose it all now, at the very last moment. "I am betrothed to another. Tomorrow, we will wed. I will accept no other man but him."

Need I remind you? I am no man, but a god! And when I have borne you away to Crete, I will change into the most handsome youth you could ever desire. In my arms, you will forget your betrothed. I will teach your mouth to sigh only for my kisses, your body to ache for my caresses . . . There will be no lover for you but me. . . ."

"No," I insisted, backing slowly away. "You cannot have me. I belong to another."

I thought of my "other" and reached out to him from the depths of my being. For me there would never be anyone else. He alone accepted me the way I was and cherished what I had striven to become—a whole person, not a fragment, a shadow, a dull chattel fit only for breeding children. Unlike most men, he did not consider me unfit for intelligent conversation or—merciful Hestia!—an opinion of my own on any subject save domestic matters, and even then, an uninformed one.

I will have you, *he disputed, his eyes flashing red with anger.* You cannot escape Zeus. If you run from me, I will hurl thunderbolts into your path. I will make the ground shake beneath your feet. I will pursue you to the ends of the earth. And when I catch you, you will lie down and do as I command.

He wanted me to be meek and docile—obedient in all things! He embodied all I thought I had escaped. Yet even as I turned to run, I knew he spoke the truth. He could do all that he threatened and more . . . There existed no one to whom I might appeal—except, perhaps, Hera, the jealous goddess herself.

"Hera!" I cried. "Hera, save me!"

Behind me, a peacock rose up in the tangled grass and spread its brilliant turquoise and dazzling green plumage. Was not the peacock Hera's symbol? In my panic, I could not remember. I fled past it, running as fast as I could. Thunder rumbled overhead. Clouds boiled out of the sky to obscure the sun and darken the meadow. My heart pounded with dread. This had to be a dream—a nightmare. It could not be true. Could not be happening . . . but I feared it was *happening.*

Stop, you rebellious and obstinate mortal! How dare you oppose me and flee my presence! From whence comes this strength to defy me? Stop, I command you!

It was not the first time I had defied authority; I had

been defying it all my young life . . . no, not defying, actually, but only struggling to be my true self . . . what I was meant to be. I ran faster still, willing my shaky legs to carry me to safety—if safety existed anywhere in the universe. The ground heaved beneath my feet. Clouds enveloped me. The thick, cloying vapor clogged my lungs and made every breath a searing agony.

"Hera! Hera!" I gasped, wondering if the proud, haughty goddess was laughing at me instead of trying to help. Yet she was a woman, too, subject to the whims of men. Surely, she understood . . .

A blinding light split the sky overhead, followed by a terrible boom! Zeus was hurling his thunderbolts.

I stopped in my tracks, suddenly blinded, uncertain which way to turn. The air crackled. On the back of my neck, the fine hairs rose. A second shaft of light stabbed the ground near my feet. The soles of my stout leather sandals sizzled and curled up around my toes. A burnt odor filled my nostrils. I swayed and toppled, falling heavily upon my side.

"I am going to die!" I sobbed, rolling over and clutching at the scorched ground. "I am going to die, and I will never see him again!"

I tried to summon Jason's features one last time— my beloved Jason! But all I could see behind my burning lids was the image of the great, white bull with his angry red eyes . . . If he did not kill me with his lightning bolts, he would gore me with his terrible horns— or else he would ravish me where I lay, panting and helpless . . .

Oh, Hera! Let this nightmare end! I earnestly beg you! Let me awaken to find my beloved Jason bending over me, smiling and teasing me for my fears!

Lightning bolts rent the earth all around me; thunder boomed. The clouds swirled over and around me . . . Far off in the distance, a voice called my name. It was trying to tell me something, but the words were muffled and unclear. I wanted to answer but could not make a sound. I feared I was dying . . . my body spin-

ning, spinning . . . hurtling through space, crashing through time . . . then, blackness. Utter blackness. The end of everything . . . the complete destruction of the world I knew.

Chapter One

Arizona Territory
June, 1885

The storm was almost upon him. Forks of lightning lit the greenish underbellies of churning black clouds scudding down from the mountaintops. The wind carried the heady, damp smell of rain. He had thought that in this land of desert, mountains, and steep, rocky canyons, it stormed so rarely as to be an unusual occurrence—yet the occasional dark pine forest, clear running stream, clump of cottonwoods, and grassy plain gave evidence of the fury bearing down upon him now.

Noah "Copper" McCord, eastern newspaper reporter and would-be biographer of the famed Apache, Geronimo, just hoped the storm would reach him in time to save his life.

Behind him, the enraged whoop and holler of his pursuers signaled they were drawing closer. On either side of his mount's galloping hooves, sprays of gravel and metallic pings told him they meant business. The poor animal beneath him was doing its damnedest to carry him to safety, but could scarcely compete against the fresher horses of the ranchers bent on catching him.

Glancing over his shoulder, Noah spotted big Ben Mellock at the head of the angry riders. It had been

Ben's suggestion to string him up from the nearest *saguaro* cactus and leave him for buzzard bait. Another man had found the incriminating article Noah had clipped from the *Boston Globe* in his gear, but it had been Ben who organized the lynch party chasing him up the mountainside.

Urging his mount to greater effort, Noah cursed his own stupidity. He ought never to have brought that article west with him—or left his journal lying about. Hell, he had thought the crude, boorish, Indian-hating settlers of the Arizona Territory mostly illiterate! Schools were primitive and few; learning to ride and shoot were far more important to them than "readin', writin', an' figurin'," and Noah finally understood why.

Damn that article anyway! In both it and the journal, he had written that the whites had only themselves to blame for creating "The Apache Problem." Geronimo's thirst for vengeance had been fed by white men who cheated and lied to him, murdered his people, including women and children, and stole his land. In sharp contrast to frontier newspaper accounts blaming everything on the Apache and claiming "the only good Indian was a dead Indian," Noah had sought to tell the truth of the matter: that the whites were largely responsible for the murder and mayhem visited upon them over the last two decades of the Apache Wars.

Shortly after the article appeared, drawing a storm of protests even in Boston, Noah had come west to get Geronimo's story firsthand before the old renegade died on the San Carlos Indian reservation where he had been unjustly confined. Upon arriving in Arizona, Noah had learned that Geronimo had escaped and fled into the mountains, leaving the entire territory in a state of uproar and hysteria.

Once again, the settlers—the ranchers especially—feared for their lives and property. What they expected a sixty-year-old man accompanied by the last of the

16

decimated Chiricahua and Warm Springs tribes to do with no horses, no weapons, and no food supplies, eluded Noah . . . yet the settlers were clearly alarmed—and all too eager to vent their ire on a presumptuous journalist newly arrived at Fort Apache to interview the Indian they had come to regard as the Devil Incarnate.

As a shot whined by his ear, Noah hunched low in the saddle and urged his faltering mount to greater speed up the mountainside. A part of him stood back from the scene, unmoved by his rising terror and the certainty he would soon be dead; the cold-blooded reporter in him idly wondered who would write his obituary back home—and if anyone would notice or care that he had disappeared from the face of the earth. The girl he had left behind with vague assurances that as soon as he had interviewed Geronimo and satisfied his craving for adventure, he would hurry back to marry might be interested, but he had no family left alive, and aside from his editor, very few friends.

Noah McCord—"Copper" to his readers and most everyone else—had always been too busy, too driven, too consumed with ambition and the lust to topple icons, to develop lasting relationships among either sex. Emily Carstairs was besotted—temporarily, he was convinced—and too good for him besides. She did not count, but Matt Potter would surely miss him. . . . Matt was his mentor, his advisor whose advice he usually ignored, his defender, his teacher . . . his one, true friend who stood by him no matter how many scrapes he got into or enemies he made.

"So long as you always tell the truth, son, I'll back you up," Matt had told him as a young, green journalist, and that was Noah's one consolation and singular pride: He *had* always told the truth.

Now, he was probably going to die for it—deservedly, many might say. Not only had he stirred up a tempest where the Apaches were concerned, but before he left Boston his last story had been a revelation of political bribery and corruption involving one of Boston's most proper, blue-blooded families. . . . In the wake of the furor this most recent exposé had created, Matt had finally conceded it might be prudent for Noah to leave town for a while, lest he turn up dead one night in an alley. So Noah had struck out for the West to gather source material for the biography of the legendary, bloodthirsty Geronimo, the last of the Apache warriors, whose fierce fight for freedom had captured Noah's admiration, imagination, and respect.

Too bad I never got to meet you, Geronimo, Noah's objective self said to his terrified one. *And too bad I never told Matt how much I appreciate and value his friendship.*

Bullets were ricocheting off the rocks now, creating a cacaphony of sound drowned out only by the boom of thunder which seemed to shake the mountainside itself.

"Rain, damn you!" Noah shouted, lifting his head to study the churning clouds.

Never had he seen a sky quite like this one—as green and murky and ominous as swamp water. When and if it rained, the downpour would completely obliterate him; it would also make firing a rifle or carbine impossible. He could feel his horse stumbling and wheezing from the effort of climbing the steep, rocky terrain. Rain was the only thing that could save him now . . . and Noah prayed for it as he had never prayed for anything in his life.

He forgot that he did not believe in prayer or the existence of an Almighty Being. He forgot that in his deepest, cynical heart, he considered man solely responsible for his own survival. . . . It was kill or be killed. Fight or die. In the battle of life, he had always been a fighter, counting the pen mightier than the sword . . . until now. Revealed at last as totally inept in basic survival skills—and a coward, to boot—

cocky, devil-may-care Copper McCord galloped blindly up the mountainside and frantically prayed for rain.

Something struck his thigh and skittered along it, leaving a crease of white-hot agony. He gritted his teeth against the cry that burst from his lungs and concentrated on keeping his seat aboard his struggling horse. His modest riding skills were not up to this grueling pace, especially when he could no longer grip with both knees. . . . The pain was too intense.

"God damn it, *rain!*" he yelled, thumping along like a sack of grain.

A wet, cold drop struck his sweaty cheek. He grinned, exhilarated by the feel of it and the sense that his luck was turning. A moment later, lightning shattered the sky and made his hair stand straight up on his head.

"You fool!" he shouted to the God in whom he did not believe. "That was too damn close for comfort!"

His cry died in the crack of thunder that struck like a whiplash over his head as the rain he had prayed for finally arrived. The clouds opened, and out poured a solid wall of water. Instantly drenched to the skin, he could not help but laugh. It was all so grimly amusing.

"Sons of bitches, I hope you drown!" he screamed at his pursuers.

A second bolt of lightning knocked him off his horse. His head struck the ground with a sickening thump and he dimly realized that one foot was caught in the stirrup, and the horse was still galloping up the mountainside, dragging him behind it.

"This is it, Copper," he told himself. "You're finally getting what people say you've had coming to you since the day your first article appeared in print."

Every bone in his body seemed to be breaking. His shirt and pants were ripping to shreds. Only the rain felt good as it pelted him full in the face *What a way to go,* he thought, grimacing at the irony of it. Then his head banged something hard and unyielding, and blackness descended.

He awoke to a cauldron of pain and the sensation that he was frying. Oh God, the heat! He knew without opening his eyes that the sun was beating down upon him—the merciless Arizona sun that at this time of year could cook a man's brains in less than an hour. He had to wake up, find shade and water, check for bullet wounds and broken bones . . . see if he was still alive. It did not seem possible. This had to be the part of hell reserved for know-it-all journalists foolish enough to risk their lives in pursuit of a good story.

He raised one eyelid and groaned from the effort, deciding it might be easier to take stock of his moving parts from a prone position, rather than an upright one. First, he wiggled his toes—sore but still there. Then he flexed his ankles. The left one was merely stiff; the right hurt like hell at the slightest movement. Gingerly, he lifted throbbing arms, hands, and fingers to explore his upper legs. Something wet and sticky was oozing from the burning crease in his right thigh. He doubted he could sit up, much less hike however many miles it was to civilization.

Fort Apache, from whence he had set out, lay somewhere to the north, but traveling in that direction might mean another nasty encounter with Ben Mellock—assuming big Ben and his foaming-at-the-mouth settlers had survived the storm the same as he had. They could be looking for him now, searching the mountainside for whatever was left of him. He *must* get up.

Gritting his teeth against the agony of moving and keeping his eyes squinted against the glare of sunlight, he maneuvered himself into a sitting position. He had been lying on a rocky incline, and the slate and shale surface beneath his hands was hot enough to sear a steak. All around him, marching up the mountainside, were incredibly-shaped rocks and boulders, large ones balanced precariously atop small ones, forming spires, pinnacles, columns, battlements, and towers. In between the fantastic formations, an astonishing variety of plant life managed to poke through the red soil and scattered stones. On a bush he dimly recognized as a *manzanita,* a lizardlike creature, striped with yellow and brown, flicked its whiplike tail and regarded him with beady eyes.

"What are *you* looking at?" he growled, secretly glad to find he was not completely alone and abandoned in this eerie, hostile environment. "Never seen a half-dead, dumb-ass reporter before? . . . Well, look your fill. You'll never see a dumber one again. I wish to God I knew what possessed me to stow that clipping in my gear, and then to let another man get within ten feet of it."

The lizard's only response was to flick his tongue at a fly rising from the mess on Noah's thigh. Several flies were buzzing around the blood encrusted wound that ran like a gash across the top of his right leg. Noah waved them away, but they were persistent and refused to leave. He sighed in exasperation tinged with hopelessness.

"If I don't die of sunstroke, I'll probably expire of gangrene—but first, they'll have to cut off my leg."

Who "they" might be he had no idea, but the very thought made him shudder. He shooed the flies away with weary determination and bent over the wound to study it more closely. It was a definite crease, but not terribly deep. Reaching for the soiled, red bandana still knotted at his throat, he removed it and retied it around the wound to deter the flies. The makeshift bandage would have to do until he located water and could cleanse the injury. . . . Maybe he would even get lucky and find his horse and the gear he had hurriedly packed while the sneaky culprit guilty of rifling through his belongings was busy telling big Ben what he had found.

In his gear, Noah remembered, was a small bottle of whisky. Half could be poured on his wound and half consumed to ease his terrible thirst and the hammering in his head. . . . But he would never find anything if he did not get moving.

Leaning heavily on the nearest boulder, Noah managed to get to his feet. Once there, he had to conquer dizziness before taking his first step. His bruised and battered body protested even the mildest of movements, but he was heartened to discover that his bones seemed capable of supporting his weight. His ankles were shaky, and he feared his right one might be broken, but it did not buckle or collapse beneath him. Maybe he had merely sprained it. Deciding that it would be hard to pull off his boots over the swelling—and even harder to get them back on—he resolved not to remove them until he reached water.

Glancing about the boulder-strewn mountainside, he anxiously scanned the scene below and tried to determine what time it was. It had to be approximately noon, for the light was dead white, bleaching the rough terrain to the color of old bones. Heat shimmered in waves rising from rocky crevices. Overhead, a turkey vulture coasted on a current of air, casting a dark shadow below as it passed by. No other living creature—neither man nor beast—appeared for as far as the eye could see. In the distance glimmered the pale green of some river-watered plain or desert grassland favored by the ranchers for cattle, but the area was too far away to do him much immediate good.

Closer to hand, the mountain vegetation displayed its adaptiveness by changing at each level of elevation: desert beargrass, yucca, and *agave* or what was sometimes called the century plant far below, *manzanita* and oak at his level, piñon, ponderosa pine, and cypress farther above, firs and aspens at the very top. The sky was intensely blue, the sun blindingly-golden, the mountaintops fantastically-shaped—as if their creator had been in a whimsical mood on the day he fashioned them.

The scene stirred Noah's soul with its elemental beauty, but he could not help wishing he knew exactly where he was. The central part of the Arizona Territory held a multitude of mountain ranges, while the Sierra Madre dominated northern Mexico. Unfortunately, no signs were posted to identify one range from another. Noah thought he might be in the Chiricahuas, south of Fort Apache and east of Tucson, but he could not be certain. After a time riding through this wild country, one mountain range became indistinguishable from another, although he did not think he was likely to forget this one, since up close, it differed so much from others.

As a newcomer to Arizona and a greenhorn Easterner, he had more or less blindly followed the ranchers. Unhappy with the army's lack of success in recapturing the Apache leader, big Ben and his men had gone out on their own to catch Geronimo, who was said to know the various mountain ranges as intimately as the settlers knew their own ranches and farms. Noah had long ago given up keeping track of where they were.

He had joined the group on the pretext of being as eager as any frightened settler to apprehend the wily old Indian and end the Apache threat once and for all—but actually he had hoped to simply be there to record the capture and talk with Geronimo before he was reimprisoned. It had not taken him long to discover that the irate settlers had no intention of permitting Geronimo's return to the reservation; they wanted him dead, and for all Noah knew, so did the army. . . . Geronimo symbolized a way of life that no longer existed for the Apache; so long as the old man lived, there would be Indians ready to ride the warpath once more in hopes of regaining their freedom—a freedom which included raiding ranches for horses and cattle, and killing all witnesses.

Noah recalled all this as he gazed down upon a landscape that looked as if man had never set foot on it, much less tried to conquer it. He had some notion of the four directions, but no idea how to get to Tucson, Fort Apache, or indeed any other civilized place. The settlers themselves and even the army relied upon paid Indian scouts to guide them through the countless arroyos, canyons, and broad stretches of waterless desert. Considering that Noah was a city man, born and bred in the East—not a rancher, farmer, or soldier—he felt as helpless as a child lost in an endless forest.

"Well, Copper, you wanted adventure, you got it," he mused aloud. "What I wouldn't give right now for something to wet my mouth besides spit."

He ran his tongue over cracked, dry lips, but the little saliva he had left failed to moisten them. It was time to start walking, but in which direction—up the mountain or down, left or right? Shading his eyes against the sun—his hat had been lost during his hasty exit from the ranchers' last campsite—he spied a shelf of rock jutting out from the mountain some distance above him. The climb would be steep, but from that elevated vantage point, he ought to be able to spot any horses or humans moving through the countryside below. With any luck, he might see his own horse grazing on a patch of greenery, calmly waiting for him to catch up with it.

A second shelf of rock above the first offered the hope of shade, for the two shelves together formed an almost cavelike structure in which he could rest until late afternoon when the sun was not quite so hot. With the ledge as his goal, he felt better about his circumstances and even managed to convince himself that as soon as he reached that high-up haven, he could better plan his next move.

Keeping a close watch among the rocks for snakes, scorpions, and tarantulas—he had been repeatedly warned about them—he began the slow, painful ascent under the broiling sun. After every few steps, he had to stop, catch his breath, and convince his aching muscles to continue. He had always considered himself reasonably fit. Women often exclaimed over his height and strength as compared to other men, and he had accepted the compliments as only his due. Now, his own weakness appalled him, and he wished for the small stature and catlike grace of the Indian scouts, who could clamber over anything without raising a sweat.

With an almost pathetic yearning, he longed for his hat to protect his skin from the sun. Being a redhead—albeit a coppery one, not a true red—his skin was fairer than most men's, and he burned more easily. The sun's glare also seemed to bother him more than it did most people; his eyes were brown, not blue, but for some unknown reason, he had always had a greater sensitivity to bright light than most people.

He wondered if the ladies of Boston—even Emily Carstairs—would find him handsome at this moment. "Handsome rogue!" or "Charming devil!" were the usual comments he overheard whenever he attended some social event, but he did not feel handsome, charming, strong, manly, or "the catch of the town," as he labored up the mountainside today. Rather, he felt weak, ill, dizzy, and disoriented, as if the entire experience were a bad dream or a sick joke his enemies had succeeded in playing upon him.

He wished he could lie down on clean white sheets and sleep for a week, awakening only long enough to drink chilled lemonade, eat cold watermelon, and make love to a woman who smelled of lavender and freshly-baked bread. Funny, what a man thought about while he dragged his weary, bruised body up the side of a mountain in the middle of nowhere. At any moment, he could get bit by a snake, stung by a scorpion, shot full of arrows, blasted by a rifle, or fall and break his leg. . . . But all he could think about were

25

his most basic needs and desires: eating, drinking, and . . .

His hand slipped as he was pulling himself upward between two boulders, and he sprawled on his face and slid several body lengths back down the mountainside.

"Copper, you stupid son of a buffalo," he muttered, spitting out gravel. "Think of what you're trying to do, instead of imagining yourself humping some poor female. The least you could do is be loyal to Emily who doesn't have the good sense to realize what a bastard you are and always will be."

He clung to the rock face a moment, trying to conjure Emily's pert features and earnest smile. The effort proved too exhausting. He never had been able to picture her in bed; that was probably the trouble with their halfhearted relationship. He was a man of deep, turbulent passions, and Emily did not appeal to him in that way. She was more like the sister he had never had. He thought of her fondly, but without the dark, hungry stirring of the ravenous beast within. For her part, Emily got red-faced and breathless whenever they kissed, but she never clung to him the way some women did, and he never tried to take advantage of her as he usually did with women. Sometimes, he wondered if he might be incapable of loving a good woman, when the bad ones were so much more tempting—and tempted.

"Get up, you dung-minded ass, or you will certainly die out here and never know the embrace of a wife or a whore again."

First, he got to his knees, then to his feet. When the world stopped tilting, he resumed climbing—advancing steadily upward, searching for the easiest means of ascent over the steep, rocky ground. It was hard going, but finally he neared the ledge. The last few feet were the most grueling, because the angle of the climb became a straight vertical. He had to find toe and finger holds, then haul himself upward by sheer force of willpower, his muscles adamantly protesting all the way.

He was shaking and winded when at last he crawled onto the rock shelf and collapsed onto his stomach. The stone felt refreshingly cool to his touch, for the ledge was indeed shaded by the overhang above it. Gratefully, he closed his eyes and rested his jaw against the coolness. When he had rested several moments, he blinked away the grit and raised his head.

Near his hand, only a hand-span from his fingertips, lay another hand—a delicate, white, feminine hand. At the end of the hand was a bare, white arm, and beyond that, the swell of a white-draped bosom.

Stiffening in shock, Noah blinked several times to clear his head; he could not believe what he was seeing. . . . Had he gone mad from the sun and the heat? Or was there really a woman lying all alone up here on the ledge beside him?

Chapter Two

If he was indeed hallucinating, it was an amazingly-realistic experience. New energy flowed through him, and he scrambled to his knees and crawled closer. A woman *was* lying on the ledge—a slender, fragile-looking creature, wearing what could only be a white nightgown, except that it was cut in a strange fashion he had never before seen on a woman, and he considered himself an expert on feminine nightwear.

The woman's throat and arms were bare, the garment held in place at the shoulders by two small, gold brooches. Extra fabric was bunched beneath her, and a red shawl of some light material skimmed her shoulders. She was lying on her back, a mass of pale brown hair—light and airy as gossamer—covering her face, concealing her features. One arm lay across her waist, and the other was outflung, the hand extended palm upward. It was the hand he had noticed when he lifted his head.

The white garment, gathered and belted at the waist, skimmed her feet, which, he was shocked to discover, sported odd-looking footgear with thick leather soles and sturdy thongs crisscrossing at her slender ankles and tied securely farther up her calves. At first, he thought she might be dead, but then he noticed the slight rise and fall of her bosom. . . . She was not dead, but asleep or unconscious.

With suddenly trembling fingers, he pushed aside

the spider's web tangle of hair, so he could see her face. Her skin was the color of milk, each feature as perfect and delicate as if it had been carved from ivory. Her lashes were the same improbable color as her hair—palest brown; they were also thick and long, lying like fans on her high, classic cheekbones. Her nose was straight, a bit long, but quite the most enchanting nose he had ever seen on a woman. Her mouth reminded him of a budded rose, the lower lip fuller than the upper, and it was temptingly tender-looking and vulnerable.

He thought she resembled a fairy princess or something painted on a Grecian urn, and for a moment, strongly suspected he was dreaming. A gold ribbon had been wound through her gossamer tresses in an obvious attempt to restrain them—but the glorious mass would not be restrained. It felt silken to his touch, and he knew her skin would feel even softer, yet he feared taking such liberties. She was almost *too* pale and perfect, as if she did not belong in the realm of mere mortals. He had never been superstitious, but his stomach muscles clenched with a strange, disquieting dread. . . . Who *was* she, and how had she gotten here?

The arduous climb to the ledge had left him more filthy and exhausted than he had been when he started out. Of course, he had started out filthy, but this young woman—girl, actually—appeared as pristine and perfect as a marble statue. Not a speck of dust or dirt marred her ivory face or immaculate gown. Only her leather sandals showed signs of wear; they looked oddly . . . burned on the bottoms of their thick soles. Amazed and incredulous, he could think of no logical explanation for how she had arrived on this desolate shelf of rock.

Chiding himself for being such a coward, he picked up her hand. It was cool and lifeless. Acting from instinct rather than decision, he began to chafe it, hoping to warm her—which was absurd, considering how hot it was, even in the shade.

"Hey, Princess. . . . Time to wake up. I don't know how long you've been sleeping or how you got here, but you need to wake up, because I need to talk to you."

He chafed her hand for several moments, and when that got no result, leaned over and tapped her cheek. He wondered if she was too close to the edge of death to come back . . . but then she suddenly stirred. Her lips parted, and a small sigh escaped them. Heartened, he tapped both cheeks, stopping just short of actually slapping her. Gradually, the color flowed back into her face, and she sighed again.

"That's it, Princess. . . . Come on. You can do it."

Her lids fluttered open, and she stared up at him in startlement. Her eyes were brown, like his, only hers were a pale, *golden* brown, and clear as a mountain stream. As he stared down at her, the thought came to him that he was gazing into the clearest, most limpid, most beautiful eyes in the entire universe.

"Jason?" she said hesitantly, her voice low and musical, like a bell chiming in the breeze.

"Noah," he responded. "Noah McCord. Though I once tried to get my mother to rename me Jason, because I wanted to have great adventures like Jason searching for the golden fleece. Then I grew up and realized there was no golden fleece and remarkably few great adventures, though I suppose this might qualify as one."

Now, why was he babbling like a fool and telling her too much about himself in the process? It had been years since he had thought of his childhood or of the strange child he had been—devouring Greek classics and imagining himself playing parts in them. He had never entrusted another living soul with that information. Indeed, he had spent much of his youth regretting—and sometimes taking pains to conceal—how "different" he was from most boys his age.

"What's your name?" he prompted, when she did

31

not respond but only gazed at him in wide-eyed perplexity.

The lovely brow furrowed. The clear eyes clouded. "I . . . I do not know," she answered. "That is, I . . . I cannot remember."

Great, he thought, a woman who's got moss where her brains ought to be. Was she ill? . . . Or just temporarily befuddled? "Well, who's Jason?" he demanded.

The brow furrowed even more. "I . . . I cannot remember that either. I know not why I mentioned the name."

Her speech was curiously formal, as if English were a second language to her, but he detected no foreign accent and found himself growing even more intrigued to learn where she had come from. "Princess, if you can't remember *who* you are, do you have any idea *where* you are?" he gruffly inquired. Perhaps she simply needed a few moments to gather her wits following whatever mishap had landed her on the ledge.

She shook her head. "I do not know this place. . . . Nor do I recognize you."

"But I must remind you of someone named Jason, or you wouldn't have mentioned his name." To hide his frustration, he offered her his hand. "Here. . . . Why don't you sit up?"

She placed her slender white hand in his, and something leaped in the pit of his stomach. Never having had that reaction merely from touching a woman's hand, Noah froze, staring with surprise into her clear, golden-brown eyes. Had it not been so unnerving, the moment would have been exciting, even sexual. He had the oddest conviction he had known this woman in the past—not just met her, but *known* her—except that he had never seen her before in his life. If he had met her, he would not have forgotten it; she was utterly unforgettable.

Very slowly, he pulled her to an upright position. Apparently oblivious to the effect she was having upon him, she gazed past him, and her eyes widened. "What

32

is this place?" she asked breathlessly. "Where are we?"

For the first time since he himself had reached the ledge, Noah noticed the view. He supposed it was breathtaking, but having already grown accustomed to the incredible beauty of the landscape, he much preferred admiring the young woman's pale, fragile loveliness to gawking at their surroundings.

Adopting a theatrical stance, he flung one arm wide to encompass all that lay before them. "This, Princess, is my kingdom. . . . Allow me to welcome you to the territory of Arizona . . . or New Mexico or Mexico, whichever the case may be."

"You are . . . a king?" she hesitantly inquired, her remarkable eyes cutting back to him. "Oh, but you are injured!"

Her hand reached out to touch his wounded thigh, which he had forgotten—as he had also forgotten his aches, bruises, thirst, and weariness. "It's nothing," he assured her. "Only a minor flesh wound."

He hoped it was minor; it had better be minor. He shuddered as her long slender fingers gently brushed the bloodstained red bandana. " 'Tis not so insignificant as you claim," she contradicted. "You have bled much. The wound should be cleaned and dressed."

"Yes," he ruefully agreed. "It should be. . . . But in order to do that, we must first find water—or at least my horse."

She raised her eyes to meet his. "You have a horse? . . . How wonderful!" From the way her face lit up, she obviously regarded horses as magical creatures.

"Had a horse," he corrected. "But you must have a horse around here someplace, too . . . How else did you get up here? A wagon could not have come this far up the mountainside. The trail is too steep and narrow. . . . And it's a bit far for you to have walked the entire distance."

"I have no horse. Horses are for men, and then only for the very rich. As for me, I . . . I . . ." she stopped, her eyes clouding with distress. When she continued, panic edged her voice. "I cannot remember how I got up here! Indeed, I cannot remember *anything!* . . . What is wrong with me? Why can I not remember?"

Gritting his teeth against the renewed throbbing in his thigh, Noah knelt beside her. "You must have some injuries, too, Princess. Let me feel your head. Perhaps there's a lump there. Maybe you slammed your head on a rock, and that's why you can't remember."

She sat very still while Noah explored her head. Spreading his fingers and combing them through the silken mass of her hair, he took pleasure in the softness of her tresses and the intimacy of the act. Gently, he parted the pale, gossamer filaments and massaged her scalp. Occasionally he brushed her fingers as she sought to help him; each time, he experienced a tingle of sensual awareness. However enjoyable the effort, neither of them discovered any lumps or swellings, and with a small, unhappy sigh, she retied the gold ribbon around the shimmering cloud of pale, shining hair.

"Just because we didn't find anything doesn't mean it isn't there. Are you dizzy?" he asked. "Have you a headache?"

"No—yes! A little, I think."

"A little what—headache or dizziness?" Loathe to take his hands from her, Noah began to massage her neck and shoulders.

"Both," she sighed as he moved around behind her and gently kneaded her shoulders. "Oh, that feels good . . . only . . ."

"Only what?" He loved the feel of her—loved touching her. Even the scent of her made him giddy; she smelled feminine and faintly flowery with a touch of lemon or some tart herb. Inhaling the delicious odor, he wondered what it would be like to bury his face in her hair and lose himself entirely.

"We should not be doing this." With a little shrug, she pushed his hand away. " 'Tis not proper."

"Proper!" he echoed indignantly. "We're stuck on a

ledge in the middle of nowhere. How can it possibly be improper when there's no one here to see us? I'm just trying to find out if you're hurt in some way."

"I am *not* hurt. . . . At least, I do not feel hurt. But *you* are. Therefore, we should be trying to do something to help you."

Exhibiting a calm determination that belied her fragile appearance, she rose to her feet, swayed there a moment, and would have fallen if Noah had not been close enough to clamp an arm around her waist and hold her upright. "Be careful!" he snapped. "If you don't move slowly, you're likely to collapse and hurt yourself worse than you already are!"

"I will not collapse," she insisted with more grit than logic. "I . . . I want to see if I can walk."

Annoyed by her eagerness to avoid his touch, Noah could not resist a verbal jab. "I sure as hell hope you can, Princess, because you're a long way from home, wherever it is."

She took a single unsteady step, then paused a moment, her eyes glistening with sudden tears. "Yes, 'tis most unkind of you to remind me of my problem. . . . I do not know where I came from, or how I got here, or even my name, do I? Undoubtedly, I will prove a great burden to you. Perhaps you should simply leave me to fend for myself. I am not your responsibility. Why should you concern yourself with whether or not I am hurt?"

Torn between anger and anxiety, he settled for contrition. "Hey, I'm sorry I snapped at you. . . . I bet you'll remember in no time. Meanwhile, I'll just call you Princess. For all we know, that *could* be your name. You sure as hell look like a princess."

"Princess," she murmured. "Somehow, I do not believe I am a princess, nor are you a king. A king would have more elegant clothing and better manners."

"All right, so I'm not a king. I'm a reporter, and reporters aren't known for their elegant attire or dainty manners."

"What do you report—and to whom?"

He snorted at her odd questions. "I write stories for a newspaper, or at least I did. At the moment, I'm working on a book. No, actually I'm stuck on a ledge with a very strange female who asks ridiculous questions."

"Now it is your turn to forgive *me*," she apologized. " 'Tis rude of me to pry into your personal affairs."

Moving away from him, she stepped nearer to the edge of the ledge—too near for his peace of mind. He grabbed hold of the gauzy, red scarf draped across her shoulders. "Whoa! That's far enough. We don't want you tripping and falling into space."

The scarf came away in his hand, and she took another step before she stopped, her attention once again riveted on the scene before her. "How beautiful it is up here! But where are all the people and the . . . the . . ."

"Farms, ranches, and towns? A long way from here, Princess. . . . I and the—uh, friends I was with—have been riding around out here for over a week without seeing any. . . . Which brings me to the reason why I climbed up to this ledge in the first place. I was hoping to figure out where we are—or at the very least, spot my horse."

She turned back to him. "But what happened to your friends and your horse? Where are they?"

"Damned if I know." For some reason, he did not want to tell her the entire truth—did not want her to know about his cowardly flight up the mountainside, praying for deliverance. "We got separated during a storm."

"Storm . . ." she said, her lovely eyes narrowing. "I . . . I remember something to do with a storm. There was . . . lightning."

"See? You *do* remember. It was the worst storm I've ever been caught in the middle of. The lightning spooked my horse. That's how we parted company. He threw me and galloped off, only my foot was

36

caught in the stirrup. I lost consciousness so I can't tell you what happened after that. All I know is he's got to be around here someplace."

"Lightning," she repeated, more to herself than to him. "The lightning was . . . terrible."

"I'm glad you remember that much. Maybe your memory's already returning. Soon, you'll recall everything, and then you can tell me how *you* wound up here on this ledge and where *your* friends are . . ." He trailed off as he noticed a worried look hovering around her tender lips. "Hey, Princess . . ."

She seemed to have forgotten him entirely. Two tears rolled down her cheeks. The impulse to comfort and reassure her swept him anew. He slid an arm around her slender waist, pulling her closer. "Hey, don't worry. . . . It will all come back to you . . ."

She gazed up at him with tear-bright, frightened eyes. "The lightning. . . . It almost . . . almost . . ."

"Struck you? Me too. Damn near fried me and my horse to a crisp. . . . But you and I survived, didn't we? We're still here. And we're going to find my horse and ride out of these mountains. Then we'll locate the nearest town and start looking for your folks. Someone will recognize you. Hell, a girl as pretty as you must have drawn a lot of attention. There aren't that many women out here, you know . . . Wait a minute. You aren't married, are you?"

He grabbed her left hand and hastily inspected it. It bore no wedding ring, and for no accountable reason, relief shot through him. He would have hated to think of her married to some jackass fool enough to have *lost* her in the Arizona wilderness. He did not like to think of her married, period.

"I, too, would like to know if I am married or not." Deftly, she removed her hand from his. "My husband, if I have one, would not approve of my being alone with you up here."

"Your husband, if you have one, ought to be shot for not taking better care of you. Whoever left you out here is going to have to answer to me when I finally catch up with him. This is no place for a pretty young woman in a nightgown, I can tell you that."

"A nightgown?" She looked down at herself with interest.

"What you wear when you're going to bed. That's what you've got on now."

"Oh . . . Oh, yes," she still sounded vague and uncertain.

He sighed and shook his head at her obvious confusion which didn't look as if it would go away in the next few minutes. "The important thing is to look over the area and see what we can find. That's why I climbed up here, and that's what I'm going to do."

"Yes, of course," she agreed. "We must study our surroundings."

They spent the next several moments examining the rough terrain visible from the ledge. The area nearest them was all mountain, sand, rock formations, deep crevices, and cacti. The scene frustrated Noah, who had hoped to spot *something* familiar, particularly his horse. He got down on his stomach and leaned far out over the ledge, but all he succeeded in doing was making himself dizzy. Sometime during the last half hour, he had begun to feel feverish, and his thigh and one ankle were now throbbing almost unbearably.

With a groan, he rolled over on his back and lay there a moment, resting. He desperately needed water. Without it, he and this odd girl stood little chance of survival—but where was he going to find a stream or a water hole? In the mountains and deserts, only the Indians could locate water with any certainty; it was said they could smell it the same as animals—another reason why whites never traveled far without the company of a good reliable scout. Yet here he was, miles from nowhere, responsible not only for himself but for a woman who didn't know her own name.

Get up, Copper, he mentally chided himself. *Get up*

38

and be the big, fearless hero and adventurer you always dreamed of being when you were a kid.

He opened his eyes to discover the princess leaning over him, her lovely face alight with concern. "Are you well? Is your leg hurting?"

"Princess, I've never been better," he drawled. "I was just resting my eyes a minute."

She gave him a smile that somehow rivaled the sun. "I know of something that will restore your energy. Down below, stuck between two big boulders, is an animal—I think."

"What?" he barked, snapping upright.

"It could be something else, but to me it resembles a horse."

"A horse!" His heart leaped. God, if it was a horse, *his* horse, he might get religion on the spot. "Where is it?" he bellowed, twisting to peer over the ledge again.

"Down there . . ." She pointed, but he could not see anything. "Do you see it?"

"No." He squinted, but still could not pick it out in the barren landscape. Then he *did* see it. A brown lump—*possibly* a horse—wedged between two huge boulders halfway down the mountainside.

"Do you think it *is* a horse?" she asked.

"Might be. Might not. Too far away to tell, but I better climb down and check."

As he got to his feet, she was wrapping the gauzy, red shawl around her head and shoulders. "I will come with you."

He was horrified. "You'll do no such thing! You'll stay right here and wait while I go down and examine whatever it is." Glancing toward the sky, he spotted several small black specks circling the spot. "It's definitely an animal of some sort, and a stuck, dead, or dying one. I'll find out which."

"What good will be served by my remaining here?" She tucked the end of the shawl into her waistband and regarded him with clear, innocent eyes that held a glint of mutiny.

"You'll save my sanity! I don't want to worry about you slipping and falling on the way down or getting bit by a snake or a dozen other things that can happen."

"I will have to climb down sooner or later anyway," she pointed out with infuriating female logic.

"Yes, but not yet—not before I decide which direction we ought to go. Up here, you've got shade, and it's relatively safe. I want you out of the sun. The last thing I need on my hands is a mad woman; who knows what the sun will do to you on top of a serious head injury?"

"I am not mad," she calmly refuted. "I have merely lost my memory. *You* are the one who is seriously injured. I should go down and check while you stay up here and rest."

"Absolutely not!" he exploded. "If I have to take that red shawl and tie your hands and feet so you can't move, you are going to stay up here and wait for my return. I'll be back as soon as possible."

Her lower lip quivered slightly, but she stood her ground. "You are being most unreasonable."

"If you think *this* is unreasonable, wait until you see me when I really get riled. I become a raving lunatic. . . . Do you understand that, Princess?"

With a toss of her head, she gazed at him imperiously. "I do not think I care to be called Princess any longer."

He stared at her in astonishment. Right in the middle of an argument, she wanted a new name? She stared back, head held high, eyes flashing golden, every glorious inch of her exuding regality.

"All right. If Princess doesn't suit your highness, then how about Agnes?"

Agnes had been his mother's name, but somehow this beautiful, haughty girl looked nothing like an Agnes . . . and the memory associations were not particularly pleasant either. His mother had died when he was thirteen, of complications following a miscarriage. Blaming his father for getting his mother pregnant in the first place, Noah had lit out on his own. Later, he had realized how unfair he had been, but by then, it was too late. His father had died, too, overcome by grief, guilt, and a weak heart. No, Noah did not want to call the girl by his mother's name—too many painful memories!

"Agnes," she murmured, as if trying on the name for size.

Damn, he could not think of a better one! There must be something he could pluck from one of the many books his mother had given him on birthdays and holidays. . . . Ah, Shakespeare . . . Old Will had been a good one for fancy women's names.

Seizing the first that came to mind, he blurted: "You can be Juliet. You look exactly like her."

"Juliet. . . . She is someone for whom you feel affection?"

He detected a slightly jealous note and grinned at the thought that she might be jealous. If he had decided to call her Emily, she might have good reason for jealousy, but he had known better than to mention *that* name.

"She's someone from a book—a play, I mean. She was young and devastatingly beautiful. Or so I always pictured her."

Her eyes softened. "Then I will gladly accept the name Juliet. It has a nice sound to it."

"Well, then, Juliet, you will stay here while I go down to see what that animal—or thing—is. Are we agreed?"

"Do I have a choice, No-ah?"

The way she said his name gave him pause. He had never heard it drawn out quite so softly, sweetly—and seductively.

"No, Juliet, you do not."

She gave him a look that was all honey and acquiescence, but her eyes sparkled with rebellion. "Then of course, I will wait here for you. . . . However, if you are

41

unable to return, I will have to climb down and rescue you after all, will I not?"

Interesting, he thought. Beneath the sweetness, she was cold, hard steel, as determined as any man. He did not doubt she *would* climb down and try to rescue him. The operative word was *try.* No slender, fragile-looking female in a nightgown could possibly succeed in such a difficult undertaking.

"I'll return," he promised. "Or die in the attempt."

With that, he saluted her and began the long, arduous descent back down the mountainside.

Chapter Three

After Noah had gone, Juliet sat down patiently on the ledge to await his return. She had been tempted to argue further but recognized the futility of trying to change the mind of an obstinate male. More accurately, she did not want Noah to waste what little strength he possessed by trying to stop her from accompanying him. Whatever he might say or think, he was dangerously close to collapse. Though his skin had been darkened by the sun, he looked pale and gray—almost haggard. Tiny lines on either side of his mouth and a dark shadow in his brown eyes revealed the presence of pain. She would have known he was hurting even if he did not move like a half-crippled, old man.

She could not help wondering how old he was— probably old enough to be her father. As filthy, bruised, and covered with abrasions as he was, it was difficult to tell much about him. She had almost screamed when she opened her eyes and found him leaning over her . . . but then she had noticed his eyes. They contained no malice—only a surprise at least as great as her own. And the shock of their meeting had quickly been replaced by an even greater shock: the realization that she had no idea of who or where she was.

When she tried to think, to remember, she got . . . nothing. No name, background, where she had come from, or who her family was. . . . A gray mist seemed to cover everything in her past. Only the present existed; she might have been born this very day and set down on this ledge to start life anew, yet she *must* have a name, a past, a family, people who cared about her. At first, she had thought she recognized Noah. Then she had realized he was a complete stranger. Would her memory come back? Or was she doomed to an insatiable curiosity that could never be satisfied—a torment of monstrous proportions?

Juliet. He had called her Juliet. It was not a bad name, and she could live with it—but how much better if she knew her own name! How much better if she could *remember*. She licked her lips, realizing only then how very dry they were. She was terribly thirsty, and her temples ached dully. Her stomach felt empty, too, but her thirst was greater than her hunger. It was a poor time to worry about the past; reluctantly she forced her thoughts to the present—and survival.

Noah must be thirsty and hungry, too. His condition was far worse than hers, yet he had to be so stubborn about allowing her to help extricate them from their peculiar predicament. Typical male, she thought, shaking her head, and then wondered how she knew what was typical and what was not, since she could not remember anything. And how did she know she must be careful about being alone with him?

Because he is a man, an inner voice answered.

There must have been a man in her life before this— or else she had received advice to that effect. She did not think she had ever lain with a man, but at the thought of it, a hot excitement flared in the pit of her belly. She *did* know what happened when a man and woman lay down together, or thought she did. They . . . copulated. Mated. Derived pleasure from each other's bodies—at least the man did. She was not sure about the woman.

The details of exactly how it all occurred eluded her, and she flushed to think of herself doing intimate things with any man, let alone the filthy, brown-eyed stranger she had just met. Still, it would be interesting to see what he looked like when bathed and tidied. His hair was a most unusual color—reddish beneath the dust and grime . . . and his features were pleasant, as was his form. She liked the broadness of his shoulders and the narrowness of his waist and hips. She also liked the fact that he was taller than she. He made her feel . . . feminine.

Enough, she scolded herself. Indulging in idle speculation about Noah McCord would do nothing to improve his or her chances of survival in this remote, challenging wilderness. Assuming that his strength soon would give out, she must prepare herself to take over the task of keeping them both alive. The first problem was finding water; it therefore seemed logical to examine the landscape for signs that might indicate a nearby water source. Perhaps moisture could be gained from the plants themselves. Some could possibly be edible. She would experiment with nibbling on a few and see. If they did not make her ill, they would not make Noah ill either.

She wondered what she could put on Noah's leg to draw out any poisons or ill humors that might have invaded the wound. Until he allowed her to tend it and she knew precisely how bad it was, she could make no plans to heal him. Instinct told her that the area's vegetation might be useful not only for food and water, but also for medicine. She would have to be careful not to harm more than she helped. Here also, she would need to experiment on herself before trying a remedy on him. Perhaps she could scratch her arm or hand to create a small, insignificant wound, then see what happened when she applied poultices made from various plants.

Restlessness seized her. Twice, she rose and peered into the distance to study Noah's progress toward the brown horse-shaped object. The first time, she saw him far below trudging slowly down the side of the mountain. The second time, he had disappeared among the boulders and rocky outcroppings. If it was his horse, the animal was probably dead, in which case they would at least have a source of food, plus whatever Noah had brought with him on the horse. A fire would be needed to cook the meat.

It was no difficult task to gather a fair-sized pile of combustible material on the ledge; Juliet only had to get down on her stomach and lean over the edge of the shelf to reach the brittle stalks of some plant that had failed to establish itself in the crevices. She picked all she could reach, scratching her hands and breaking a fingernail in the process. Finding two flat pieces of rock from which a spark could be struck took longer. She did not question how she seemed to know what to do and what to look for; she simply did it, letting instinct and common sense guide her. It was safer that way—not so threatening. Whenever she probed the gray mist in her mind, all she got for her trouble was a worsening of her headache.

By the time she had finished, she was exhausted. Shading her eyes against the sun's glare, she looked for Noah but did not see him anywhere below. Nothing moved on the vast, sunbaked landscape; the only other living things were the tiny, black specks wheeling in the air above the distant brown shape.

She swallowed a yawn, then realized it was foolish to deny herself the rest she so badly needed. She should sleep now so she would have the energy to tend Noah when he returned. Succumbing to the irresistible urge to lie down and close her eyes, she picked a spot as far back in the shade of the ledge as she could get. Still, it was incredibly hot. Her garments stuck to her skin. Her hair felt damp and heavy on her neck. No breeze stirred the silent, still air. No sound broke the silence. Rolling onto her side, she let herself doze . . . and that was when she heard the distant, muffled ringing of chimes.

I heard voices murmuring in the distance—the low, happy exclamation of women greeting each other after a long separation, the gruff, jovial greetings of men joking with one another. I was a child again spying on grown-ups and listening to the voice of my father inviting an old friend into the andron, *the room set aside exclusively for male entertainments. My mother was urging the visitor's wife up the stairs to the* gynaeceum, *the private abode of the womenfolk—the gilded cage, as I thought of it. The tomb.*

Here my mother spent all her time. Here she spun and wove and entertained her friends. Like other women of our class, she organized her household and directed her slaves and found what contentment she could in a life strictly proscribed by tradition and my father's dictates. Oh, the gynaeceum *was a pleasant enough place, being large and well furnished with long, low wooden couches, tables, and pretty wall-hung tapestries my mother had made—but it was still a place of confinement.*

My mother rarely left it. She rarely left the house itself, except for occasional religious or family celebrations or to do small bits of personal shopping. Even on such exciting occasions, a slave always accompanied her, and she could not spend past the modest amount women were limited to by law. Sometimes my father permitted her to visit friends, but mostly she stayed in her gynaeceum, *trying to make a proper young woman of me, to mold me into her image. . . . How I hated that place! I much preferred trailing after my brothers when they were home, particularly Nicias, who delighted in my cries of wonder whenever he described the city, the marketplace, and the* gymnasium *where boys learned mathematics, science, history and politics.*

Once he had taken me exploring without my parents' knowledge, and that one trip had opened my eyes to all that I was missing as a female of the upper class. Had I been born poor, I would have been able to do my own marketing in the agora and gone whenever I wished to stand in awe before the huge bronze statue of Athene Promachos, Athene the Champion, made by the sculptor Pheidias. It stood atop the Acropolis and could be seen by sailors returning to the port at Piraeus.

After that brief taste of freedom and forbidden knowledge, I burned with dissatisfaction at my lot in life and was forever escaping into the vineyards, where I could at least enjoy the golden air and the bright blue sky. On the fateful day of "The Visit," as I later came to think of it, I slipped into the central courtyard and hid behind a wooden pillar. I hoped my mother would not notice my absence right away, send for me to be shown off, then have a slave whisk me out of sight for the rest of the afternoon. I prayed she would simply forget about me, and I could spy on the young man the visitors had brought with them.

He was still a boy actually, but older than I, and being male, much more interesting than any females who might have come to see my mother. He had a most arresting face, dark hair, and lively dark eyes. In the manner of most young men, he wore a thigh-length, ivory-colored tunic, belted at the waist with a tasseled gold cord, and tall, stout sandals laced all the way to the knee. They were the sort my brothers wore while learning to ride horses—another activity forbidden to women.

The only thing marring the young man's attractive appearance was his scowl. He looked unhappy, and I wondered why. If he would only smile, he would be most handsome. Breathlessly, I waited to see if he would follow his elders into the andron. At the doorway, he paused, glanced into the central courtyard, and discovered me peeking out at him from behind the pillar.

His scowl vanished, to be replaced by a white-toothed grin. Startled, I stepped backward to better conceal myself. Then I heard the young man telling his father he would join him in a moment. I held my breath, waiting for him to pass the pillar. Instead, he came around the side of it and slowly looked me up and down, shaking his

48

head at what he saw. I hid my bare feet beneath my chiton and wished I had not touched the ribbons in my hair with my sticky fingers after I had stolen a honey cake from the kitchen.

"You are the daughter of the house?"

Swept with shyness, I could only nod. My father's guests almost never spoke to me—or even saw me. Only my mother's friends knew who I was. Once in a great while, I was allowed to play with visiting daughters, but never with sons, and I was dumbstruck that this tall, good-looking youth should single me out for his attention.

"I guess I do not have to worry about you for a while yet." Cocking his head, he grinned even wider, if that were possible. "You are only a baby."

"I am not a baby!" I protested, stung by the accusation. "I am nine years old."

"A baby," he affirmed with a satisfied smirk.

"How old are you?" I was too angry to remember my shyness or that I had no business speaking to a male guest in my father's household.

"Almost seventeen," he responded with a cocky self-assurance that infuriated me. "Old enough to be invited to attend your father's dinner party."

"But not old enough to wear a long tunic, instead of a short one." I gazed pointedly at the telltale garment marking him as a boy, not yet a full-grown man.

"You have a saucy tongue in your head," he snorted. "I am not sure I like that."

"I do not care if you like it or not. I am nothing to you, nor are you to me."

His scowl returned. "I wish that were true, but sadly, 'tis not. Our fathers are friends and business associates. My father buys the wine made from your father's grapes . . . Do you know so little of what goes on under your own roof?"

"I . . . I . . . know something of my father's doings," I hesitantly admitted. Actually, I knew more than most girls but was not sure I should say so. I was, after all, a *lowly female and not supposed to eavesdrop behind pillars. "Of course, I do not know as much as my brothers who are training to take a place at his side."*

"No, you are training to become someone's wife—and from what I overheard this morning, I am the one our parents have decided will be your future husband."

My mouth dropped open. This was the youth I would one day wed?

"Well you may gape at me like a startled fish," he said. "I myself was greatly surprised to hear of it . . . and even more surprised to learn I was invited along with my parents to visit here today."

"But . . . but . . . I'm only n—nine," I stammered. Then I realized what he was implying, and my pride prompted a quick defense. "You have no wish to marry? Is that why you object to me?"

"I certainly do not wish to marry a saucy little maiden who hides behind pillars spying upon her betters. Another young woman has caught my eye. She is the daughter of my teacher, a renowned sophist who is coaching me in the art of public speaking."

"The daughter of a sophist is not well-born enough to be your wife," I pointed out with a practicality that would have pleased and astounded my mother. "Besides, 'tis not your choice to make. The decision belongs solely to your parents—and mine."

This had been drummed into me since my birth: Girls were possessions to be traded from one man to another to enhance the family fortunes. This was their duty. They had no say whatever in deciding their futures.

"She is the only one I can ever love," the young man passionately declared. "Fortunately, I have plenty of time to change my father's mind. As you pointed out, you are far too young to marry. Nothing will be done until you are at least fifteen."

I knew he spoke the truth and was glad the time was still so far away. Still, it wounded my female vanity to learn he did not much like me—and indeed, loved another. Somehow, I had always assumed that whomever

I married would be smitten by my great beauty and fall to his knees in adoration the moment he first saw me. My mother despaired of my beauty as much as my practicality, but I dreamed of proving her wrong one day.

"Perhaps I do not want to marry you either," I said. Hands behind my back, I leaned against the pillar with as much disdain as I could muster. Unfortunately, the effect was spoiled by the necessity of having to tilt back my head to look this arrogant boy directly in the eye. "You are too serious to be my husband. I want someone more . . . friendly."

"Hah! You want a playmate!" he exclaimed with a laugh. "That proves you are only a child."

He reached out to tweak a strand of my hair, the bane of the slave responsible for taming it, but I slapped his hand away. "I do not want a playmate for a husband! Rather, I want someone who will love me as much as Paris loved Helen."

Nicias had been kind enough to tell me that tale, and I thought it most romantic.

His brows arched in surprise. "What do you know of Helen of Troy?"

Glaring at him, I proudly announced, "I may be a girl, but I know more than most girls my age. I sometimes spy on my brothers' lessons."

"Do you also want to cause a war like Helen did, little spy?"

I tossed my head. "Perhaps . . . It might be interesting to have armies fighting over me. A woman's life is usually so dull and boring . . . nothing but spinning, weaving, sewing garments, overseeing the slaves . . ."

I thought with venom of all those tasks I was supposed to love and did not. Raw wool made my arms itch, and on a hot day, it made me sneeze.

Again, he burst out laughing. "Great Zeus! 'Tis a rebellious maiden my father has picked for me to marry! Do you not realize that a quiet, industrious wife is all a man wants? If he desires companionship and wit, he has hetairai *to entertain him.*"

Young as I was, I knew what a hetaira was. Whenever my father invited hetairai to entertain his guests, my mother wept silently in her chambers and would not smile for days afterward. Of course, I had spied on them, too, as they came and went, and I knew they were pretty and laughed a lot. "My husband will have no need for a hetaira," I declared. "I will learn how to play a lyre and kithara, and I will be able to tell entertaining stories far better than any hetaira."

His brows rose, and he looked quite superior. "That is not all a hetaira does, little one."

"What else is there?" This drew another amused chuckle, to which I responded, "Whatever it is, I will learn to do it better. My husband will cherish me above all others. He will not leave me to weep alone in my gynaeceum, while he feasts with his friends in the andron."

"You are amazing—truly amaz . . ."

"Jason! . . . Where has that boy gone off to?" a man called out from the direction of the andron.

"I have to go." The young man darted a nervous look over his shoulder. For all his brimming confidence, he, too, had to bow to authority. "I have tarried long enough, and my father bids me return. He will be angry if I am not there in time for the serving of the meal."

The enticing odor of food wafted through the courtyard—food for the two separate feasts, one for the women, and one for the men—and any possible hetairai who might have been invited.

"I have to go, too, Jason. The next time you come, maybe we can visit again."

"Maybe," he said, this time succeeding at ruffling my sticky-ribboned hair with his strong, brown fingers. "You are more interesting than I thought you would be, little one. Do you know that your father's vineyards adjoin the lands of my father? That is probably why they think a marriage between us would be so advantageous."

"No, I did not know that," I admitted. *"If 'tis true, perhaps I will see you sometime, for I often walk in my father's vineyards. 'Tis the place where I go to escape, where no one can find me. . . . 'Tis how I get out of spinning and weaving."*

He laughed a third time. When he laughed, he appeared extremely friendly, kind, and playful—everything I could wish for in a husband, if indeed I was fated to marry. I liked to see Jason's smile and hear his laughter. It made my insides feel warm and tingly. Nor did I mind that he was so handsome a youth. . . . I would have hated to have to marry some wrinkled old man, as most young women were forced to do. Indeed, the more I thought on it, the more pleased I was that my father was not considering such a match. I had been taught that maturity in a husband was a quality to be desired above all others. My own mother was far younger than my gray-haired father.

"Goodbye, little rebel. . . . Grow up some, and maybe I will not mind so much marrying you—if I cannot have the one I love."

Love. He loved someone else. . . . But I could surely make him fall in love with me—could I not? I had at least six years to try. He took himself off then, and I sought to sneak out to the vineyard before anyone could catch me, but one of the slaves grabbed my arm.

"Where are you going?" she hissed. *"Your mother sent me to fetch you. I have been looking all over for you."*

"Oh, Atossa," I begged. *"Please tell her you could not find me. Do not make me go up to that stuffy old gynaceum."*

She clung tightly to my arm. *"I'll have my ear pulled if I don't take you. . . . But look at you! You are hardly fit to be seen. Your chiton is all smeared and dirty, your hair a proper nesting place for rats. What is to become of you, girl? No man will ever want a stubborn, willful, little naiad like you for a wife, and then what will you do?"*

She hauled me off to clean me up, but I knew she was not really angry. She had called me naiad, *her pet name for me.* Naiads *were spirits of nature who lived near water or waterfalls. They were generally thought to be happy and kind. My brother Nicias always called me* Nymphet, *a pet name derived from nymph, also meaning a spirit of woodland or water, often chased or loved by both gods and mortals. My father called me little* dryad, *meaning tree nymph—but only when he was pleased with me. He was not often pleased.*

"This is the creature who will one day advance our family fortunes?" he sometimes complained to my mother when he was upset over something I had done— or not done.

" 'Tis not easy, but I am developing her," my mother would always answer. "She will be sweet, biddable, and proficient in the household arts, I promise you."

I thought of that promise as Atossa made me presentable to join the ladies in the gynaeceum. *And I thought of Jason. I thought of Jason most of all.*

Slinging two heavy saddlebags off one shoulder and a rifle and cartridge belt off the other, Noah stopped to rest a moment before beginning the final leg of the long hard climb back to the ledge. It was late in the day, and he was trembling from a combination of weakness and exhaustion. At least, he was no longer thirsty; upon first reaching his poor dead horse, he had drunk deeply from one of his two full canteens. Remembering the horse, he sighed. The animal had apparently died after becoming wedged between the big boulders where he had found it. Something must have frightened it—causing it to bolt madly into the narrow opening, where in its frantic efforts to turn around and extricate itself, it had only succeeded in multiplying its injuries.

Noah regreted its demise, but in all probability, he would have been unable to save it, even had he arrived earlier. At least one of the horse's forelegs was broken. Not wanting the buzzards or other predators to destroy his gear, he had then spent a good hour stripping the still warm carcass of everything valuable and hiding what he could not carry back with him to the ledge on this trip. His first priority was to save everything edible. Aside from the bottle of whiskey he had brought along, he had a sack of dried beans, a small quantity of coffee and sugar, a packet of sun-dried beef, and a handful of carefully-horded peppermint drops—all bought from the trading post at Fort Apache. These and his canteens constituted his "emergency" rations, which he had prudently kept hidden from the ranchers on the off chance that one day he might need them.

In all his previous news-gathering exploits, he had always tried to be prepared and think ahead. This usually meant carrying a small pistol on his person and/or a knife strapped to his calf in case he met with hostility or violence. Though he knew little or nothing about surviving in a wilderness, he had attempted to prepare himself as best he could. That preparation was paying off now—providing he could get all his booty back up to the ledge. One saddlebag contained all his foodstuffs; the other held everything else, including his journal, a clean shirt, a warm leather vest, and a small dented coffee pot. His saddle, saddle blanket, and bedroll had had to be left behind for another journey.

Sitting on a rock in the late afternoon sunshine, elbows propped on his knees, Noah bowed his head and rested it on his hands. He felt dizzy and lightheaded, but resisted thinking about his injuries or exhaustion. Later, after he reached the ledge, he could rest, take off his boots, and tend his aching thigh. His thoughts turned to the swig of whiskey he had promised himself; never had he so desired a single long swallow of anything, as he did the fiery Mexican distillation of the *agave* plant, called *aguardiente,* which he had bought at the post.

Not normally a drinking man, he disliked feeling out of control and having his powers of concentration weakened—but he longed for sweet oblivion now. The pain, weariness, and danger of his present situation weighed heavily upon him. . . . He was half afraid he had been hallucinating. Maybe he had only dreamed the existence of that girl up on the ledge; maybe he would find that she was gone now—had never really been there. However, if she *did* exist, she was surely thirsty and hungry, and that realization finally prompted him to struggle to his feet, pick up his things, and start the difficult climb upward. Halfway to the ledge, he found he could not negotiate the steep terrain carrying saddlebags, rifle, cartridge belt, and canteens. Loathe to leave the food and water, he hid the rifle, cartridges, and one canteen in a shallow crevice and continued on without them.

Arriving at the last toe and finger holds of the near vertical rock face, he called to Juliet to help him by taking the saddlebags, which he intended to hand up to her. There was no response. Certain now that he had imagined everything, he made a supreme effort, tossed the saddlebags onto the ledge, and wearily crawled up after them.

Juliet lay huddled by the wall, but before he could check on her, he had to rest again. Sparing a few moments to catch his breath, he then crawled over to her. Her color was good, her breathing regular. She was probably worn out. Stretching out beside her, he rejoiced that he had not lost his wits, after all. She really did exist—and was as beautiful as he remembered. He did not intend to sleep, but decided that a brief rest could not possibly hurt. Juliet had, he noticed, assembled the makings for a fire, which solved at least one of his problems—how he would cook the coffee and beans. Succumbing to the impulse to close his eyes, he was rudely jolted when Juliet suddenly muttered something in her sleep. Instantly wide awake, he raised his head and strained to listen.

"Jason," she said softly. "Oh, Jason . . ."

That was it. Just three small words. But the way she said them convinced Noah that Jason was someone very important—someone she held in high regard. He hoped she would say more, but all she did was sigh, and the sigh seemed more ominous than her mention of Jason's name. Jason was *definitely* someone she cared about, and Noah discovered that he did not at all like the idea that she loved some stranger named Jason. . . . Could he be a friend or a relative—a brother, perhaps?

No, women did not sigh over their brothers or friends. This Jason meant something to her, and Noah had a fierce urge to throttle the man, whoever he was. It seemed grossly unfair. Of all the things and people Juliet had so thoroughly forgotten, why should this Jason alone have the power to breach the wall in her mind and invade her dreams?

He debated whether or not he should awaken her and once again demand to know Jason's identity. Awake, would she remember? And if she did, would she tell him? He decided to try a more subtle approach.

"Juliet," he whispered. "Where is Jason? Tell me where he is. How do you see him?"

Juliet frowned. "Through the leaves," she said. "I see him through the leaves. . . . Oh, he is so handsome—the most handsome boy—man—I have ever known!"

At least she wasn't in bed with him! Noah's relief died abruptly as Juliet muttered something that made his hair stand on end.

"Jason! Jason, come here! No one will see us. . . . Jason, come here!"

Noah waited a minute, and when she said nothing more, he impatiently prodded: "Well? Is he coming?"

Juliet sighed and rolled over. She did not speak again, and Noah lay rigid and frustrated, wondering if he would ever learn who the hell Jason was and what he meant to Juliet.

Chapter Four

"Where is the horse meat, No-ah?"

Noah awoke with a start, the simple question catapulting him out of the drowsiness to which he had succumbed. Rubbing his eyes, he sat up. It had grown quite dark, but a small fire in the center of the ledge crackled merrily, illuminating the amazingly lovely young woman kneeling beside him.

"No-ah, where is the horse meat? I thought to cook it while you slept, but I cannot find it. Did you not bring some back with you? I thought surely you would if the animal was dead, which it certainly seemed to be."

"Yes," he responded, trying to clear his fogged brain. "The horse was dead . . . but I never once thought of the meat. I can't eat the flesh of a poor animal I once rode."

"Why not?" Juliet rocked back on her heels and gazed at him curiously. The firelight made a shining nimbus of her pale hair, so that it resembled spun gold and glistened with a life of its own. His hand itched to touch it.

"Because . . . the horse's name was Bud," he answered irrelevantly. "I bought him when I arrived in the territory. He didn't like me at first, but after we got to know each other, we got on well together."

"I can understand that you felt affection for such a grand creature . . . but he is dead now. We are alive and hungry. Why should the horse's flesh go to waste when it could serve a worthy purpose?" Juliet waved a slender hand at the merry little blaze behind her. "I prepared this fire in anticipation of fresh meat to cook."

Noah blinked in astonishment. He had not expected her to be capable of such efficiency—or practicality. Much as he hated to admit it, she was right. The food in his saddlebags would not last long; they ought to eat the horse meat first and save the dried food for later. . . . Never mind that the idea of eating "Bud" turned his stomach.

"I should have thought of it," he sheepishly conceded. "By tomorrow the meat will probably all be spoiled."

"Not if we retrieve it early in the morning." She tugged her red shawl more closely about her fragile shoulders. "The cold night air in these mountains will keep the meat from spoiling. We will butcher what we can tomorrow and dry some of the meat in the sunshine. Then it will not all go to waste."

"Good idea," Noah agreed, though he wondered how he would ever be able to climb back down the mountainside and carve up his horse come morning. His head was throbbing, his ears ringing. The night air did not feel cold to him; it felt peculiarly warm, as if the sun were still beating down upon him. He had no idea how long he had slept. He hadn't planned on falling asleep, yet apparently had collapsed like a dead man.

"We do not have enough fuel to cook the beans I found in your leather bags," Juliet continued. "I do seem to remember that beans take a long time and must be soaked first. It will take all night to soften them. As for the rest of what you brought, I am uncertain what to do with it. I am sorry, but I find none of it familiar."

The whiskey, Noah remembered. What he needed was a hearty swig of *aguardiente*. "Hand me the bags," he said, feeling too weak to get them himself. "I know of something we can drink to make us feel better."

Rising gracefully, she brought him the heavy saddle bags, and he rummaged around in the one that contained the bottle of whiskey. A moment later, the fiery, wonderful liquid was burning a path down his tight throat. "Aaaah," he sighed, as the liquor took hold and soothed him. "That's just what I needed. Here, you try it. If you're cold, it will warm you."

Palming the mouth of the bottle, he handed it to her. She took it dubiously in her long, slender fingers. "What is this drink? It has a strange, sharp smell."

"And an even sharper taste. You'll like it. I promise."

Noah watched as she drank from the bottle, then coughed and spat the whiskey on his boots. "Oh!" she gasped. " 'Tis terrible stuff! It burns my mouth and throat."

"You just need to get used to it before you can appreciate its medicinal qualities." He reclaimed the bottle and helped himself to another long swallow.

"If 'tis a medicine, then perhaps we should use it on your injuries rather than drinking it. 'Twas getting dark when I awoke, but I did notice that the wound on your upper leg looks as if it could become most serious."

"I'll splash some on it later. Right now, I prefer to drink my medicine."

"You should at least eat, No-ah. Have you nothing in those bags that can be eaten without being cooked?"

"Matter of fact, I do." Setting down the bottle, he rummaged in the bags until he found the packet of dried beef. Grinning, he opened it and held up a piece. "This should ease your hunger. It tastes like boot leather but ought to fill the hole in your belly. A cup of coffee would help, too. . . . Do you remember how to make coffee?"

She shook her head no, leaning closer to gaze curi-

61

ously at the strip of beef. "If you will only tell me how to do it, I will gladly make the coffee."

Handing her the beef, he deliberately let his finger-tips touch hers. As before, he felt a jolt clear to his boots from the brief contact. Or maybe he was just imagining the heady reaction. It must be the whiskey, he told himself, relieved to discover such an easy explanation. He did not let himself dwell on the fact that he had not been drinking whiskey the first time he touched her.

"Easier to show than tell," he drawled, carefully withdrawing his hand.

As quickly as possible considering his exhaustion, he dumped coffee grounds, water from the canteen, and sugar into the small dented coffee pot. He never had been too particular about measurements, but he knew what he liked—strong coffee well laced with sugar, and tonight, with whiskey. He hoped another shot of it would help dull the pain in his head and thigh before he had to doctor the wound. He really was not feeling well. When he handed Juliet the coffeepot, his hand shook like an old man's.

"Put this on the fire. Just set the pot right down in the middle, but be careful when you remove it, or you'll burn your fingers."

"How will I know when the coffee is finished?" she inquired with a tilt of her golden head.

He wondered that she could not remember even so simple a thing. "It will start to boil over. Then you take it off the fire, let it sit a few minutes so the grounds can settle, and pour it out. . . . Hell, I only brought one cup," he recalled, digging through the bag for it. "We'll have to share it. I never planned on having company, you see. I thought I would only need one if I got in trouble with the ranchers and had to set out on my own. One kettle, one pot, one cup, one set of utensils—just the bare essentials for a single man alone."

She paused to look at him, the coffeepot suspended

in both hands. "And that is what really happened? There was trouble between you and your friends?"

Now, how had she finessed that out of him? The whiskey must be making him muddle-brained. He set down the cup with a clunk. "Yes, that's what really happened, but if you don't mind, I'd rather not discuss it. Doesn't concern you anyhow."

She gazed at him a long silent moment, then rose and set the coffeepot on the tiny fire. When she returned and sat down near him, he had to bite his tongue to keep from apologizing. He suddenly wanted to explain everything, even his shame at being so afraid and desperate. But at the moment, he did not feel up to it. The urge to stretch out on the ledge and sleep was becoming irresistible.

She reached for his saddlebags. "You should use these leather bags to pillow your head, then you must try and rest while we wait for the coffee to boil. . . . You do not look at all well." She withdrew his folded vest and shirt and handed them to him. "Here. . . . Put these on first to keep you warm."

He took the vest but gave her back the shirt. "If you're still cold, *you* put on the shirt. I should have brought the saddle blanket and my bedroll back with me too, but it was too damn much to carry. . . . Don't worry about me; I feel hot, not cold."

" 'Tis probably fever. You must lie down and rest. You must keep warm." She pushed him back to lie with his head on the saddlebags, then covered him with the shirt and the vest. "Sleep now, No-ah. I will take care of everything."

"You can't," he muttered, fighting the inertia stealing over him. "You're just a woman—a girl really. And you've lost your memory . . . and you're dressed in a nightgown."

He thought he saw the flash of a smile in the darkness. "None of these things will keep me from doing what must be done. I am not a child but a woman full-grown, and I am not injured as you are. Trust me, No-ah. I will take care of you."

He wanted to jump up and insist that *he* be the one to take of *her*, but his body refused to obey. Despite the nap he had just taken, he could no longer keep his eyes open. "Wake me when the coffee's ready," he mumbled and closed his eyes.

Worried that he was truly sickening, Juliet laid her palm on Noah's forehead. It was hot to the touch—and so was his jaw when she ran her fingers down the lightly stubbled surface. Fever was indeed upon him; instinct told her she must keep him from becoming hotter. Rising, she went to the fire and removed the coffeepot. The water inside it could be better used to cool him than to make the stuff called coffee, she decided, doubting that Noah would awaken again tonight to drink the brew he had requested.

Returning to his prone figure, she again knelt beside him, set down the coffeepot, and lifted the hem of her gown. Using the edge as a rag, she dipped it into the pot of water, wrung it out, and proceeded to wipe Noah's face and forehead. Fortunately, the sugar and grounds Noah had added to the pot had settled somewhat; the water itself was only slightly warm. As the sweat and grime disappeared from his features, Juliet inhaled sharply. Noah was not old—far from it! He could more accurately be described as young and handsome.

In sleep, his expression had softened, revealing a vulnerability where there had only been cynicism. The line of his jaw suggested stubbornness, but his mouth showed a sensitivity that quite surprised her. His nose was elegant, his brow noble. She could imagine him fighting great battles and making fine speeches. She already knew he possessed a forceful personality and liked having things his own way. Now she suspected he was a leader among men and a great success among women.

Whatever he was, he was most certainly ill. She ought never to have let him exert himself as he had today. The wound in his thigh had not yet been dressed and might already be suppurating. While the fire provided light, she must tend it.

Wasting no more time, she began stripping off his lower garments so she could examine the injury. This, too, proved enlightening. Handling a man so intimately—even a man who had no idea what she was doing—was a revelation. He was so very . . . masculine, all muscle and lean hard planes that bore only a faint resemblance to her own physical topography. Carefully ignoring that part of him that both worried—and intrigued—her the most, she concentrated on the ugly-looking crease that marred the otherwise perfect formation of one sturdy, hairy thigh.

He stirred as she cleansed it. She worried she could not get it clean enough to withstand infection. Already, it smelled bad when she lowered her head to sniff it. Then she remembered Noah's whisky. . . . Fetching the bottle, she unstoppered it and dribbled it onto the gash. Noah stiffened and cried out, thrashing his head from side to side, but mercifully, did not come fully awake. He had sunk into feverish oblivion, and she was glad the pain did not penetrate his consciousness.

Completing her ministrations, she wrestled Noah back into his clothing. By now, the fire had died down, and darkness shrouded the ledge. Starlight illuminated only one corner of it near the front. She could do no more for Noah or herself until daylight. She lay down near him, her hand brushing his arm which seemed to be shaking slightly. He was shivering. She had already covered him with everything they had; the only other available remedy was to warm him with her own chilled body.

Moving closer, she huddled against his side and felt

comforted. If something threatened them during the night, Noah would be of little use, but at least he was another human being. She was not alone—though perhaps it would be better if she were. It would never do to become too attached to Noah. She had a life of her own somewhere—family and friends who were wondering what had happened to her. She had commitments and responsibilities. She had a past . . . someplace, with someone. She could never rest—never be happy or content—until she knew what that past was. Until she knew who *she* was.

A surge of deep frustration threatened to rob her of badly-needed sleep, and her head began to throb unbearably. Willing herself to relax, she thought once more of Noah. Beneath the dirt and grime, he truly was an attractive man. Tall, handsome, and well-made. Though she dare not permit herself to become attached to him, she could see no harm in enjoying his company and sharing his body warmth. Until they returned to civilization—wherever and whatever civilization was—he needed her, and she needed him. Besides, the more she concentrated on the present, the less threatened and insecure she felt about the unknown past.

The next day, Noah could not recall if Juliet had awakened him for coffee or not. He remembered flinching and crying out as Juliet—or somebody—did something painful to his thigh, and he recalled drinking water and feeling hot, then shivering with cold and wondering why the bed beneath him was so hard and uncomfortable. With some effort, he realized that he was not lying on a bed, but on a ledge in the middle of a wilderness in Arizona, or maybe it was New Mexico. . . . Wherever it was, he was sick and hurting and occasionally delirious, and every so often, Juliet put the cup to his lips and forced him to drink.

After that, it grew cold and dark again. He would

have frozen had she not cuddled close to him, held him tightly, and murmured soothingly in his ear. Once, he awoke in a sweat, certain his mother was taking care of him, sponging his forehead and feeding him, as she had done when he was ill as a young boy. However, this woman did not smell like his mother who had been partial to lavender scent. She smelled better than his mother, but he could think of no one else who would care for him like this, when he was so weak, dizzy, and unable to care for himself. Whoever she was, he resolved to make it up to her, because he had an awful feeling that were it not for her, he would die before he woke up.

His next conscious thought was a realization of annoyance that someone was again making him drink— and the hot liquid burned his tongue.

"Please drink this, No-ah," a soft voice pleaded. "It will give you strength. You *must* drink it."

Juliet. It had been Juliet caring for him all this time.

He obediently swallowed and discovered she was right. The hot liquid was thick, rich, and reminiscent of beef, though it had a peculiar hearty flavor all its own. Each mouthful imparted vigor.

"Ah, that's good," he croaked, sounding like a bull frog. "What is it?"

"Broth. Good, nourishing broth."

His eyes flew open. He was drinking broth made from the meat of his poor old horse, Bud.

Juliet smiled encouragingly. The rising sun had stained her face, hair, and garments a soft rosy color, but the red shawl hung limp and wrinkled off one shoulder, and the white nightgown was soiled and rumpled. Her hair was wild and unkempt, as if she had not had time to care for it properly. A dark smear marred the purity of one cheekbone; she had the look of a woman who had been working unceasingly.

"How long have I been lying here ill?" he growled, disgusted with himself.

"Several days. . . . For a time, I thought you might

die, but I was determined not to lose you. I have cared for you as best I could, considering how little I can remember. . . . Do you think you can eat beans? I cooked a small quantity in hopes you would awaken hungry."

"Maybe later. I'm not up to beans yet. . . . How are we doing on water?"

"The container in which you keep the water is full," she said proudly. "Last night, it rained, and I collected as much as possible. I then used some to make broth from the horse meat I am drying."

"You climbed down from the ledge and butchered that carcass all by yourself?" Noah was astounded. The dark splatters on her white nightgown must be dried blood, he realized.

As she saw where he was looking, her golden-brown eyes twinkled with amusement. "It was a messy job, and much of the meat went to waste, but yes, I butchered the dead horse. I have cooked a large quantity, so it will not spoil, and the rest I have cut into strips and laid along the edge of the ledge to dry in the sun."

Noah was even more astounded. He had thought only Apache women capable of such grueling labor. "How did you know to do all that? . . . And what was I doing while you did it?"

Momentary panic swamped him. For a devastating instant, he understood how Juliet must have felt, waking up and being unable to remember anything.

"You were sleeping—or delirious." She smiled, a most radiant smile despite her bedraggled appearance. "I cannot tell you how I knew what to do; I only did what made sense at the time. . . . Do you know that in your delirium, you sometimes talked about a woman named Emily? Who is this Emily, No-ah?"

"Emily! Why . . . she's no one important. Just a girl I knew back East."

Juliet's smile faded. "You mentioned her name several times while you were raving with fever. Therefore she *must* be important."

"No more important to me than you claim Jason is to you," Noah countered. "You've mentioned Jason twice in your sleep."

The rosy glow faded from Juliet's elegant cheekbones. "I have told you I cannot remember this Jason or whether he was important to me or not. That is the truth. However, you can obviously remember this Emily. I can see in your eyes that you do. Why do you not wish to tell me about her? If I could remember Jason, I would tell you all I know."

Could she possibly be jealous? The notion pleased Noah. Obviously, she did not want him to be attached to any other female. Little did she know he had avoided such attachments like the plague! . . . And he was not about to get attached now, he reminded himself.

"Emily's the girl back home who wants to marry me . . . but I don't want to marry her—or any woman. I like my freedom too much. . . . However, I do thank you for nursing me through this crisis. I don't know what I would have done without you."

"You would have died," she said simply, turning away and busying herself with the empty cup and the cooking utensils. "The wound in your thigh became red, swollen, and angry-looking. Each day, I poured some of your medicine on it. I also made a poultice of the spines from a plant I found growing a little way down the mountainside. It seemed to help, so I crushed its spines and put them into your water. That, too, seemed helpful."

"You doctored me with a strange plant you found?" Ignoring a wave of dizziness, Noah rose up on one elbow. "How in hell did you know you weren't going to poison me instead of cure me?"

She gave him a level look over one shoulder. "Because I first tried these remedies upon myself. They did me no harm, so I did not think they would harm you. Plants are often beneficial. I cannot recall how I know this or which ones are and which are not, but I do know it. The plants around here are strange to me, but I am slowly learning their properties."

"You are really quite amazing!" Noah lay back down on his saddlebags. "I've never met anybody like you."

"I have good instincts." She smiled modestly. " 'Tis fortunate, is it not, since my instincts are *all* I have?"

Noah quelled the impulse to offer comfort. He owed her a great deal and he was grateful, but the obligation made him feel suddenly wary and uncomfortable. He wasn't accustomed to owing anybody anything. "I wouldn't worry about it, if I were you. In time, you'll recover your memory."

"I hope so, No-ah. I cannot help dreading what will become of me if I do *not*." She began tidying up the ledge. " 'Tis so . . . bothersome. I look at an object such as this one," she picked up his rifle, ". . . and I do not know what it is or how it is used."

"That's my rifle, and you had better put it down. That thing over there is my cartridge belt. Both are dangerous. What are you doing with them? I thought I left them . . ."

She interrupted with a smile. "I knew they must be yours. I found them down the mountainside." She motioned toward the edge of the ledge. "And I brought them up here to keep them safe."

He watched her, dumbfounded. Everything she said and did surprised him. Were it not for her, he would probably be dead by now. "I'll . . . help you," he offered, only a little reluctantly. "I'll explain things to you . . . and if we get off this ledge alive and make it back to Tucson, I won't just dump you there and forget you. Someone somewhere knows about you; I'll help you find your folks and get medical attention. . . . Hell, it's the least I can do after the way you've helped me these last few days."

"Tucson? What is Tucson, No-ah?"

The question jolted him, opening his eyes to just how naïve and helpless she really was. "It's a town,

70

Juliet. A place with people and buildings. . . . It's civilization, one of the few places that can even pass for civilization in Arizona."

"Arizona . . ."

"Here . . . where we are. This is the Arizona Territory. At least I think it is. I could be wrong."

"At least, you can make a good guess." She smiled ruefully. "I cannot even do that. You see how frustrating losing one's memory can be."

He nodded, feeling her frustration as if it were his own.

She sighed. "Ah, well, I must not dwell on it. That's why I so much enjoyed helping you, No-ah . . ." She gazed at him from beneath the opulent sweep of her gold-tipped lashes, the longest lashes he had ever seen. "Doing what needed to be done kept me from being anxious over my own problems. . . . Perhaps you should rest now. Sleeping is a good way to regain one's strength."

"I do feel as weak and helpless as a newborn kitten," Noah confessed. "I can't recall ever having been this useless. But I don't intend to baby myself for long. Our water won't hold out through a leisurely recovery period. Neither will our food. We're a long way from Tucson and civilization. The sooner we get started on our journey, the better."

"You know best how you feel, No-ah. Whenever you are ready to leave, you have only to say the word, and we will go. The decision must be yours."

Noah narrowed his eyes, studying her. She sounded meek and deferential, but her actions these past few days revealed a strength that simultaneously impressed and disturbed him. As he had suspected, there was far more to her than initial impressions suggested. She appeared fragile as glass, yet she had taken charge and saved his life, butchered his dead horse singlehandedly, experimented with plants and found one that had helped him, caught and stored rainwater, retrieved his rifle. . . . It was almost eerie how she had known what to do and calmly done it. By now, most women of his acquaintance would have succumbed to hysterics.

If the truth be known, she scared the hell out of him.

"I'll be ready in a day or two," he muttered, needing to assert himself.

"If you insist, though I do think we should wait until the meat is dried. If we are careful, our water will last. Perhaps tomorrow I can search for another source of water. I did not want to leave you while you were . . ."

"No!" He cut her off midsentence. "You aren't going anywhere! It isn't safe to be wandering alone in these mountains and canyons . . . or in the desert areas. A cougar could get you or a pack of coyotes, or even the Indians."

"I am not afraid. 'Tis only the lightning I fear—not the living creatures who share this beautiful land with us."

"You damn well better be afraid! Beautiful or not, this land is harsh and unforgiving. One mistake and you're done, finished . . . wiped off the face of the earth. Promise me you won't go off by yourself again and risk getting lost or hurt."

"I did not get lost or hurt while you were delirious," she stubbornly reminded him. "And I had no choice but to go off by myself. If I had not, you would have died, and the horse's meat would have been wasted."

"I don't want you going off alone again!" Noah insisted in what passed for a shout in his weakened state.

"All right, No-ah," she acquiesced, though he wondered if she really meant it. "But you must promise me we will not leave for Tucson before you have regained your strength. I would not have you collapsing on the journey because you tried to do things too quickly."

"I won't collapse on the journey." Noah clenched his teeth in irritation. "I promise you I won't collapse."

72

Chapter Five

"Jason! Jason, over here!"

It was late afternoon, and the workers had all left the vineyards. I was the only one there, and I could not believe my good fortune at having discovered Jason walking alone on his father's land only a stone's throw away from where I stood among the grapevines. I had come so often, hoping to catch a glimpse of him—perhaps even to talk with him—but although I had seen him several times, he had not seen me. Once he had been with his father, and I was too afraid to call out to him; the other times he had been too far away to hear my cautious summons.

This time, he did hear me. He stopped in his tracks and looked up from the wooden tablet he had been studying intently. I stepped out from behind a row of vines and waved to him. He grinned when he saw me, and my heart nearly burst from excitement. . . . Great Zeus, but he was handsome! Better in person than I had imagined when I lay on my couch at night, dreaming of him, wondering how it would feel to be married to such a well-favored young man.

Slowly—much too slowly—he walked over to me, meeting me beneath a raised trellis tall enough to make an arch overhead. "Ah, here is my little spy again. . . . What a naughty creature you are, hiding among the vines to catch me unawares. Your parents would not be pleased to learn where you are at this moment."

"My parents will not find out," I retorted, bending to pick up the white cat curling around my ankles. Zeno always followed me about. One of my most trusted companions, he now obligingly provided something to do with my hands while I talked to Jason.

After all the times I had visited this section of the vineyard in hopes of just such a meeting, I suddenly felt shy and awkward, uncertain what to say or do. Zeno promptly curled up in my arms, purring contentedly, and I hugged him to me, thereby avoiding looking Jason directly in the eye. As if he knew that he discomfitted me, Jason laughed softly.

"I see you have a way with animals," he noted. "What is your pet's name?"

"Zeno." I raised my eyes to meet his and relaxed somewhat. Dare I hope that he loved animals as much as I did? "He is really a most marvelous cat. He knows when I am happy and sad. He even knows when I am lonely. All I have to do is think of him, and he comes to me, appearing at my side moments later."

"Nonsense. A cat cannot guess your mood. I'll bet he only comes because he's hungry, and he knows you will feed him. From the looks of him, you must feed him all the time. Rarely have I seen a fatter feline."

" 'Tis not nonsense. Zeno does know my moods. And I know his. The same as I know the moods of many other animals and birds. 'Tis not difficult; all I have to do is close my eyes, and I can feel what they are thinking."

"That's impossible," Jason scoffed. "You are only imagining such a thing."

"No, I am not. 'Tis true!" I was upset that he did not understand. It was suddenly very important to me that he did understand. My family and servants knew of my affection for animals, of course, but they did not know how far it went or that I had discovered I could communicate with them in this way. They would only laugh if I told them—but Jason must not laugh. Of all people, Jason must understand even if he did not share my emo-

74

tions. I could not bear it if he belittled me, as my father so often belittled my mother!

"Look. I will show you." I closed my eyes a moment, concentrating very hard on the warm, rumbling body in my arms. "Zeno is telling me that he wishes to take a little nap. He fatigued himself chasing birds away from the ripening grapes this afternoon."

Jason's erupting laughter made me open my eyes again. "He fatigued himself, did he? What an imagination you have, little spy!" Then, seeing that I was angry, he ceased laughing and said placatingly: "But I am certain you are a wise, sensitive mistress to your beloved Zeno. 'Tis obvious he enjoys your company. Such solicitude shows you have a kind and gentle nature, an excellent quality in a young woman."

Somewhat mollified, I allowed myself a small smile. "Zeno adores me, and I adore him," I agreed, deciding to let the matter drop for now. "What is it you have written on your tablet?"

Jason glanced down at the tablet he still held in his hands. "Oh, 'tis nothing that would interest you . . . just a verse I am memorizing. An educated man must be able to quote the great poets in his conversation. Therefore, I am constantly studying extracts of poetry. My father and teachers assign them to me. However, 'tis too difficult to concentrate in our noisy household, so when I want to memorize, I go for long walks by myself."

"I may be young and female, but still I am interested," I eagerly assured him. "Will you read the poem to me?"

His eyebrows arched. "You—a mere girl—are interested in poetry?"

"I am also fascinated by mathematics, science, politics, and history, even as you are . . . but 'tis not considered necessary for a woman to learn these subjects. But as I told you before, I have spied upon my brothers at their lessons, so I am not completely ignorant. I just wish I could learn more. I have requested my own kitharistes, but alas, my parents will not allow me to have one."

"You begged your parents to provide a teacher of music and poetry especially for you?" Jason's dark eyes betrayed his amazement.

"Yes, but they refused. Did I not also tell you the first time we met that I wish to learn all the ways of entertaining, so that my future husband will not be tempted to take his pleasure among the hetairai? I cannot understand the reasoning of my parents—indeed, of most everyone. Why should a woman be denied the opportunity to learn, if she so desires it? She will be a much more interesting companion to her husband if she is not kept ignorant all her life. . . . Do you not agree?"

Cocking his head, Jason appeared to think a moment. "Yes . . . I do agree," he finally said. "It makes no sense at all for a woman to be illiterate and stupid. Though you must admit that education for women is a revolutionary idea. Neither your parents nor mine would condone it. A woman has her own responsibilities; our parents would say that you should learn your wifely duties and leave intellectual matters to your husband."

We had begun walking down a row of vines, passing from deep shadow beneath the trellis into bright sunlight between the rows, and the play of light on Jason's face enthralled me. I was reminded of the beautiful marble and bronze statues I had seen in Athens with Nicias. He had sneaked me into the Parthenon, and I had marveled at its treasures. I recalled none so fine as Jason's profile gilded by sunlight.

"I would not attempt to usurp my husband's authority simply because I knew how to play a lyre or quote poetry or write with a stylus on a waxed wooden tablet," I said. "Nor would I neglect my duties. . . . But why must all my time be spent learning boring tasks that slaves and servants can perform every bit as well or better than I can? I had rather be a friend and companion to my husband than a menial slave. If I cannot discuss poetry with him, will he not seek companionship with someone who can?"

Jason halted and looked at me: "You know we are

76

probably discussing you and me, not some hypothetical husband and wife. Your parents and mine intend for us to marry someday. That day I came to your house for dinner was so your father could take my measure. He has also dined at our house several times. When he comes, he displays an unusual interest in me. None of my father's other friends show the least desire to learn the opinions of a green young man, as my teachers delight in calling me."

I faced him and earnestly lay my hand on his arm. "Then, if we are to wed one day, you must tell me what you prefer, Jason—a timid, industrious wife or one who can converse with you on a wide variety of topics? If you prefer the former, you had best look elsewhere for a wife. Tell your father you refuse to consider me. But if you prefer the latter, then you must help me to educate myself to be a worthy and interesting companion."

Jason's look was incredulous. My boldness had clearly astonished him. Perhaps I should have held my tongue, but I was too young and headstrong to practice discretion. And I was jealous of all he knew—all that I had been denied. I felt the same jealousy toward my brothers, both of whom liked to tease me about my insatiable curiosity. The older one particularly—not Nicias—could be most cutting. . . . Would Jason be so cruel? I desperately hoped he would not be, because I did so want to please him and make him fall in love with me. And I wanted to be able to love him. Yet how could I do that if he scorned my ambitions and intellect?

He reached out to ruffle my hair as he had done on our first meeting. "I would prefer that you be yourself, little rebel, and if that means learning poetry, why then, I think you should study poetry."

My heart thudded with happiness at his answer. In that moment, I began to love him. Not another young man in Greece would have responded similarly. "Then will you teach me what you are learning?" I pleaded. "For there is no one else whom I can ask. My brothers only ridicule me."

77

"Now, how can I do that—when it is forbidden I should even be talking with you like this?"

"I will meet you here from time to time!" I blurted out, inspired. "You can say you are coming here to study, and I can simply disappear as I so often do!"

He laughed. "So you are a schemer, too! I might have guessed. . . . Very well, my little schemer, I will meet with you occasionally here in the vineyard . . . but not too often. I would not like for our parents to discover what we are doing. My father would beat me if he knew I was meeting you in secret."

"Oh, you will not be sorry, Jason! I will tell no one. When you come, I will even help you study! There must be something I can do to help you . . ."

"You can listen while I discourse," he suggested loftily. "In that way, you will learn from my arguments and give me an opportunity to reconsider them before I try them out on my teachers. . . . Do you think yourself capable of learning from arguments?"

"Oh, yes, yes, Jason! I am most capable! . . . What a splendid idea! With all the experience you gain from arguing with me, you will be a wonderful orator one day. . . . By listening and questioning, I can help you, and at the same time, you will be helping me."

"I doubt not you will be a good audience. However, you must not be too critical. Sometimes you must challenge me, as my teachers do, but only if you are absolutely certain I have gone astray somewhere in my reasoning."

This was more than I ever dared hope for—to be treated as an equal. To be counted worthy of an opinion. To have that opinion gravely considered. I set down Zeno and clapped my hands with glee. "Oh, this will be perfect, will it not?"

"Perhaps. . . . It will either be perfect or the most foolish thing I have ever done."

"It will not be foolish," I hastened to assure him, embracing him in my exuberance.

Laughing, he held me away from him with one hand

78

and kept hold of his tablet with the other. "You had better go home now before someone comes looking for you."

"But you have not yet read me the poem on your tablet!"

"Next time, little schemer. . . . Next time, I will read several poems to you, including one of my own creation, and you will tell me which you like best and why."

" 'Twill be your poem I like best, Jason! I am sure of it!"

I ran home in a rosy haze of happiness, knowing I would count every moment until the next time we met. When I arrived there, my mother put me to work spinning wool on a distaff and using a spindle to stretch out the thread. It was unbearably tedious, and my hands and arms promptly broke out in a rash. Itching, scratching, and wiggling, I complained.

"Hush, now!" my mother snapped. "A good wife must learn to spin wool. If you do not impress your husband with your domestic accomplishments, he may decide to divorce you and bring shame upon both you and your family."

That was my mother's worst fear—that she herself might be divorced and a cause for shame and scandal. All a man had to do to divorce his wife was make a formal statement in front of witnesses. And he always kept the children. It was much more difficult for a woman to end a marriage; no woman could take legal action on her own behalf or anyone else's. Nor could she inherit or own property, take part in the running of the government, or conduct business transactions. She was always controlled by her nearest male relative—father, husband, son or brother . . . and she lived in terror of offending him.

When I married Jason, I would not have to worry about my place in his life. He would treasure me for my conversation, my wit, and my appreciation of poetry. He would never notice—or if he did, he wouldn't care—that

I could not spin wool. So I spun dreams instead . . . and all my dreams were of Jason.

"Damn it, you're dreaming about him again!"

The angry comment caused Juliet to snap upright and rub the sleep from her eyes. As she did so, she discovered that the sun had already risen and so had Noah. He was kneeling beside her, glaring, his expression rife with accusation and annoyance.

"Are you all right?" She feared he might be feverish again. His face looked unnaturally red and congested. "You are not ill, are you?"

"No, I'm not ill! I'm damn bloody well fine! Just wonderful, thank you! I'm only stuck on a ledge a million miles from nowhere with a female who can't remember her own name and who keeps dreaming about some guy named Jason and claims she can't remember him either!"

There was nothing she could say other than what she had responded the first time he had complained similarly—and that had been precisely nothing. Noah was obviously on his way to recovery and fast regaining his strength. She could smell coffee boiling, and he looked as if he had made some effort to smooth down his unruly red hair and tidy himself to greet the morning.

"I cannot help it I cannot remember my dreams, No-ah." She was trying to be patient but felt irritable herself. She had explained all of this to him before; she simply could not remember the dreams she apparently had almost every night.

"You mentioned Zeus this time. I know who Zeus is—but do you?"

"Zeus?" She wracked her brain; the name meant nothing to her.

"Zeus is a Greek god, and you said 'Great Zeus!' as if you knew all about him. . . . Ever hear of Athene or Aphrodite? How about Pluto and Persephone?"

She shook her head, not answering. It was futile to discuss this subject when he was so irrational and accusatory.

"Well, if you're ever going to remember anything, it will probably be Jason—because Jason is the name you say the most. I wish to hell I knew who he was and what he means to you."

"So do I," she agreed morosely. "Then you would not be angry when I cannot remember."

Noah ran his hand through his coppery hair and sighed. "Hell, I'm sorry. It's just so damn frustrating. Surely, you can recall *something* of what you were dreaming."

She sat very still, thinking. "I was in a vineyard . . . The grapes were ripening, the sunlight filtering down through the leaves and dappling the earth below. . . ."

"Yes . . ." he prompted. "Then what?"

She frowned. Her head ached. She wished he would not pressure her so much. "I do not know. I was waiting for something . . . or spying on someone."

"Jason," he grumbled. "It had to be Jason. But what would you be doing in a vineyard?"

"I do not know. I do not *want* to know. . . . What difference does it make? 'Tis only a dream, No-ah. It has nothing to do with here and now."

She really did want to remember. She was trying. But she did not like the person Noah became when they spoke of these matters. She hated the look that came into his eyes. He became like a stranger; gone was his easy smile, his good humor . . . his patience. His face became dark and brooding; he almost frightened her.

"It has everything to do with here and now, Juliet. Your dreams are the key to who you are and how you got here. They're all you have left of the past. . . . I don't think you're trying hard enough; there must be some other details you can recall."

Juliet studied his dark, handsome face, his angry

eyes. In an intensely masculine way, he was beautiful even when he was scowling. And his body was lean, hard, and impressively muscular. She had discovered that rough-hewn muscularity during the time she had taken care of him and seen to his most intimate physical needs. . . . Then he had disturbed her only a little, for he had been so ill. Now, as he recovered and grew stronger, his masculinity was much more evident— and extremely disturbing. More and more, she found herself watching him, noting the width of his shoulders or some other physical detail, and . . . waiting. But waiting for what she could not have said.

"Yes . . ." she finally sighed. "Now that I think on it, I can recall other things. I was . . . excited. Elated, perhaps. I was glad to be there in that vineyard. I was happy."

"Happy about what?"

Noah bent nearer. She could not help noticing the reddish curling chest hair poking out of his shirt front. She glanced away, embarrassed and strangely breathless. They were so close together—so alone—with no one at all to see them in these mountains. Anything might happen. He was growing stronger every day, every hour. Soon, he would be stronger than she . . . and her feelings for him would be more difficult to control. She had no memory of this kind of thing, no experience; she only knew there was danger in his nearness.

"I cannot remember!" she cried, jerking away from him. "Why do you press me? When I do remember, I will tell you."

He sat back, regarding her with a deep frown. "Have you ever heard of Homer?"

"Homer?" The word resonated with familiarity.

"You *have* heard of him, haven't you? Once upon a time you knew all about him—probably read the *Illiad* and the *Odyssey,* the same as I have."

"I do not know what you are talking about." She

turned her back. "The name does sound familiar, but what it means or what he did, I have no idea."

His hand clamped down on her arm and he twisted her around to face him. "Juliet, don't you see? Jason and Zeus are names from Greek history. Zeus was a god and Jason a character from a Greek legend. I remember his story from my youth, when I was fascinated by tales concerning all things Greek. Adventure and fantasy laced the legends and poetry of that ancient time. I can't explain it, but when I read them, I felt as if I was actually there. . . . I *lived* all the tales and legends. You must have done the same. You must have been a lonely, unusual child, just as I was—and somehow those tales stayed buried in your mind and are now resurfacing in your dreams."

It all sounded too strange and fastastic. She could not accept it, though she supposed one explanation was as good as another for why she kept dreaming about someone named Jason.

"Tell me about this Jason," she urged, distracted by the flare of light in his deep brown eyes. When he was excited, his dark eyes glowed, and she had the odd sensation that she could lose herself in his eyes and never find her way out again. Her glance dropped to his mouth—that firm, arrogant mouth. What would it be like to be kissed by that mouth? A wave of heat consumed her. Embarrassed, she sought to banish the thought.

"Tell me everything you remember about Jason," she insisted.

"Well, now, let's see," he said, drawing up his knees to sit beside her on the ledge. "As I recall it, Jason was the only heir to the throne of Iolcus. When he was still a baby, his uncle stole the crown and banished Jason and his father. The uncle—Pelias, I believe his name was—announced that Jason could reclaim his place as heir only if he fetched the golden fleece from Colchis."

"The golden fleece? You mean fleece such as comes from sheep—*that* kind of fleece?"

Jason shot her a sideways glance. "You see? You haven't forgotten everything. . . . Maybe you're the daughter of a sheep farmer and my tale will jog some other memories. Yes, fleece such as comes from sheep, only this fleece came from a special golden ram, provided by Hera to aid Phrixus . . ."

"Hera . . . that name sounds familiar, too." Juliet thought hard for a moment, but only succeeded in worsening her headache. At least, the headache banished her passionate thoughts. "Go on . . ."

"What happened to the ram is a whole other story. All you need to know at this point is that its precious golden fleece was at a place called Colchis, and Jason was supposed to fetch it and bring it home. The first thing he did was build a ship, which he called the *Argo*. Next, he assembled a crew called the Argonauts. Then he visited King Phineus to ask his advice on dealing with the dangers that lay ahead. . . . Phineas said he would help Jason and his crew, but only if they would aid him in getting rid of the Harpies, birdlike creatures who . . ."

As Noah told the tale, Juliet listened intently. To her amazement, she discovered that she knew some of the tale before Noah related it. Knew about the Clashing Rocks which guarded the Straits of Bosphorous, crashing shut whenever a ship tried to pass through them. Guessed ahead of time that Jason would never be faithful to Medea, the witch who helped him along the way and demanded his everlasting love and loyalty in repayment . . . but *how* did she know these things?

Perhaps it was exactly as Noah claimed: She had read the tales in her youth, and now, they were resurfacing in her troubled dreams.

"There," Noah concluded. "Now you have the story of Jason and the Golden Fleece."

She thought a moment and then said, "A great tragedy, was it not? For all his adventures, Jason died an outcast, an unhappy mortal doomed to sorrow by his own ambitions."

"That's not how I see it." Noah leaned forward earnestly. "Most people live lives of utter boredom and predictability. Jason led a life of unremitting adventure and lofty aspiration. He had great goals, and he achieved them. Just because he lost everything in the end doesn't mean his life was all for naught. While he lived, he reached for the highest. . . . I give him credit for that if nothing else."

"But he never experienced true love!" she argued. "No matter that Medea could be cruel and capricious, she *loved* Jason to distraction. Yet he betrayed her. As soon as he got what he wanted, he threw her over to marry a simpering little princess. Neither Jason nor Medea were happy or successful. They both had serious character flaws, which was why they ended up miserable," she finished with a toss of her head.

"What a romantic you are!"

"And what a cynic you are! Since you love adventure so much, I presume you relish our present circumstances?"

Noah drew back with a grimace. "No, I don't. Indeed, it's long past time we left this ledge and started for Tucson. I feel well enough now, and if we don't leave soon, we're going to run out of water. I say we should collect our belongings—everything we can carry—and set out this morning."

At the mention of Tucson, Juliet's stomach lurched. A premonition of impending disaster swept her. She wished she could remember Tucson—remember anything—anything at all. She felt lost and frightened. Tucson meant nothing to her; yet it seemed to mean everything to Noah. Tucson was a world apart—one she did not know. One for which she was unprepared. There, she might find out about her family. She might also find out . . . nothing.

She touched Noah's arm. "Are you sure, No-ah? You feel strong enough to attempt this journey? As I told you before, I can search for water while you remain here resting. Another day or two won't matter."

He misinterpreted her concern. "You don't regard me as hero material like Jason, do you?" he snapped, getting stiffly to his feet. "Well, in my own way I've been searching for the Golden Fleece ever since I was old enough to figure out that life is what you make it, not something that *happens* to you while you're busy looking the other way. . . . Hell, yes, I'm ready to start for Tucson. And I'll get us there one way or another."

"No-ah, I did not mean to offend you . . ." She scrambled to her feet. "I do have confidence that you will get us there. I am filled with confidence."

"Like hell you are! You probably wish my name was Jason. *Then* you might have more faith in my abilities."

"But I do not know this Jason! He is not real to me! I cannot even recall his face!"

Noah stopped and looked at her, a smile turning up the corners of his mouth. . . . How she loved it when he smiled! It transformed his whole face and personality. The rough, hard edges seemed to melt away. Deep within her, another melting occurred. Even her knees seemed to liquefy.

"'You honestly can't?'"

"But I thought you wanted me to remember!" she exclaimed, confused.

"Oh, I do and I don't. Guess I'm afraid that if and when you do remember, I'll be hard put to compete with the guy."

She grinned at that. Noah could compete with anyone—it thrilled her that he wanted to compete. "I think we should forget about Jason and live one day, one hour at a time."

His smile faded. "You're right. We've got one hell of a journey ahead of us, and it's going to take all our stamina and strength to make it. We shouldn't waste time worrying about anything else. When we get to Tucson, there will be plenty of time to tackle our next problem—finding out who you are and where you come from."

"And whether or not I am already committed to someone else," she added softly.

His eyes narrowed. "That, too. Not that it makes a difference to me personally, you understand, since all we are—or ever will be—is two people caught in unusual circumstances."

Oh, Noah, she thought, as he turned away. How can you be so jealous one moment, and so distant the next? Did he care at all? she wondered. It did not seem so, yet at times, she thought he did. Nor could she sort out her own conflicting emotions. She was helplessly attracted to Noah. One could even say she *desired* him. But the uncertainties of her past made her wary of giving her heart to any man. If she did belong to Jason or some other man, she did not want to betray him—especially not with a cynical rogue who cared little or nothing about her!

Chapter Six

Noah was sweaty, exhausted, and thirsty. For the last hour, all he had been able to think about was the single swallow of water he and Juliet had agreed to allot themselves when the sun passed the meridian and began its downward slide toward the west. Soon, they would stop and rest—and drink from their carefully horded water supply. If they did not find more water in the next day or two, they would die of thirst.

He refused to dwell on the possibility. It had been five days since they left the ledge. They were now trudging across a broad, cactus-studded grassland, headed in the direction of Tucson. Or if not Tucson, he hoped to stumble across some ranch, farm, or fort that dotted the region, or perhaps one of the rivers, the San Simon or Gila that bisected the area. If they were lucky, they might encounter the Southern Pacific Railroad tracks or the Gila Trail, the western wagon route to California. Noah remembered crossing and recrossing it several times in company with big Ben Mellock. Tucson was a major stopping place for both the railway and the Gila Trail.

Ben and the ranchers had been searching the entire area from Fort Apache to Mexico. Since Fort Apache lay northeast of Tucson, Noah had concluded that the best chance of encountering civilization was to head roughly northwest. Unfortunately, assorted mountain ranges, canyons, foothills, and deserts hindered the direct route, and he had to decide whether to climb, cross, or go around these obstacles. Considering that they were on foot and he was still limping from his recent injuries, it would be a miracle if they made Tucson before summer's end. Along the way, they must find food and water and also avoid hostile Indians and vengeful ranchers.

They had to keep moving; to stay in one place on this dry, open plain was to court disaster . . . and Noah was not about to die after all he had survived thus far. He was determined to reach Tucson, locate Juliet's family or someone who knew her, and still get a book out of his adventures. It might be too late to tell Geronimo's story, but people back home should still be interested in reading about the land that had spawned the wily old Apache. Noah was just the man to tell them. . . . Before setting out with big Ben, he had familiarized himself with the most plentiful plant and animal species of Arizona, and he now considered himself an expert on burning hot days, freezing cold nights, and scenery that took away a man's breath. He could write a book just on the subject of dehydration.

Glancing back over the top of the bedroll lashed across his shoulders, he saw Juliet trudging resolutely some distance behind him. She had her head down to watch where she was going. Her red shawl swathed her arms, shoulders, and face so that she appeared shrouded and ready for burial. Slung over one shoulder, she carried the saddlebags. One of the two canteens dangled from the other. He adjusted his own burdens—rifle, cartridge belt, bedroll, canteen, several items taken from the saddlebags to lighten them, and a packet of the remaining dried horse meat.

Their food was holding out well; neither were able to eat much after a day's hard march . . . but the canteens were woefully light. Even so, Noah would have stopped and taken a drink then and there, were it not for the painful prospect of shaming himself in front of Juliet. She never complained, whined, or wept about their many discomforts. Disgustingly cheerful, she seemed to have absolute faith in his sense of direction. He wished he could be as certain he knew how to get them both to Tucson. . . . Of course, how could she have argued about directions when she had no memory of ever having been there?

She was altogether an amazing creature. He mentally listed her assets which included an ethereal grace and beauty that made it difficult for him to keep his mind—and hands—where they belonged. At night in the cold moonlight, she became an enchantress whose cloud of pale hair glimmered enticingly. By day, wrapped like a mummy, she displayed a quiet courage and perseverance that impressed him every bit as much as her beauty. He had come to know her well over the past five days and found himself admiring nearly everything about her.

Because of the cold mountain nights and the limitations of a single blanket roll, they slept near each other—lying without touching but close enough so that he could feel the heat radiating from her slender, sweetly-curved body. He could hear the slightest sound she made and always awoke when she talked in her sleep. At such times, he would lie rigid and unmoving, straining to hear every word. Sometimes, she laughed or giggled like a child and once recited something that sounded like a poem. Occasionally, she babbled a strange gibberish that might have been a foreign language—Greek perhaps?

Noah relished these moments as giving him information and insight into her character, plus the possibility of learning something that would enable him to identify her. . . . He also found the episodes extremely frustrating. Hardly a night went by that she did not mention Jason's name at least once. He was beginning to wish he could strangle the nocturnal intruder. Jason threatened his budding, albeit reluctant feelings for Juliet. Despite his best efforts to keep his distance emotionally as well as physically, he had grown protective of her. Found himself worrying over whether or not she was hungry, thirsty, or getting sunburned. Could her strength hold out through the arduous journey? His worst fear was that he might have to watch her die out here and not be able to do a thing to help her. . . . She was his responsibility, and he did not like this Jason hovering in the background, waiting to claim her as his own.

But there was nothing he could do about Jason, except ignore him and trust that Juliet's dreams would soon turn to *him*. When they did, he hoped she would want him to put his arms around her in the night and hold her close, maybe even do more than just hold her. . . . Damn, but he was thirsty! He couldn't even think about sex because of his damn thirst!

Juliet must be thirsty, too. For *her* sake, he would stop, permit them both to drink, and rest while the sun was so hot. Despite what she thought, it was foolish to keep going during the midday heat. She had pointed out that they could not afford long rest periods during the prime travel time of the day. Because of the danger of a fatal slip on the uneven, rough terrain, they dared not keep going at night. Just this once, a brief rest could not hurt, Noah decided.

Mind made up, he stayed where he was and waited for Juliet to catch up with him. Pushing back a fold of her shawl, she gazed at him inquiringly. "What is wrong, No-ah? Why are you stopping?"

"Thought you might need a drink of water. It's damn hot with the sun beating down on us."

Smiling, she shook her head. "Thank you for your concern, but I can make it a little farther."

Beneath the dusty, dirty shawl, her face resembled a fresh-plucked rose. Lightly sheened with perspiration—"dew" the ladies back home would call it—her skin was perfect, her mouth a tender Cupid's bow. He could not keep his body from responding to her nearness. His heartbeat accelerated, his palms grew sweaty, and his pants constricted him uncomfortably.

"I'm glad you're such a stalwart heroine," he growled, annoyed at his lack of self-control. "Trouble is *I* can't make it any farther. I feel like a boiled lobster."

"A lobster? That is something to eat?"

"Damn fine eating. I could eat a half dozen or so about now. Dripping in butter and accompanied by an ice-cooled drink."

He slung down his belongings as soon as he could get his arms free of the lashings. Then he sat down on a large rock and reached for his canteen. Juliet regarded him soberly, then she, too, divested herself of the saddlebags and her own canteen. But she did not drink from it as he did. He felt guilty as the hot, brackish water slid down his parched throat.

"Now, tell me the truth, Juliet. Aren't you just a little thirsty?"

She nodded. "Yes, but our water is almost gone, No-ah. I will wait and drink tonight."

"Like hell you will! I drank, so you've got to drink. We're in this together. We share what we've got—drop for drop—until it's gone."

"No, truly I am not *that* thirsty, No-ah. You may have my share, if you like. I will wait, as I said."

Setting down his canteen, he grabbed hers, unstoppered it, and held the leather-covered container out to her. It was an army issued piece of equipment he had bought at Fort Apache. The letters U.S. were stamped on it. "Drink. Don't argue with me. Just drink. Otherwise you might collapse in this heat."

She seemed to find the uplifted arms of a nearby *saguaro* cactus unusually fascinating. It was a magnificent specimen, taller than Noah himself, its arms starkly green against the brilliant blue of the sky. He had heard that *saguaros* lived more than a hundred years, but at the moment, the longevity of the plant failed to interest him.

"Come on, Juliet . . . please. I mean it. You need the water. Even a mouthful is better than nothing."

She sighed. "All right, No-ah . . . if you insist."

She took the canteen, lifted it to her lips, and drank a very small swallow. Noah doubted she got a whole mouthful. "More," he snapped. "That wasn't enough."

She lowered the canteen and licked her lips. "That was more than enough. I feel quite refreshed now."

"You can't remember what refreshment is, and neither can I." He stoppered the canteen, laid it aside, and took off the red bandana knotted around his neck. It was a spare he had kept in his saddlebags, but now it was nearly as dirty as the one he had used to bandage his thigh wound. "Here . . ." he said, offering it to her. "Wipe your face."

She took the kerchief and daintily dabbed at her brow. A dirty smear promptly appeared on her forehead, marring the pristine purity of her skin. He did not tell her about it; trying to remove the dirt would probably only make matters worse. Grunting, he took back the cloth and wiped the sweat from his own forehead. Sharing a bandana seemed like an intimate act. Fumble-fingered, he retied it around his neck with a strong sense of connection to Juliet. Her sweat and his had mingled; he had a sudden mental image of their two wet bodies sliding across each other. Incredibly, considering the heat, a little shiver raced down his spine.

He stood up again. "Let's find some shade and rest a few minutes. The sun is roasting my brain."

"Only for a few minutes," Juliet cautioned. "I thought we agreed to keep going through the daylight hours."

"We did, but I've got to get out of this sun for awhile. I'd be all right if I had my hat."

"Why don't you tie your kerchief around your head for protection?" Juliet suggested as they headed toward a narrow gorge between two walls of rock rising up to form a flat-topped mesa on the sunbaked plain. A slight overhang of ochre-colored rock shaded several large boulders below. It was the only respite from the sun for miles around.

"Good idea. Might try it. My nose is near burnt to a crisp."

"If I see any more of that plant from which I made the salve for your sunburn, I will make it again. It soothed your burnt skin, did it not?"

"Saved my life," Noah grudgingly agreed.

Before he had adjusted to the fierce sunshine in his hatless state, he had thought he would go mad from the pain of that first bad sunburn. In her practical way, Juliet had observed his agony and calmly done something about it. From a plant he thought was called an aloe, she had broken off some spines and made a paste of the moisture it contained. Her success had simultaneously amazed and annoyed him. Since she could not remember her own name, he felt *he* should be the one with all the answers. He may have learned the names of many desert and mountain plants, but it was Juliet who had unlocked their secrets.

"Keep your shawl wrapped tight around your face and shoulders," he advised her. "You're fairer than I am; your skin will curl up and peel right off like the skin of an onion."

"I have been most careful, No-ah. My *himation* does an excellent job of protecting me."

Noah stopped dead in his tracks. "Your *what?*" He swung around to face her. "What did you call that red shawl?"

The golden-brown eyes peering out of the garment in question looked perplexed. "I do not know. What *did* I call it?"

"You called it a *himation,* whatever the hell *that* is!"

"A *himation,*" she slowly repeated. "I cannot tell you what it means—or why I said it. The word somehow rolled off my tongue."

"It's Greek! I bet it's Greek, and you know other Greek words, too. Maybe that's what you mutter in your sleep. You must have gone further than I did and studied the language extensively. I gave up on it after a few tries with a tattered little dictionary. I bet you knew someone who actually understood and spoke the language."

Brow furrowed, eyes unhappy, she considered the suggestion. "Perhaps I did study Greek, No-ah, but I cannot remember. I assure you I do not know the meaning of the word *himation.*"

"It means your red shawl. Obviously, it means that. It's damn weird you'd remember something so insignificant. . . . Why not your real name? Or the place where you were born? Or the name of your parents? . . . Out of all the things you might have chosen to remember, why did you pick that?"

"Because I did not *choose* to remember anything! The word just came to me. Perhaps it means nothing, and you are making something out of nothing."

"Maybe I am. . . . Oh, sit down. Lean back and rest. We're both going mad from the sun and the heat."

Throwing down his gear, he stamped his feet to scare away any snakes or scorpions, then sat down and leaned wearily against a second large boulder cluttering the narrow gorge. During the rainy season, this would be a perfect place for one of the flash floods he had heard about from the ranchers. At the moment, the gorge was dry as dust.

"Do not be angry with me, No-ah." Juliet still stood in front of him, shouldering her heavy burdens, the least of which were the saddlebags. "I cannot help it I am unable to tell you how or why that word burst from my mouth."

Noah struggled to subdue his irritation. He could not explain why her mysterious background bothered him so much. "I know . . ." he finally sighed. "It's not your fault. Just put down your gear and rest."

Feeling like a rotten lout, he closed his eyes. "I'm sorry I get so mad at you. I just want to understand your obsession for everything Greek."

"If I do have an obsession, which I am not certain

I do, it should not make you angry. Did you not admit that as a child, you had one, too?"

He slitted his eyes to look at her. "Yes, but I was strange and different. My obsession was a distinct oddity in my youthful character. You can't have had the exact same obsession. I just don't think it's possible."

Juliet eased off the saddlebags and sat down on the rock beside him. *"Himation* might not even be a Greek word."

"Then again it might. . . . Lacking a dictionary or a handy Greek scholar, we have no way of proving whether it is or is not, do we?"

Sighing deeply, he let his eyes drift shut and dozed a little. Even beneath the jut of rock, it was terribly hot. He was still thirsty, his mouth parched. Thoughts of cold, refreshing lakes and icy rivers filled his aching head. . . . He dreamed of swimming in them, gulping them down, bathing in them, dunking Juliet in the cold, cold waters. He wished they could have stayed in the mountains where the nights made the days more bearable.

A snarling sound woke him. Growls and hisses punctuated the still, hot air. Noah shook himself fully awake and automatically reached for Juliet, slumped against the rock beside him. Not twenty feet away, a cougar crouched in the rock-strewn gorge, its tawny yellow coat almost the same color as the boulders. The animal paid them no heed; it was watching the half dozen or more doglike creatures slinking around behind it. Lips drawn back over sharp yellow teeth, the cougar screamed and swiped at the coyotes. They leaped out of the way, then crouched and slunk nearer, snapping at the cougar and making long low growling noises deep in their throats.

"Juliet, don't move!" Noah whispered as she stirred and sat up rubbing her eyes. "I'm going to try and pick up my rifle without attracting their attention."

"The big cat is hurt, No-ah! That is why they are after it. Its front paw is bloody."

"Don't move, I said!" Noah grabbed for his rifle. Before he could raise it, Juliet jumped off the rock and hurried toward the fracas, her slender body blocking his line of fire. *"Juliet!"*

Noah could not imagine what she thought she was doing. He wanted to stop her, but his legs—like his mind—refused to function. Fused to the rock, he gaped as she walked calmly to the cougar, laid her hand on its large tawny head, and frowned reprovingly at the coyotes. The animals froze and stared at her. Then the largest coyote—a big, tan, black-sprinkled fellow with tiny eyes and a lolling tongue—gave a sharp yelp, spun around, and fled with his tail between his legs. He disappeared among the rocks and boulders farther up the gorge, and his companions wasted no time following.

Juliet patted the big cat on the head, gazed long into its yellow eyes, then nodded slightly. Something seemed to pass between them—some agreement or understanding. Then the cougar bounded in the opposite direction, its injured paw apparently forgotten. With a smug satisfied smile on her face, Juliet strolled back to him.

"He will be all right," she said. "He simply tore open his paw on some of that hairy cactus you call *cholla,* and the smell of blood excited the coyotes."

Noah bolted to his feet. "You could have gotten yourself killed! What in God's name did you think you were doing?"

"Why . . . stopping a fight—a *potential* fight. That is all. I knew they would be surprised to see me, and their surprise would cause them to reconsider their intentions."

"Those animals aren't human, for God's sake!" Beside himself with fury and the chilling fear that she might have been torn to pieces right in front of him, Noah was shouting at the top of his lungs.

Juliet lifted her chin defiantly. "They understood what I was asking of them. They are not stupid, Noah."

"They may not be, but *you* are!" Noah raked his fingers through his hair. He wanted to pull it out. "Just how do you account for this astounding ability to communicate with wild animals?"

Her golden-brown eyes darkened. "I cannot account for it. I simply knew what to do and did it. To thank me for my interference—which saved him from a bad fight he might have lost with his sore paw—the cougar told me where to find water."

"What?"

"He told me where to find water," Juliet pointed to the canyon wall rising almost straight up from the depths of the gorge. "Up there. . . . Somewhere up there is water."

"Are you insane? I didn't hear that cougar say a damn word. This whole thing is ridiculous. Animals can't talk. And I didn't hear *you* utter a single word either."

"I did not have to say anything out loud. I spoke to them with my thoughts, No-ah. Just because you do not understand how I did it does not mean it cannot be done." Juliet walked past him and calmly began gathering her things.

"Where in hell do you think you're going?"

"To find water." Hoisting the saddlebags over her shoulder, Juliet carefully rewrapped herself in her red shawl—her *himation.* "I am going deeper into the gorge. There I will climb the canyon wall and find the water that has been keeping alive the coyotes, the big cat, and whatever other animals live around here."

Noah leaped after her. "Juliet, this is foolishness! Surely, you see that. It was pure luck and coincidence that those animals ran away without attacking you. There's a logical explanation for everything that's happened. Give me a minute. I'll think of exactly what it is."

99

Juliet faced him with the calm deliberation that he had come to dread as well as admire. "I am going to look for water, No-ah. The big cat did not lie to me. I am sure I can find it. Before this, I should have thought to ask the birds and animals where the water is. As long as there are other living creatures around us, there has to be water. . . . I am ashamed I did not think of it sooner. 'Tis one more thing I have forgotten—that I can understand the thoughts of animals, and *they* can understand *my* thoughts."

"Anyone listening to you would think you were insane—completely mad, Juliet! I don't know what happened between you and that cougar and those coyotes, but whatever it was isn't natural or normal. You're making it all up in your head. If you climb the wall of this canyon, you're going to exhaust yourself and make me mad as hell."

"You do not have to come with me." She regarded him unblinkingly from the cowl of her shawl. "When I have found water, I will call down to you."

"If you're going to do this stupid thing, I'm coming with you! I cannot allow you to go off by yourself, and you damn well know it!"

Her expression remained grave, but a smile trembled on her lips. "I would be delighted if you accompanied me," she said, smooth as butter.

"Permit me to get my gear first, your highness," he snapped sarcastically. "Then you may lead the way."

When she discovered there was no water to reward her hard climb, she would realize she had imagined everything. Cougars and coyotes couldn't talk. . . . Still, it was amazing that they had *seemed* to exchange thoughts with Juliet. He had never seen anything like it. . . . He might not have seen it at all. In this heat, he might be hallucinating, conjuring up the animals and even Juliet herself.

Chapter Seven

Water—there it was! Water was bubbling out of a crevice in the rocks not far from the edge of the steeply sloping wall of the canyon. Juliet laughed aloud. She had not been wrong. Looking into the big cat's yellow eyes, she had known that water was nearby. . . . He had been drinking somewhere. Noah would be so pleased—or maybe he wouldn't be. He did seem to hate it when he could not understand her. Little did he know she hated her own mysterious secrets as much, or more, than he did!

No one who had not experienced it could understand how depressing it was to be unable to remember one's past or to understand how one knew things. However, none of that mattered at the moment. . . . All that did matter was the wonderful sound of water gurgling up out of the rocks, spilling over them— water! Clear, fresh, cool . . . the source of all life.

Juliet peered over the precipice to look for Noah. The climb through the gorge and up the canyon wall had not been as difficult as the one leading to the ledge where they had stayed for so long, but it had been steep enough to cause her heart to thump loudly in her ears. Noah's darkly-tanned face was red from the effort as he picked his way among the boulders, rocks, and prickly growth, searching for handholds to help himself. . . . Why had they not noticed that more plants grew here and of a different variety than elsewhere in the canyon? The lush growth alone was a sign of moisture.

Struck with an irresistible idea, Juliet quickly divested herself of the saddlebags and her canteen, then got out the little dented coffeepot. Filling it with water, she leaned over the precipice and tilted the pot so the water poured out and cascaded on top of Noah's head. He let out a yell that echoed through the canyon.

"Water, No-ah! It's right up here! Wonderful, glorious water, just as I told you, and the big cat told me."

Kneeling, she refilled the pot and drank deeply, then splashed the water on her face, hands, and down her bosom. . . . It felt marvelous. Better than marvelous. The sensation was exquisite.

"Damnation! There *is* water!" Arriving on top, Noah dropped to his knees beside her.

She began splashing him. He laughed and splashed back. Shrieking and shouting, they had a delightful few minutes soaking themselves. Finally, Noah held up his hand. "Take it easy. We better stop. Might use it all up before we've even filled the canteens. Let me drink some first."

He stretched out on the rocks and buried his face in the bubbling spring. It really was not much water, Juliet realized, scolding herself for wasting a single drop. The spring erupted between the rocks, wet them for a short distance running downward on the uneven surface, then disappeared into a crevice. . . . There might be an inexhaustible supply trapped in the bowels of the mesa, or there might be very little.

She crawled the length of the streambed and put her ear to the crack where the spring disappeared. She could hear water falling on rock somewhere inside the mountain. Sitting back on her heels, she wondered if it would be possible to locate the place where the water was falling.

"That cougar didn't tell you where to find water," Noah scoffed, coming up beside her. "You found it by studying the growth on this side of the canyon. Green

102

plants—more than just *cholla* and prickly pear—dot this whole area, so you knew that water had to be here somewhere."

Something twisted deep inside her; he did not believe her! Did not understand. She did not fully understand it herself, but somehow, through the cougar, she had *known* where to look for water. The plants had had nothing to do with it.

"Believe what you wish, No-ah. I have no wish to argue. Let us see if we can find where the water goes from here."

They spent the rest of the afternoon searching, but all they found was a rocky cave set high in the wall of the canyon. At the back, a narrow passageway led deeper into the bowels of the mountain, but it was too late in the day to go exploring.

"We'll spend the night here," Noah announced. "Let's gather fuel to make a fire. This might be the den of that cougar; a fire will keep him out."

Juliet sniffed the dank, stuffy air of the cave. She detected no odor of cat—or coyote either. If the cave had ever sheltered animals, it was now abandoned. She helped Noah assemble dried *mesquite* branches and other thorny tinder, then watched while he took out one of the magical skinny sticks, which when struck against rock produced a flame. This was a much quicker way of making a fire than striking together two flat rocks to make an elusive spark, but she had brought the rocks in the saddlebags just in case. Not many of the magical sticks were left.

While Noah's back was turned, Juliet slipped out of the cave and returned in near darkness to the little spring to fill the cook pot with water. They had already filled the canteens and the coffeepot, but she wanted desperately to wash more thoroughly. She hated being dirty all the time and hoped to persuade Noah to leave her alone in the cave for a bit, so she could remove her clothing and truly cleanse herself.

On her way back to the cave with the water, she was

startled to hear a loud whoop. A moment later, Noah came dashing out of the cave, followed by a swarm of small black shapes. Wings flapping, they rose into the red-streaked sky, where the sun had just set.

"Bats!" he exclaimed, disgusted, as she came up. "Did you see them? They flew out of that narrow passageway at the back of the cave."

"That means there *must* be an inner chamber. To-morrow, we will find it."

"Not me. . . . I'm not going into some chamber full of bats." His voice held a note of fear. He was almost trembling.

Had her hands not been occupied, she might have soothed him with a quick embrace. Instead, she walked past him to enter the cave. "I will ask them not to disturb you, No-ah. I will tell them you are afraid."

"I'm no such thing—don't you dare tell them that!" Noah followed her back inside the cave, but he did not get too close to the back of it, she noticed. "Not that I think for one minute that you can talk to them anyway."

She set the pot down near the fire. "Would you care to test my abilities? Perhaps I should call them back again."

He glared at her. "Don't be ridiculous."

She thought she heard a faint flapping sound. One last bat might still be in the passageway. "There's another one coming. I will call him to me."

No sooner had she said the words when a huge bat with an enormous wingspan swooped and dipped between her and Noah. A big old fellow, the bat homed in on her thoughts as if the two of them were dear old friends. Noah stood petrified. Obviously, he wanted to run but did not want to leave her. "Good God," he muttered. "It's the Granddaddy of all bats."

She implored the bat not to go near him, and it did not. It only soared and circled in the narrow confines of the cave. Noah withstood it for several silent mo-ments, but the color all drained from his face, and his tanned skin got whiter and whiter. Then he tore off his shirt and wrapped it around his head. A moment later, he ripped it off and wrapped it around *her* head.

Whenever the bat swooped near him, he ducked. "If you can talk to the damn thing, tell it to go away!" he hollered.

Biting back laughter, she took pity on him. "Depart now, my friend," she said in a low voice, and the bat winged out of the cave.

Noah slowly unwound the shirt from her head. For the first time since she had met him, he looked sheepish. "Bats can get tangled in your hair, you know."

She did not say a word. There had been no real danger of that happening, but Noah's efforts to protect her, to put her safety ahead of his own, deeply touched her.

"I still don't believe you can talk to them," he scoffed, shrugging back into his shirt.

She only smiled.

"Aren't you going to say anything?"

"Thank you for caring, No-ah." She knelt down beside her pot of water. "Will you leave me now? I desire a few moments alone before it gets altogether dark."

"Leave?" he echoed disbelievingly. "You want me to leave?"

"I wish some privacy." She pursed her lips together. Must this sweet, obtuse man be told *everything?* "I have brought water back from the spring, and I would like to bathe."

"Oh. . . . Well, in that case, I'll go bathe myself, back at the spring."

She unwrapped the *himation* and shook out her hair. "Thank you again."

"Women!" he muttered, stomping from the cave.

She smothered her laughter. He, too, would be clean, she thought. For the first time in their relationship, they would both be clean—and at the same time. A wild fluttering began in her chest, as if a horde of bats had taken flight within her. Sternly she reminded herself of how annoying Noah could sometimes be. How was it possible that he could also be so endearing . . . and exciting?

They had bathed—albeit in a limited fashion—and they had eaten. Noah had even shaved the reddish, rough-looking beard from his face. Tonight, they would not have to worry about chance thunderstorms or other threats, except maybe harmless bats. Juliet doubted she would awaken even once to find Noah staring anxiously into the darkness, head cocked to detect anything dangerous. A cheery fire illuminated the interior of the cave, casting flickering shadows on the ochre-colored walls. It was time to lie down on the bedroll beside Noah . . . and Juliet could not bring herself to do it.

She sat with knees drawn up, arms wrapped around them, chin resting on them, while she gazed into the leaping flames. She did not look at Noah, but she was intensely aware of his presence. He lay on his side, already stretched out on the blanket they used to cushion the ground, the second blanket bunched at his feet ready to be drawn over them both once she had joined him on the makeshift bed.

She longed to join him—but she was afraid.

They had spoken little since he had come back into the cave, his hair dripping wet, his handsome features rosy from a thorough scrubbing. Occasionally, their eyes met, and what she read in Noah's dark, hungry eyes told her he felt the same way she did—tense, nervous . . . and expectant. Something was going to happen between them. She knew it with the same certainty that she knew the sun would rise tomorrow, and the day would be hot and dusty.

What she could not decide was whether or not she should allow it to happen. Noah wanted her. She could sense his hunger as surely as if he had spoken.

She recognized and could not help responding to his desire. It was an attraction as old and elemental as the mountains surrounding them. But dare she permit any intimacy between them? Noah had never said anything to indicate his feelings for her, and she scarcely knew how to evaluate her own feelings. Their circumstances were so unusual that neither could rationally assess the attraction they felt or the connection that already existed.

They had been thrust into each other's company and forced to rely on each other, fueling a relationship that might never have blossomed in other circumstances. And then there was the major complication: Juliet did not know her own self, much less Noah. Thus far, he had shared little of his previous life, and she had had nothing to share with him. In many ways, they were still strangers. She could awaken tomorrow morning recalling that she was wed or promised to another man and not free to commit herself to Noah.

Assuming for a moment that she *was* free, she could not decide if she would choose to spend the rest of her life with him or not. He could make her laugh and he stirred tender emotions, but he could also rouse her anger. He was arrogant—conceited, actually—and believed that his way of doing things was better than hers and probably anyone else's. He seemed to have a low regard for females in general; he consistently failed to acknowledge her capabilities, even when her skills and talents obviously outstripped his.

Given all that, he was a unique and wonderful man. Ignoring his own fears, he did try to look out for her, and despite the odds against them, he was doggedly determined to find the way back to civilization. She admired his gritty courage and knew she could rely on him. Thus far, his gruff galantry had kept him from asserting the masculinity she found so appealing . . . but tonight he had reached his limits. Tonight, he would make an issue of his needs, and she would have to decide how far to go with him.

"Aren't you coming to bed?" Noah murmured into the hollow hush of the cave.

"Soon. Go ahead if you wish, No-ah. It has been a long day; you must be weary."

"You've got to be as tired as I am—or worse. I'm a man, after all, and widely accounted the stronger of the species."

Smiling to herself, she forebore to correct his misimpressions. "I know very well that you are a man." She peeked at him from beneath her lashes.

Oh, yes, he clearly *was* a man. In his recent ablutions, he had again removed his shirt and neglected to replace it. His bare chest and upper arms bulged with muscles. Dark, reddish hair—darker than the hair on his head—covered those muscles, shading the white areas untouched by the sun. The triangular pattern on his chest seemed to point downward into his britches, and she could not help remembering what he had looked like *down there,* when she had undressed him to tend the wound on his thigh. At the time, her musings had not been sexual. Now, they were, and a blush heated her cheeks.

"Come here, Juliet . . ." His compelling dark eyes were watching her intently, as if he had mastered the art of reading her thoughts all of a sudden—thoughts she had rather keep private.

She gazed at him directly. "What do you want, No-ah?"

He said nothing for a moment, only continued to watch her, his eyes skimming her hair, her mouth, and the swell of her bosom. "I just want to be near you—to have you near me." His voice was low and cajoling. "We're all alone, Juliet, and I want—I *need*—your softness and your warmth."

She needed *his* also, but if she permitted him to hold and caress her, it would not be enough for either of them.

"I am flattered that you find me appealing, No-ah. But I think it safer I remain where I am."

108

"Safer? Do you fear me, Juliet? I would not harm you. Surely, you know that by now."

He sounded hurt. Juliet knew a moment of contrition; she had as much as told him she did not trust him, when the truth was she did not trust herself.

"You would not wish to harm me. I know that, No-ah. But we would both be hurt if . . . if we became lovers and then learned that I belong to someone else."

"We may *never* learn that. Fact is we may die out in this wilderness without ever discovering who you are or making it back to civilization. . . . Why shouldn't we hold and comfort each other in the night? You don't find me repulsive, do you?"

Startled, she raised her eyes to his. "Oh, no! I do not find you repulsive in the least."

He grinned—a rather superior, but charming grin. It occurred to her that he must have planned to lie half naked on the blanket, calculating the effect such a provocative pose would have on her. "Then why don't you come join me? All I want to do is hold you—put my arms around you and keep you warm. It's ridiculous for us to sleep night after night without touching each other. For one thing, it's cold."

"It will not be cold tonight, No-ah. This mountain is not that high, and we have the fire—and the cave. We are amply sheltered from the wind."

"I am cold *inside,* not outside. I need your warmth, Juliet. What harm can there be in that? You won't be cheating on Jason just to let me hold you."

Jason. She had momentarily forgotten him—could not remember him in the first place, or understand why she kept dreaming of him. She could summon no face to go with the name, because when she awoke, even when she was able to recall vivid snatches of her dreams, the one thing she could not see was Jason's face.

" 'Tis true that Jason means nothing to me now—but someday I might remember him, and *then* I would feel badly if I had cheated on him."

Noah scowled. "It isn't cheating simply to stay warm. I've already told you I won't hurt you. I won't rape or attack you or do anything you don't want me to do."

That was precisely what she feared—she *would* want him to do more than hold her. She wanted him to do more right now. She wanted to melt into him, inhale his scent, touch and explore his hairy chest and bulging muscles—and see what would happen next.

"I will lie down beside you as usual," she finally said. "But you may only put one arm around me. Nothing more."

If he did more, she might not be able to resist him.

"All right. I'm willing to bargain. I'll only put one arm around you—but first, you have to let me kiss you."

"Kiss me?"

"One kiss . . . that's all I ask, Juliet. Maybe neither of us will feel anything if we kiss, and then all this fuss and bother and examination of conscience will be for nothing. We'll discover we aren't really attracted to each other. We can go on as before, but without the temptation."

She leaned forward to better see his face in the flickering firelight. Was he teasing? Poking fun at her? The corners of his mouth looked suspiciously twitchy. But his eyes held a wonderful yearning; when she herself wanted it so much, how could she possibly refuse?

Rising, she went to him and knelt down on the blanket. "I will give you one kiss, No-ah, but only so we may sleep in peace this night. There can be no intimacy between us, not tonight or any night. You yourself must realize this. You belong to someone named Emily, and I . . ."

"Emily! Emily has nothing to do with this. This is between you and me. Here we are, in the middle of nowhere. . . . We may never encounter other people again. We might die out here. All I ask is a bit of comfort and warmth, a little drop of compassion

. . . not a lifetime commitment, Juliet. It's a bit premat- ture for that, don't you think?"

It was, and she was being foolish.

"I said I would kiss you and I will, No-ah," she acceded. "But you must show me how to do it. Remember, I have no memory of kissing. I may never have kissed before."

He grinned. "I'd be happy to instruct you in the delightful art." He lay back on the blanket, gazing up at her, then grasped her shoulders and gently drew her down on top of him. The feel of his body against hers came as a shock. She tried to draw away but he held her fast. "First, you have to get comfortable, or it won't be any good. Relax. Stretch out. A kiss is always better if all our other parts fit properly together."

She felt a slight tremor of suspicion. "This is how it is always done? With the woman lying on top of the man?"

"Always," he told her solemnly. "But there's one exception."

"And what is that?"

"When the man lies on top of the woman. Would you prefer that position?"

"No! Oh, no!" It seemed much safer the way they were.

"Well, then." He wrapped his arms around her. "Let your body go all soft and yielding. I'll hold you a moment until you relax."

She did not think she could ever relax with him holding her. Keeping her pinioned against him, he began to stroke her back and shoulders. "Stretch out on top of me," he urged, his nose buried in her hair, his lips teasing her earlobe. "You'll see. It's much better that way."

She unfolded her legs and gingerly obeyed. He was all hard muscle and flat plane, yet warm and comfortable, much better than the hard ground. Her breasts flattened against his chest, and the rest of her body seemed to fit perfectly into the cradle of his body. She tried to relax, but it was difficult with her senses spinning. She inhaled the scent of him, a dizzying combination of woodsmoke, man, and the salve she had made for his sunburn.

She wiggled a little lower to bring her mouth closer to his. He groaned slightly. Fearing she had hurt him, she lifted herself on her elbows. "What is it? What is wrong? Am I too heavy?"

"No . . ." Her hair muffled his voice as he pulled her back down on top of him. "No, you just feel so damn good. We should delay the kiss for a few minutes and simply enjoy holding each other."

"But I am not holding you; you are holding me. And I do not wish to hurt you."

"I promise you. Nothing hurts . . . well, almost nothing. What *does* hurt is a pleasant discomfort."

She lay perfectly still and gradually became aware of swells and bulges on his body that she had not noticed at first. Something hard and warm was pressing between her thighs. She wanted to rub against the hardness to ease the pressure in her own nether regions, but suspected that such an action might be improper. So she lay utterly still, absorbing sensations, while Noah hugged her closer still and nibbled her earlobe.

That, too, was a pleasant feeling, but she bucked in surprise when she suddenly felt his hot wet tongue. "Is licking my ear a part of kissing?" she demanded, shivering slightly.

"Yes," he murmured. "It's a prelude to it. Before I take my kiss, I want everything that leads up to it."

Kissing must be quite a delicious experience, if all this leading up to it felt so nice.

Noah's hands began to roam her body—one holding the upper half of her clamped tightly to him, the other sliding lower to palm her bottom. The intimacy of the act shocked her. "No-ah, do not touch me there. I am certain it cannot be proper."

"God, Juliet," he muttered softly. "You're so soft

and warm and sweetly rounded. You're so wonderfully feminine, sweetheart."

Sweetheart. She liked the sound of that, and her protests died on her lips. He kneaded her bottom for a moment, his breath hot on her ear, then he pushed down on her buttocks . . . Strange! She did not remember him being so big down there—not that she had examined him closely—but he was certainly big now. And hard. When he surged upward against her, her thighs clenched in reaction. The core of her throbbed and tightened.

One hand moved upward to cup her face. "Now, Juliet . . . I want to kiss you now. Tell me you want it, too."

Breathless, she could only nod. Never had she felt such excitement—such warmth and wonder. Her blood pounded through her veins. Her heart galloped.

"Open your mouth," he whispered.

She parted her lips. Their breath mingled. He raised his head, tilted it slightly, and pressed his mouth to hers. Surprisingly, their noses did not bump. Then his tongue plunged deeply into her mouth. This she had not expected. She tried to raise her head.

"No . . ." he breathed, pressing her head back down. His tongue twined with hers. It filled her mouth, moving in and out, in rhythm with his hips thrusting upward. His hand clutched her bottom. His chest hair abraded her nipples. She could feel the heat of him through her clothing. He rolled over, so that he was now on top and she on the bottom.

He kissed her eyelids, nose, and cheek. Kissed her hair and forehead. She sensed that his control had slipped, and she was spinning out of control along with him. She could scarcely breathe. She began kissing him back. Kissing everything she could reach with her lips. His mouth reclaimed hers, his tongue urgently seeking her tongue. His hand found her breast. In his eagerness, he tore at the fabric covering her bosom.

His sudden ferocity alarmed her. She broke the contact of their mouths. "No-ah! No-ah, stop!"

He did not stop. Did not seem to hear. Fear welled up in her, making her frantic. "No-ah!" She choked on his name and struggled desperately. "No-ah, listen to me!"

Chapter Eight

It took a moment for Noah to realize where he was and what he was doing—practically ravishing Juliet. She was now beating on his back with her fists and calling his name.

"No-ah, stop! Stop it, please!"

Horrified, Noah levered himself off her. Juliet's beautiful golden-brown eyes were wide with terror, her cheeks flushed—she was terrified! And with good reason. Her gown had a wide gap in it where he had torn it free from the pin at her shoulder. The fabric itself was ripped, revealing an exquisite pink and white breast that quivered beneath his gaze. Quickly, Juliet covered herself. Then she rolled over, hiccupping on a sob.

"Oh, Juliet. . . . Oh, God, I'm sorry . . ." He tried to gather her into his arms, but she flinched away from him. He was sick with self-loathing.

"Juliet, I never meant for things to get out of hand like this. . . . Sweetheart, I swear it. I lost my head, that's all. I could kill myself for what I did. . . . Juliet, look at me. Please, Juliet, say you forgive me."

He sounded like an insincere, babbling fool but could not stop himself. His behavior appalled him. Now, Juliet would never trust him, never be at ease with him again. He had betrayed her trust. And the worst of it was, he did not understand how it had happened. He had never lost his head with a woman before—never come so close to forcing himself on one. One kiss . . . one little kiss was all it had taken . . . and he had gone off like a rocket, like a whole boatload of fireworks in Boston harbor on the Fourth of July.

He had damn near raped his sweet little Juliet. His golden-eyed beauty who knew nothing of men and their passions, or if she ever had known had completely forgotten. . . . Damnation! He was a low-lying snake, the lowest of the low. He ought to be castrated like a squealing pig, hung by his balls over a slow-burning fire, buried in an anthill up to his neck . . .

" 'Tis not your fault, No-ah," Juliet murmured, keeping her back to him.

"Not my fault! The hell it isn't!"

"I should never have agreed to kiss you. I knew it was a dangerous thing to do; still, I wanted to do it. Therefore, 'tis all *my* fault."

Noah reached for Juliet and roughly turned her over on the blanket. She would not look at him and kept her eyes tightly closed. Tears squeezed out from beneath her delicate eyelids and slid down her reddened cheeks. At the sight of her tears, he really wished he could kill himself.

"I knew better," she whispered. "You are not to blame. You would never have taken such liberties had I not given my permission."

"Nonsense! Bull feathers! . . . I am a swine, do you hear me, Juliet? Open your eyes and look at me! It's not your fault, it's mine! I don't know what came over me. I've kissed women by the dozens, but I've never torn off their clothes or frightened them half to death."

Her eyes snapped open. *"Dozens* of women have lain on top of you and let you lick their earlobes and put your tongue in their mouths?"

"Well, maybe not dozens, but I've kissed a bunch of them . . . and that's the amazing thing. Not one ever made me lose control like I did a few minutes ago. Not one. Only *you,* Juliet."

"Then you see? 'Tis all my fault," she said, shaking her head. "Oh, I am so ashamed."

"Damn it! You are not to feel guilty over something *I* did. I'm the guilty one. I behaved like an oversexed schoolboy; the whole thing just got away from me."

"I do not understand. Is it common among schoolboys to kiss women and tear their clothing? Do their parents permit such things?"

"No, but—oh, forget it. The point is, I'll never paw you like that again. I'll never tear your clothing. By God, Juliet, I swear it. From now on, I'll treat you with respect."

They both looked down, discovered that her breast was once again showing, and hastened to cover it. Noah's hand shook as it collided with Juliet's.

"We must never kiss each other again," she said earnestly. "You must swear we will never kiss or lie on top of each other again."

Noah's heart sank. "Never?" he croaked, wanting more than anything to soothe her with kisses.

"Never," Juliet insisted. "Swear it to me, No-ah."

"All right, I swear it," he agreed, crossing his fingers behind his back—and his toes, too, for good measure. Next time, he promised himself, he would be more gentle. Next time, she would think he was an angel. He would kiss her so gently that fear would never cross her mind. She'd be thinking only of sweet surrender. If he had not handled this like such a perfect ass, she never would have panicked in the first place. He would probably be sheathed inside her sweet body right now, taking them both to paradise and back.

"Do you forgive me?" he asked, disgusted with himself but already planning his next move.

"I forgive you—but only because you have sworn to me it will never happen again."

"My violent attack on you won't," he promised, and this time, he meant it. Next time he kissed her would be very different, indeed.

117

"Then let us go to sleep, No-ah. . . . If you wish, you may put one arm—one arm only—around me."

This was more than he had dared hope for, considering his beastly behavior. "Thank you, Juliet."

Much chastened, he lay down next to her. She turned onto her side, facing away from him. He drew the blanket over both of them, then inched closer, fitting himself around her. That was a mistake, for her soft bottom was dangerously near his groin. He wanted to pull her closer, but knew that if he did, he would be right back where he started—on the brink of losing all control.

"I said you could put your arm around me," Juliet reminded him, her voice as soft as a caress.

"I was just about to do that." Gingerly, Noah moved closer and encircled her slender waist with his arm. How in hell was he supposed to sleep like *this?*

Juliet sighed. "That feels very nice."

He lay there rigidly, battling every base instinct he possessed. It was pure torment to be this close to her, especially when he now knew what it was like to be closer. Once again, he wanted to abandon all restraint and do what his body was urging him to do. But he dare not frighten her twice in one night. When Juliet finally surrendered to him, he wanted her pliant, willing, and intoxicated with passion, even as he was. He wanted everything she had to give. . . . Therefore, he must be patient.

"Good night, No-ah," she breathed on a sigh.

"Good night, Juliet." He hoped to hell she would soon go to sleep.

Not long after, she did, but he lay awake a long, long time, far too excited—and miserable—to sleep.

I had grown up. I was no longer a child worshiping Jason from afar, but a young woman. I wore my hair piled on top of my head, fastened in place with ribbons or a scarf, and I had a gold diadem for special occasions.

118

I still did not relish spinning or weaving, but I had learned to tolerate disagreeable tasks and seek solace in my dreams and secret accomplishments.

Today, my hair ribbons were purple to match my purple chiton, *which was cut fashionably in the Doric style. A gold girdle, gold earrings, and brooches completed my attire. I thought I looked especially sophisticated—almost of an age to marry. The time was drawing close when my future would become a topic of discussion and final planning. My parents still had not told me whom they had chosen for me, and I would have to be careful to act surprised when they finally revealed that Jason was the one. Jason and I were good friends now, meeting often in my parents' vineyard, sharing confidences, exchanging opinions, poring over poetry, arguing history and politics. . . . He was my dearest and closest friend—he had taught me so much! Alas. . . . He was not yet my lover. That is to say he had not yet fallen in love with me or expressed joy that we would one day wed.*

This bothered me enormously. Long ago he had ceased being infatuated with the daughter of his sophist, *but from time to time, he became smitten with other young ladies and wrote passionate poetry about his feelings. Sometimes, he recited the poems to me, and sometimes he refused. I wanted him to write poetry to* me *and* me *only, but thus far, he seemed to regard me only as his friend—an amusing child whose antics and opinions made him laugh. My heart ached with love for him—and all he did was laugh at me!*

But not today. Today, he would not laugh. I had first bathed, then rubbed my entire body with precious oil of myrrh that my mother kept in a flask shaped like a human foot. After that, I had donned my new and very grown-up finery. For the first time, I had applied cosmetics, a bit of paint "borrowed" from my mother. My mother's maids had thought it amusing that I was finally taking an interest in my appearance. They had teased me unmercifully. I had been taking pains with my ap-

pearance for some time now, but no one, including Jason, had noticed. Today, he would notice. I was tired of being thought of as a child and determined to be accepted as a woman. Today, he would finally fall in love with me!

As I crept down the steps on my way out of the house, I met my mother—the last person I wanted to see. Usually, she would cast her eyes upon me, sigh, and shake her head. Then send me to the gynaeceum. *This afternoon, she stopped on the stair and slowly looked me up and down. For the first time in a long time, her eyes lit with approval.*

"Daughter, you have become a woman."

I waited, expecting at any moment to have my plans for the day destroyed. To my great astonishment, tears glistened in her amber eyes. "You remind me of myself at your age—so pretty and vibrant. So eager for life."

My surprise must have shown on my face, for she continued: "Oh, do not look so astounded! I, too, was once young and full of dreams. You do not think so, do you? But 'tis true."

I wondered what dreams she could possibly have had, for I knew she did not dream as I did. She could neither read nor write her own name, and she could never have recited a long epic poem. Perhaps she had dreamed of creating fine cloth and tapestries, which was what she did best. The chiton *she wore was a marvel—pale yellow to complement her brown hair—and patterned with her own design of tiny leaves, flowers, and birds. Bits of gold sparkled along the borders of the garment. Truly, it was a masterpiece.*

"Your father is right to think of you as his little dryad," *she continued. "For you are beautiful, gentle, and good. You are also elusive as a tree nymph, coming and going like a breath of air."*

I held my breath wondering what next she would say. This was the most praise I had ever received from my mother, and I expected some cloaked reprimand regarding how elusive I had learned to be. Her next words shocked me even more. "I regret I have oft been so harsh with you, Daughter, but a woman must learn her place in society. She must not pine for what can never be; do you understand what I am trying to say?"

I did and I did not. She had never spoken to me like this before, never let me glimpse her as a person, not just my mother. "I hope I shall not disappoint you," I said, for I wanted her approval—had despaired I could ever win it.

She smiled, and I suddenly wanted to hug her. Her smile was beautiful. "You could never do that. Despite all my rantings, I love you, Daughter. The day is coming when you will leave here and begin your own family. Think kindly of me then, and remember all I have tried to teach you."

I realized in that moment that she had done her best. Had done all she knew how to do. Neither of us could help it that I was so different and thus so rebellious. "I love you, too, Mother!" I threw myself into her arms and managed a quick kiss and a hug before she pulled back in embarrassment.

"Yes, well . . ." she dabbed at her eyes. "Be about your business then."

Before she could change her mind and assign me to some boring task, I darted past her and down the steps. "Where are you going?" she cried. "Do not forget we have company coming."

"Just out for a walk! I will not forget!" I flung back over my shoulder.

Marveling at the warm encounter, I hurried through the vineyard and finally arrived at my accustomed meeting place with Jason—the arched trellis that screened us from prying eyes. Jason was not yet there. I peered through the greenery, watching for him. Finally, he came, no longer dressed in the short tunic of a youth, but wearing the ankle-length garment that proclaimed him a man, the son of a rich man. Over the saffron-colored tunic, he had fastened a sky-blue chlamys, a short cloak usually donned for hunting, riding, or traveling. . . . I prayed to Aphrodite, goddess of love, that it was not for the latter reason; if he went away and forgot me, I could not bear it!

Jason's long strides soon brought him to the trellis. He laughed as he ducked beneath it and found me waiting for him. "Ho, little one! I knew you would be here. . . . Forgive me for being late but I have been riding my friend's fine new mare."

"Then you are not going anywhere! Traveling, I mean," I burst out, clumsy-tongued as usual when first I saw him.

"Nay, I am going nowhere, little one. . . . But what about you? I scarcely recognize you; you look so pretty and grown-up this afternoon."

I blushed to the roots of my hair. He had noticed! Sweet Zeus, he had actually noticed! "Thank you, Jason. . . . No, I am not going anywhere either. However, we are having guests this evening. The family of my father's friend, Anytus, will shortly be arriving. So I cannot stay long."

Jason sat down on the small wooden bench that lined one side of the trellis. It had been provided as a shady resting place for the overseer of the vineyard and was where we sat when we pored over Jason's poetry.

"Anytus? I have heard of him," Jason said, cocking his head. "He has a son about my age."

"Yes, he is coming, too, so my mother told me." I sat down beside Jason, as close as I dared, so that our knees almost touched.

"He is?" Jason frowned. "Why would Anytus's son be coming to visit your family? I myself have not been invited for a long time."

"I have no idea, Jason, but my father has lately been doing a great deal of business with Anytus, while your father has been purchasing his wines from other vineyards."

"That is only because he was upset over those few spoiled barrels from last season. You remember—our fathers exchanged harsh words over it. But I had thought everything was smoothed over now, and they were friends again."

"I am sure they are still friends." A feeling of unease crept over me. "Still, Anytus has come often to our house of late—and this time, he is bringing his entire family, including his son."

Jason suddenly rose, his dark eyes angry, his mouth drawn downward. "I do not like it. When a man brings his son to visit the family of a beautiful young woman, there is usually a reason other than mere friendship."

"A beautiful young woman? Do you mean me?" His obvious jealousy pleased me.

"Of course, I mean you! Who else would I mean? No, I do not like this at all! Perhaps your father is reconsidering whether or not he wishes to have me as a son-in-law."

I jumped up too, as agitated as Jason. "He would never do that! No, I am sure he would not."

"But he's never formally told you that I am to be your husband, has he? Just as my father has never formally told me; he has only insinuated it."

"Insinuated it! I thought 'twas definite. You said it was definite."

"I said it had been discussed. I did not say it had all been decided. Your father will go where he can to make the best alliance. My father will do the same—and neither you nor I will have a thing to say about it."

"Oh, no, Jason! That cannot be! I will refuse to marry anyone but you. I will run away first. I will weep, tear out my hair, scar my face with my nails . . ."

"Hush, hush, now. . . . Do not upset yourself." He drew me into his arms and held me close against his broad chest. I could hear his heart thudding against his rib cage. My own heart beat in unison. "We are leaping to conclusions. We do not know for a fact that Anytus and your father have marriage in mind for you and Anytus's son."

"Then why haven't my parents told me that you are the one they have picked out for me? Why hasn't your *father told you? When winter comes, I will be fifteen. That is not far away. Many families plan their daughters' weddings when the girl is fourteen or younger."*

He drew back to look at me, and his hands came up to cup my face. "You will soon be fifteen?"

I nodded. He examined me slowly then, as my mother had done, looking me up and down as if really seeing me for the first time. I waited breathlessly for his reaction.

"I should have guessed you would soon be fifteen. . . . You have become a ravishing beauty. And your body has filled out . . ." His glance strayed down the front of me, lingering on the swell of my breasts, noting the flare of my hips. I grew warm beneath his intent scrutiny.

"Yes, you have become a woman, little one. You grew up while I was looking the other way."

"At other girls," I chided. "I have been waiting a long time now for you to notice me."

"I am noticing you now, little one, and I find you most appealing." He ran his finger along my lower lip. "One could even say I find you delectable—like a ripe, juicy fig waiting to be savored." He inclined his head, and his lips brushed mine, gentle as the wing of a moth. "Ah, I knew it. . . . You taste delectable, too—what a fool I have been not to have recognized your womanhood sooner!"

Joy flooded me. I was dizzy with it. I had dreamed of this moment, and now it was finally happening. He was seeing me as the woman I had become, not as the child who had simply amused him. I cast caution to the four winds, stood on tiptoe, and boldly pressed my mouth to his. I wanted a real kiss, my first kiss, a kiss I could dream about during the night and relive with all the longing, passion, and love bubbling in my soul.

He wrapped his arms around me and gave me that kiss. When we broke apart for air, we were both trembling. The feelings coursing through me left me weak and shaken. Jason himself looked stunned.

"Sweet Zeus! You have bewitched me!" He chuckled hoarsely. "Who would have guessed it? I have been searching for passion—for a love to consume me ut-

terly—in the bold, wayward glances of a dozen or more pretty women. Yet here it was all the time, in my little spy and rebel, my eager little scholar . . . in the last place I expected to find it."

"I have loved you forever, Jason," I admitted, too intoxicated with happiness to pretend a shyness I did not feel. "I have loved you since the day I first saw you in my parents' house."

"And I must have been falling in love with you! Great Zeus, but I did not know it! I never once guessed it—not until this minute. I am like a blindfolded man who never realized his handicap. At last I see you as you really are—rather, as you have become."

I clung to him, dizzy with happiness. "What am I, Jason? Tell me what I am—who I am. I am not sure I know anymore. When I am with you, I become a different person altogether. I am so alive—so filled with joy and gladness!"

He gazed down into my eyes with an expression that could only be described as reverent. "You are the most beautiful girl in all Greece, the loveliest creature in all of the universe. Either that, or I have been struck by one of Eros's golden arrows. I am dazzled."

I laughed in delight. "It must have been Eros. I am no beauty, Jason. My hair is too pale and unruly, my eyes too unremarkable, my nose too large, my mouth too small . . ."

"You are perfection, and I will hear none of your dissembling. Your hair is the finest gossamer. I swear it is spun from moonbeams." He pressed his lips to my hair. "Your eyes are like the stars or planets, shining golden in an ebony sky." He kissed my eyes. "Your nose is exquisite . . ." He kissed my nose. "And your mouth . . . ah, your mouth . . ."

His lips closed over mine. As we shared our second real kiss, my heart overflowed with delight. We were together now; nothing could part us. I would marry Jason and spend the remainder of my days loving him, sharing poetry and animated conversation. . . . I would *not wind up like my mother, bound to a man I had not met until the day of my wedding, then living my entire life in a* gynaeceum, *shut off from all things fascinating and worthwhile.*

I wound my arms around Jason's neck and kissed him with the fervor of years of unreciprocated feeling. His hands raked my hair, tumbling the arrangement that had taken my maid half the morning to achieve. I did not care. . . . This was Jason, my one true love. This was the moment I had been awaiting all my life.

A shrill scream pierced my happiness. Jason guiltily thrust me away from him. "Merciful Hestia!" a woman cried. "What are you doing to my daughter? Unhand her this instant! Why . . . it's Jason! My own neighbor's son—ravishing my virgin daughter!"

"Mother!" I protested. " 'Tis not what you think! He but kissed me; that is all!"

Desperately, I tried to explain, but my mother was wild-eyed and furious. She was not about to listen.

"I came to look for you!" she shrieked. "To speak with you again before our guests arrived—to tell you that we have chosen a husband for you, and he will be here within the hour! And this *is what I find! . . . Look at you! Your hair is undone! Your face flushed—your eyes glittering. . . . Oh, you are ruined . . . ruined . . . ruined!"*

"Ruined . . . ruined . . . ruined . . ." Juliet muttered in her sleep.

Noah snapped upright and leaned over her. The fire had long since died down, but a shaft of moonlight streamed into the cave, illuminating Juliet's troubled face.

"We did nothing wrong," she said clearly. "You cannot accuse us of wrongdoing when it felt so right. . . . No! Do not send him away! I love him, do you hear me? I will have no other. I care not what you do to me—you can cast me out into the wilderness, but I will marry no other but him! . . . Jason! Jason, do not leave me! Oh, Jason . . ."

Tears streamed down Juliet's cheeks. *Real tears.* She flung her head from side to side, her hair whipping wildly about her. Over and over, she called Jason's name. Fearing that she would harm herself in the violence of her grief, Noah gathered her into his arms. He tried to soothe her, then to awaken her, but she was locked in her dream, unable to respond. She wept and cried and clutched at his neck. He did not know what to do except to hold and rock her. Each time she whimpered Jason's name, he died a little inside. She was plunging a knife into his chest, stabbing him repeatedly.

He could no longer deny the truth that she had loved this Jason, heart and soul. Something had happened, and her parents had sent Jason away. Apparently, they had discovered her in Jason's arms—perhaps in his bed—and had thrown her out or abandoned her in the wilderness for the sin. . . . God, if they had done something like that to Juliet, he would kill them when he found them!

It seemed too incredible—too impossible. But what other explanation could there be?

You cannot accuse us of wrongdoing when it felt so right . . .

She had given this Jason what Noah wanted for himself. He had thought her a virgin; apparently she was not. That should have made him feel better about his own intention to seduce her, but somehow, it only made him feel worse. Where was this Jason now? Had he taken off for a safer climate when he discovered he had stirred up a tempest?

Whoever he was, wherever he was, he did not deserve Juliet. She deserved only the best, a man who would love, honor, and cherish her every day of her life. A man who would give her children, protect her from the world's cruelties, build her a pretty little

127

house with a white picket fence around it . . . not a man like *himself,* either.

He was a cold-blooded, hard-hearted newspaperman, jumping from story to story, ready to go anywhere, anytime, to dig up the ugly truth about people. The last thing he needed was a wife like Juliet. . . . He had not been able to commit to a sweet, besotted young woman named Emily; how in hell could he commit to a confused, befuddled girl in love with another man?

Gradually, Juliet's sobs died away. Her tears ceased to flow, and she slumped against him in boneless exhaustion. Gently, he lay her down again, curled up next to her, and cuddled her close. If only she were not so beautiful, so defenseless and vulnerable, keeping his distance would be a hell of a lot easier. He would just have to try harder . . . and he would have to have a talk with her about this dream tonight, tell her what he had found out about her past. He owed her the truth, as much as he could give her; she loved a man named Jason, her parents had disapproved and tossed her out on her pretty little behind—and Jason, the bastard, had taken off for parts unknown.

Chapter Nine

Awakening the next morning, Juliet was immediately anxious. She had had a bad dream involving Jason. She could not remember any of it, but something frightening and worrisome had happened. Then she remembered the scene the previous night with Noah and wondered if it might be the cause of her anxiety. He had apologized and done nothing during the night to frighten her, but still she felt scared and lonely.

She lay still, savoring his warmth at her back. One arm encircled her waist, and his breath caressed her neck, providing a comfort and intimacy that pleased, rather than alarmed her. He had been right that it was foolish for them to sleep apart, without touching. She needed the security of his arms around her. She wanted and needed *him,* but could not allow herself to take what he was offering. Not until she had solved the riddle of her past did she dare plan for the future. . . . Still, it would be so nice to turn over and gently awaken Noah with soft, ardent kisses.

Avoiding looking at him, she removed his arm, stretched, and yawned. The sun was well up. While Noah still slept would be a good time to explore the narrow passageway at the back of the cave. Rising from their makeshift bed, she wrapped her red shawl about her shoulders and took a few items from one of the saddlebags. Then she walked quietly to the rear of the cave and stepped into the darkened passageway. It was cool, dim, and shadowed, but enough light filtered down from wide cracks in the rock overhead to illuminate the narrow passageway. It twisted and turned several times before opening into a spacious chamber that was even larger than the cave itself.

She heard the sound of splashing water before she saw it—a thin stream pouring down from the center of the ceiling and pooling in a shallow basin of rock. Enchanted, she spared not a minute searching for the bats that had startled Noah. Here was a natural bathhouse, complete with running water and privacy! She could have a real bath, not a fumbled wash in a dented cookpot.

Setting down her things, she stripped off her garments. The wet rock surface was slippery. She quickly discovered that sitting down at the pool's edge was the best way to take advantage of the bath. Leaning forward, she dunked her head under the water spilling into the pool and eagerly scrubbed her hair, using the thick cake of soap Noah kept in his saddlebags. Until he had told her the purpose of the soap, she had thought it was something to eat—like the wonderful peppermint drops they had horded and savored, one by one, until they were gone.

As she rinsed away the yellowish lather, delicious shivers rippled down her spine. The water was delightfully cold and refreshing, better than it had been on top where the sun had warmed it. Having filtered down through rock, it was sparkling clean, and she washed and splashed with grateful abandon, eagerly anticipating showing the hidden pool and waterfall to Noah.

He had been so doubtful that the spring went anywhere, other than to disappear between the rocky crevices. How satisfying to be able to prove the great cynic wrong! After washing to her heart's content, Juliet spent several moments combing out her hair with her fingers. Along with the soap and several other

130

grooming articles, Noah had brought a small comb in his saddlebags, but it was unequal to the challenge of long hair curled into hundreds of small, tight ringlets. She smoothed the mass back from her temples, intending to tie at to the nape of her neck with the grimy bit of ribbon she still had left.

"Don't tie it back," Noah suddenly said.

Heart pounding, she grabbed the first article of clothing she could reach, her red *himation*. Quickly, she wrapped her naked body, then scrambled to her feet beside the shallow pool. Grinning from ear to ear, Noah stood at the mouth of the passageway.

"Don't let me stop you," he drawled. "Just pretend I'm not here—only don't tie back your hair. Let it tumble freely down your back. You look like Aphrodite rising out of the sea in her clam shell; you're so pink and white and perfect . . ."

"And who are you—Adonis? You should not be spying upon me in my bath," she scolded.

"How can I help it? Like Adonis, I, the humble mortal, am smitten by the beauty of the goddess . . ."

"I am not Aphrodite, and you are not Adonis, and this is most definitely not the island of Cythera."

"Cythera?"

"Where Aphrodite was born from the sea," she explained without thinking. "Four beautiful girls called the Seasons met her and gave her clothes and jewels to wear, including a magic golden girdle which made her irresistably attractive to all who looked upon her."

"Ah, yes, I had forgotten. How amazing that you have not! . . . What else do you remember, Juliet?" Like a cougar stalking its prey, Noah moved toward her.

She frowned. As usual whenever she tried to concentrate, her head throbbed unbearably. Where had all that information about Aphrodite come from? "N-nothing. I-I do not recall another thing. Nor do I know where I heard the story."

"Juliet," he sighed, and she sensed that something

bad was coming. "Last night you talked in your sleep again, and I think I know some of what happened to you now."

Suddenly chilled, she clutched the *himation* to her bare breasts. "Do not tell me. I am not sure I wish to hear it."

"Sweetheart, you loved a man named Jason, and your parents caught you with him. Apparently, they were furious and sent you away. Or else you ran away to escape their wrath."

She digested this for a moment. "And Jason? What happened to him?"

"He left you. He didn't stay around to suffer the consequences. You kept calling for him to come back. And you wept because the bastard was gone."

"Oh . . ." Her flesh felt cold and clammy. A wave of nausea swept her, and her teeth began to chatter.

"You're freezing," Noah said, walking closer. "You'll catch cold."

She grabbed up her remaining garments and her heavy sandals. "Leave, and I will put on my clothing."

He glanced regretfully at her red *himation,* which clung to her damp body like a second skin. "Do I have to? I would much rather stay and help you dress. I haven't had much training as a lady's maid, but I learn fast. That's one of my best traits. Show me something once, and I've got it forever."

"You must leave immediately, No-ah. There can be no future for us—not while I cannot remember my past. Whoever I am, I love a man named Jason."

"Loved. You loved a man named Jason, and he isn't here anymore. When you needed him, he didn't stand by you. Why should you remain loyal to a man you can't remember, one who abandoned you? You don't owe this Jason anything, Juliet. I doubt very much if he was worthy of you."

"But what are you offering me, No-ah? Do you really want a woman with such a peculiar flaw? What if I wake up one day remembering everything? What if

I still love this Jason, even though he's left me? Maybe he had good reason to leave. . . . We do not yet know the whole story. Perhaps there is more . . ."

Noah grabbed her arm, and she had to hold on tight to her clothing and sandals, lest she lose everything. "Perhaps there *isn't* more," he countered. "All I know is that I want you, Juliet. It's torture to be near you and not be able to touch you."

"You touched me last night! You put your arm around me as I slept."

"You know what I mean; I want to touch you as a man touches a woman he cherishes, a woman for whom he cares a great deal . . ."

She noticed he did not say *loved*.

"I want to touch you all over, Juliet, and give you a pleasure I doubt you've known in the past. . . . I can be gentle. I swear I won't hurt or frighten you. Oh, sweetheart, let me make love to you here and now . . ." He put his arms around her, drew her to him, and buried his face in her wet hair. "I want you so much, Juliet. I need you. You are so beautiful. In all my life, I've never encountered a more beautiful woman or one that I desired so much."

She leaned against him, wishing he would say that he loved her, not only that he desired her and found her beautiful. She wanted him to pledge himself to love and cherish her always. Then maybe, she could set aside her fears and succumb to the desire that plagued them both.

His hands dropped to her hips and held them steady while he rubbed against her lower body, his arousal hot and hard between them. All manly strength and sweet temptation, he pressed his lips into the hollow where her neck met her shoulder. "Sweetheart, put down your things. I want you naked. I want to worship your nakedness . . . my Juliet. My Aphrodite."

He had said the wrong thing. Once again, he had reminded her of the past about which she knew nothing, except what she babbled in her dreams. The past separated them like an unbreachable wall. They could see each other and touch fingertips across the top, but they could not truly embrace or become one—not while the wall loomed between them, filling her with doubts and hesitations.

"No-ah, I cannot do it! I cannot let myself love you yet—nor accept what you are offering. . . . Please understand. I *want* to, but I cannot."

He drew back angrily. "Why not, damn it? What have you got to lose that you haven't already lost to that sod, Jason?"

Now, his words were blows to her heart, bruising and punishing her. "You think I am no longer a virgin—that I gave myself to Jason. Therefore, I am a woman of no virtue, one you need not love in order to take your pleasure! That is what you think, is it not?"

"I never said that!"

"You do not have to say it! I can see it in your eyes."

"How the devil can you see it, when I'm not thinking any such thing?"

"Because you do not say you love me! You only say you want to *make* love to me!"

He stared at her, scowling, as angry and frustrated as she had ever seen him. But he did not deny it—and he did not say he loved her. He only glowered, seeming at a loss for words.

She turned away from him. "Leave me, No-ah, and let me dress. Virgin or not, I will not give myself to a man I do not love, a man who does not love me. If you cannot say the words, you must not feel them. There is lust in your heart, not love. In my own heart, there is great loneliness. . . . I can bear it. I *will* bear it. What I cannot bear is to lose my self-respect, as I will surely do if I lie down with a man who cares nothing for me."

"I *do* care for you! But why does a man have to sell his soul just to make love to a woman? I like you. I want you. You like me. You want me. Why can't we keep it simple? Why complicate things with promises we may not be able to keep? Sure, I can tell you what

134

you want to hear, but how do I know I'll be able to deliver?"

He feared commitment. She should have guessed as much. He wanted the pleasure without the responsibility—but then he was not the one who might get pregnant. "What if your brief pleasure produces a child, No-ah? What then?" she asked calmly, though she felt anything but calm.

His face paled. She had brought him up short. "A woman doesn't necessarily get pregnant every time a man touches her. Besides, I can always withdraw before I plant my seed in you."

Juliet was shocked. She did not know these things— had never known them. Still, even if she could be sure she would not get pregnant, she would not want to mate with a man in the cold manner he was describing. If she gave herself to Noah, she would never want to give him up. She would belong to him and he to her. She would *want* to bear his children. She might not remember her past, but she did have some notion of right and wrong. People were not supposed to behave like animals, mating without thought, tenderness, or respect for each other and the new life they might be creating. How empty and meaningless!

"Leave me, No-ah. I have no interest in your brief moments of selfish pleasure. Or if you will not go, I will." Leaving the grooming articles where they lay, she started to step around him but he cursed under his breath and blocked her.

"I'm not the only one who might enjoy it," he shouted. "Damn it, woman, you're turning down something lots of women would give their right arms to have! I don't proposition just *any* female, you know, and I've never failed to satisfy one. Guess I'll have to settle for a cold bath in a cold cavern to cool my ardor. But I want you to know that this is a first for Copper McCord. You're heartless, Juliet—do you know that? You haven't an ounce of feeling in you . . ."

135

Jerking up her head, she almost dropped her armload. "Oh, no, No-ah. 'Tis not *I* who have no feeling. 'Tis *you*. . . . Yes, 'tis *you*. You guard your heart well. You never let a woman get too close to you, do you? Oh, you speak pretty words designed to weaken her resistance, but you do not say the words she longs to hear in such situations."

"Should I lie to you then? Is that what you want? All right. . . ." He sank down on one knee, folded his hands, and gazed at her soulfully. "I love you, Juliet. I'll marry you tomorrow. . . . There." He got up again. "Now I've said the magic words every woman wants to hear, even when she doesn't believe them and knows the guy is lying through his teeth. Now, will you come back here and take off that damn red shawl? When it's wet, it doesn't hide much anyway, and what I can't clearly see, I can sure as hell imagine."

"No," she said, shaking her head and backing away from him. His mocking cynicism appalled her. This was a side of him she had not seen before—at least not so blatantly. She found it much more frightening than his loss of control the night before; this time, he was very much in control and entirely too calculating.

"Mock me, if you wish, No-ah, but one day I will know the joy of freely loving a man who loves me back. One day, I will gladly take off my *himation* for the one man I will cherish above all others. Until I meet that man, I will save myself and not squander the only true gifts I possess—my love and my loyalty. I especially will not waste those gifts for the sake of a few hours—or moments—of physical satisfaction."

Noah's lips compressed. His dark eyes flashed. His face flushed as red as his hair. "You're saving yourself for Jason," he snapped. "Why don't you admit it? I'm not good enough for you. You want the man of your dreams—not a flesh and blood human who's less than perfect. . . . Do you realize we might die out here? We might never find Tucson or your beloved Jason. Then all your moralizing and self-denial will have been in

136

vain. . . . And you know what, Juliet? When we're both laying there dying, I'm going to find the strength to lean over and ask you a question. And that question will be: Tell me, sweetheart: *Was it worth it?* Are you glad you defended your precious virtue? Or are you wishing you had let yourself live a little while you had the chance?"

"I will wait for you in the cave."

Her lips were quivering, and tears threatened, but she bit down hard, so he would not notice. He did not fight fairly; he made her doubt everything in which she thought she believed. She had never met a man like him—or if she had, she did not remember and had learned nothing from the experience. He had her half believing that *she* was in the wrong, not him!

"Run along now, little ice princess. You're right about one thing. You're not Aphrodite; you're a cold, little bitch. You flaunt your bare ass in my face, and then tell me I've got to be a good boy and *respect* you! Well, I'm a man, damn it! Not a fantasy from a dream world. But maybe that's how you like your men— from a safe distance, where you can control them."

"You are hateful!" she spat. "Crude, boorish, and hateful! I have flaunted nothing in your face, and my dreams are the last things I can control! Just because I will not give you what you want, you make ugly, spiteful comments and accusations. I despise you, Noah Copper McCord! I wish you had never discovered me on that ledge, and I did not need you to help me find Tucson or my family. It would be better for us both if we had never met!"

"You can say that again," Noah growled. "But just remember that *you* want it too. You just won't admit it."

Juliet fled the inner chamber and the truth of his terrible cutting sarcasm.

* * *

137

Noah stood glaring after her for a long, dismal moment, then finished stripping off his clothing. He plunged into the little pool, seized the soap, and thoroughly scrubbed himself. His passion had long since died—killed by Juliet's disdain. She had rejected him—actually rejected him!—thrown his regard for her back into his face. Like most women, all she wanted was a wedding ring and security, a man to look after her forever, not the man himself.

Day after day, he had to watch her, smell her, live in close proximity to her . . . slowly go mad with his pent-up passion. What did she think he was—a marble statue? He had feelings; of course, he had feelings! He was burning up with feelings. She was the one who calmly floated through the day, surmounting one obstacle after another, never losing her temper, never surrendering control. Only in her dreams did she show any fire or passion. . . . It all went to her dream hero, Jason. Clearly, she preferred illusions to a *real* man.

If that's the way she wanted it, from now on he would ignore her. Treat her as coolly as she treated him. When they got to Tucson, he'd dump her faster than she could say Arizona. She could damn well locate her own family and her lover as well. He certainly wasn't going to go searching for that asshole Jason to tell him Juliet was free to marry whenever he wanted.

Climbing out of the pool, he tugged on his dirty clothes. Lord, but they stank! Maybe that's why Juliet wasn't too eager to let him get close to her. Despite all his recent bathing, he still smelled like a polecat. Disgusted with himself, he jumped back into the pool and scrubbed his shirt and pants while they were still on his body. In the heat, they would soon dry. Next time he came to the wilderness, he would bring more clothes— and more food and water. He'd bring a pack horse, too, to carry it all . . . and he would strictly refrain from climbing up on ledges where he might find a beautiful, stubborn girl mysteriously linked to ancient Greece.

Chapter Ten

Three days and nights passed, and Juliet did not speak to Noah. Nor did he speak to her, except for a brief growl when he wanted to communicate some directive, such as "We're stopping here for the night," or "Watch out for that prickly pear."

They were no longer in the mountains, but had entered a dry, arid valley of baked earth, sagebrush, *mesquite,* and cacti. There was no respite from the sun and no water. Various mountain ranges surrounded them. Trees marched up the side of one, but it would take days to reach it, and they'd be going in the wrong direction. Distances were deceiving. Noah had claimed at the outset that they could cross the valley in three days, but Juliet doubted they had gone halfway.

On this, the fourth morning, she had a heavy heart and a throbbing head. The silence and tension between them was making her ill. She could tolerate the heat, the sun, the barrenness of the land, the brackishness of the water in their canteens, the hunger cramps, the grit in her hair and garments, the blisters where a sandal strap had rubbed her flesh raw . . . but she could not bear another moment of Noah's cruel indifference. By day, he ignored her and at night slept far enough away that she shivered with cold and a dread that he might leave her.

She had had enough. As he picked up his gear and started off without even looking back to see if she was following, she stood and shouted at him. "No-ah! No-ah Copper McCord!"

He stopped but did not turn around. "What do you want? We've got to cover as much ground as possible before the sun saps our energy."

They had learned to slow down when the sun reached its zenith. If shade was available, they stopped to rest. Yesterday, there had been no shade, not even a single, solitary *palo verde* tree to shield them from the burning sun. Today would likely be the same.

Juliet inhaled a deep breath of the dry desert air, still cool at this hour, but soon to become as hot as the inside of an oven. "I will not walk another step if you do not turn around and talk to me, No-ah. I am a human being. I do not deserve the misery you have been inflicting upon me these past few days. You are a cruel man, No-ah Copper McCord."

He planted one booted heel in the dust and slowly pivoted. Three days growth of beard obscured his face—a face as brown as the leather of his boots. The rising sun glinted off his reddish-colored hair, which he had not bothered to comb this morning. He looked like a wild man. "Me? Cruel? . . . You think I'm the one who's cruel? Funny, I thought it was you. You haven't spoken two words in three long, hellish days."

"Neither have you."

"Oh, I recall saying a few things, but you never responded. You made it a point *not* to respond. And I'm not stupid; I got the message."

"What message? I sent no messages."

"You despise me!" he thundered. "You'd leave in a minute if you could find your own way to Tucson."

"That is not true, No-ah. I have simply been angry. So have you. We cannot continue like this. I will die if I have to spend another day in silence, with you refusing to look at or speak to me."

"Hell, you're going to die anyway!" He dropped his gear and strode back to her. "By tonight, we'll be out of water. We're already out of food; I haven't seen

140

anything but a few lizards and a rattlesnake the last few days."

She had not realized things were so bad. Had assumed they would find all they needed. Noah would make things right for them. "I am sorry. . . . I did not know." Her eyes filled with tears. "I . . . I have been too miserable to notice."

"Well, *I* noticed. If we don't find water today, we're finished, Juliet. There's probably water in those mountains up ahead, but we'll never get there. It's taking a hell of a lot longer to cross this damn valley than I thought it would."

"Then we will walk faster. We will not stop to rest. If we have the energy, we will run. . . . We can do it, No-ah! But you must not be angry with me anymore. I cannot bear your anger."

He clamped his hands around her waist and hauled her to him. "Ah, hell, Juliet. . . . I'm sorry I'm such an ass. If you hadn't said something, I'd have spent today just like the last three. I'd have wasted our last rational moments together. We would have died being mad at each other."

"Yes, yes, we were both wrong." She hugged him tightly, reveling in the feel of his arms around her. "I am so sorry, No-ah. I should not have said those nasty things."

"And I shouldn't have pushed you to have sex with me. I shouldn't have mocked you . . ."

"You no longer wish to have sex with me?" she murmured into his chest.

"Hell, yes, I do! But . . . but I don't want you to feel bad about it. Or guilty. I do *care* for you, Juliet—more than I've cared for any woman. Truth is it scares the hell out of me!"

"I understand, No-ah, truly I do."

"How *can* you when I don't understand it myself?" He took her face in his callused hands and stroked his thumbs along her cheekbones. "Juliet, I'm *afraid* of loving you. Maybe it's because I don't know who you are or where you come from . . . but I *do* know who *I* am—and it's not the sort of man who can settle down and be happy living behind a white picket fence."

"A white picket fence?" She had no idea what one was or why he should fear it so much. Was it a cage of some sort?

"Don't you see? That's what women usually want—pretty little houses and gardens behind little white picket fences. Even out here in the wilderness, the first thing a woman wants is to make everything neat and tidy—a picket fence around every cactus. But I'm not a neat and tidy man. I can't live like that; I'd be tearing out my hair within a month's time. What's worse, I'd be making *you* miserable because I was miserable."

"I do not want a house inside a picket fence, No-ah. All I want is to have you smile at me. To know that you care."

"I *do* care, damn it!"

"Then you will look at me and talk to me. Together we will make it to the mountains and find water and food."

"We'll make it," he said, grinning down at her. "Now that I know you're not angry with me anymore, I feel like a man again instead of a whipped dog."

She threw her arms around him. "We *can* do it, No-ah! You must believe it! If we believe strongly enough, we can make anything happen."

He hugged her hard. "If you say so, sweetheart. I just wish we'd meet a handy cougar or some coyotes. Maybe they could tell you where to find water in the middle of a cactus patch."

They clung to each other for a long, wonderful moment, and then Noah reluctantly set her away from him. "Let's get going. The sun's getting hot already."

They gathered up their things and set out across the wasteland. This time, Juliet's heart felt lighter than air. Noah offered her his hand, and she joyously took it. Her elation lasted throughout the morning and well into the afternoon. By the time the sun was setting, it was gone. The green-clad mountains were still a long way off. They had spotted only one other living creature the entire day: a piglike animal Noah called a *javelina*. It had snorted at them and run away. She had had no chance to talk to it.

"We'll stop here for the night," Noah croaked, his voice hoarse from thirst.

She nodded, unable to speak. They had drunk nothing since noon and then only a small swallow of water. She felt weak and shaky. Her legs were trembling. She sank down on a small flat rock while Noah cleared a spot for their bedroll, unrolled the blankets, and laid them out side by side. Other than the rock and a patch of thorny *ocotillo* nearby, the land was perfectly flat beneath the darkening sky. In the distance, the mountains rose—purple, blue, and black in the fading twilight. Brilliant shades of red, orange, and rose streaked the sky. Stars winked on the horizon.

It was going to be a beautiful night. A quarter moon was already rising. It would be their last night before thirst and the desert heat robbed them of strength and eventually claimed their lives. By tomorrow night, assuming they were still alive, they would be unable to appreciate the beauty of the desert night.

Noah rummaged around in the saddlebags, then came to her, pulled her up from the rock, and led her to the blankets. "Sit down. . . . We'll have our last drink of water and our last meal."

"I thought we already had our last meal," she whispered. "I thought our food was all gone."

"Not quite. I saved these." He opened his palm to reveal two dirty, sticky peppermint drops. "Thought we might as well go out in style. I've been dreaming of these damn peppermint drops for days. No sense saving them any longer."

"Oh, Noah . . ." was all she could get out.

They sat side by side on the blankets and contemplated the nearly empty canteen. There could not be

143

more than a few swallows left. Noah opened the container and held it out to her. "You first."

Obediently, she took a mouthful of water and swished it around her mouth for a moment, wetting all the corners, then letting it slide down her throat. It was wonderful.

"Now, you . . ." she urged.

He did the same, waiting even longer before swallowing. He handed her back the canteen. "There's still some left. Might as well finish it off. Waiting until morning won't make me any less thirsty. I could drink a whole lake without stopping."

"We'll share it, drop by drop. Maybe it will give us strength to walk a little farther yet tonight."

Noah shook his head. "Nope. This is as far as we go tonight. We're both too exhausted to move another step."

Silently, she agreed with him. Her trembling had ceased, but she still felt light-headed. Thankfully, her hunger cramps had eased. The water had helped renew her strength. She did not want to think about what would happen tomorrow and watched approvingly as Noah took another swallow. He handed back the canteen.

"Drink the rest now. I've had enough."

Obediently tilting the canteen to her mouth, she was surprised by yet another small rush of water. She saved some for him, but he would not take it. "Finish it. I'd like to die knowing I was a gentleman at the very end."

He grinned, a slightly crooked, endearing grin. It made her realize how much she had grown to love him since he had found her up on that ledge. She had seen no other person but him—and wanted no one else with her now. Noah was all the company she needed. He filled up the emptiness inside her. If she had to die soon, she was glad it would be with him.

He handed her a peppermint drop. "Now, eat this.

. . . Let it melt in your mouth. For a last meal, it's not bad."

" 'Tis truly marvelous," she sighed after concentrated tasting and sucking. "Thank you, No-ah."

They said nothing for a while, savoring the aftertaste of the peppermints which lingered long in Juliet's mouth, leaving it fresh and tingly. Noah lay back on the blanket and gazed up at the stars. "If this is the end, Juliet, I'm glad it's with you, happening like this. We'll try to make it to the mountains tomorrow, but if we don't get there, at least we'll have had tonight. Now that you're not mad at me anymore, I suspect it's going to be the best night of my life. Just look at those damn stars . . ."

He took her hand and squeezed it, then lifted her fingers to his lips and kissed them. "Knowing we might die soon, I'm not so afraid to say I love you, Juliet. I do, you know. You're the first woman I've ever said that to—other than my mother. I'm ashamed to say I didn't tell her very often. But then, I assumed she would live forever."

Juliet wondered about her own mother and knew a moment of deep sadness. "What happened to her?"

"She died when I was young. I saw it as a kind of desertion . . . as if she'd had a choice about leaving me. . . . Let's not talk about it now. I want to talk about *us* instead." He rolled over on his side to face her. "I said I love you, Juliet—but you haven't told me how you feel."

She looked down at him, lying there watching her so intently. Starlight illuminated his face and eyes, and his expression told her how important the question was. "I love you, too, No-ah."

"And you won't ever desert me?" he asked quietly. "Not even for Jason?"

"Jason means nothing to me, No-ah. He is not here with me now. Tonight, there is only you . . ."

With slow, deliberate movements, she began to unwind her *himation* from around her head and shoul-

145

ders. She laid it aside, untied the ribbon from her hair, and fluffed out the unruly mass around her shoulders. Then she undid the brooches that held her garment in place and removed the cinch at her waist. She paused a moment, gathering her courage, then exposed the upper half of her body to him. Noah did not move until she had finished undressing.

"You're certain this is what you want, Juliet?" He sat up and reached out a hand to caress her hair and push it back from her face.

"Tonight may be the only night we will ever have, No-ah. I do not not want to die without having loved you. I *want* to be your woman. I want it more than I have ever wanted anything."

His glance dropped to her breasts, bared for him in the starlight. "Ah, God, Juliet. . . . You are so beautiful, so perfect. Lie back and let me love you, sweetheart. I'll be gentle, I promise."

"I know you will, No-ah." She lay back on the blanket and watched, fascinated, as he undressed.

Above and behind him, the stars shone brilliantly—too many to count. The clear light silvered his hair and body, outlining his splendid masculinity. The cooling air brushed her nakedness, but the warmth from the sand at her back kept her from shivering. Then Noah moved over her, shutting out the starshine and bringing his own warmth.

He began by kissing her—soft, gentle kisses that fell on her hair and forehead, feathered across her closed eyelids, and brushed her nose and mouth. She shivered as he nosed her neck and nibbled down her collar bone. His mouth found her breasts, and she arched her back and whimpered with pleasure as he kissed and suckled the throbbing mounds.

He was gentle but forceful, coaxing responses she had not known were hers to give. It was all new to her, yet somehow familiar—the way he touched and caressed her, the feelings he evoked, the emotions he stirred. She began exploring his body with the same eagerness and joy. They rolled together, fitting hardness to softness, glorying in the differences between them, eager to discover them all.

"Lie still . . . relax . . ." he crooned, rolling her beneath him, then catching her hands by the wrists and pinning them above her head. "I won't be rushed or hurried, Juliet. If this is the only night we will ever have, it must be perfect."

Already quivering with need and hunger for him, she craved union but had only a vague notion of how to achieve it. "No-ah, I want you," she whispered. "I want you so much."

"And you shall have me, sweetheart, but only when you're ready. . . . Close your eyes. Don't move . . . just feel. Feel how much I love you, sweetheart. Feel the pleasure I can give you . . ."

As he murmured into her ear, his hand searched her body, seeking out the most sensitive, intimate spots. His fingers discovered all her secrets. They dipped between her thighs, stroked and rubbed, titillated and teased, parted and entered her. . . . And all the while he kissed her and murmured endearments, telling her how beautiful she was, how sweet and tender, how warm, moist, and . . .

"Juliet . . . By God, you're a virgin!" His fingers stilled and he lifted his head to gaze down at her with startled eyes.

"Is that so important to you, No-ah? If it is, then I am glad of it . . . It means I never gave myself to Jason, no matter if he does dominate my dreams. You will be the first, No-ah. . . . How I wish I could be the first for you!"

"You *will* be," he assured her, "The first woman to whom I have given my heart as well as my body . . ."

He resumed kissing and stroking her, building her need to dizzying heights, making her shiver, quiver, and moan . . . and still, he held off taking her. She ceased to lie still and acquiescent. She boldly clasped him and attempted to guide him into her.

"Juliet, no! Not yet, my love . . ."

"Yes, No-ah. . . . Now, please. Take me now."

He rose up over her. She felt him probing and eagerly opened her thighs to him. He pushed part way inside her, stretching and widening her. A sensation of pain mixed with the pleasure. She did not fear the pain; it was a small price to pay for total unity. She lifted her hips and surged upward against him. With a strangled groan, he sank into her. The pain became sharp . . . tearing . . . then gradually faded as he remained sheathed within her but unmoving.

"Sweetheart, is it too bad?" he asked, breathing hard as if he had just run a long distance. "Can you bear it?"

" 'Tis over now," she sighed. " 'Tis not unbearable."

"I didn't want to hurt you. I tried not to hurt you."

"I know. But now we are one, and I am so happy, No-ah!"

"You will be happier yet, Juliet. I guarantee it."

Very slowly, taking infinite care, he began to move within her. She lay perfectly still, savoring the sensation, discovering that what should have hurt did not, so long as she did not fight it or tense her muscles. The pressure began to build, the pleasure returned—elusive and shimmering, enticing her along a path she had never before trod. Noah kissed her as he thrust long, slow, and deeply. He pushed his tongue into her mouth and mimicked his body's movement, making her head spin.

She felt herself dissolving inside, melting and sliding. . . . She moved against him, tilting her hips to take more of him into her, surging upward, meeting his thrusts with her own strength and power. She clung to him, wept, and cried out with the force of her feelings. A tide of ecstasy engulfed her. Pleasure sang in her veins; she was vibrantly alive.

As her pleasure peaked and exploded, Noah stiffened against her and gasped her name. Tears wet her cheeks. She held and rocked him as he collapsed on top of her. Gazing up at the stars, she knew she had experienced the grandest, most wonderful moment of her entire life. . . . She had never done this with another, never shared this exquisite rapture, never given nor received so much before. If she died tomorrow, she would die happy and fufilled, satisfied that she had experienced one of life's greatest mysteries . . .

Closing her eyes, she drifted into sleep. Sometime before dawn, Noah awoke her with more kisses, more lovemaking, more ecstasy and rapture. His lovemaking banished the chill of the desert night. Afterward, they dressed, then drew one of the blankets over themselves and slept again, wrapped in each other's arms.

When next she awoke, her first thought was that she did *not* want to die today; she wanted to live. She wanted a lifetime of loving Noah. Intending to tell him this, she opened her eyes—and discovered that she and Noah were no longer alone. The sun had already risen. Silhouetted against its blinding brilliance stood at least a dozen men—long-haired, half-naked men with slashes of white paint streaked across their dark cheekbones and brightly-colored bandanas tied about their foreheads.

The whinny of a horse was the only sound, and her own voice came out softly and hesitantly, laced with her sudden fear. "No-ah . . . No-ah, wake up. Someone has found us."

Chapter Eleven

"Apaches!" Noah's tone betrayed alarm, but for a moment, no one, including the Apaches, did anything.

Juliet had time to look at the strangers and wonder about them. They radiated a stunning ferocity; not one was smiling in greeting, and all held weapons. As a people, they were very different from herself and Noah. They had dark, unfathomable eyes, straight black hair, and deeply-bronzed skin. Several wore only short, waist-to-knee length garments and soft-looking, bootlike footwear. One fellow was dressed in trousers and a bright red shirt, with a long brown cloth tied around his waist. Others wore vests and clothing similar to Noah's. Cartridge belts crisscrossed the bare chests of most of the Apaches. Brightly-colored bandanas held back their hair.

Despite the occasional similarities in dress, these men were far more primitive than white men; Juliet sensed that they lived close to the land and probably knew animals as well as she did. Their horses knew what was expected of them; they stood quietly in the background—one man easily controlling several—while others simply stayed by their masters, awaiting the next command. Juliet relaxed a bit, but Noah's tension was rapidly mounting. She did not have to look at him to know what he was thinking; he expected violence. She wanted to tell him to remain calm. Calmness was everything. Without it, they did not stand a chance.

"Don't say or do anything, Juliet. Let me handle this." Noah still lay on his back in the tangled blankets, his rifle not close enough to be of any use. "Geronimo!" he said clearly and deliberately. "Are any of you Geronimo?"

One of the Apaches said something. His eyes lit with recognition. Repeating the word Geronimo, Noah moved to get up. Immediately, four Apaches grabbed him. One pulled out a wicked-looking knife and held it to his throat.

Juliet jumped to her feet. "Stop that! Put that knife away!"

Another man slipped behind her, effortlessly hooked an elbow about her neck, and bent her backward. At the same time, he pressed a skinny long blade into her throat, its cold edge nearly piercing her skin.

"I said let me handle this." Noah did not move a muscle. Amazingly, he seemed to recognize the need for calmness while she grappled with rising panic. "I've got to make them understand that we come in peace and just want to see their leader, Geronimo. . . . Ahhh!" he gasped, as one of the Apaches cruelly twisted his arm behind him.

Juliet struggled to quell her fear and think clearly. *Do not consider these men your enemies. Think of them as wild creatures and gentle them through your thoughts.*

She understood that she and Noah were about to be killed; the Apaches would slice their throats as quickly as the coyotes had attacked the cougar. In the animal world, predators acted on instinct when they scented blood. So also had the Apaches responded violently when they sensed her and Noah's fear. Closing her eyes, she concentrated on reaching into the mind of the man who held her. *We mean you no harm. Free us and we will prove it to you.*

After a long, tense moment, the Apache eased his

hold on her neck, but kept a firm grip on her upper arm. She opened her eyes to find him staring at her, a perplexed frown creasing his forehead. It was the opportunity she had been awaiting. She gazed steadfastly into his eyes. The other Apaches began abusing Noah, but she ignored them. Loud thumps signaled the administration of harsh blows. Each time the Indians landed a particularly good one, they grunted with satisfaction and Noah groaned.

The sounds tore at Juliet's heart, but she gazed intently into the black-as-night eyes of her captor and concentrated on exchanging thoughts with him. She worried she might not be able to reach him. He was a complicated man, not a simple animal. Hatred and hostility radiated from him. Whatever kindness or gentleness he possessed was deeply buried beneath layers of anger. He wanted first to frighten her, then to make her suffer before he killed her. . . . Only she would not allow it. By sheer force of determination, she would shame him into acknowledging their shared humanity.

After a few minutes, the Apache glanced away. He lowered his knife and quickly stepped back from her. Muttering something under his breath, he gestured to two comrades who were holding horses and watching Noah's futile struggles. Then he let loose with a string of gibberish Juliet could not decipher. Immediately, the men stopped beating Noah, and Noah fell heavily to the ground.

The man who had been holding Juliet pointed to her, gesticulating and shaking his head. Another man asked a question, and the answer did not please him. He gave Juliet a fearful look and moved back several paces. Suddenly, all the Apaches were wary of her; she had succeeded in reminding them that it was wrong to kill innocent people, but the danger was not yet over. She could not control these Apaches as easily as she had the coyotes.

"What in hell did you do to them?" Noah lay doubled up on his side, his face contorted, his breathing labored.

She ran to him and knelt at his side. "No-ah! Did they hurt you badly?"

"Feels like they b-busted my ribs—besides d-damn near killing me."

She reached out to touch him, but the Apache whom she had stared down—a big, bare-chested fellow with a blue cloth tied around his forehead—thrust his rifle barrel under her nose.

"D-do what he says," Noah gasped.

"I will try, but I cannot understand him."

"Don't try, just do it!"

Juliet slowly rose to her feet. The Apache glared at her a moment, then to her great astonishment, said clearly: "You . . . prisoners. We take . . . Geronimo."

"Geronimo," Noah grunted. "Damn, we've found him. . . . Rather, he's found us."

"Who is Geronimo?" Juliet whispered.

"He's . . ." Noah started to say, but the Apaches grabbed him, dragged him upright and bound his hands behind him with a thin, narrow strip of leather. They made a loop of rope, dropped it over his head, and dragged him toward a nearby horse. Juliet expected them to do the same to her, but Blue Bandana, as she decided to call him, fetched a white horse with a circle of red paint around one eye, and gestured that she should mount it.

She went to the horse, touched its muzzle, and peered deeply into its eyes, letting it know she meant no harm and would be its friend. The animal blew air through its nostrils and nuzzled her hand while the Apaches muttered among themselves. Blue Bandana unceremoniously lifted her and set her astride the horse's back, then he mounted a second horse—this one a dark brown with white hand prints all over its body—and set off leading her horse behind him.

All of the Apaches mounted, a couple sharing a horse and one keeping a tight grip on the rope around

154

Noah's neck. Only Noah was still afoot. He could barely stand upright.

"He will never be able to keep up!" she protested, but the Apaches never even looked back as they rode out at a brisk trot.

Juliet sought to transmit some of her own strength and energy to Noah. She focused her entire being on the effort. The trick seemed to work, for Noah rallied. He had to run to keep from falling and being dragged by the neck, but run he did—for a surprisingly long time, given the beating he had just suffered.

When Noah finally fell, the Apache holding his rope uttered a cry of disgust and rode back to him. Noah was twice his size, but the wiry little man picked him up, dumped him face down over the back of his horse, and leaped up behind him. Then everybody rode hard for a range of mountains in the opposite direction from the ones toward which Noah had been leading them.

By the time they stopped in the early evening, they had reached the foothills of the mountains, and Juliet was dizzy and near fainting. Her horse gave a glad whinny and before she could dismount, followed the other horses to a trickle of water cutting through the bottom of a gully. She might never have noticed the tiny stream on her own; now she gladly slid to the ground and collapsed to her knees beside her thirsty friend. Greedily slurping the water on her hands and knees, Juliet then wet the end of her *himation* and wiped her gritty face and eyes.

She looked around for Noah. The Apaches were all drinking or watering their horses, but Noah lay on his side unmoving, a short distance from the stream. She hurried to him as fast as her shaky legs could carry her.

"No-ah, wake up. There's water here. You must get up and drink."

Blue Bandana strode over to her and stood scowling down at Noah. "No water. . . . None for Red-Hair."

155

Juliet rose to confront him. "Yes, water! He will die if he does not get water."

The Apache gave Noah a contemptuous kick in the ribs. He spat something in his own language and turned away in disgust. Juliet dropped to her knees. "Noah, wake up! Please, you must!"

Noah stirred and groaned. Juliet hooked both hands under his armpits and tried to drag him into the gully toward the thin trickle of water. The Apaches found her efforts amusing. They gathered around, laughing and hooting. No one offered to help. She suspected they would derive a gleeful satisfaction from watching Noah die of thirst.

Incensed, Juliet rose to her full height and stared them down. She put all of her anger and contempt into it, letting them know exactly what she thought of their misplaced humor and cruelty. She gazed long and hard at each man in turn, all thirteen of them. One by one, the Apaches fell silent, unable to hold her gaze. And Juliet thanked whatever divine being had provided the mysterious inner knowledge that enabled her to intimidate them.

After a few moments, the Apaches turned away, busying themselves with setting up camp. Two men emptied Noah's saddle bags and grunted their disappointment at the meager contents. The Apaches had appropriated everything—including their blankets. One was now wrapping himself in the very blanket she and Noah had slept under the previous night.

Recalling those wonderful hours beneath the stars, Juliet bit back a sob. Fate had given her and Noah one more day together—one more night—and she resolved to keep him alive somehow. Eventually, she managed to drag him to the water's edge. First, she splashed water on his face and neck. He jerked and mumbled incoherently. When he had regained a degree of consciousness, she assisted him in drinking. After he had drunk his fill, he flopped back in her arms. His brown eyes opened and wearily scanned her face.

"Juliet. . . . They haven't hurt you, have they?" He did not sound like himself. His skin was the color of the clay at the bottom of the gully.

She shook her head. "No, nor will they. They fear me. I looked into their eyes the same way I looked into the eyes of the cougar and the coyote."

Noah's lips curved in a ragged grin. "Then you've betwitched them. . . . Thank God for that. If I don't make it, just go on bewitching them. Stay alive, Juliet. They said they were taking us to Geronimo. Sooner or later, the soldiers will catch up with them. When they do, let them know you're white as soon as you can. Tell them what happened to you—as much as you can remember. They'll take you to Tucson and help you find your family."

"But I do not understand, No-ah. Who is Geronimo? Why are the soldiers searching for him?"

He sighed. "I should have explained all this to you before. Don't know why I didn't. . . . Geronimo is the last Apache leader, and these are the last free Apaches on this entire continent . . ."

Juliet listened carefully while Noah told her briefly and succinctly about Geronimo and why he himself had come to Arizona. She was amazed—and not a little hurt that he had been so reticent about his past.

"Why did you not tell me all this before?" she asked, keeping one eye on the Indians who had made a fire and were beginning to cook something over it in Noah's black caldron.

"Never came up, I guess. . . . With your lost memory, what would have been the point of frightening you with lurid local history, sweetheart? The whole territory is in a turmoil over Geronimo's escape from the San Carlos reservation. . . . He's said to be a cold-blooded murderer. Don't know if his people will kill me or not, but if I live to meet the old renegade, I'm going to try and talk him into trading us to the soldiers in exchange for some of his own people. Maybe I can persuade him to give himself up. If he doesn't, he'll be hunted down and slaughtered. The ranchers and settlers in the territory don't want him imprisoned; they want him dead. They damn near killed me when they found out I wanted to do a book about him—telling *his* side of the story."

"I really do not know much about you, No-ah, do I?" she sadly inquired.

"What you don't know isn't important, sweetheart. All that matters now is staying alive. The Apaches unwittingly saved our lives today; whether we'll live to see tomorrow is anybody's guess."

Juliet did not agree that her ignorance was unimportant. She had spent the previous night in Noah's arms; they had shared hunger, thirst, and assorted other perils. Yet he had never told her about Geronimo and his quest to interview the Indian. Nor had he described exactly what had happened with the ranchers or revealed much about the life he had led in a place called Boston. Her feelings were hurt. If she could have remembered her own past, by now she would have told him everything. However, now was not the time to dwell on the disappointments of their relationship.

"I will help you out of this gully, No-ah. Then I will see if I can shame the Indians into feeding us."

"Sorry, but I don't feel too hungry just now. Those braves did a hell of a job working me over."

"Yes, but if you don't eat, you'll never make it to tomorrow. Come along," she urged, sliding her arm around his waist.

It took some effort, but Juliet finally managed to get Noah settled against a large boulder not far from the campfire where the Indians were eating and talking in their incomprehensible language. No one was paying attention, so she started to untie Noah's hands and remove the rope from his neck. Blue Bandana shouted at her, his hand moving to the knife sheathed at his waist. Scrambling to her feet, she marched over to him, folded her arms, and demanded: "Food. We must have food."

Thirteen pairs of fierce black eyes intently watched her. Blue Bandana frowned and tossed his long black hair in annoyance, but Juliet refused to back down. She made eating motions with her hands and repeated her request. Blue Bandana silently turned his back to her. Offended by his rudeness, Juliet wasted no more time with diplomacy. She stalked to the cookfire, grabbed Noah's cup from a nearby rock, and scooped out a hefty portion of the caldron's contents.

None of the Indians made a move to stop her. Their faces and eyes were utterly impassive, their thoughts impossible to guess. She focused her energy on assuring them she meant no harm, but at the same time, they must leave her alone. They did, and flushed with triumph, she calmly walked back to Noah.

The next two days were long and exhausting. Day and night, they rode across the plain, stopping only once for a brief rest. Soon they left the plain behind. Impenetrable ravines and hills covered with *mesquite, ocotillo, saguaros,* and other thorny cacti cut up the foothills through which they now rode. But it was not all bad. As they reached the higher elevations, dense patches of cypress and pine gave off a tangy odor that reminded Juliet of the mountains where Noah had found her. The smell and the cooler air were most pleasant.

Even more pleasant was the feel of Noah's arms around her waist as he rode the white horse behind her. The Apaches were in a great hurry to get wherever they were going and so did not waste time mistreating Noah while they traveled. They had untied his hands so he could ride; however, Blue Bandana kept a firm grip on the animal's reins, never once permitting Juliet or Noah to touch them.

"I love the scent of these trees." Juliet kept her voice

low so as not to attract the attention of their captors.

They were riding through a patch of pines, and it was cool and shady. Water gurgled and splashed somewhere nearby. After so many days of desert heat and silence, the sound alone refreshed her.

"They're called ponderosa pines," Noah muttered, adjusting his hold on her waist. Occasionally, he slumped against her, almost causing her to lose balance. Then he would realize what he was doing and abruptly straighten. Juliet knew he was hurting and seriously weakened from the lack of food and sleep—she herself felt weak—but she could do nothing about it, except distract him with conversation.

"The vegetation is quite different from what it was a few days ago out on the plain. If we had had horses, we could have made it here ourselves."

Noah did not respond. Did he think she was criticizing him? "What other trees have you spotted?" she asked, to keep the conversation going.

"*Manzanita,* oak, what they call mountain mahogany, and some scrubby cork. . . . Farther up above are firs and aspens. If you want to know more, you'll have to ask the Indians. That's all I recognize." He sounded weary, as if he wished she would quit. If she did, he might succumb to brooding despair.

"What mountains are we now approaching? Do they have a name? Do you know it?"

"Damned if I can tell you. Geronimo used to hang out in the Chiricahua and Dragoon Mountains, same as Cochise, another Apache leader who's dead now. When Geronimo escaped from the reservation at Fort Apache, the U.S. Army and the ranchers searched for him first in the mountains near there, then worked their way south. The army supposedly brought reinforcements into Fort Bowie overlooking Apache Pass. We combed the pass but didn't see any sign of him. The ranchers and I split off and rode farther south. About the time we started back north, I lost track of where we were. I still don't know where we are, but I

160

wouldn't be surprised if these were the foothills of the Sierra Madre in Mexico."

Juliet turned to look at him over her shoulder. "Do you really know where Tucson is, No-ah? Or were you only guessing?"

He gave a short bitter laugh. "Guessing, but it was an educated guess, Juliet. I knew if we kept heading north, we were bound to run into something—stumble across some sign of civilization. Between the mountain and desert areas, forts, rivers, railroad tracks, and ranches dot the region. . . . Only it's damn easy to miss 'em, especially on foot."

He trailed off, sighed deeply, and rested his head on her shoulder. From the very beginning, their situation had been far more grave than she had realized. She was glad the Indians had found them—providing they did not decide to kill them. It was up to her to prevent that. Only her mysterious "gifts" could stop the Apaches from taking revenge on her and Noah for all the wrongs done to them by others. And Noah was more at risk than she.

One good thing about the past few days was that she had not once had one of her disturbing dreams. Too much had been going on in her life to worry about the past. Her lost identity was a problem to be solved at a later time, when the fight for survival had been won.

She and Noah rode the rest of the day in dreary silence. Toward nightfall, they reached the Apaches' camp, high in the mountains. Tall pines and fir trees framed breathtaking views, but the village itself struck Juliet as poor and simple. A collection of rude, dome-shaped huts made of mud and sticks, covered over with long grasses, made up the Apache homes, and there were not many of them. Half-naked children, tired-looking women, and a handful of old folks, all chattering in the Apache tongue, spilled out of low doorways.

At the sight of Noah and Juliet, the people stopped in their tracks and stared. Then a small boy picked up a stone, and with a loud, belligerent cry, hurled it at Juliet. She ducked, and it missed her, but immediately, everyone surged forward—hands clawing, mouths shrieking, faces congested with rage. As Juliet was pulled from the horse, Noah toppled backward. There was no time to think, react, or defend themselves. . . . The Apaches clearly hated them and meant to kill them then and there.

Chapter Twelve

Blue Bandana uttered a sharp cry, caught Juliet's hand, and yanked her off to one side. The crowd's fury then fell on Noah. No match for anyone, least of all outraged women and children, he disappeared beneath the flailing figures. Jerking free of Blue Bandana, Juliet sought to help him, but several moments passed before she finally managed to get between Noah and the wild-eyed creatures bent on pummeling his chest and scratching out his eyes. At the first pause in the attack, Noah rolled into a ball and lay there, panting, trying to catch his breath, while Juliet shakily straightened and fought to regain her breath and her composure.

The villagers had surrounded them. In the sudden quiet, she could hear the creak of the pine trees swaying in the wind. Her gaze fell upon the angry women; they were all dressed similarly in two-piece garments, long skirts that skimmed their ankles and tops that brushed their hips. Some wore beaded necklaces, earrings, and rows of fringe on their sleeves or bodices, but even the fanciest among them impressed her as being poorly clothed. The colors of their garments had faded; some were torn and tattered. Few were clean.

Despite the evidence of poverty and harsh living, the Apaches exuded a fierce pride. Like their men, the women and children had long black hair, erect carriages, and snapping, black eyes. They radiated grace and agility. The children were mostly naked, even the

163

girls, except for a simple cloth about their waists which hung down to cover their loins. Juliet was reminded of fleet-footed deer one rarely caught a glimpse of—only these deer had a predatory air at odds with their underlying timidity and shyness. It was an intriguing mix, and a personal challenge to her.

She located the boy who had thrown the rock. He was standing directly in front of her and scowling as if he meant to cut out her heart. Dropping to her knees before him, she gazed into his eyes. *We come as friends. Do you understand? Friends.*

The effect upon him was stunning—and much more immediate than it had been on his elders. His eyes widened. He hazarded a tentative smile, then a friendly grin. Had he been a puppy, his tail would have wagged. He erupted into excited chatter. Other children pressed in more closely, eagerly responding to Juliet's silent message. They were as easy—easier—to conquer than the coyotes and the cougar. Smiling, Juliet held out her hands to them. A little girl with enormous wondering eyes clasped her fingers and giggled.

Then one of the women said something in a disapproving tone. Startled, the children guiltily jumped aside. Juliet rose. The adults would not be so quickly won over as the children; she should have known as much. The women stared. Black eyes hostilely examined her hair and clothing. Disapproving mouths curved downward. The silent perusal lasted for several heart-stopping moments, during which no one spoke or moved. Juliet sensed their conflict. Curiosity warred with hatred. Suspicion wrestled with the desire to be friendly. The Apaches realized she was different, but the grown ones resisted her silent communications.

A new voice—one she had never before heard—broke the silence. Even before she saw who had spoken, Juliet recognized the ring of authority. The women and children stepped aside to permit a short, stocky man to approach. Juliet's first impression of the newcomer was that there was no softness in him, no gentleness. He differed little in general appearance from the other Apaches—having a similarly round face, darkly-bronzed skin, and black hair and eyes. But in the set of his mouth and the intensity of his gaze, he differed greatly.

His mouth might have been carved from stone. It was tough and unyielding, slashed on either side by deep grooves. Small, closely-set eyes regarded her impassively, but within their depths, dark emotions burned and smoldered. Juliet knew without being told that this man had suffered greatly. Anguish and deep sadness stamped his expression. Mixed with the sadness was arrogance and cruelty.

As he walked toward her, she noticed his clothing—a red and white striped shirt, a darker red bandana knotted at his throat, a loose blue garment tucked around the cartridge belt at his waist, tan trousers beneath it, and tall brown footwear of the type most of the Indians were wearing. On his head was a brimmed hat with a blue band around it. He wore it crooked, dipping down over one malevolent eye.

He seemed to look right through her. Try as she might, she could not penetrate his concentration. It was as if he saw her without actually seeing her. Glancing past her, he spotted Noah still lying on the ground. His lip curled contemptuously. Juliet stepped in front of Noah to shield him from this imposing man, who could only be Geronimo.

Reaching out a gnarled hand, Geronimo impatiently shoved her to one side and stood gazing down at Noah, as if the sight both pleased and offended him. Turning toward Blue Bandana, he uttered a low, gutteral growl. Blue Bandana responded at some length, and Geronimo nodded and prodded Noah with his toe. Noah opened his eyes. His mouth formed a single word: "Geronimo."

This amused the Apache chieftain. He grinned widely and said something to his people. Other grins

165

appeared. Geronimo's faded as quickly as it had come. He barked a command, and Blue Bandana and several other Apaches jumped to obey. They seized Noah's arms and began dragging him away.

"Wait! Where are you taking him?" Juliet grasped Geronimo's sleeve.

Giving her a scathing glance, he removed her hand from his sleeve and turned away. Deprived of an answer, Juliet sought to follow the braves who had taken hold of Noah. They dragged him to one of the round-shaped dwellings, and hauled him inside. When she bent to enter behind him, they barred her way, indicating with a nod that she was to go with the women and children who had accompanied her in a small avid group.

"I will stay with him" she announced, but Blue Bandana shook his head and pointed to the women.

One woman seized her elbow. Another grabbed her free hand. The children chattered and twittered like a flock of excited birds. An old woman with a missing front tooth uttered a short, sharp command. Juliet understood that she could not stay with Noah but dreaded leaving him alone. More damage may have been done to him during this most recent skirmish; without examining him, she had no way of knowing. He needed food and water—would it be given to him? Or would they simply kill him as soon as she turned her back?

Two of the Apache braves took up a protective stance in front of the dome-shelter, and Juliet had no choice but to retreat with the women. They took her to another of the shelters and bade her crawl inside. It was growing dark; inside the shelter, it was even darker. She sat down on some sort of grass mat. Several people crawled into the hut behind her. She could see little of the interior but had no difficulty hearing people settling themselves around her. They breathed and scratched. Someone belched. A child giggled.

Exhaustion stole over her, numbing her emotions.

Her muscles ached from the long hours of unaccustomed riding. Her stomach grumbled. She sighed and leaned back against the wall of the shelter. Whatever was going to happen would happen, and she could not stop it, at least not tonight. If Geronimo wanted them to die, they would die. If he permitted them to live, they would live. In the darkness and her present state of depletion, she could do little to help Noah or herself. She must be patient and gather strength. She must hold fast to the belief that a moment would eventually present itself when she could plead their case to the Apache chieftain.

Later, much later by Juliet's confused reckoning, she was roused from her stupor and urged outside to a clearing in the middle of which burned a fire. The blaze was small, but its light illuminated the darkness of the cool mountain night. Its heat had cooked food in a large kettle hanging from a wooden rack. Shadowy figures—women and girls—moved back and forth serving food. A woman motioned Juliet to a log and handed her Noah's cup filled to the brim with something hot, steaming, and savory-smelling. Juliet sat down and lifted the cup to her mouth, then abruptly lowered it. . . . Where was Noah?

A commotion off to one side caught her eye. Several braves were laughing and talking—and kicking something or someone. Juliet squinted in order to see better. A man crouched on his hands and knees in front of them. Every time he tried to rise, the Apaches kicked his hands or legs out from under him, and he fell to the ground, whereupon they poked him with sharp sticks to make him rise again.

Juliet rose, rapidly crossed the clearing, and arrived just in time to witness Noah sprawl on his face and lay unmoving while two young men prodded him in the ribs. Ignoring his tormenters, she sank to her knees beside Noah, set down the cup, and turned him over on his back. The young men silently watched. All conversation around the campfire ceased. Not a word was spoken as Juliet slipped an arm beneath Noah's head.

His eyes were closed, his breathing labored. Taking the cup, Juliet pressed it to his lips. "No-ah, here is refreshment. Drink quickly now, before they stop me."

He opened his eyes and gazed up at her. The flickering light revealed his torment, and her heart twisted painfully in her breast. "Can't . . ." he gasped.

"You must! Hurry!"

She tilted the cup so that some of the liquid ran into his mouth. Noah drank. She lifted her gaze to the men who had been mistreating him, daring them to stop her. She would feed Noah if they killed her for it. They would have to kill her to stop her. One of the young men made a sudden motion with the stick, as if he meant to poke Noah again.

"Touch him, and I will curse you," Juliet snapped. "Your enemies will chase you to the ends of the earth. You will suffer and die a lonely, misbegotten death."

Her powers did not extend to harming people—at least, not that she knew—but the Indians were unaware of that. The young man she had threatened seemed to recognize a warning when he heard one. With a grunt, he withdrew the sharp stick.

"Strong medicine . . ." a voice said behind her. She looked up to see Blue Bandana standing over her.

She thought he meant the food swimming in broth in the cup; then it occurred to her he might mean herself.

"You . . . strong medicine . . . Shaman Woman," Blue Bandana gravely pronounced. "Look in man's eyes. See heart. Drive out wickedness."

"Your people should be ashamed of the way they are treating this man. You must tell Geronimo not to allow him to be abused anymore. This is savagery of the worst sort."

"Hah! Better dead," Blue Bandana scoffed, giving

Noah a negligent kick. "No good white man. Geronimo think save to trade. I think better dead."

Juliet remembered Noah telling her that given a chance, he would try to bargain with Geronimo. Geronimo had apparently already thought of it. "This man has done nothing against the Apaches. He came to this land to talk to Geronimo. He searched for your leader, but could not find him. He comes as a friend, not an enemy. Your chief should listen to what he has to say."

"No white man friend," Blue Bandana disputed.

"This one is. And he would be a better friend, if you would let him. He . . ." Juliet struggled to recall what Noah had told her regarding his work. He reported things. He talked to people and wrote down what they said so that other people could read it. He had wanted to write about Geronimo, but she did not know how to explain all this to Blue Bandana.

"White man no friend," Blue Bandana stubbornly insisted.

Noah finished the broth, and Juliet felt his hand touch hers; his fingers were trembling. And his handsome face was so battered and bloody that his own mother would not have recognized him. She set down the cup with unnecessary force. "I must get him cleaned up! I must see to his injuries."

"No. Leave him. Come see Geronimo now."

"I do not wish to see Geronimo at this particular moment. This man needs immediate care. I intend to give it to him."

Noah's eyes sought her face. "Go . . ." he croaked, fixing her with an intent gaze. "T-tell Geronimo . . . I can help him with the soldiers. Warn him about the ranchers. They will kill him, if they f-find him first. . . . Juliet, t-tell Geronimo."

Every instinct Juliet possessed screamed at her to stay and protect Noah from the Indians. Yet if she went and spoke to Geronimo, perhaps he would order the Apaches to leave Noah alone . . . to stop abusing him and let them go free. This was her chance to plead with the Apache leader, but still, she hesitated.

"Juliet, go . . ." Noah's bloodshot, swollen eyes pleaded with her.

"All right," she finally said. *"All right.* But if anyone touches you, if anyone harms you, they will answer to *me."* She glanced up at Blue Bandana. "Tell them that. Tell them I have power and I will use it if they harm him."

Blue Bandana's mouth thinned. "Geronimo's power stronger. His power greater than any white-eyes. Better you not threaten Geronimo, or he destroy you."

Geronimo must be very powerful indeed, Juliet thought, for Blue Bandana to have such confidence in him. She wondered if the Apache chieftain could share thoughts with animals. "I am not making threats," she said in a soft, calm voice. "I am telling the truth. Please translate my warning for your friends."

"I translate," Blue Bandana conceded with a scowl. He lapsed into his own language. Listening, one of the young men leaned back on his elbow, effecting a casual pose, while the other yawned, rose, and disappeared into the shadows.

Blue Bandana nodded to Juliet. "You come now. No one touch Red-Hair."

"I will return as soon as I can." Juliet told Noah. Gently, she lay his head on the ground.

He grabbed her hand and squeezed her fingers, his grip surprisingly strong. Reassured, she rose and accompanied Blue Bandana to a different sort of dwelling set off to one side by itself. Made of animal hides stretched across poles, it was wide at the bottom and narrow at the top. A flap of animal skins covered the doorway. Juliet bent a little, pushed aside the flap and entered.

Inside, a small fire blazed in the center of the circular structure. Mats and skins covered the floor. Drawings of hunt scenes and animals adorned the walls.

Baskets, clay jars, and weapons stood neatly along the sides. The sense of orderliness surprised Juliet—as did the man seated near the fire. Geronimo seemed much less fierce here in his own home. He gestured for her to sit down. She knelt and sat back on her heels. Blue Bandana and several other man came into the dwelling and also sat down. No one said anything for a long moment, and then Geronimo began to speak.

"Geronimo say welcome tipi," Blue Bandana translated.

This, then, was a tipi. She wondered what the other dwellings were called—the dome-shaped, grass-covered ones.

"This man Naiche, son of great Apache chieftain, Cochise." Blue Bandana nodded toward one of the men who looked taller than Geronimo, and somehow more noble and elegant. He had prominent cheekbones, steady eyes, and an aquiline nose. Naiche gave Juliet an inscrutable look, not friendly, not hostile. She judged him a quieter, less intense personality than Geronimo.

Blue Bandana spoke again. "This Nana." He nodded toward the oldest of the gathered men. "This Chihuahua," he nodded to a third. "This Mangus . . ."

As he finished, Juliet asked: "And you? What is your name?"

Blue Bandana seemed surprised at the question and responded with a string of incomprehensible syllables. She decided to keep thinking of him as Blue Bandana. He, too, was taller than Geronimo and possessed his own brand of fierceness, tempered by a quiet reserve and thoughtfulness that made communication less a chore with him than with the others. He held her gaze a moment, then looked away as another man burst into the already crowded tipi.

Younger than the others, the intruder had naught but a cloth to cover his nakedness. Tight-lipped and grim, he sat down next to Nana. Blue Bandana gave a grunt of disapproval and muttered: "This White Antelope."

Juliet surmised that these were the leaders of the Apaches—or what was left of them. She estimated that there could be no more than 150 in the camp, the majority women and children. She dearly hoped she would be able to convince them to deal kindly with Noah—and to heed his advice about surrendering.

Geronimo spoke, interrupting Juliet's thoughts.

"Geronimo want know where you and Red-Hair come from," Blue Bandana translated.

"Fort Apache," Juliet answered, reciting Noah's history, since her own was such a muddle. "Before that, Tucson, and before Tucson, Boston."

"Boston!" Geronimo echoed, his brows lifting.

"Where Boston?" Blue Bandana demanded.

Juliet gave a slight shrug. "I do not know . . . east, I think."

"You shaman there?"

"I . . . I am," she agreed, not sure what a shaman was but loathe to arouse suspicion that she really had no remarkable powers. "I am important to my people," she added on inspiration. "And so is Red-Hair. Our people will want us back. They will deal kindly with you if you return us."

Blue Bandana translated, rousing a snort from Geronimo. Silence descended. Then Nana spoke, and after him, Naiche, Chihuahua, and Mangus. Only White Antelope said nothing. He only stared at her, making her uncomfortable as he watched her every move. She could sense his fascination with her hair. He reached out to touch it before she could pull away. Perhaps he had never seen a white woman before.

"What are they saying?" she asked Blue Bandana.

"Make talk-talk," he responded. "You speak *Español?*"

She shook her head. She did not think she did.

"Red-Hair speak *Español?*"

"I . . . do not think so."

"Too bad. Geronimo speak it. So do many Apaches."

"But what are they saying?" Juliet repeated, growing anxious.

Blue Bandana gave her a level look. "No like white man stay here in *ranchería*. Like better kill."

"No, it would not be better to kill Red-Hair! He came to Arizona to learn the truth of Geronimo's story. Not all white men think Geronimo is bad. Red-Hair does not. I know he doesn't." Juliet hoped she was making sense. Noah had told her so little. She longed for more details to convince them. "They should talk to Red-Hair."

Blue Bandana made a sound of contempt. "Time for talk-talk done. Now white men kill all Apaches. Apaches kill all white men. Even if possible talk-talk, Apaches no can believe white man talk. White man talk all lies. All tricks."

This confused Juliet. Had the Apaches been lied to? Had they been tricked in the past?

Geronimo suddenly turned to her, biting out a question.

"Geronimo say many sick in camp. You shaman. You heal."

"What?" she did not immediately understand. "Who is sick?"

"Geronimo decide what do with you and Red-Hair. While he decide, you heal sick." Blue Bandana regarded her implacably. "You savvy?"

"Savvy?" She took a guess at what he meant. "Yes, I savvy. But . . . but what about Red-Hair? Red-Hair is hurt. I must heal him, too."

Blue Bandana and Geronimo conversed for several moments. Nana added his opinion. Naiche also spoke.

"No see Red-Hair," Blue Bandana finally announced. "He stay wickiup."

"Wickiup?"

"House . . . like tipi. Stay wickiup. You not heal Apaches, Red-Hair die. You die, too."

That was plain enough, Juliet thought. If she did not cooperate, Noah would pay the price. So would she.

"I will try to heal your sick, but my medicine may be different from yours. It may not work."

"Better work. You shaman. Look in heart. Send away bad spirits."

Now Juliet understood. The Apaches apparently believed that sickness was caused by evil spirits entering the body. They wanted her to look into the eyes of their sick and make the evil spirits depart. The challenge was daunting—and dangerous. If she could not meet their expectations the Apaches would undoubtedly kill her and Noah. However, if she did meet them, they had a slim chance of staying alive. Realizing she had no choice, she smiled and nodded, pretending a confidence she did not feel.

White Antelope suddenly leaned forward and touched one of the pins at her shoulder. As he did so, his fingertips brushed her breast. The startling contact caused Juliet to jump. Gazing into her eyes, White Antelope grinned and muttered something to Blue Bandana.

"White Antelope like you. Like pale hair. Like gold eyes. Good hunter. Strong fighter. Have no wife."

"N-no wife?" Juliet repeated, fearing the implications.

"No wife," Blue Bandana affirmed.

As Juliet scooted farther away from the young brave, he grinned more widely. Geronimo laughed. When the Apache leader smiled, his face lit up. For a moment, he looked gentle and human. But when his smile disappeared, the savagery returned.

"Geronimo say you start now. Take you wickiup sick squaw. You heal."

"B-but . . ." Juliet started to argue, but Blue Bandana was already rising.

"Come. Want keep Red-Hair alive, you come."

Chapter Thirteen

The wickiup to which Blue Bandana led Juliet was not far from Geronimo's tipi. It, too, had a small fire inside, contained by a ring of stones. Beside the fire, an old woman lay on a woven mat, her face turned toward the blaze, her wrinkled hands extended toward its heat. Accompanied by Blue Bandana and two younger women who crowded on either side, Juliet knelt down near the sick woman and searched for signs of illness.

She felt the old woman's forehead but detected no unnatural warmth. The woman's skin was unusually cold. Her tangled white hair partially obscured her face, and Juliet gently combed it back with her fingers. The old woman did not so much as raise her eyes to look at Juliet. Oblivious to her surroundings, she stared unblinking into the fire.

"Tell me about her," Juliet urged Blue Bandana. "What are her symptoms?"

"Not eat. Not drink. Family say she dying. Not want live."

"But . . . is she ill? Does she have pain?"

"Body not sick. Spirit sick. Husband dead. Sons dead. Only daughter left. Last son killed by *Nacoya.*"

"*Nacoya?*"

"Mexicans. Mexicans and Apaches long time make war. Since before white man come."

"If she does not wish to live, no shaman can help

175

her. She is very old. Perhaps it would be a kindness to let her die if she wishes it."

"Not so old. Only little old," Blue Bandana disputed. "Hair turn white when husband and first two sons die. Then last son die. Now she refuse eat." Blue Bandana's eyes softened in the firelight. A deep sadness radiated from him.

"How long ago did her son die?"

He held up five fingers. "Five days. Son ride out scout Mexicans. Mexicans shoot. He ride back camp. Die next day. Mexicans kill whole family. Now kill mother, too."

"Poor woman." Juliet wondered how she could possibly help the still, silent figure lying beside the fire. She passed her hand in front of the old woman's eyes, but the woman neither blinked nor glanced away from the flames.

"Daughter no want lose mother. Lose too much. Father, brothers, first husband. You save mother for daughter."

Juliet was about to ask which of the younger women was the daughter when she discovered the answer for herself. One of the women was gazing at the old woman with a sorrow too great to contemplate. The young woman did not weep or speak, but the slump of her shoulders and her quivering mouth communicated her grief and worry.

"Tell her I will try," Juliet said. "If I can reach her mother and call her back to the living before she slips away from us entirely, I will do so."

"Good," Blue Bandana grunted. "That good."

Aching in every muscle of his body, Noah lay sprawled on his stomach in the dark. After Juliet had fed him and been led away, the Apaches had dragged him into one of their dwellings and departed. It was dark and stuffy, but he welcomed the darkness. The Indians had left him unbound, providing the perfect

176

opportunity for escape. Gathering his strength, Noah sought to turn over, but his body would not obey. He had been pummeled, prodded, and beaten so severely that any movement was agony . . . but he was alive. And as long as he still lived, he had to do what he could to save himself and Juliet.

He had thought of more advice to give her, more arguments to present to Geronimo. The Indians would not listen to him, but they would heed her. They respected her strange powers and held her in awe; she must not hesitate to use that awe to protect herself. . . . Had he told her that? He could not remember. He must find her—and help her to persuade Geronimo to surrender.

Setting his teeth against the pain, Noah managed to get to his knees. After several moments of breathless exertion, he gained his feet and stumbled toward the opening of the shelter. A faint reddish light indicated that a fire still burned outside. When he got to the doorway, he had to grab hold of the doorposts on either side to keep from falling. Pain clawed at his sides and back. Even the tiniest movement intensified his dizziness and disorientation. Stiff as ramrods, his arms and legs refused to function, and he could hardly see out of his swollen eyes.

Hoping to catch a glimpse of pale hair shimmering in the firelight, he peered out of the shelter. Juliet had been taken to Geronimo, he suddenly remembered, but he had no idea which hut belonged to the old chieftain. As unobtrusively as possible, he stepped outside and stood there swaying, desperately trying to remain upright and hoping no one would notice him. A child saw him, shrieked a warning cry, and pointed in his direction. Figures rose from beside the fire, and Noah groaned with frustration. He could not fight them in his present condition; neither could he hurry back inside the wickiup.

The first Apache to reach him placed his palm flat on Noah's chest and shoved. Noah could not catch himself . . . could do nothing except fall. He landed flat on his back, every bone in his body jarring from the impact. Four men swarmed over him, grabbed his hands, and stretched them above his head. They lashed his wrists together and fastened them to one side of the hut. They spread-eagled his legs and tied them to separate posts on the opposite side of the hut. He lay helpless and furious, rendered as useless as a trussed-up pig.

The trussing had been accomplished with a maximum of speed and a minimum of conversation. One of his captives then fetched a torch and held it over him; in its wavering red light, the faces of his tormentors twisted in contempt and loathing. Their eyes burned into him like red-hot coals.

"Dog!" a big fellow spat in English.

He kicked Noah hard between his outspread legs. Unable to help himself, Noah arched his back and cried out. Sparks danced before his eyes. He nearly lost consciousness. Almost but not quite.

"Soon you die, Red-Hair."

Noah did not recognize the man who spoke; his English was heavily accented with Spanish. Not among those who had captured them, he did not look in the least disposed toward kindness. Sweat popped out on Noah's brow. Fear gripped him. He recalled what he had always supposed were exaggerated tales of Apache cruelty, but they did not seem so exaggerated now. He had heard that somewhere in their long battle for freedom, the Apaches had mastered the art of inflicting exquisite pain and could prolong a man's death for days on end.

"Savages . . ." he gasped, straining at his bonds.

The imprudent response earned him another kick—this one so vicious that blackness descended. As he lost consciousness, Noah almost sighed with relief. His last coherent thought was that maybe he could goad them into killing him quickly . . . but if he died, what would become of Juliet?

*　*　*

Juliet held the bowl of broth to the old woman's lips and gently urged her to drink. Old One, as Juliet had decided to call her, clasped shaky hands around the bowl and obediently opened her mouth to take a small sip. . . . Victory! Juliet grinned at Blue Bandana and Old One's daughter, both of whom were smiling, flushed with the triumph of the moment. Old One hesitated, taking her time about swallowing. Juliet murmured encouragement and gazed deeply into the old woman's eyes. Focusing her energy, she sent another silent message.

You can do it. You must do it. You have grieved too long and too hard. Now you must eat so that you will live and not bring sorrow to those who love you.

Old One nodded and drank again. Gaining entrance to her thoughts had been a great challenge to Juliet, for the woman had not wanted to be called back to the living. . . . Expending enormous amounts of mental and emotional energy, Juliet had finally persuaded Old One to reconsider her resolution to die. Now Juliet herself felt totally depleted. If Geronimo himself lay dying, she doubted she could save him. The power had all but left her; she needed rest before she could invoke it again.

"You good shaman," Blue Bandana told her with a grunt of satisfaction. "Make wife plenty happy."

"Wife?" Juliet inquired.

Blue Bandana indicated Old One's daughter with a sly twinkle in his eye. "Wife. Old squaw mother-in-law."

"You did not tell me this," Juliet chided as she helped Old One finish the broth in the clay bowl.

"If you know, maybe not help," Blue Bandana explained. "Maybe too angry you and Red-Hair captured."

Juliet set down the bowl and gave Blue Bandana her

full attention. "Since I have helped, will you now let us go? Will you speak to Geronimo on our behalf?"

Blue Bandana shrugged. "Where you go? These mountains far from white men. Desert lie between. Better you stay here, heal sick Apaches."

"You could take us back to our own people. You know how to find water in the desert."

Blue Bandana made a slashing motion with his hand. "No. Must stay here. Fight soldiers. Soldiers kill Apache or take prisoner if they catch. Not good idea I take you to them."

Juliet rose, allowing Old One's daughter to assume the task of ministering to her mother. "Tonight I am too tired to speak to Geronimo again, but tomorrow I should like to do so. In the meantime, will you protect Red-Hair and not let the young men harm him?"

"This I do for Shaman Woman. Red-Hair no die tonight."

"Thank you. . . . Now, if there is somewhere I could sleep . . . I am so very tired."

Blue Bandana crooked his finger at the woman who had been helping Old One's daughter.

"This E-clah-heh, second wife of Naiche, son of Cochise."

"Second wife?"

"Other wife Ha-o-zinne. Very pretty. Very young." Blue Bandana grinned at her astonishment. "Important chief need more than one wife."

Juliet recalled that Naiche had been with Geronimo in his tipi and did seem to be a man of great importance. Geronimo himself had shown Naiche grave respect. Apache customs were certainly interesting. She smiled at E-clah-heh; the young woman had a pleasant face. With her large dark eyes and generous mouth, she was actually quite pretty.

"I am delighted to meet you, E-clah-heh."

E-clah-heh took Juliet's arm to lead her from the wickiup. "Wait!" Juliet said. "What is *your* wife's name?"

Blue Bandana grinned and uttered a many-sylla-beled word Juliet knew she would never be able to remember. "In white man's tongue mean Smiles-A-Lot."

Smiles-A-Lot proved the meaning of her name by looking up and smiling a most beautiful smile.

"She say thank you. You good woman, Shaman Woman."

"Tell her it was my pleasure." To Juliet, Blue Bandana, E-clah-heh, Smiles-A-Lot, and Old One were not savages or Apaches anymore; they were ordinary people—friendly and attractive, and she hoped that some of their warmth toward her would rub off onto Noah. Tomorrow she intended to ensure that it did. With a last smile at her newfound friends, she allowed E-clah-heh to lead her from the wickiup.

The next morning, Juliet awoke early to an empty hut. Discovering that she was alone, she snapped up-right in chagrin. Something spilled off her lap. Look-ing down, she discovered a small leather pouch lavishly decorated with white, blue, and yellow col-ored beads. Obviously, it was a gift, and her heart lifted with gladness. Surely, the Apaches would not be giving gifts if they meant to kill her or Noah.

Last night had raised her standing in the tribe, and today, she would again speak to Geronimo, this time from a position of more influence. As Juliet rose from her sleeping mat, E-clah-heh entered the wickiup, saw that she was awake, and motioned for Juliet to follow her. The woman—girl, actually, seemed much younger in the light of morning. She collected a few items from a corner of the wickiup, then took Juliet's hand to lead her outside.

"Wait a moment, E-clah-heh." Juliet pointed to the pouch lying on the woven floor mat. "Did you bring that for me?"

E-clah-heh shook her head, then shyly giggled.

"If not you, then who did it? Smiles-A-Lot? Blue Bandana?"

She realized that E-clah-heh could not understand what she was saying, nor would she recognize Juliet's own special name for the Indian who translated. E-clah-heh looked predictably perplexed, but then a thought seemed to occur to her. Tugging on Juliet's hand, she led her to the doorway of the wickiup and pointed to something outside. Juliet poked her head out to see who or what it was.

Not far away, near a tall pine tree, squatted White Antelope. E-clah-heh gestured to the pouch and then to the young man. Juliet needed no translator to understand that White Antelope had brought the present and put it where she would be certain to discover it when she awoke. She pulled in her head before White Antelope spotted her. This was a complication she had not expected; the young man must seriously mean to court her if he was already bringing her gifts!

She must discourage his interest immediately.

Retreating into the interior of the wickiup, Juliet snatched up the pouch, then marched past a surprised-looking E-clah-heh, exited the shelter, and carried it to the squatting Indian. Arriving at his feet, she unceremoniously tossed the pouch on the ground in front of him.

White Antelope leaped up in surprise. His glance darted from her to the rejected gift and back again.

"No," she said slowly and emphatically. "I am not interested."

For good measure, she shook her head vehemently.

White Antelope looked down at the pouch. His mouth thinned. His eyes darkened. "Sha-man Wo-man . . ." he growled haltingly. "You. Me. *Yes!*" This apparently exhausted his supply of English words. "Yes!" he repeated, to emphasize the point. "Yes! Yes!"

"No," she insisted. "Never. I belong to Red-Hair."

He did not seem to understand, so she pointed to the

182

red shirt he was wearing and then to her hair. "Red-Hair. Savvy? Red-Hair."

His eyes lit with comprehension, then narrowed in anger. "Red-Hair?"

It was a question, affirming what she was telling him. She nodded. "I belong to Red-Hair. I am Red-Hair's woman."

She did not know how else to say it; she only knew she must make him understand that she had no interest in becoming his wife. She was already Noah's wife—not officially perhaps, but in every way that counted. Their last night together before being captured marked the union between them, made the bond irrevocable. There would be no one for her but Noah; and she fervently hoped there would be no one for him but her.

"*Kill* Red-Hair!" White Antelope made a threatening gesture, raising his fist high in the air and shaking it. He scowled as if he meant to do it within the next few minutes.

"No, you must not kill Red-Hair!" Alarmed, Juliet looked around for Blue Bandana, but to her dismay, did not see him. Nor did she remember which wickiup belonged to him and Smiles-A-Lot. "E-clah-heh!" she cried. "E-clah-heh, help me!"

The young woman simply stood there, watching everything with wide, black eyes. Other Indians left their wickiups to investigate the commotion. Dogs began to bark. Children gathered. Geronimo himself stood in the entranceway of his tipi, but made no move to say or do anything.

"Kill now!" White Antelope's upper lip curled back, giving his face a feral, predatory look. His hand dropped to the knife sheathed at his waist. Spinning on his heel, he strode purposefully toward a particular wickiup which Juliet surmised held Noah.

She ran after him, grabbing at his arm. "No! You must not kill him! *Please* do not kill him." She spun back toward the gathering crowd. "Geronimo! Geronimo, stop him!"

Geronimo stood silent, his round face expressionless. The powerful Indian chief did not intend to interfere. Juliet searched the crowd and finally spotted Blue Bandana leaving a wickiup in company with Smiles-A-Lot. She ran to him. "Stop White Antelope! He is going to kill Red-Hair! You promised to protect him. . . . Stop White Antelope!"

Blue Bandana gaze traveled past her. Juliet whirled to see White Antelope pausing outside the wickiup. One of several men waiting at the entranceway barked a question. The man's hand rested on his knife, as if he did not wish to be excluded from whatever excitement—or violence—was about to take place. Blue Bandana began to speak. He spoke for what seemed like a long time. Geronimo then asked several questions. Blue Bandana responded.

Heart pounding, Juliet searched the face of each man in turn, wishing she could understand. Then Geronimo motioned to a boy who stood watching with avid interest. The boy ran off. Moments later, he returned leading a horse—a reddish-colored horse that limped as it came toward her. The boy brought the horse to Juliet and silently held out the animal's lead rope.

Geronimo pointed to the leg the horse had been favoring. She deduced that she was supposed to cure it.

"You help Geronimo's war pony," Blue Bandana said. "Geronimo great shaman. Great war chief. But no have time for some things."

Juliet could not restrain her anger. "I have already helped your mother-in-law. Is that not enough?"

"Must help others, too. Must prove power to Naiche and Geronimo."

"And if I help the horse, will they then spare Red-Hair?"

"Yes. But may still give you to White Antelope."

"I am not a possession to be given to anyone. I am a woman—Red-Hair's woman. He is my man. It is the same relationship you have with Smiles-A-Lot."

"You are one?" Blue Bandana entwined two fingers together and held them up.

"Yes," Juliet answered, holding up her own hand and entwining two fingers. "We are one, even as you and Smiles-A-Lot are one."

Blue Bandana nodded and explained her situation to Geronimo and Naiche who had come up silently, accompanied by E-clah-heh. Juliet smiled her thanks to the young woman for having gone to fetch her husband. Naiche then issued an order, and two braves brushed past White Antelope, entered the wickiup, and returned a few moments later, shoving Noah out in front of them. Noah stumbled and fell to his knees. Bleary-eyed, his face black and blue, he looked worse this morning then he had the previous night.

Juliet bolted toward him, but had not taken three steps before Geronimo himself seized her by the shoulders and restrained her.

"No," Blue Bandana told her. "No touch. Apaches no harm Red-Hair. Only ask question."

Juliet ceased trying to break away from Geronimo's unyielding grip. Trembling, she stood silent, aghast at what they had done to Noah. His hands were bound, and he appeared incapable of walking or even standing. He knelt blinking in a shaft of bright sunlight pouring through the pine trees. Juliet had never seen him in worse condition.

"Red-Hair!" Blue Bandana shouted.

Noah straightened and lifted his head. Showing no fear, he gazed at his captors with the cool, mocking insolence she knew so well. Her heart swelled with a sudden, fierce pride. Noah had been beaten and abused, but he had not been broken. His puffy eyes scanned the gathered Indians, found her, and lingered. A grin curled his swollen lips.

"Morning, Princess . . ." he greeted her, the words more beautiful than any she had ever heard.

"Red-Hair!" Blue Bandana repeated. "Answer truly. Shaman Woman is your wife?"

"Sh-shaman Woman?" Frowning, Noah stumbled over the unfamiliar name.

"They mean me, No-ah. I told them you were my husband. You must confirm it."

"Wife," Noah grunted. "Juliet . . . Princess . . . wife." His strength suddenly deserted him, and he pitched face first onto the ground and lay unmoving.

"That was yes," Juliet assured the onlookers. "He meant yes."

"Fight!" The single word exploded in Juliet's ear. "Must fight!"

"Fight who? What do you mean?" Juliet twisted in Geronimo's grip. "Who is going to fight?"

"Red-Hair . . ." Blue Bandana said. "White Antelope. Want same woman, must fight. Winner be your husband," he added unnecessarily.

Juliet was horrified. "How *can* he fight? Look at him! You have beaten him so badly he cannot stand, let alone fight. Have you no sense of fairness?"

Geronimo muttered a string of syllables.

"Seven . . ." Blue Bandana held up seven fingers. "Give Red-Hair seven days. . . . Then he fight."

"Seven days! That is not enough time!" Juliet broke free from Geronimo and ran toward Noah. White Antelope stepped into her path and shook his head.

"No see. No touch. Seven days," Blue Bandana said. "It decided. Shaman Woman heal horse. Help sick. Red-Hair fight White Antelope in seven days."

"He cannot possibly be strong enough to fight in seven days," she protested. "This is ridiculous. You want him to lose so you can keep me here to be your healer. You will force me to marry White Antelope."

"Shaman Woman belong Apache now. Help people of Naiche and Geronimo. Help all Chiricahua Apaches. Red-Hair have fair chance. Fight in seven days."

Two of the watching Apaches advanced on Noah and picked him up by his hands and feet. As they carried him back inside the wickiup, a small hand plucked at Juliet's sleeve. It was the young boy leading the red horse. Again, he offered the rope to her. She took it with a sense of dread and outrage. Seven days was not enough time. Noah would not be strong enough. And they would not let her near him . . . not that she could transmit strength to Noah even if she had access to him. Though they had been attuned to each other since the moment they first met, it was a different sort of unity than the one she drew upon to heal sick creatures or calm violent ones.

Her power could not scale Noah's barriers; he was smarter and more clever than the Apaches—perhaps educated was a better word, but that very education seemed to stand between them, giving him layers of complexity unknown to animals or primitive Apaches. . . . Still, she tried to reach him as he was carried from sight.

Be strong, No-ah! Do not give up. I love you, and I will fight for you in my own way. . . . I will not let them kill you. Before they can do so, they will have to kill me.

Chapter Fourteen

The seven days passed all too quickly. During that time, a small band of Apaches led by Chihuahua departed from the *ranchería* and were attacked by other Indians working for the U.S. Army. Juliet learned from Blue Bandana that one woman had been killed, fifteen women and children captured, and many horses taken. The survivors straggled back to camp, and she was called upon to treat several injuries. Fortunately, none were life threatening.

Not a day passed that the Apaches did not bring a person or animal who was ailing in some way. . . . Each day, she laid hands upon the horse, dog, child, or adult and tried to impart a measure of her strength. She gazed into their eyes, spoke to them from her heart, and attempted to ease their sufferings. For the most part, she succeeded at providing relief, if only temporarily, and the Indians were pathetically grateful. Living in the shadow of constant danger, having only limited opportunities to hunt or forage, they had few comforts and low expectations, tending to bear things without complaint—things that Juliet herself found impossible to accept.

One old man had a terrible malady eating away at his lungs. He frequently coughed blood, and Juliet could do little for him. The old man's death was drawing near; looking into his eyes, Juliet realized that he knew it as well as she and unlike his family, had made his peace with it. She had Blue Bandana question him, and he admitted that he wished to live ". . . only so long as my people are free. When the day comes that they can no more roam the mountains, if I am not already dead, I will die."

Freedom was dearer than life to all of the Apaches. They constantly celebrated it—men, women, children, the young, the old. At night around their campfires, they told tales of a glorious past—riding, hunting, raiding, and roaming the mountains. They often mentioned Usen, the unseen sky-spirit, who gave them strength, health, wisdom, and protection in their fight for freedom, though the deity disdained any actual interference in the petty quarrels of men.

By day, small groups of warriors took turns riding out each morning to scout the soldiers who were searching for them. Campfires were kept small and unobtrusive, children exhorted to play quietly, and the women had everything ready to break camp at a moment's notice. All of this stirred Juliet's sympathies, but she had little time to worry about the Apaches' problems when her own were so pressing. Each morning, as soon as she awakened, she spent several moments concentrating on Noah—sending him her energy. E-clah-heh and Smiles-A-Lot both assured her that Noah was getting stronger, eating well, and exercising daily outside the wickiup. But she was not permitted to see or speak to him. Until the fight between Noah and White Antelope decided her future, she could communicate with Noah only through her mind and heart.

She agonized over whether he was receiving her silent messages or not. It frustrated and angered her that she could penetrate the minds and hearts of Indians and animals, but could not reach the one person who meant the most to her. She worried that Noah would not be strong enough to defeat White Antelope and wished she could prolong the hour of their confrontation; at the same time, she longed for the week to be over, for the tension was unbearable.

On the morning of the seventh day, E-clah-heh, Smiles-A-Lot, and Ha-o-zinne awoke Juliet with much giggling and chattering. Blue Bandana was nowhere in sight, but through gestures, the three women indicated that Juliet was to accompany them to a nearby stream to bathe, after which she was to don the garments they had brought for her. With some surprise, Juliet noticed the pretty, festive clothing the women themselves were wearing.

E-clah-heh had a brilliant, billowing red skirt, topped by a bright yellow blouse decorated with fringe and beads. Smiles-A-Lot flaunted blue and red, enlivened by curious, beautifully-rendered designs. Ha-o-zinne wore green and purple. The traditional soft Apache footwear, which Juliet had learned were called moccasins, encased their feet. The trio expressed excitement over the clothing they had brought for her. Juliet examined it in amazement. The skirt was the color of the sky, and the top the shade of desert sand. The top was fine, soft buckskin, elaborately fringed and sewn with tiny beads along the bodice and wide sleeves. Moccasins to match completed the outfit, along with several strands of small, shiny beads in various colors.

Knowing how valuable the clothing must be to the impoverished Indians, Juliet was reluctant to accept the lavish gifts. But E-clah-heh insisted that the new garments were for her. Apparently, the Apaches regarded this day of the fight as a special day on which everyone would be wearing their finest.

Departing the wickiup, Juliet saw that the entire camp was up and stirring, but she did not spot either White Antelope or Noah. Not that she had expected to see Noah, considering the care that had been taken over the last week to ensure that she had no opportunity to speak to him. Other women and girls joined her three companions and accompanied them to the stream that provided water for drinking, washing, and bathing. Everyone but Juliet had a happy time splashing each other and washing themselves in the warm, pine-scented air. Juliet was too worried about the upcoming fight to take part in the revelry, but she did wash her hair, scrubbing and rinsing it Apache fashion, using a soapy substance produced by the yucca plant.

When she left the stream, the women helped her to comb out the tangles. As her skin dried, they assisted her in dressing in the new clothing. Juliet was glad to be rid of her old and filthy garments, but she did want to keep the two gold brooches. On impulse, she gave one each to E-clah-heh and Smiles-A-Lot, her two closest friends in the camp, in exchange for all they had given her. The two were delighted with the gifts and eagerly fastened the jewelry to their own clothing.

The bathing finished, Juliet was taken to the wickiup where she had been staying—the one belonging to E-clah-heh, Ha-o-zinne, and Naiche, though Naiche spent little time there. E-clah-heh and Smiles-A-Lot indicated that she must remain there until they came for her. Today, it seemed, she would not be asked to do any healing, nor would they expect her to help with preparations for the feast. A feast was obviously in the offing. A hunting party had gone out the day before and returned with a mule deer, a pronghorn antelope, and several rabbits, and the women had busied themselves gathering wild foods, as well as bringing out staples gathered and dried some time in the past.

Juliet sat down on one of the woven mats in the wickiup and tried to control her nervousness and rising sense of dread. She studied E-clah-heh's beautiful basketry and many examples of weaving that decorated the simple shelter and gave it character and warmth. Apache women, she had discovered, were wonderfully skilled in twining burden baskets, weaving rugs, tanning hides, and making household implements and utensils—all this in addition to the everyday tasks of cooking, food-gathering, caring for children, and hauling firewood.

In the short time she had been with them, Juliet had developed a great admiration for these hard-working females who never seemed to spend an idle moment, but were always busy doing something to enhance the well-being of their families. The Apaches may have fallen upon hard times, but plenty of evidence existed to prove that they were a resourceful, highly artistic people. Juliet had come to respect and appreciate their culture, but if Noah died at their hands, she knew she would quickly learn to hate them. She could never remain as their healer, married to White Antelope. Besides, they already had a powerful shaman— Geronimo. His power was different from hers, but still a unique gift. She sensed that the old Indian embodied all that the Apaches revered; Naiche was the head chief, but Geronimo exemplified the freedom-loving Apache soul.

Sitting there, waiting for the fight, Juliet prayed to whatever deity ruled her past and continued to oversee her present. She begged for wisdom and strength— especially the strength to aid Noah in the fight though she wanted neither man to be killed. So great was her concentration that she lost track of time and barely heard the sounds coming from outside the shelter . . . Eventually, they intruded upon her consciousness. She raised her head, listening, and her heart leaped into her throat.

A great commotion had begun, the Indians shouting and making noises of approval or disgust. Muffled thuds, grunts, and the sound of heavy breathing carried into the wickiup. Scrambling to her feet, Juliet rushed to the entrance of the shelter, only to find her way barred by Blue Bandana.

"Let me see," she begged.

"Stay wickiup," he commanded, frowning sternly. "Await . . . outcome."

"But I *must* see!"

193

She pushed past him and caught a glimpse of Noah and White Antelope warily circling each other in the cleared area in front of the wickiups. Both men were barefoot and wore only knee-length breechcloths. Noah's body gleamed whitely in the sunshine, and his hair shone red as fire. His face was grimly intent. He stood taller than White Antelope and appeared more muscular, but White Antelope was lithe, trim, and surefooted. No bruises marred the perfection of the Indian's bronze body. He moved quickly, a coyote circling a wounded cougar.

That was all she saw before Blue Bandana shoved her back into the wickiup and drew the skin covering across the entranceway. Determined to overcome her helplessness, Juliet sank to her knees and began praying in earnest. Closing her eyes and folding her hands tightly together, she drew upon every shred of power she possessed to send her strength to Noah. She would gladly have given her life to help him, but she did not know if anything she did could make a difference. . . . Unless Noah opened his mind to her, it would not.

Noah! she cried from the depths of her being. *No-ah! No-ah! No-ah!*

White Antelope sprang at Noah and hit him hard in the midsection, toppling him backward into the dust. Noah's rib cage shuddered from the impact, and he fought to keep from groaning aloud. Despite better treatment during this past week, he was still weak and sore—no match for the virile, healthy young Indian intent upon killing him with his bare hands.

Straddling Noah's chest, White Antelope clamped his fingers around Noah's jugular and pressed his thumbs against his windpipe. Mustering all his strength, Noah rolled over on top of him. He succeeded in dislodging the Apache's death grip, broke free, and regained his feet. Once again, the two men circled each other, searching for an opening or sign of weakness.

There were no rules for this sort of fighting; Noah only knew that he must fight to save Juliet. If he lost, the Indian would have her, take her into his wickiup and make her his woman. Noah himself would be killed if he was not already dead. That much had been explained to him by the translator. Noah did not intend to let White Antelope win, but he doubted he could beat him—weak as he still was. . . . Somehow, he must find the strength.

Sweat poured from his flesh to mingle with the grease the Apaches had rubbed on his body. The grease prevented him—and White Antelope—from getting a good grip on each other. He longed to plunge into a cold stream and cool himself, as the Indians had let him do each morning before dawn of the past seven days. The cold water had invigorated and revived him, preparing his muscles for the rigorous exercise that followed. After his bath, the Apaches had made him run all the way down the mountain and then back up again. They had kept pace beside him, hardly raising a sweat while he panted and labored like an old sick dog.

The Apaches had an odd sense of fairness. In a single week, they had done what they could to prepare him for this fight. Noah suspected they wanted a good show before they killed him, and by God, for Juliet's sake, he was going to give it to them! As he lunged at White Antelope, he wondered where she was—where they were hiding her—and if she knew that he was fighting to save them both. During the last week when he wasn't exercising, he had been kept bound hand and foot inside the wickiup. He had only the translator's word to reassure him that she was not being mistreated.

White Antelope easily avoided him, spun around, and kicked him in the lower back. Noah sprawled on his face, rolled quickly to avoid being pinned, and found White Antelope once again straddling his chest. This time, the Indian used his knee to shut off Noah's air while he held down Noah's hands. For a single, chilling moment, Noah thought it was all over. Then, from somewhere—he knew not where—he mustered the strength to dislodge his attacker. Scrambling to his feet and panting from the effort, he backed off slightly to give himself time to prepare for the next onslaught.

A headlock, he thought. He had to get the Indian in a headlock and hang on for dear life.

Don't rush him. Let him rush you. Let him think you're tiring. Let him see you're afraid. Taunt and tease him. Then when he comes at you, catch him unawares . . .

Noah reminded himself to watch out for White Antelope's feet. The Indian could do amazing things with his feet. He did not wrestle like a white man, playing by white rules. He wrestled like an Apache, and he meant to kill.

Round and round they went . . . Noah dodging White Antelope's kicks, then mocking him in a tone that needed no translation. The young Indian's face grew redder and redder as his anger mounted. The sun's heat punished them both. Noah forced himself to watch and wait, to be patient, to guard his waning strength. He made no fast moves. Gradually, White Antelope grew reckless and overconfident. At long last, he rushed Noah, as Noah had known he would, without calculating the consequences. Lowering his head, he charged like a ram.

Noah steeled his legs for the impact, took it full in the stomach, reeled backward . . . but managed to catch the Indian's head in the crook of his forearm. It was now or never. Bracing his legs, he tightened his hold. White Antelope struggled. Noah squeezed harder, teeth clenched, muscles straining. White Antelope dug his fingers into Noah's thigh, causing a terrible cramping sensation. The frantic Indian entwined one leg around Noah's, seeking to shift him off balance. Noah hung on. He heard the other Indians shrieking and shouting. They began jumping up and down like demons. Noah felt his strength ebbing. . . . Blackness hovered at the edge of his consciousness.

He thought of Juliet . . . fair, fragile Juliet. Juliet with her hair spread out across the desert floor, opening her arms to him, whispering words of love and encouragement. He could not let go. *He would not.* In a burst of determination, he squeezed harder still, ignoring the excruciating pain in his thigh. Red sparks danced before his eyes. The world went black. He felt himself falling. Hands clawed at his arms and shoulders. Still, he would not let go . . . he would not let go . . . he would not let go.

One moment, there was noise and shouting—a cacophony of shrieking voices. Then there was silence. A deep, resonating silence. Juliet rose from her knees. The fight was over. Someone had won; someone had lost. She stood waiting, not bothering to approach the entranceway. They would come soon enough to tell her the outcome. She prepared herself. She would be stoic as an Apache; she would let no one see her grief, if grief was indeed her lot this day. She had done her best, and now, she must accept her destiny.

"Shaman Woman," Blue Bandana said behind her.

Slowly, she turned. Blue Bandana, Geronimo, Naiche, and the old man, Nana, filed into the wickiup. Their faces told her nothing. Looking at her, they said nothing. She glanced from one to the other. Geronimo's eyes sought hers. He gave the slightest nod—as if acknowledging her powers. His English was limited, but she had learned that he understood and could manage a few halting words. . . . It was Geronimo who told her the news.

"You . . . win."

"I win?" she questioned. The truth dawned. She turned to Blue Bandana for confirmation.

His lips quirked grudgingly. His eyes smiled. "To-night . . . you . . . Red-Hair . . . same wickiup." He held up two entwined fingers. "Two people. Make one."

Juliet's heart nearly burst, but she dared not rejoice before she knew the answer to her next question. "White Antelope?"

"Still live. Throat . . . sore." Blue Bandana touched his own throat.

"Shall I come and fix it?"

"No . . . Geronimo fix. Smiles-A-Lot help. You . . . make ready for tonight."

"I am sorry White Antelope's throat is sore, but I am not sorry he lost." Juliet touched Geronimo's arm. " 'Tis as I told you. I am Red-Hair's woman. I belong with him—not White Antelope. I hope you will now listen to what Red-Hair has to say, for he is your friend, even as I am."

Blue Bandana translated, and Geronimo's head jerked in assent. "I . . . listen," he said.

Juliet wanted to shout for joy. Elation coursed through her. "Thank you!" she cried, impulsively seizing his hand and carrying it to her cheek. "Oh, thank you!"

His eyes locked on hers. She was sure she saw a flicker of emotion in those sad, tortured depths. "Now, may I go see Red-Hair?" she begged.

"Tonight . . ." Blue Bandana gravely informed her. "Tonight you see."

It was quite late that night before Juliet was allowed to leave the wickiup. All smiles and giggles, as excited as if this were a wedding, the women came to escort her. Perhaps in their eyes it was a wedding, Juliet surmised, for the women fussed over her, straightened her clothing, slipped several bead bracelets over each wrist, and poked at her hair. When her appearance finally satisfied them, they fastened a soft narrow piece of leather over her eyes as a blindfold and led her out of the wickiup amid a gale of laughter.

The delicious scent of roasting meat assaulted her nostrils. To her left, a fire crackled. As the women led her around it, she could feel its heat. People jostled her on every side. The tone of laughter suggested jokes of a ribald nature. Finally, the little procession came to a standstill, and someone lifted Juliet's hand and held it out. Another hand—warm and strong—clasped hers; at the same moment, her blindfold was removed.

She found herself facing Noah—a clean-shaven, handsome Noah dressed as she was in soft, buttery buckskin with elaborate fringe. His eyes twinkled as he gazed down at her. "I think we are being married," he said softly, grinning. "Not being Apache, I can't be sure, but it looks and feels like a wedding celebration."

Juliet was so happy to see him that she could not immediately answer. At last, she blurted: "Geronimo said he would listen to you now."

Noah's grin widened. "I know. The guy who translates told me."

"Blue Bandana. . . . I call him Blue Bandana."

Noah lifted a brow. "Very appropriate. I've heard his real name but I can't seem to pronounce it."

"Nor can I. 'Tis why I gave it to him."

They stood foolishly grinning at each other, uncertain of what to do next, until Blue Bandana himself came pushing through the crowd. Like nearly everyone else, he was in a jovial mood. "This . . ." he said, pointing to the wickiup in front of which they stood. "You wickiup. Belong Shaman Woman and Red-Hair now."

"This is ours?" Juliet exclaimed, delighted.

Blue Bandana nodded. "You . . . Chiricahua Apache now. Live own wickiup."

"But . . . but we wish to return to Tucson, do we not?" Juliet questioned Noah in a whisper.

"Not yet," Noah whispered back. "This is my big chance. This is why I came to this country. We'll stay

199

with the Apaches for a bit so I can interview Geronimo—and persuade him to surrender."

Juliet searched his face, noting the excitement and satisfaction there—not apparently all due to their reunion. "This is what you want, No-ah?"

"Hell, yes. . . . Since I won that fight today, they've been treating me like a damned king. We've got to stay for a while, Juliet, and take advantage of this rare opportunity."

Wherever Noah was or wanted to be was fine with Juliet, though she had expected him to be more anxious to return to his own people. "We will stay then," she agreed. "If this is what you want."

Smiles-A-Lot held back the skin at the shelter entrance in invitation. They were about to enter the wickiup when an angry shout stopped them. Heads swiveled. All eyes sought the lone, defiant figure on horseback who had just emerged from the darkness. It was White Antelope. He urged the horse into a trot and did not signal for a stop until he was almost on top of them. In his free hand he held a rifle which he brandished and waved in the air while he spoke.

The fire in his eyes and the scowl on his face emphasized his bitter speech. He spoke in a low rasping voice that carried only because everyone had fallen silent. While he was speaking, Geronimo stepped out of his tipi and stood listening in the flickering firelight. When White Antelope had finished, he sat back on his horse and glared at Geronimo as if awaiting a response. The reply never came. Geronimo simply gazed at White Antelope and sadly shook his head. The brave then jerked his pony around and galloped off in a cloud of dust.

"What did he say?" Juliet murmured, swept with uneasiness.

Blue Bandana's mouth had lost its smile, his eyes their sparkle. "He say Geronimo regret this day. No more friends. No more brothers. He go join enemies of Geronimo . . . come back defeat Chiricahuas."

"Oh, I am so sorry!" Juliet burst out. Then, seeing Noah's look, she hastily added: "Not sorry he lost the fight, but sorry that White Antelope has turned against his own people."

"Don't be sorry," Noah muttered. "The loss of a follower—a man who knows the location of this camp—is another good reason why Geronimo should surrender before he's found and wiped out."

"Camp gone by time White Antelope return," Blue Bandana grimly disputed. "Tomorrow, change camp. You watch. Geronimo order."

And Geronimo did order—swiftly and precisely. He then pointed to Noah and Juliet and added another command.

"Geronimo say enjoy tonight," Blue Bandana told them. "Because tomorrow all travel."

Noah tugged on Juliet's hand, drawing her toward the entrance of the wickiup. "Shall we?" He nodded toward the interior.

Not saying a word, Juliet entered the wickiup ahead of him.

Chapter Fifteen

A small fire inside the shelter illuminated an array of baskets, mats, skins and household utensils. Juliet recognized the handiwork of Smiles-A-Lot, Ha-o-zinne, and E-clah-heh, as well as many of the other Apaches she had helped during the past week. Greatly touched, she lovingly fingered the objects that represented so much sacrifice on the part of the gift-givers.

"I cannot believe they mean for us to have these things," she told Noah. "They live so simply and have so little themselves."

Noah did not seem interested in the furnishings of the wickiup. "In the morning, they'll probably take them all back again," he grunted, watching her intently.

She bent down to examine several large, finely-worked baskets. "No, they will not do that. The Apaches are a good and generous people, No-ah."

"So I always believed until they beat the breath and very nearly the life out of me."

"That was only because you are a white man, and they are bitter; now, they have accepted you."

"We'll see." Noah's tone conveyed doubt. "Right now, I care little for the Apaches. It's *you* I want to think about, Juliet. Are you all right? They did not mistreat you, did they?"

As she straightened, he came up behind her and slipped his arms about her waist, turning her around to face him. Excited by his nearness, she allowed herself the luxury of studying his dearly-loved face. He seemed older somehow, familiar but also strange, A new maturity stamped his features. It seemed an eternity since last she had seen or touched him.

Shaking her head in answer, she ran her fingertips along the line of his stubborn jaw, skimmed his arrogant nose, then traced the sensual lips that always made her think of kissing. His dark glowing eyes reflected the same warmth and heat as the firelight. As she gazed into them, a slow heat began to build deep within her. Her body reminded her of how long it had been since she had known Noah's touch and how close she had come to losing it forever.

"Do I look as if I have been mistreated, No-ah?" she whispered on a sigh. "The Apaches have taken me into their tribe and made me one of them. I am their shaman woman now. I, too, am an Apache."

He frowned. "No, Juliet, whoever and whatever you are, you are not Apache. You are first of all a white woman; after that, you're *mine.*"

"Yours," she repeated, not quite believing it. "Am I really yours, No-ah?"

She needed to hear him reaffirm the love he had expressed for her out on the desert, when he thought they would die soon. Had he really meant it? True, he had fought for her, but he had also been fighting for his own life. Now that his life was spared, and he could think about doing what he had originally come to this land to do, she needed for him to confirm her place in his present and future. She could not forget that it had taken him much longer to commit to her than it had taken her to commit to him.

"Yes, you're mine, sweetheart," he murmured, pulling her closer and pressing her head into his shoulder. "And I am yours. Shall I say the words to make it legal? There are no witnesses, no church, and no minister, but we can speak our vows without them. To me, it will be just as binding."

"Oh, No-ah . . ." She hardly dared hope that he really meant to wed her here and now.

Tilting up her chin, he solemnly searched her eyes. "I, Noah, take thee, Juliet, to be my lawfully wedded wife . . . to have and to hold, to love and to cherish, from this day forward . . . until death do us part."

She smiled at him through a blur of tears. "Such beautiful promises."

He chuckled. "You're supposed to make the same promises, only you also agree to obey me."

She leaned back in surprise. "As your wife, I am to obey you? I must promise this?"

A sly twinkle lit his eyes. "That's the way the marriage ceremonies I've attended always go."

"I do not think I should promise something I may not be able to do, No-ah. I will try, of course, but if you demand the unreasonable, I may have to disobey. . . . However, I will gladly say what you said. I, Juliet, take you, No-ah, to be my lawfully wedded husband . . . to have and to hold, to love and to cherish, from this day forward . . . until death do us part."

"I didn't think you would agree to obey, but at least I tried." He gave a long drawn sigh, picked up her hand, and kissed her curled fingers. "Now, I'm supposed to put a ring on your finger and kiss you properly. Unfortunately, I haven't got a ring."

"We do not need a ring to seal our bond. We are husband and wife, No-ah. We will seal our commitment by the giving of our bodies to each other."

"Great idea! Don't know why I didn't think of it myself," he wryly exclaimed. Wrapping his arms around her waist, he nuzzled her neck. "Ah, Juliet . . . I can't tell you how much I've missed you this past week. You were all I thought about while I was hurting. You helped block out the pain."

She pushed him away, suddenly remembering. "But you still must hurt, No-ah! And I have not yet examined you or assessed the extent of your injuries."

"Then you will have to examine me now, won't you?

I have all kinds of bruises that need kissing, my love. I've got aches and pains only your tender ministrations can heal."

"I tried to send you strength and healing, No-ah. Did you not feel it? I have helped the Apaches, horses, and dogs, but *you* are the one I wanted to help most, and you always seemed so far away from me. I could not be certain I was reaching you; tell me you felt it!"

He encircled her waist with his hands and pulled her close so that her breasts were crushed against his chest. "Yes, I felt it. I sure as hell felt something. Your love gave me strength, sweetheart. Just thinking of you gave me an energy I can't otherwise explain. I don't understand your gift or how you do it, but I certainly don't deny its existence."

"Oh, No-ah!" She threw her arms about his neck. "I am so glad! I prayed that you would let me help you— that you would open your heart and mind to me!"

"And now will you open to me, sweetheart? Will you be my wife and let me love you?"

"Yes, oh, yes," she breathed, trembling but eager.

He set her away from him long enough to lead her to a beautiful rug with red and yellow designs outspread beside the little fire. There he knelt down and drew her downward to kneel facing him.

"Let me undress you," he whispered. "I want to see you naked, Juliet, with your pale hair tumbling all around you."

Her heart pounded. Shyness swept her. Here in the privacy of the wickiup, what they were about to do seemed a wholly new experience, something they had never done before. Perhaps it was the words they had spoken or the realization that the moment was so special . . . so incredible. By now, they could have died a dozen times, but still they were alive, and they had this precious night to enjoy their love and all it meant to them. They could take their time . . . endless sweet time to savor each lovely moment.

"Do you not want to eat first?" she questioned.

"There is food laid out for us on the other side of the fire. You must be hungry, No-ah."

She herself was too excited to eat, but Noah had fought a hard battle. Perhaps, he should eat and rest before they celebrated their union.

"You bet I'm hungry," he growled, entwining his fingers in her hair and dragging her closer. "Hungry for you, woman. . . . If you don't let me love you soon, I'm going to rip off those pretty new clothes and devour you on the spot."

All thoughts of the roasted meat and other delicacies prepared by the Apache women fled. Juliet leaned forward and offered Noah her mouth. He kissed her as though he was starved for the taste of her. She lost herself in sensation—the sweetness of his mouth and tongue. The clean male scent of him. The hardness of his body. The texture of his hair as she raked her fingers through it. His wonderful warmth.

They kissed until her head was spinning, but she could not get enough of kissing. It was agony to tear her mouth from his long enough to let him remove her upper garments and his own. When he had done so, he clasped a breast in each hand and knelt a long moment simply gazing into her eyes, while she absorbed the feel of his hands on her. Gently, he pulled her closer, so that her sensitive nipples grazed his chest hair, and she felt his heart slamming against her own heart.

As he resumed kissing her, she reached down and fondled the bulge in the front of his trousers. She wanted his warmth and hardness, his marvelous masculinity, deep inside her. Wanted all of him, muscle, bone, and sinew. Wanted him so much that she was weak and light-headed, her limbs trembling and quaking.

He leaned her backward on the rug and bent over her. His mouth found her breasts. She gasped as he began to lick and taste her. His mouth knew all the wondrous ways to make her body respond, to open to him, to soar with him, to fly above earth and clouds.

He kissed, suckled, and bit. He made her ache and throb. She clawed at his back and whimpered shamelessly, begging for more.

Somehow, the rest of their clothing disappeared. With mouth, hands, and body, he worshiped her nakedness. They kissed and tasted every quivering part of each other. Arms and legs entwined, they murmured endearments until passion obliterated rational speech. The universe narrowed to Noah's mouth and hands. When he finally entered her, Juliet arched against him, each thrust a penetration of soul and body. A glorious union.

He drove into her with a pounding rhythm that shattered her senses. Her release was a blinding cataclysm. She heard a woman crying "No-ah! No-ah!" and scarcely realized that the impassioned cry had burst from her own throat. At almost the same time, Noah shuddered and rocked against her. Then all was silent, except for the thunderous beating of their hearts.

After several long moments, Noah stirred above her, shifting his weight so he would not crush her. "Too fast," he murmured. "I'm sorry, sweetheart, we did it too fast. I had intended to make it last longer, but once I started, I couldn't seem to stop."

For Juliet, it had been perfect; she could not understand why he was apologizing. "We can do it again," she offered. "If you are displeased, we can practice until you have no cause for complaint."

He gave a short, amused chuckle. "Not yet we can't. And I didn't mean to complain or imply that I'm displeased." Lifting his head, he kissed the tip of her nose. "I'm anything but. Loving you is like . . . is like . . . experiencing a little bit of heaven right here on earth, sweetheart."

She was not sure what he meant. "What is heaven, No-ah?"

Gently, he brushed a strand of hair from her face. "Heaven is where we go when we die . . . if we've been good, that is. It's . . . well, it's a place of perfect peace and contentment. It's the ultimate happiness. All we could ever want. At least, that's what I've always heard. When I was a boy, I pictured it as a land of green meadows, lofty mountains, waterfalls, clouds and rainbows. A magnificent place, not unlike Arizona where even the desert is beautiful. Only heaven has angels. The angels sing and make lovely music . . . and there's God. I quit believing in God and angels a long time ago, but loving you makes me remember heaven and almost makes me think it might exist after all."

Juliet was intrigued. "Do you think there really is such a place? How wonderful that we might go there when we die!"

His smile turned grim. "You might go there. I doubt I will. I haven't been all that good, Juliet."

"Maybe I have not been good either," she mused. "Maybe losing my memory is punishment for something very bad that I have done."

"I can't believe you've ever done anything bad," Noah snorted.

"Do we go straight to heaven or—or wherever else we go—after we die?"

"I don't know. I never interviewed a dead person before. Might be an interesting experience." He grinned. "Maybe we come back as something or someone else first. I myself wouldn't swear to the possibility, but I did read somewhere that we live several lives before we go to heaven or hell—the other alternative."

"Several lives?" Juliet pondered that and found it a fascinating notion. She wondered what she herself had believed before she lost her memory and who she might have been in some other life, not just before she became Juliet, but even before that, in the far distant past. "Tell me more about this heaven. . . . If it feels anything like what we just did, I most definitely wish to go there. But of course, it would *not* be heaven, if you were not there to make love to me."

209

"That's a brilliant idea. Could be my bargaining point with God, if He really exists." Noah dramatically raised his eyes skyward. "You have to send me to heaven, God, because Juliet won't be happy unless I'm with her, jumping her bones—I mean her spirit—every now and then."

She laughed with pleasure at his teasing. She loved it when he teased and the little lines of cynicism and mockery disappeared from his handsome face. "If I do get to heaven first, No-ah, that is exactly what I will demand—that you be sent there to join me."

"If you promise to get me into heaven for all eternity, I promise to give you regular doses of heaven while you're here on earth, sweetheart." Still grinning, he rolled off her. "But before I can deliver any more heaven, I'll have to eat first. . . . Ouch!" He rubbed his ribs. "Damn, I keep forgetting my sore spots. Don't think my ribs got broken, but they did take a hell of a beating, and my little skirmish with White Antelope didn't help any."

"Oh, let me see!" she cried, sitting up. "I will lay hands on them and make them feel better."

"No, no . . . forget it. Don't practice any more of your wily shaman tricks on me. From now on, I'd appreciate it if you only used conventional methods. This other stuff makes me uncomfortable."

"But . . . my powers are a part of *me,* No-ah. You should not disdain them."

"I don't disdain them. As I said before, I just don't understand them. In my world—the world we're going back to as soon as we leave the Apaches—you can't use them, Juliet. People will look at you strangely and think you're bewitched. They won't understand either. It's all right to act a little weird around Indians and animals, but you can't go staring into white people's eyes and talking to them without words or they're going to be afraid of you and shun you. I don't want that for my wife, sweetheart. It's bad enough we'll have to deal with the problem of your lost memory without adding one more thing to set you apart from normal human beings."

In all his naked, masculine splendor and arrogance, Noah rose and walked to where the food had been laid out on the mat across from the fire. He did not look at her. Did not see that he had deeply wounded her by rejecting the very essence of who and what she was—a woman who may have lost her memory but still possessed the rare ability to help others with the gift of being able to talk to them in her head and heart. . . . Did he actually expect her *not* to use her powers once they returned to his people? How shortsighted and unfair!

All the joy of the night drained out of her, and she felt suddenly lost and cold. Yet she did not know what to say to him or how to explain what he had done to her.

"Juliet?" He held out a piece of roasted antelope meat. "Here, sweetheart, you better eat this." He slanted her a loving, roguish glance. "If we're going to find heaven again tonight, we have to replenish our strength."

She could have told him that there were other ways to gain strength besides eating—could have reminded him that she had sent him all her strength during his fight with White Antelope. That was probably why he had won—but instead, she only reached out to take the meat from him. He should have known these things for himself. If he truly loved her, he *would* know them. . . . Who was she anyhow that she even possessed such powers?

Chimes. The chimes were ringing on the breeze, filling the inner courtyard with their delicate, fluting notes. It was a happy sound, much at odds with the angry voices rising to drown them out. My stomach churned with dread and tension. Darkness and menace filled my world. I feared I might be sick on the cobblestones.

"You have disgraced us!" My mother shrieked. "Stealing out to meet Jason behind our backs!"

"I told you; we did nothing wrong."

"I do not believe you! I saw the two of you embracing. I witnessed the look on his face. Your own face, your eyes . . . the passion was unmistakable. Jason has stolen your innocence! He has ruined you for your future husband. You have destroyed all our plans for you!"

I wanted desperately to make my mother understand. To have her smile at me with tenderness and empathy as she had earlier that very day. For one fleeting moment, I had felt at peace with her. I had glimpsed her heart, and she had glimpsed mine. Now, we were once more strangers—or worse yet, enemies.

"We did not do anything wrong," I insisted. "I swear this to you."

"Liar! Fallen woman! You are worse than a hetaira!"

My mother's hand came up so quickly I did not see it, but I felt the blow and reeled backward from the impact. My cheek stung like fire. As I rubbed it, my father stepped between me and my mother.

"Enough! Violence solves nothing. Besides, if you mark the girl, she will be of no use to any man. No one will want her. Not even that young cur, Jason . . ."

Yes, he will. He will still want me, I thought, dazed but defiant. I am your daughter, I wanted to tell my father—not just "the girl." I am a person, not a possession to be awarded to the highest bidder.

"You are right," said my mother. "I am distraught. I must get hold of myself. We must think what to do. No one but us knows of this. If we act quickly, we can have her married to Anytus's son before Anytus hears of the incident from servants or from Jason's family. Once the marriage has taken place, Anytus will have to live with it. He is a reasonable man; he will keep to his end of the bargain and not spoil your previous arrangement."

"But I will not marry Anytus's son! I do not care what arrangements you and my father have made. Did you

not hear me when I said I would marry only Jason, and he will marry no one but me?"

My mother's hand sprang up once more. Never had my mother struck me; now, it seemed, she could not resist the impulse.

"Wait . . ." My father was coldly reasonable, an imposing figure of authority in his beautifully embroidered, ankle-length white tunic. He stroked his short gray beard. "As you said, we must think on this. Perhaps there is another answer. Until my quarrel with Jason's father, our two families had planned for this union. . . . We must not forget that. 'Tis a fact that might work to our advantage."

"But my husband, the man does not speak to you anymore! You have not done business together in a very long time. Jason's father will not want an alliance with our family now."

"Perhaps he will not want it, but he could be made to see the benefit, the same as I do. And if Jason himself is willing . . ."

I could not hold my tongue. "Jason is willing, Father! Ask him and you will see."

"Hush, you disobedient, ungrateful child! Have you not done enough to your father and me, not to mention your brothers? Do you know so little what is at stake here?"

"How can she know? We have kept it secret from her." My father ran his hand through his thinning hair and sighed. He suddenly looked older; just as I had grown up without Jason noticing, my father had grown old, and I had not noticed. " 'Tis a father's duty to safeguard his family and provide for them. It sorely batters my pride to admit even now that we teeter on the brink of financial disaster."

"Financial disaster! What is it, Father? Is that why you wish me to marry Anytus's son—because he will one day be richer than Jason?"

My father sighed. "That and because the alliance will immediately help us. Little dryad, you must have no-

213

ticed that we have had a poor crop several years running. Neither the quantity nor quality of our wine has been as it should be . . . yet our expenses remain constant. The vines must still be tended, servants and slaves must still be fed. . . . Anytus has offered me and your brothers the opportunity to diversify and expand. In addition to a thriving export business, he owns lands in another district, and with our knowledge of wine production and merchandising. . . . Well, what does it matter now, if you will not consent to marry his son? There will be no alliance and no expansion. Another bad season, and our family will be ruined. Your brothers shall have to seek their fortunes elsewhere."

"Oh, Father, I am so sorry! I did not know!"

"You see now what you have done, you foolish girl?" my mother exploded.

"But what about Jason's father's land?" I cried. "Could we not expand in that direction? Was that not your original intention? Surely, you can resolve your difficulties with Jason's father and proceed as once you planned—then we could all be happy!"

"I do not know," my father said, stroking his beard. "After such bitterness, it may be impossible to mend the rift between us."

"Oh, Father, please try!" I went down on my knees before him and clung weeping to the hem of his tunic. "I beg you, Father! I have loved Jason for nearly as long as I can remember!"

"How long could that be?" my mother snorted. "How long have these secret meetings been going on?"

"Since we were children," I admitted. "Since the day he and his father first came to our house. You were thinking of marriage between us then; I know you were. Jason overheard his parents talking. At the time, he hated the idea, and it has taken me all these years to change his mind. Truly, I never dreamed I was behaving improperly. I expected you to be pleased to find us so eager to wed."

"You think I should be happy that your Jason no

longer opposes a union with our family," my father dryly observed.

"That is what I have been trying to tell you, Father. He does desire this union. Talk to him, and you will see!"

"First, I will think on it." Placing his hands on my shoulders, my father helped me rise. "I will also speak to your brothers. We all need time to accustom ourselves to these new developments."

"None of this would have happened, Father, had you told me what you were planning."

"Bah! You are only a female. Men do not consult with women on issues of such major importance."

"Perhaps they should!" my mother snapped, her ire finding a new target. She glared at my father, the first time I had ever seen her challenge him. "We have more than wool in our heads—and on our minds. If you took a moment to consult with us now and then, you would discover that for yourself."

My father's brows lifted in surprise. "Indeed . . ." he said, as if seriously considering the possibility. He waved a hand in my direction. "Now get you to your chambers, Daughter, while your mother and I consult on how to handle Anytus and his son who will be arriving at any moment, anxious to meet you."

"Oh, Father, thank you . . . thank you!" I wept, kissing and hugging him.

I left my parents staring at each other and went obediently to my chambers. Anytus and his family arrived shortly thereafter. They did not stay long; indeed, they departed without eating the meal that had been prepared for them. A servant brought me fruit, olives, and a wedge of cheese, but could tell me nothing, other than that the recently-arrived guests had left in anger, Anytus himself muttering that my father had behaved abominably and stained his good name by negating their agreement. He also claimed that my father ought not to accept the advice of women on such important issues.

I was amazed and gratified that my mother had apparently stood up for me, and that my father had lis-

215

tened to her. I waited breathlessly for one of them to come to me, but they did not. When the entire household had retired, I slipped out into the moonlit night and ran through the vineyards. Jason would be there; he had to be there. Had to realize that I would come as soon as possible to tell him what had happened.

He did not disappoint me; he was there, brooding in the dark shadows of the trellis. With a joyous cry, I flew into his arms. "Jason! Oh, Jason!"

"Did they beat you? Have they cast you out? I have been so worried." He kissed my forehead—then my hair, eyes, and cheeks. He gathered me close and held me, stroking my back and shoulders. "Sweet Zeus, I have been frantic! In his wrath, I feared your father might do you great harm. It would be his right. As your father, he could take your life, and none could gainsay him."

" 'Twas not my father who struck me, but my mother. I have deeply wounded them, Jason, and I am sorry, but I cannot be sorry I love you. Oh, Jason, there might be a chance for us after all! My father is going to speak to your father. . . . My mother advised him to send Anytus and his son away, and he did."

"He did? I cannot believe it! 'Tis better than I had dared hope for . . . Ah, little one, if you had not come tonight, I would have come for you. Now that I have found you, I will not lose you. . . . I had planned to enter your house under cover of darkness, take you from it, and make you my wife before any could stop us . . . For your sake, I would sacrifice even my inheritance."

I put my hand over his mouth. "Let our fathers work it out, Jason. They were friends many years ago; once they had plans for us. I pray they will rebuild their friendship and again make plans."

"It could happen," he agreed. "I should like to join our lands and learn from your father how to plant vines and make wine. I would enjoy working alongside your brothers to enable all of us to prosper. 'Tis is a logical

216

step to benefit both our families. Had our fathers not quarreled . . .''

I stood on tiptoe and stopped his speech with a kiss. I had an overwhelming need to kiss him, to reassure myself that he was real and substantial, not a creature conjured up from moonlight and my own desires. He gathered me closer and deepened the kiss. He pressed against me, and I felt the intrusion of his maleness. A shiver ran through me. I ached with the need to be close to him, closer than we had ever been before.

Whimpering deep in my throat, I opened my mouth to his kiss. The savagery of it both thrilled and vaguely alarmed me. His hands molded me to him. Heat flooded my body. My blood raced. A wildness overcame us both, and we kissed and embraced with heady abandon—tasting, clawing at each other, writhing together, trying to achieve a unity that clothing would not allow.

His hands avidly explored me through my garments. His tongue probed deeply as he thrust against me, his body hard and insistent, demanding everything I had to give.

"Jason. . . . Oh, Jason!"

The world was spinning too fast, veering out of control. I lost myself to physical sensation; a tide of fire raged inside me. I wanted to see his face—gaze into his eyes, tenderly kiss his mouth, whisper endearments and compliments. But there was no time; it was all hunger, need, and blazing, dark passion. Like a dazzled stranger in a wonderful but terrifying new land, I trembled with fear and urgency. His hands impatiently tugged at my garments. Fabric tore. His wildness stunned me; this was a Jason I no longer knew.

"Jason . . ."

Something in my tone must have alerted him that something was wrong. Abruptly, he stopped and let go of my tunic. His breath came in great gasps. "No . . ." he panted. "No, you are right. I will not take you like this. Out here in the vineyards. . . . No, we will wait. I will marry you properly. We will secure the permission of *our families. I will honor and respect you. You are the mother of my future children; I will not treat you like a common whore."*

"Jason, my dearest love, Jason . . ." I could not say more. He was proving his love for me, living up to my ideal, being the man I had always believed him to be. And yet . . . and yet . . . I could hardly wait until the night of our wedding! Then it would be right—this glorious savage desire that threatened to destroy all restraint and carry us away.

"I love you, Jason. I will love you forever, until the day I die, and beyond into whatever awaits us."

"I love you the same. . . . Go home now, little one. Leave here before I lose control and despite my noble intentions, drag you down to the ground with me."

"Yes, Jason," I replied with a meekness I seldom felt and even more rarely displayed.

The moonlight dappled his hair and face as I touched my fingertips to my lips, kissed them, and then transferred the kiss to his lips. If I did more, I knew I would be lost again. There would be no stopping. Fighting my own impulses, I turned and fled.

Chapter Sixteen

"You dreamed about Jason again last night, didn't you?"

The question held accusation, rather than curiosity. It was early morning. Thinking Noah to be still asleep, Juliet had been gathering together all of their belongings. Geronimo had said they would move camp today, and she wanted to be ready. Now, heart pounding with dread, she turned to face her irate husband; Noah did not look at all happy. Nor was she happy. For a time, she had been able to forget that she had a bothersome past waiting to destroy her contented present. She could not forget it this morning.

The total substance of the dream eluded her, but she vividly recalled exchanging kisses and caresses—experiencing the hot flood of desire—with the mysterious Jason. She could not remember Jason's face, could not picture what he looked like, but she knew she had loved him with her entire being, exactly as she now loved Noah.

She paused in the act of picking up a basket. "Yes, No-ah, I dreamed of Jason again."

"Dreamed of him how? Where were you this time, and what were you doing?"

She dared not tell him what they had been doing. If she herself felt guilty and considered her behavior a betrayal, how much worse would he view the entire situation! No matter that she had no control over what she had been doing or feeling in the dream, Noah was jealous and angry.

"Juliet, you're blushing, and you look guilty as hell. Does that mean what I think it does?"

She averted her face. How could he be so perceptive? She had not said a word, yet he already knew. He could see right through her.

"Juliet, come here."

She toyed with the basket, her hands trembling with nervousness.

"Damn it, I said come here!"

She looked up and met his gaze. His eyes seared her soul. He rose from the rug and stalked toward her, then grabbed her hand and hauled her to her feet.

"Juliet, what were you and Jason doing in that damn dream of yours? Why can't you tell me?"

She could hardly find her voice. "We . . . we were . . . doing exactly what you are thinking," she finally got out.

"God Almighty!" he swung away from her, back rigid, mouth twisted in fury.

As if she needed further proof of his ire, he kicked at the sleeping rug and sent it flying against the wall of the wickiup. Then he turned back to her, looking unusually large and menacing in the confines of the small dwelling. Shirtless and bootless—sometime after their last bout of lovemaking, he had put on his trousers—he regarded her as he might a rattlesnake who had slithered into the wickiup during the night.

"Does Jason satisfy you better than I do?" he grated between clenched teeth. "Is that why you dreamed of him—because I failed to satisfy your physical needs?"

"Of course not, No-ah. You *know* I was satisfied. It was a wonderful night. A . . . a taste of heaven. But I cannot control my dreams or explain them. I know not why I dreamed of Jason again. I had hoped I was done dreaming of him."

"What if you're *never* done with it? What if you

keep comparing the two of us and decide that's he's the better lover, the better man for you altogether?"

"I do not compare the two of you!"

"No? Tell me, Juliet, how did you feel in Jason's arms? Did he make you quiver, shiver, and moan? Tell me exactly what he did and how it made you feel. You see? You can't *help* making comparisons on so important an issue."

"No-ah, stop it! I do not want to think about Jason. I did not want to dream about him. I hope I never discover who he is and why he haunts my dreams! *You* are all I care about!" She rushed to him and threw her arms around him. "You are the one I love, No-ah— not this Jason! Jason does not matter to me in the slightest."

"No? Just what the hell do we do if we one day discover that you're married to the bastard?"

"I cannot be married to him. You yourself said I was a virgin. That proves I was never married."

"Well, maybe you were—*are*—engaged to him. And maybe when you regain your memory, you'll discover that you're deeply in love with him. Then where will *I* be, Juliet? Which of us will you choose?"

"I will choose you, Jason—I mean No-ah!" She clapped her hand over her mouth, appalled that somehow she had made another terrible slip of the tongue. Jason's name had popped out of her mouth, just as she had unwittingly called her red shawl a *himation*.

Noah's eyes narrowed dangerously. A muscle leaped in his jaw. In that moment, she thought he must surely hate her. His love had dissolved into something ugly and twisted. "I knew I should never have let myself care for you," he growled. "I knew all along it couldn't work between us. Jason's got a hold over you I'll never be able to break. Whether or not you tossed your skirts for him, you sure as hell let him get close to you. He *owns* you, Juliet. You've never moaned *my* name in your sleep. Obviously, I'm not the man with whom you want to spend the rest of your life; he is."

Juliet could *not* remember dreaming of Noah, although as she was waking up this morning, Noah and Jason had seemed all mixed up with each other. It was Noah she had thought of with her first conscious thought—Noah's kisses and caresses she remembered best.

"I am not responsible for my dreams," she protested once more as a sense of helplessness overwhelmed her. "I only know that I love you—and only you—when I am awake. You are the one I want to be with always, forever and ever. Can you not be satisfied with that, No-ah?"

"If that's all you can give me, I guess I'll have to be satisfied, won't I? I get you during the day, and your precious Jason gets you at night. Somehow the three of us will just have to learn to be one big happy family."

"Do not say these hurtful things, No-ah. Jealousy is a powerful, destructive emotion. If we let it, it can destroy love altogether."

"It won't be my jealousy that destroys our relationship; it will be your willingness to tolerate this secret lover."

" 'Tis not my fault, No-ah! You must not blame me for that which I cannot help!"

"Can't you help it, Juliet? Sometimes, I wonder . . ." Noah grabbed for his shirt and boots. "Look, I've got to get out of here. I can't take this anymore."

She ran after him as he headed for the doorway. "Where are you going?"

"To see Geronimo," he snapped over his shoulder. "Maybe he'll make more sense than you do."

"No-ah!" she cried as he stalked out of the wickiup. "Please, No-ah, wait!"

But Noah did not wait, nor even glance back at her. Juliet would have followed him and continued the argument, but as she stepped outside, she saw that most of the wickiups had already been dismantled, horses stood loaded, and the women were rushing to break camp. E-clah-heh and Smiles-A-lot waved to her; she could do nothing without attracting attention. The argument must be postponed. Noah was in no mood to listen or be reasonable anyway; giving him the opportunity to reconsider his foolish jealousy might be her best and only recourse.

Noah ignored Juliet all the rest of that long, hot, busy day. He knew he was being unfair, and she was not at fault, but he could not bear to look at her. The thought of her belonging to someone else—caring so much for him that she dreamed of being in his arms only hours after making love to *him*—made him physically ill. He was bleeding inside, the pain worse than any he had ever experienced. He needed to distract himself or he might start howling like a maddened wolf.

He spent the day near Geronimo, riding a horse given to him that morning by Blue Bandana, while the Indians climbed high into the Sierra Madre in search of a new campsight. He had suspected that this was the Sierra Madre range, but did not really know for certain until Geronimo confirmed it with a silent nod. The old chieftain refused to be drawn out by Noah's questions and further insulted him by engaging Blue Bandana in a conversation Noah could not follow. Greatly disappointed, Noah fell back among a group of Apache braves forming the second line of the procession of fleeing Indians.

There, he was greatly surprised to discover someone else besides Blue Bandana who understood and spoke English.

"Me—Running Horse," the young man said, thumping his chest emphatically. "You savvy?"

Noah looked him over carefully, wondering why he had not seen—or perhaps not noticed—the fellow before this. Running Horse was a striking specimen of the best physical attributes of the Apaches, small in stature but muscular, athletic, and graceful as he sat astride a surefooted little mare he controlled with no apparent effort other than the pressure of his knees.

"I'm Noah," Noah informed him, to which the brave gave a short, negative shake of his gleaming, shoulder-length black hair.

"Red-Hair. . . . You Red-Hair. Defeat White Antelope. Running Horse hear all about fight."

"Then you weren't here for it. That's why I didn't recognize you. You're new to the camp."

"Not new—one of best, most loyal Apache warriors. Gone scouting soldiers. Return to see tribe ride out. Wife, Half-Moon, tell me story."

"You mean about me and Shaman Woman, as my . . . uh . . . wife is called." It felt strange to Noah to call Juliet his wife, yet he supposed that was what she was now. He had sworn a vow; he had committed himself. Done exactly as he had promised himself never to do—tied himself to a woman, and worse yet, to a woman in love with another man.

"Yes, Half-Moon say Shaman Woman *mucho* powerful. Heal those Geronimo not heal. You, Red-Hair, fight good fight. Nobody think you win, but you do. Surprise everybody."

Noah shrugged, not wanting to admit that he had been the most surprised of all. As tired as he felt today, he was glad he did not have to fight any more Indians—especially not Running Horse. He had a hunch that the young man would make a most formidable adversary. Running Horse's black eyes were studying him with keen interest and discernment.

"Not good rider." Running Horse's lip curled. "No beat Apache riding horses."

Noah watched the way the young Indian sat his spotted mare and had to agree. Running Horse was an extension of the animal; the two were one in a way Noah had never imagined man and horse could be.

"Maybe I'll get better just watching you."

Running Horse grinned, accepting the compliment

GET
FOUR
FREE
BOOKS
(AN $18.00 VALUE)

ZEBRA HOME SUBSCRIPTION
SERVICE, INC.
120 BRIGHTON ROAD
P.O. Box 5214
CLIFTON, NEW JERSEY 07015-5214

as only his due. He had strong white teeth, and when he grinned, his serious features revealed a wealth of good humor. Noah decided he liked him, especially after the Indian replied with a twinkle in his eye; "Maybe. Red-Hair stay long enough among Apaches, I teach him many Apache things. Red-Hair must learn shoot bow and arrow—kill silently. Save bullets for when really needed."

"I'd like to learn all that. Truth is, I want to learn everything I can about your people and the way they live. I want Geronimo to tell me the story of his life."

Running Horse frowned. "Why tell story of life? Apaches already know. White men, too. All men hear of great Apache shaman and war chief, Geronimo—same as hear of Cochise."

"Yes, but they don't know the story from Geronimo's point of view. That's why I came to this country—to learn the truth about Geronimo and to tell it to other white men. I believe that once whites learn the truth, they will try harder to make peace with the Indians and stop plotting to take their lands."

Running Horse snorted. So did his mare who was tossing her head at a tumbleweed blowing across the rocky terrain. "Whites no listen. No want listen. Want land instead. That why Apaches fight and run. Want stay free."

"I can understand why you might think that way." Noah guided his own horse around a pile of small boulders. "Still, I want to talk to Geronimo. I hope to persuade him to surrender before all of you are killed. The day of Apache freedom has ended. Whether you like it or not, you must negotiate for your survival and live in the places the whites have set aside for you."

"Geronimo no want hear that. I no want hear it," Running Horse responded in a peeved tone. "You white man. Not understand Apache love for mountains and desert. Apaches cannot leave this land. It given us by Usen. If we leave, we die."

"You will die if you stay. Geronimo does not accept this, but it is true. You must all try and accept it."

"You not Apache. Impossible you understand. That why Geronimo not speak to you. You want follow Apaches, better you not speak of surrender. Make Apaches angry."

With that, Running Horse urged his horse to a gallop and left Noah sitting quietly in the saddle, pondering what the young Indian had said.

Two days later, the Apaches found a place to camp that was better than the last place. Commanding a less obstructed view of the surrounding mountains, it was high on a wind-protected knoll tucked between two lofty peaks. The tangy scent of pine and spruce trees filled the air. A waterfall splashed in a silver skein from one of the peaks and formed a pool of crystalline water ideal for drinking and bathing. E-clah-heh and Smiles-A-Lot helped Juliet build a new wickiup, and she in turn helped to build their shelters. First, they lashed together young saplings to make the frames for the dwellings, then they covered them over with skins and beargrass. Not content to stop there, they went on to throw up *ramadas*—open-sided structures that provided shade but allowed for outdoor living.

It amazed Juliet that the women could work so fast and efficiently; in a matter of several days, the village had disappeared from one site and reappeared on another, whole and intact. Only long practice had made such a feat possible.

As night fell, Juliet retired to the new wickiup to await Noah. They had not had any privacy nor slept together since that first night of their reunion. Nor had Noah sought her out among the Indian women and children, who kept separate company from the men while they were on the march. She could not be certain he would even come to her, for he had had nothing to

226

say on the journey and had not smiled at her the whole time.

He spent his time either with Blue Bandana or with another young man whose name she had learned was Running Horse. Running Horse had a wife named Half-Moon, but the young woman was so shy that Juliet usually saw her only from a distance. E-clah-heh told her that Running Horse had been off scouting, and his young wife therefore stayed close to her husband's family. Half-Moon herself had no relatives in camp. Her blood kin had all perished in the interminable skirmishes between the Apaches and their enemies.

Juliet wondered whether Noah would join her in the wickiup, or if he would take his evening meal with his male companions as he had done on the journey. Tonight, there was no communal cookpot. Each family had prepared their own food. The baskets given to her by the women contained precious dried staples—*mescal,* which resembled squash, yucca, walnuts, and deer meat. Smiles-A-Lot had also given her a generous portion of tiny sweet nuts painstakingly gathered from piñon pine trees. Noah was expected to furnish fresh meat for their wickiup, but no hunting had been done on the journey as Geronimo had wanted to make certain the tribe left no traces of their passage into the high country. Tomorrow, perhaps, a hunting party might go out, and Noah would be invited to accompany them.

As Juliet sat on the rug beside her tiny fire, her heart ached with the painful realization that Noah might not be coming. Obviously, he was avoiding her and the possibility that he might overhear her muttering about Jason in her dreams again. Since the last dream, there had been no others, but that was no guarantee she would not dream of Jason this very night. If only she could learn to keep silent, Noah would never have to know about her dreams! She was disgusted with herself, but also with him for being so unreasonable.

She sat until the fire died out, and still, he did not

come. Anger festered in her soul; did it mean nothing to him that she was his wife, waiting for him in their shelter? How dare he treat her this way! He was mean, stubborn, and cruel, and someone ought to point out his faults to him. *She* ought to do so and she would!

Suddenly eager to confront him, she rose and left the wickiup. Outside, the air was cold. This high in the mountains, the nights already hinted of summer's passing. Undeterred by the chill, she hastened toward a small campfire around which lounged a number of men. Neither Noah, Geronimo, Naiche, Blue Bandana, or Running Horse were there, but she suddenly spotted Geronimo coming out of a nearby wickiup, followed by Noah.

"Geronimo, wait!" Noah was saying, as he pursued the Indian leader. "Why won't you talk to me? I don't mean to offend you, but I'm getting damn sick and tired of being ignored."

"Red-Hair!" another man called. Squinting, Juliet saw Running Horse. "Red-Hair, stop!"

Noah halted and swung around to face the younger man while Geronimo continued toward his tipi and entered without a backward glance.

"You not show respect," Running Horse scolded. "Ask too many questions. Insult Geronimo. I warn you, Red-Hair."

Noah tossed his head in a gesture of frustration. "But why won't he tell me anything, Running Horse? Why does he let me stay here if he never intends to talk to me? All I did was ask about his early life. I never got a chance to mention that I think he should surrender. He never let me get that far."

"Red-Hair permitted to stay because of Shaman Woman. She strong medicine. Bring luck to Apaches. Geronimo medicine growing weak. Apaches growing weak. Once we were as leaves on oak tree in summer. Now leaves have fallen; only few remain. Apaches need strong medicine of Shaman Woman."

Juliet froze, not daring to move a muscle. She had

not realized that Running Horse could speak English so proficiently. This was the first time anyone had ever verbalized her importance to the Apaches. How could she possibly meet their expectations? She could cure their ills, but she had no power to stop the soldiers from attacking. If anything, she and Noah depended upon the Indians for survival, not the other way around.

"So that's it," Noah grumbled, his face a mask of anger. "I suppose I should have guessed. The old man will never confide in me, will he? He'll never accept me the way he does Juliet—his precious Shaman Woman. He won't listen to a word I say."

"You white man, not Apache. No can trust yet."

"Yet? You mean he does trust *some* whites?"

Running Horse nodded. "Some, not many. When Geronimo know you better, he trust you."

"There isn't time for him to get to know me better. Tell me what I can do now to make him trust me. I would be his friend. I would give him good counsel. There must be something I can do to prove myself."

"When dawn comes, Apaches ride," Running Horse said, eyeing Noah intently. "You ride too."

"Ride where?" Juliet burst out. "Where are the men going tomorrow?"

A sense of dread swept her; wherever they were going, there would be danger. Noah might get hurt.

"Attack *Nacoya*," Running Horse grunted.

"Mexicans," Noah explained, finally noticing her and not looking too happy about her interruption. "They're going to raid a Mexican settlement for food, horses, and whiskey. That's what the leaders were discussing tonight."

"You must not go with them, No-ah! There will be killing and bloodshed."

It was almost too dark to see his face, but the straightening of his shoulders and the firming of his mouth conveyed his intentions. "I have to go with them. I have to prove myself to Geronimo. Otherwise, nothing I say will count. He'll dismiss all of it."

"In time, he will talk to you, No-ah. If you are patient, you will win his trust, even as I have."

"I haven't got your skills, Juliet. And time may be running out on us. Don't forget White Antelope. They say he's a great tracker. He'll bring the soldiers into the mountains. That's why the Apaches need more horses, so they can escape if they have to."

"They already have horses!"

"Yes, but having extra means having fresh ones to elude their pursuers. That's how they do it. First, they hide the women and children. Then they lead the soldiers on a merry chase, changing horses frequently so they can't be caught."

Juliet suspected he was only trying to distract her. "No-ah, do not go! Do not involve yourself in this fight. I thought you wanted the Apaches to make peace." Heedless of Running Horse who was watching and listening to everything, she stepped nearer and placed her hand on Noah's arm. "You are not a warrior. You are not trained to do battle as they are. You will be killed!"

He gave an exasperated snort. "Have a little faith in me, Juliet. I may not be Jason, but I can survive a raid or two. To the Apaches, this is child's play. I'll simply watch and do what they do."

"And will you kill if it becomes necessary? Promise me you will not kill anyone, No-ah!"

"If someone tries to kill me, I'll do my damndest to kill him first, Juliet." Noah turned to Running Horse. "Count me in, friend. I admit I'm not fond of attacking Mexicans—or anybody else for that matter—but I'll do whatever I must to prove myself to Geronimo."

Running Horse's teeth flashed in the darkness. "Be ready at dawn, Red-Hair. Tomorrow, you become Apache."

"No-ah!" Juliet cried, but Noah pivoted on his heel and strode toward their wickiup.

She followed, intent on pressing the argument and restating her case, but at the doorway, he stopped and blocked her way.

"If you say one word to try and talk me out of this, I'll find someplace else to sleep, Juliet."

She felt as if he had struck her. "You would . . . you would sleep somewhere else?"

"I'd sleep *with* someone else," he snarled. "Why not? You do."

So he had *not* gotten over his jealousy.

"Not w—willingly," she managed in a trembling voice. "You already know that."

"Do I? But that's the point, isn't it? I don't know any such thing, and it's tearing me up inside."

"No-ah, you *must* believe me. You are the only one I love. It matters not if I regain my memory and learn who Jason is, I will *still* love you. Only you."

"How can you be so sure, Juliet? Before, I wanted you to regain your memory. Now, I don't. I'm suddenly afraid. . . . Hell, I've spent most of my life trying not to care, telling myself I don't need people, and then along you come and turn my whole world upside down. Why did you have to make me start *needing* you, Juliet? Why do I have to care so damn much? This Jason . . . if he's real . . . if a part of you still loves him . . ."

"No, do not say it! 'Tis *you* I love, No-ah! 'Tis you who are here with me now! The past does not matter—I swear to you it does not. Come, I will prove it to you . . ."

She grabbed his hand and pulled him into the wickiup. Once inside, she threw herself into his arms. This time, she did not wait for him to take the lead and show her what to do. She herself fed the flames of their passion, stoked the fires, awakened the slumbering beast inside them both. She kissed him as if she would die if they ceased kissing. She clawed at his clothing. She made their joining fierce and savage, reflecting her determination to banish Jason forever from the secret recesses of her mind and heart.

She wanted only Noah, craved only his strength and power deep inside her. . . . For her, there would never be another lover; he was sun and moon, stars and rainbows, thunder and windstorm. He was the heaven he had told her about. She would not let his jealousy destroy them. In the crucible of desire, she would burn away the past and every dream or memory that tied her to it.

Chapter Seventeen

Despite Juliet's protests, reiterated as Noah rose in the predawn hours to join Running Horse in preparation for the raid, Noah rode out at first light with the rest of the warriors. He was even dressed as an Apache—clad only in a breechcloth, his skin and hair stained by a dark juice Running Horse had brought him. Red war paint streaked his chest and cheekbones. A strip of buckskin held back his hair, and knee-high moccasins protected his feet.

This was the Apache way—riding out at dawn, stripped of encumbering garments, loaded down only with weapons and modest provisions. His rifle and ammunition had been returned to him, and he carried the army-issued Springfield encased in a fringed leather pouch fastened to his saddle. Some of the Indians—Running Horse included—rode bareback, but Noah did not trust his horsemanship skills enough to attempt that. He only hoped he would not disgrace himself. Whatever happened, he intended to keep up.

The descent through the mountains was exhilarating. He was so caught up in the excitement of the coming raid that he forgot to be afraid as they galloped through narrow passes and down rocky inclines that would have terrified him in full daylight. Fortunately, his horse was an experienced war pony; all he had to do was hang on. Daylight came, and they slowed down but kept a steady pace, stopping only once to water the horses in a stream cutting through the foothills.

All that day and well into the night they rode. When they finally stopped, Noah was so stiff and sore he could barely climb down from his horse. He assumed that everyone would fall asleep as soon as possible, but soon discovered the foolishness of that notion. After first assuring themselves that no one else was in the vicinity, the Apaches gathered fuel, then held a war dance by the light of the fire. To the beat of a deerskin tamborine called a *esadadedne,* they chanted and prepared themselves for the coming battle. Geronimo invoked the spirits of the mountains to give them strong arms and keen eyes.

With detailed accuracy, he recalled the various depredations of the hated Mexicans, and Noah heard firsthand how Geronimo's mother, Juana, his first wife, Alope, and his three small children were slaughtered by the Mexicans near a little town called Janos, where they and their band had been invited to trade. Tears glistened in Geronimo's fierce black eyes as he reminded his brothers of the Mexican practice of offering bounties for Apache scalps and enslaving Apache women and children. Another of Geronimo's wives, Chee-hash-kish, was even now a slave somewhere in Mexico.

Throughout that long night, the Apaches danced around the leaping flames, and Noah learned more than he wished to know about the history of violence, betrayal, and bloodshed between the Apaches and the Mexicans and the Apaches and the whites. He had heard many of these stories back home in the East, but they had always been whitewashed, the terrible incidents blamed on the Apaches themselves. Now he was hearing them from the Apache point of view, and for the first time, he understood the depths of the Indians' anguish and why they were so determined to remain free.

Watching the shuffling, twisting figures in the flickering red light, he could imagine himself one of them, could appreciate their need for revenge. In the past, he had been distantly sympathetic. That sympathy had now turned to personal outrage. In some strange mysterious way, their fight had become *his* fight. He was no longer merely an interested onlooker; he was as close as he could get to becoming a true Apache.

In the rose-washed dawn, they remounted their horses and galloped across a broad flat plain. Screaming the Apache war cry, they rode into the rising sun. By midafternoon, they reached their destination, an isolated Mexican ranch with a corral full of sleek, fat horses. Geronimo led them to a copse of green-barked *palo verde* trees, in which they hid themselves and settled down to watch and wait.

Throughout that second night, Noah dozed fitfully. His stomach churned with dread of the morning to come. The Apaches remained hidden until just before daybreak and at dawn, attacked the ranch. Howling like avenging angels, they swept down upon the inadequately defended settlement. Sleepy Mexicans poured from the ranch's outbuildings, but were no match for the swift-riding Apaches. Arrows flew. Rifles blasted. Smoke shrouded fleeing figures.

Noah surprised himself with his own ferocity. Suddenly realizing that he was actually trying to kill people, he joined Running Horse who had been assigned the task of stealing the horses. Never having stolen anything in his life, he quickly assessed the situation and followed Running Horse's lead. Riding at breakneck speed, twisting and turning like a jackrabbit, Running Horse rode straight for the line of Mexicans attempting to shoot him down. The Mexicans knew why the Apaches had come, and they raced to save the horses, but Running Horse paid no heed to whining bullets or shouted threats.

With singular purpose, he rode for the gate of the corral while the horses whinnied and milled about inside. Ducking low in the saddle, Noah followed, and together they opened the gate and let the horses free. Shots rang out all around them. Puffs of dust kicked up from the earth on every side. Miraculously, neither of them were hit. Noah never thought of the danger; he concentrated on keeping his seat and herding the horses ahead of him.

While Geronimo and the other Apaches raided the storehouse, Noah and Running Horse drove the band out onto the plain. It was the most exciting thing Noah had ever done—better than seeing his name in print above a provocative article. It came close to making love to Juliet. Fleeing across the plain in the golden light of the rising sun, Noah wanted to shout with elation. He tilted back his head and gave a full-throated Apache war cry.

Galloping beside him, Running Horse echoed the cry, then leaned over and slapped Noah's thigh. The young man's grin stretched from ear to ear. His eyes shone with victory. Drunk with his own triumph, Noah gave another great whoop, and they fled across the plain, driving the stolen horses ahead of them.

When at last they pulled up, far ahead of the other Apaches, both Noah and his pony were lathered. Sweat ran in rivulets down Noah's face; his knees were shaking. He searched for Running Horse and discovered the brave riding toward him with a magnificent stallion in tow behind his little spotted mare.

Wiping the sweat from his eyes with his palm, Noah studied the animal Running Horse had so proudly captured and separated from the rest of the herd. The horse was white with patches of brown and black splashed across his sleek muscular body. He had a finely-shaped head, large brown eyes, and a glorious black and white mane and tail. Though the rest of the horses were panting and blowing, their legs slightly wobbly, this one pranced effortlessly, every movement graceful and elegant. He snorted and blew through flared nostrils, protesting the curtailment of his freedom.

A rope halter encircled the stallion's head, attached to a lead rope in Running Horse's hand. Running Horse rode straight to Noah, stopped, and held out the rope.

"This for you. Best horse in herd. You help capture; you get first pick."

Noah stared, awed by the stallion but not wanting to admit it. This was clearly a most valuable horse.

"Go on, take." Running Horse shook the rope. "No want this one, pick another. Hurry. Before others come."

"I want him," Noah acknowledged, uncertain what to do with the animal. He took the end of the lead rope, then had to hold tight as the stallion reared and pawed the air.

He came down with a scream of rage, his hooves thudding against the hard-packed earth. Noah had to let go of the reins of his own horse in order to keep hold of the stallion. Running Horse laughed.

"Best horse anywhere. Plenty spirit. You deserve, Red-Hair. Ride almost as good as Apache today."

"He's wild and unbroken," Noah muttered in what had to be a gross understatement. The stallion nearly yanked his arm from the socket. "I doubt he's ever been ridden."

"What name you give?" Running Horse blandly inquired.

Noting the distinctive patch of black surrounding one baleful eye, Noah had no hesitations. "Patch," he said, the name coming to him like a lightning bolt. "His name will be Patch."

"Patch," Running Horse echoed approvingly. "Next time we raid you ride stallion. No white man or Mexican catch you."

"You're undoubtedly right," Noah agreed. "If he doesn't kill me first, he'll make a splendid mount. The question is, what do I do with him in the meantime?"

"Let go free. He no leave mares. Follow back to camp and stay hidden with other horses."

At their present camp, the Apaches had designated a small mountain plateau as a place of forage for their precious ponies. The grass would not sustain them forever, but at the moment it grew green and long, fringing a tiny but adequate water hole. In the harsh terrain of the Sierra Madre, it was the best to be had. Noah smiled to himself; he could not wait to see Juliet's eyes when he rode up leading this magnificent beast. Then he frowned, recognizing his need to impress her. He remembered his jealousy—that corrosive emotion that kept eating away at his happiness and eroding his trust in Juliet.

He wondered if he would ever be free of it. No matter what logic he applied to banish the feeling, it would not stay banished. He knew it could destroy him and all the love he felt for Juliet; it was making Juliet miserable, too. But he could not seem to stop the bitter comments that rose to his lips and brought such sadness into her beautiful golden-brown eyes.

He was suddenly exhausted. His muscles throbbed with weariness and the strain of the long hours on horseback. He could summon no enthusiasm for the homeward journey and had to force himself to smile at Running Horse who had lost none of his elation over the success of the raid.

"They come!" Running Horse cried joyously, indicating the arrival of the rest of the Apaches with a nod of his head.

Spinning his mare around, he cantered off to greet them.

When the Apaches rode into camp amid cries of gladness and shouts of greeting, Juliet hurried out of the wickiup as eagerly as any of the other Apache wives. Her eyes searched the returning warriors. When she did not immediately spot Noah in the throng, she began counting heads. . . . Yes, as many men had returned as had ridden out. Noah had to be among them.

Picking up her skirts, she ran past the wickiups gathered beneath the pines and hurried toward the commotion at the far end of the village. At last, she spotted Noah leading a prancing horse with brilliant patches of color splashed across its white coat. The Apache women and children were all exclaiming over it as they welcomed the returning—and apparently highly successful—warriors.

Horses whinnied and stomped, children shrieked with excitement, but Juliet had eyes only for Noah—and the incredible horse he had brought back with him. Other braves were handing around jugs, barrels, and sacks of plundered goods, and gesturing behind them to indicate an entire herd of newly-captured horses. Noah had nothing in his hands except the lead rope of the multicolored horse who was becoming difficult to manage in the noise and confusion.

As the stallion reared, the Apaches pressing close on every side scattered. Noah's horse nervously edged sideways. Juliet rushed forward to help. As she ran, she started talking to the horse—sending her thoughts winging toward it. The animal sensed her efforts to calm it and froze, body trembling, ears perked in her direction. A light sheen of sweat glistened along its massive chest.

Knowing the danger was past and she had the horse's attention, Juliet slowed to a walk. A silence fell over the Apaches as they watched her approach Noah and his prize. The Indians seemed to realize what she was doing, but Noah only watched her in puzzlement, his gaze flitting from her to the horse and back again, as if he did not believe what he was seeing—or did not *want* to believe it.

Juliet walked up to the stallion and gently stroked its muzzle. The horse arched his proud neck and nuzzled her. Leaning forward, she breathed gently into its flared nostrils, exchanging a breath of greeting. Within moments, the animal gentled and ceased to be nervous or threatening. Noah's eyes sought hers; she read a grudging admiration in them.

"I've named him Patch for the ring of color he's got around one eye," he said as if nothing unusual had happened.

"He is beautiful," she acknowledged. "So strong and powerful, yet graceful, too. He was surely someone's pride and joy."

"I did not have to shoot anybody to get him," Noah declared, his tone defensive. "But I did steal him from his rightful owners, and I don't feel the least bit remorseful."

"Perhaps they were not his 'rightful' owners. He looks as if he belongs among the Apaches, not the Mexicans or anyone else."

"He belongs to me," Noah said. "I am going to train him. Running Horse has offered to help."

She noticed he did not ask for her help, nor did he thank her for the assistance she had already given. "I am glad you have come back safely," she murmured, wishing he would show more delight at their reunion. "I missed you while you were gone," she added softly.

His reply was even softer. "And I missed you, Juliet."

Their eyes met and held; the air crackled between them. It would always be so—this helpless longing, this sensual awareness, this leaping flame of desire. Around them, the Apaches began to chatter again. Families claimed husbands, fathers, and brothers. Only Juliet and Noah stood motionless and silent amid the confusion, their glances fused together.

"I will take Patch to join the other horses, and then I will come to the wickiup," Noah finally said. "Go there and wait for me."

She nodded, well aware of what would occur in the wickiup. They would draw a skin across the entranceway and spend the rest of the day in each other's arms. Whatever their problems, whatever their worries and fears, they had only to embrace, and all else would be forgotten. After their lovemaking, Noah would probably sleep, but she would remain awake. She dared not risk spoiling his homecoming with another unsettling dream.

That day marked a turning point in their relationship. Noah went out of his way to avoid mentioning Jason or speculating about her mysterious past, and Juliet did the same. They lived as the Apaches did—one day at a time—giving no outward appearance of worrying or planning for the future. It was a time of temporary peace and plenty. The raid had provided not only horses, but food supplies, ammunition, and whiskey. Both they and the Apaches were set for a while.

During the day, the men worked at training horses; making new lances from *sotol* trees, bows from mulberry branches, and arrows from reed; cleaning their Winchester or Springfield rifles; and preparing the young men and boys for their lives as warriors and hunters. The braves challenged each other to run up and down the mountainside with a mouthful of water, which they were not allowed to swallow, the exercise supposedly teaching them how to control their breathing while running in hot weather. They then spent long hours on their stomachs studying animal tracks, Noah beside them, learning Apache ways along with the youngsters.

When Juliet was not busy with healing duties, she took up basketry and studied Apache methods of cooking and sewing. She became proficient at setting up and taking down a wickiup with little or no help. Apache girls did this as a game, each trying to be the fastest. No one ever pointed out to them that one day their lives might depend upon the skill, but it was understood. They must be able to remove all traces of a campsite within moments of an alert.

At night, the Apaches gathered around campfires—kept small for safety's sake—and listened to the tribal elders recount stories of Apache history and religion. The Apaches worshiped many spirits, believing that everything in the world had a spirit, and that certain members of their tribe were blessed with the ability to communicate with those spirits. Geronimo was one of those members, and so—according to the Apaches—was Juliet.

Noah always looked doubtful and uncomfortable during these discussions, as if he did not believe it, but Juliet realized that this was how the Apaches were able to explain and accept her unusual gifts. It was how they fit her into their world. Now, she and Noah were discovering how to fit into the world of the Apaches.

Noah's writing utensils had been lost, but the Apaches returned his journal, the precious book in which he wrote things down so he could remember them later. Each night at the campfire, he scribbled away in his journal with a piece of charcoal—until E-clah-heh showed him how to make signs and symbols with a small pointed stick dipped in plant dye. Thereafter, Noah used the stick and dye to write down the stories of the Apaches, becoming especially excited over the ones involving Geronimo's personal history.

Geronimo spoke more freely now in front of them, and they were fast learning the Apache language. No longer did they always need Blue Bandana or Running Horse to translate for them. Together, they heard how Geronimo had received his name. His mother had named him Goyathlay, meaning He Who Yawns, but in a battle with the Mexicans, he had shown such ferocity that the Mexicans started shouting the term, Geronimo.

"Name mean courage. Bravery," Old Nana proudly informed the enthralled audience.

Shielding his mouth with his hand, Noah leaned over to Juliet and whispered, "That's not what it means. The Mexicans were actually calling upon San

242

Jerome, one of their saints—a holy person—to whom they pray for protection."

Juliet hid a smile, thinking she liked the Apache version better. She was learning many things at the nightly campfires. Geronimo's was not the only name that had come from people the Apaches hated. Another great Apache leader, Mangas Coloradas, had also received his name, Red Sleeves, from the whites. He had died at the hands of his enemies while on a peace mission. Half the Apaches around the campfire bore names given to them by whites or Mexicans—and all had lost friends or relatives to these same people.

It was a curious and tragic situation, indicative of just how much the Apache language and way of life had been influenced by association with foreigners. The Apaches had also incorporated the foods—and the vices—of their enemies into their everyday lives. Geronimo himself had a weakness for fiery Mexican whiskey. Whenever the warriors got to drinking instead of talking, Juliet and Noah retired early to their wickiup. The whiskey made the Indians quick to quarrel and pick fights with one another, even among the closest of friends. In addition to the whiskey captured on the raid, they occasionally brought out *tizwin,* an Apache concoction that had much the same effect.

Tizwin was made from fermented corn. A plump woman named Huera, the wife of Mangus, excelled at its production, and the brew was used for many religious observances. On the reservation, *"tizwin* drinks"*, as they were called, were prohibited, along with wife-beating or the cutting off of the tip of a woman's nose in cases of adultery. The Apaches found these rules insulting, intrusive, and restrictive—all the more reason to rebel against white control.

Aside from those few nights when the Indians drank, life in the high Sierras was almost idyllic—a pleasant interlude before the storm, as Juliet was to think of it later. Noah's body grew lean, hard, and strong, his hair lengthened, and he became a skilled rider under Running Horse's tutelage. Whenever Juliet chanced to glance up from her work to discover him silently watching her, his eyes inviting her to a secret tryst in the wickiup or in a grove of pine trees away from prying eyes, she found it hard to breathe. . . . She loved him so much! She wished these precious days would never end but feared that their contentment and happiness was temporary, a fragile thing, doomed to be destroyed either by a dream, some other reminder of her past, or a physical threat.

Occasionally, she *did* dream, but managed to hide the fact from Noah. Once, she dreamed of a happy scene with her parents in which they gave her permission to wed Jason, and once she had a disturbing dream involving a white bull, of all things! She could put none of it together, nor determine whether she had actually gone ahead and married Jason or was only betrothed to him . . . nor could she remember Jason's face. Try as she might to recall it when she awoke, she discovered it was impossible to resurrect a single person or event from her past—unless the dreams really *were* her past, as Noah suspected.

She tried not to think too much about it. It was easy to adopt the Apache philosophy of savoring today and letting tomorrow take care of itself, but the past continued to haunt her. Like the Apaches, she was unable to reconcile her present with her past and to live in harmony with the realities of either. She learned to nurture a bittersweet appreciation for the beauty of the moment and nursed a secret dread that too soon everything would be lost, not only to her but to her dear friends.

During the rest of that long hot summer, the Apaches did suffer occasional devastating losses. One confrontation occurred not far from camp, when the U.S. Army under the command of Captain Wirt Davis ambushed four of Geronimo's scouts and killed two. A week later, while Juliet was off with the women gathering materials to make baskets and Noah was hunting with the warriors, a large party of army Indian scouts overran the *rancheria*. A woman and a child died in the fracas. Old Nana was captured, along with Huera, Geronimo's entire family including his two most current wives, Zi-yeh, and She-gha, and all of his children with the exception of one warrior son. According to the frightened witnesses, they were carried screaming and fighting down the mountainside.

Upon their return, the Apaches, Noah among them, set off to recover the captives and were able to steal some of them back. Geronimo regained She-gha, and the band found some Mescalero women to replace the other lost wives. This cold-heartedness shocked Juliet, until she realized that in the carefully-balanced Apache system, both men and women were essential to Indian survival. Still, the encounters cost the tribe fully one third of their women and children. Twice more, the disheartened Apaches moved camp, the second time less than a half day ahead of their pursuers. The bounty of previous raids rapidly dwindled; when food grew scarce, several old war ponies had to be slaughtered to feed everyone.

At summer's end, the Apaches headed into New Mexico. They threw up their wickiups one day and tore them down the next. As tensions mounted and everyone grew short-tempered, Juliet just barely managed to avoid another serious argument with Noah—until the afternoon she happened to open Noah's journal to see what he had written in it and made the shocking discovery that she could not read.

Chapter Eighteen

"What do you mean you can't read it?" Noah practically shouted at her. "The method for producing dye from Devil's Claw cactus is written right there in plain English. I wrote it all down when E-clah-heh described it to me." He pointed to a string of symbols that made no sense to Juliet, then tapped on the spot for emphasis.

"This is written in the language we are speaking now?" she asked, beginning to be frightened.

This was the first time she had ever looked inside his journal—the first time she had needed something she knew was recorded there. She had wanted to please him by volunteering to make a new batch of dye for him to replace what had been destroyed during the last raid and instead, had only made him angry. . . . Why had they both assumed that she knew how to read? Maybe she had known at one time but forgotten it, along with everything else in her misbegotten past.

"You mean you can't even tell that it's English?" Noah's brows rose. "Take the book outside and look at it in the sunlight. You must be able to recognize something."

"I can *see* it perfectly well here in the wickiup," she retorted. "But I cannot understand it. What do these symbols mean, No-ah? What is this one here?"

"That's a *D,*" Noah snorted. "For Devil's Claw. Don't tell me you can't identify a single one of those letters. I won't believe it. You've read history; I know you have. You've read all about the Greeks, for one thing. You told me you did."

"No, I did not tell you that, No-ah. You assumed it. And because I could not remember how I came to know about the Greeks, I assumed you must be right. Now, it appears you are wrong."

Gazing down at the open book, she squinted and cocked her head. She turned the journal upside down and studied it from that angle. Nothing helped. No matter which way she looked at them, the symbols meant nothing. To her, they resembled the irregular tracks of an insect or tiny animal. She could not understand how Noah could glance at them and see instructions for plant dye.

"What are you doing?" he demanded, turning the book right side up. "Do you think it would be easier if you stood on your head? Maybe you should lie down and balance the book on your stomach."

The sarcasm in his tone pricked her pride and made her feel foolish and ignorant. " 'Tis obvious I am simply trying to irritate you and admirably succeeding in the effort!" she shouted at him. Chagrinned at her outburst, she lowered her voice and strove to continue in a normal tone. "I wish I could read this, No-ah. I never knew I could not. But then this is the first time I have tried to read since . . . since I woke up on that ledge."

"Well, try harder, damn it! People don't 'forget' how to read. Once you've learned the skill, you've got it forever."

Undeterred by his continuing nastiness, she continued to pore over the book's pages. It was hopeless; the symbols were incomprehensible.

"Give it here!" Noah snatched the journal from her hands. "If you can't read, you can't read. But it beats the hell out of me how you can know so much about ancient Greece if you didn't learn it from a book somewhere. . . . What am I going to do with you, Juliet?

248

Sometimes, I think you'll turn me into a foaming-at-the-mouth madman. I'll start howling at the moon and wake up one morning not being able to remember my *own* damn name. Right from the start, this whole thing about your lost memory has been absurd. It's downright unbelievable, and I've had more than enough of it."

Wounded to the quick, Juliet jerked back from him. "I was only teasing a moment ago, No-ah. I am *not* trying to irritate or infuriate you. That was never my intention, I assure you. Your anger pierces me like an arrow to the heart."

"Oh, hell, I'm *not* angry. What I am is . . . frustrated! I get paid to dig into people's backgrounds and discover the truth about them, Juliet. It's how I make my living. Now, when it really matters, my skills count for nothing. After all this time, I still don't know you. I should be able to figure you out from the clues you drop, the way you act, your unconscious mannerisms, your responses to things. . . . I keep watching and wondering, but all I do is get more confused."

He shoved his journal back into the leather case in which he kept it and returned the case to its spot near the wall. "Just listen to the way you talk, for example. You don't speak like an illiterate, backwoods country girl. You sound like someone who's been taught by an excellent teacher. You know words like *himation,* which means you *had* to have read the classics and studied about Greece just as I did. Your education and background *must* have been similar to mine."

His confession that he was frustrated at not being unable to untangle the mystery of her past did not make his impatience or anger any easier to bear. Juliet wanted to lash out at him. Wanted him to know what it felt like to be the victim of unfair attacks.

"If I disturb you so much, why do you remain in this wickiup, No-ah? I no longer want you here. I refuse to share your sleeping rug any longer—not until you apologize for the way you have treated me."

"The way I've treated you! What about the way you treat me? You could have told me before that you didn't know how to read or else had forgotten it. Why did you wait to spring it on me like some big damn surprise? Is it any wonder I lose my temper?"

"I did not wait to spring this on you. I am as surprised as you are. I am *more* surprised. Think how you would feel if you opened a book and could not understand it. Think how frustrating it is for me. What other things will I discover that I have forgotten or do not know? To live like this is most unsettling. It makes me afraid. And your anger only makes matters worse. You are my world, No-ah. My present and future. Do you not realize that I can endure anything so long as I have you? When you are angry, I feel as if you have gone far away, and I am alone and frightened. I dread what will become of me."

A moment of silence ensued, at the end of which Noah groaned and opened his arms to her. "Juliet . . . sweetheart. . . . Oh, little one, I'm sorry. Please forgive me."

He enfolded her in his warm, strong embrace and held her tightly, his chin resting on her head. "I can be such an ass at times. I only get this way because I love you so much, and I'm afraid of losing you. I keep thinking that something is going to happen or someone is going to come along and snatch you away from me. One day you'll remember everything, and it will change how you feel about me. You'll never want to share a sleeping rug with me again. I'll be nothing to you; I don't deserve you anyway. I've never felt like this about anyone before, and I've done bad things to women. I've used them, Juliet. Took them for my own pleasure and tossed them aside like . . . like yesterday's garbage. Before you, I really only cared for one other woman—my mother. Every woman since I've treated with contempt. Why, I never even bothered to tell Emily Carstairs—the closest thing I ever had to a sister—that I'll never marry her. Losing you would be a just punishment for my past cruelties to women."

"You are not going to lose me, No-ah!" She clung to him, loving him even more, if that were possible, after his sweet apology. "Do you think I would ever willingly let you go? *Never,* my dearest love, never."

Pressing herself against him, she kissed him full on the mouth, then seized his hands and placed them on her breasts. Only when he was touching her intimately could she feel safe again. He lifted her blouse so he could caress her nakedness, then yanked up her skirt so he could part her legs.

He made love to her standing up, then drew her downward to lie beneath him on the rug. As always, his lovemaking obliterated all her doubts and fears. Lost in passion, she could forget the precariousness of their relationship. . . . How *did* she know so much about Greece if she had not read about it in some book? The land and culture so vividly portrayed in her dreams resembled nothing she had seen in *this* land. Maybe Tucson would look more familiar, she consoled herself. Maybe it had beautiful pillared villas, marble statues, tinkling fountains, grape arbors, and olive groves. Maybe she would recognize everything and feel at home there . . . find her family and Jason . . . and lose Noah in the process.

She trembled and arched more strongly against him. She met his thrusts with fevered thrusts of her own, took him into her, gave him all she possessed, and then found more to give him. She could not live without Noah. Pray God or Usen or whoever else was listening that she would never have to!

The next morning, Running Horse came early to fetch Noah. "Red-Hair, come quickly! Last night, Yellow Coyote return from scouting soldiers. He say bluecoats not far from here. White Antelope leads them.

He tracking us here. We meet in council now. Decide what to do."

Juliet rolled over in alarm. Bakeitzogie, or Yellow Coyote, could not have been mistaken about the soldiers or White Antelope; he was said to have the eyes of an eagle. The whites called him Dutchy. He knew many white men and occasionally scouted for the army himself. On such occasions, he led the army away from his fellow Apaches. One time he had deliberately drunk too much Mexican *mescal,* and his bout of drunkenness gave the tribe time to escape.

Planting a quick kiss on her forehead, Noah hurriedly dressed and left the wickiup. By the time he returned, Juliet had risen, bathed, prepared food, and was eagerly awaiting news of the council's decision.

Noah slid his arms around her waist. "Sweetheart, I'm afraid we're moving camp again."

"That is no problem," she assured him. "I have done it so often now I can take down the wickiup in a matter of moments and build a new one with my eyes closed, as quickly as E-clah-heh and Smiles-A-Lot."

"But can you do it all without me?" he gently asked her. "Running Horse has been assigned the task of tracking the army's movements, and Geronimo now trusts me enough to let me go along to help."

"You! But No-ah, you are not Apache! They have trained since childhood to ride like the wind and disappear just as easily. For you, it will be too dangerous, especially with White Antelope in the vicinity. You will be caught, perhaps even killed!"

He slanted her a wounded glance. "Juliet, you must learn to have more faith in me. What do you think I have been doing all this time? I can ride almost as well as Running Horse now; I can run up and down mountains with my mouth full of water. I can go all day and not get tired. Running Horse has asked that I accompany him, and Geronimo and Naiche have consented. I am honored by the appointment, and I am going."

"Oh yes, I realize you must go!" she wailed. "The

Apaches have given us so much, and we owe it to them. But I am so afraid for you, No-ah."

He hugged her to him. "Don't be, sweetheart. No matter where you and the Apaches wind up, we'll find the camp again. Until we do, Patch will take good care of me. The soldiers will never be able to catch him. If you don't trust me, at least trust my horse. Go and talk to him if you wish. He'll assure you that we won't be caught."

"You are mocking my abilities again, No-ah!"

He chuckled. "No, I'm not, sweetheart. I mean what I say. Patch knows how you feel about me, and he'll bring me back safe and sound. . . . Just don't belittle *my* abilities. I've learned to be a good Indian in the time we've lived among the Apaches."

"I know you have, No-ah," she admitted in a weary tone, then struggled to display more optimism. "I have watched with pride as you have overcome every challenge and conquered every obstacle. You are a great man, No-ah; in my eyes, there is no one greater. You are a king among men."

He laughed outright. "That's carrying it a bit far, honey, but I always did appreciate flattery. Stay close to Geronimo, little one, and if the opportunity presents itself, remind him that I still think surrender is a better idea than this constant running. As you know, I've tried to tell him this, but he refuses to listen. He still thinks I lack a full appreciation of the Apache point of view."

"I will do what I can, No-ah, but he will not heed my advice either. He respects me, yes, but only when it comes to healing. In all other areas, I am merely a female intruding upon the domain of men."

"He should be more open-minded—like me." No-ah grinned. "My mind is always open to suggestions from the fairer sex, especially when those suggestions come from you."

"No, you do as you please, No-ah, and I fear you

253

always will. 'Tis I who must make all of the accommodations in order for us to get along."

"Then accommodate me before I go, wife." Inclining his head, he nibbled along the edge of her lip. "Give me one last memory of your sweet body to take with me."

She reached for the hem of her blouse. "Yes, oh yes . . ." she murmured, only too eager.

"Red-Hair!" a voice barked from outside. "Come! We leave at once. Dutchy already gone to get horses."

"I'll be out in a moment," Noah sighed, regretfully turning away from her. Before he could leave, she grabbed hold of his arm.

"Dutchy? He is going with you?"

Noah picked up his rifle and gun belt. "Only part way. The council has decided that he will return to Fort Bowie and resume his services as a scout to the army. We need him more than ever now. He can accuse White Antelope of leading the soldiers astray."

"But will the soldiers not suspect what *he* is doing?"

"They might. But then Apaches often disagree among themselves. The soldiers never know who's telling the truth and who's lying to protect his friends. While they debate the issue, Geronimo and Naiche will lead the tribe to safety."

Juliet lowered her eyes to hide the welling of her tears. She *knew* this trip was going to end badly. "The Apaches will never be safe, will they, No-ah? Always they will be running and hiding, only a step or two in front of their enemies. They have no time to hunt, dry meat, or gather the wild foods they need to survive the winter; they have no time to plant and harvest their own crops. They must raid continually to gain fresh horses, ammunition, and clothing. The women scarcely have time to bear their children or recover from childbirth. . . . How much longer can they live like this, No-ah? 'Tis too harsh a life for the very old and the very young."

"I know it, sweetheart. That's why I keep trying to

convince Geronimo to surrender. Until he does, we'll stand by him, and I'll keep recording Apache beliefs and customs—and also attempting to get his whole story. We're witnessing the destruction of an entire culture, Juliet. I can easily foresee a time when the Apaches will have disappeared from the face of the earth."

"Do not say that, No-ah! It cannot be true! What kind of people are the whites, that they can so heartlessly destroy another race?"

"We're greedy, my love. We want the land of the Apaches. And we want everyone else in the world to be exactly like us—to eat, dress, look, and think like us. If they won't—if they refuse—we'll either drive them out or kill them."

"Sweet Zeus!" Juliet gasped, horrified by the realization that he was right.

A scowl crept across Noah's handsome face. "Zeus?" he questioned. *"Sweet Zeus?"*

"Forget I said that! Oh, forget it, No-ah! 'Twas only a slip of . . . of the tongue. Put it out of your mind, or we will soon be fighting again."

"God help us all," he muttered. *"God,* not Zeus. Our personal situation isn't much better than that of the Apaches'. I have the strangest feeling we haven't got any more time than they do."

She clung to his arms. "Do not make such terrible statements and then go off and leave me, No-ah!"

"All right . . . all right," he soothed, drawing her close one last time. "Let's bury our fears again and remain optimistic. Before you, I never knew what optimism was. Now that I'm acquainted with the feeling, I'll do anything to keep from wallowing in pessimism and cynicism, the way I used to do."

He gave her one last kiss—and then he left her sitting alone in the wickiup, wondering what would become of all of them.

* * *

Under cover of darkness, on hands and knees, Noah followed Running Horse and joined him in the protective shelter of a large, flat boulder. There, they stretched out on their stomachs and lay still, hoping no one had noticed them. They had crawled on their bellies to within a stone's throw of an army encampment—close enough to hear every word the soldiers were saying.

Noah was cold and wet. Once again, the desert had surprised him, this time with a deluge that flooded the arroyos and canyons. From the soldiers' conversation, he knew that the blue-coats were as miserable as he was, though he would never have stooped to complaining as they were doing. Apache stoicism had finally rubbed off on him; he had learned to tolerate both the heat and the cold. He had even convinced himself that it wasn't still raining—yet the air smelled of moisture and tasted of it. Moisture ran in rivulets down his bare back.

"Damn blasted rain," swore a nearby man. "First, the desert roasts us, then it freezes us. Next, it's surely gonna drown us. Jake, you think it's rainin' up there in the mountains where them devil Apaches are hidin'?"

"Prob'ly," a voice replied. "I bet it's rainin' in Tucson an' Fort Bowie, too. Hell, it's raining' all over the territory. When it finally gets t' rainin' out here, it rains like hell."

"We git anywhere near them Injuns, I'm gonna shoot t' kill, instead of takin' prisoners. I ain't fixin' t' go through this again. I agree with the ranchers and settlers. Only way t' deal with Injuns is t' wipe 'em out alt'gether. I hope they *don't* surrender, 'cause if'n they do, we're gonna have t' protect them. But if they keep runnin', we kin shoot 'em down and git this over with."

"Settle down, man. General Crook's patience is runnin' out, too. If they don't surrender sometime soon, we'll get orders to kill instead of catch 'em."

"Yeah, but we can't do neither if we don't never git close to 'em. This damn country's so rough I sometimes think we'll never find 'em. Hell, even the scouts can't always pick up their trail. Or else we can't trust the damn scouts. Could be they're just leadin' us in circles—givin' Geronimo all the time he needs t' escape."

"True, but if it weren't fer the scouts, we'd git lost and die out here ourselves. Not only us, but the horses, too. Injuns are the only ones who know this country and where t' find water, grass, an' game when we need it."

"Well, we got more'n enough water right now! Got water in my boots, in my bedroll, in my hat, down the back of my neck . . ." There was a plopping sound, as if someone was emptying water out of something.

"Aw, quit your belly achin'. T'morrow we go up in the hills and set up that heliograph we brought with us, and then we can signal back and forth from the mountaintops an' let the whole damn army know when we find something. You mark my words—it'll be the heliograph that causes Geronimo's downfall, an' I bet he ain't never heard of it. Or if he has, he don't understan' what it's used for. With the heliograph, we can finally keep track of him and warn the Mexicans and settlers where he's headed. Best of all, we can send troops t' ambush him. Geronimo don't stand a chance against us now. The heliograph has sealed his fate."

So the U.S. Army had finally gotten around to setting up stations for the new invention, Noah thought. He had heard about the instrument before his arrival in Arizona. First used by the British in India, the heliograph was designed to transmit signals by means of the sun's rays reflecting off a mirror set atop a tripod. The heliograph was claimed to be a far superior invention to the telegraph for use in combat, because no lines existed to be cut. The Apaches had quickly learned to shut down telegraph communications by cutting the wires and then splicing them back together with twine so the breaks were difficult to locate. However, they could not stop messages from being sent by heliograph.

Noah remembered reading that the heliograph had been tested in Arizona at Fort Whipple six or eight years ago, and heliograph stations had then been erected at Fort Huachuca and other sites. Until now, their use had been limited. Now it appeared that the army meant to rely upon them—bad news for the Apaches who depended upon the lack of communication among their enemies. Bad news for Geronimo.

Noah had heard more than enough to convince him that time was running out for the Indians. He signaled to Running Horse that he was ready to leave, but his friend insisted upon remaining for a few more moments. They overheard more complaints—about the food, the discomforts, and the harsh army discipline. Then another nugget of gold reached Noah's ears.

"Hey, Jake! What you think about that rumor that Lieutenant Davis is gonna give General Crook whatfor about the way the Injuns have been handled—and then he's gonna resign his commission?"

"I 'spect that's exactly what's gonna happen. I hear tell it ain't only the lieutenant who's unhappy and wants t' quit. Al Seiber, the chief of the Injun scouts, don't like bein' told by Washin'ton how t' run his business neither. For that matter, Crook hates them Washin'ton busybodies as much as anybody."

Discord among their white pursuers might work to the Apaches' advantage, Noah thought. It might buy the Indians a bit more time to make up their minds to surrender and then to arrange it so that they would not be slaughtered. Noah had half a mind to walk into the army camp right this minute and start bargaining with the detachment's commander. But he was not in charge here; that honor belonged to Running Horse. And because Running Horse was his friend, he must talk it over with him first. He must convince him that something had to be done and soon—before the ranchers and settlers found Geronimo or the soldiers themselves lost all patience.

Chapter Nineteen

"No!" Running Horse cried. "What you thinking, Red-Hair? Apache no can walk into army camp and make peace with soldiers. They shoot before he open mouth."

Noah took a deep breath before continuing. They had left the army encampment on the plain below, and their horses were now picking their way up a mountain path in the rainy darkness. "They won't kill us if we approach them in peace, letting them know that we just want to negotiate."

"You wrong, Red-Hair. No can trust white men. They kill Mangas Coloradas when he go to their village to talk peace."

"These aren't townspeople or miners angry about Apache raids, Running Horse. They're cold, wet, miserable soldiers who just want it to be over, so they can go home. Most of them don't even live in the territory. They have no families here. They're willing and eager to make peace."

It was too dark to see Running Horse, but a sudden motion suggested he was shaking his head. "No . . . not our place negotiate peace. That for Geronimo, Naiche, and tribal council to decide."

"I wasn't suggesting that we bind the people to anything. I was only saying we should try and set up a meeting between Geronimo and Naiche and General Crook—or Lieutenant Davis. Or anybody at all. We need to talk to the soldiers, Running Horse. Talk is always a better solution than running and shooting. If the Apaches keep running, the soldiers will keep shooting. Unless your people agree to negotiate, you face annihiliation."

"No good negotiate. Whites make promises, then break them. They say 'ho Apache'! Go live on reservation. No hunt because game all gone. No follow game because game leave reservation. No plant corn and melons because ground won't grow things. Or maybe it flood and wash away crops. Water bad. Make Apaches sick. Ground bad. Make crops die. But don't worry, Apache, we give you food. We give you clothing. . . . Then give food with worms in it. Bring blankets with holes; give knives that not cut. Supplies come late, sometimes not come at all. Only thing Indian can do all day is drink *tizwin*— no can ride, hunt, or care for own people. Must sit all day and look at walls of wickiup. No longer be a man. . . . No, Red-Hair! No more negotiate. Apache must be free or die. No can live like white man want."

"Listen to me, Running Horse. I know that things have not worked out in the past, and reservation life has its problems. But we can change that. I can help change it. I can tell the world the truth about the reservation and the broken promises. I can talk about the problems. Not all whites are bad. They will listen and be outraged. Conditions will improve. Your people can be taught new things—new ways to survive and prosper in the white world. You can't fight them, Running Horse. You're going to have to join them."

"You go make talk-talk, Red-Hair. Not me. Maybe they listen to you. You, too, are white. Maybe they not kill you. But they kill me and my brothers. Or if they not kill, they let ranchers and settlers do it. Army not protect us from bad white men who want see all Indians dead."

Noah felt he must make Running Horse understand—must make him realize that peaceful surrender was still possible, and that the army *would* protect the Apaches. Eventually, even the ranchers and settlers would listen to reason; what no one would tolerate was continued raiding, stealing, and murdering. That aspect of Apache life must end and good riddance. Raiding was no longer a viable cultural institution. Horses, cattle, and other things the Apaches needed must be obtained through less violent means—and never mind how thrilling it had been to ride in and take them, then gallop back across the plains to dance a victory dance among family and friends.

"I will go to them dressed as I am now, Running Horse. When they see me, they'll think I'm Apache. But they won't shoot. You'll see. They'll let me talk to them. I'll tell them that the Indians want peace but are afraid to return to the reservation. I'll explain that Geronimo fears nothing will change, and things will be worse than before."

"Geronimo and Running Horse *not* afraid. We want be free! That why we and other Apaches stay out. That why we fight . . . run . . . raid. Better to die living free than live locked up on white man's reservation."

"I'll prove to you that you're wrong about the whites, Running Horse. Tomorrow night I'll prove it to you. I'll walk unarmed into the soldiers' camp and see if they're willing to talk to Geronimo. If they are, we can go back and try to persuade Geronimo and Naiche to meet with them."

"This your decision. Not mine. I no persuade Geronimo make talk-talk. When they shoot you, I take body of Red-Hair back to Shaman Woman. This all I promise. This all I can do."

"So be it then," Noah snorted, and turned his attention back to the rain-slickened mountainside that Patch was so carefully negotiating.

The following evening, an hour or so before dark, Noah tied Patch behind a stand of *mesquite* in the

263

shadow of the Dragoon Mountains where the soldiers had made camp. He took off his gunbelt and the sheath holding his knife. He stripped himself of everything but his breechcloth and moccasins. He was now ready to face the soldiers. But before he could step from behind the brush and head for the encampment, Running Horse placed a hand on his arm and spoke in a low, earnest voice.

"Do not go, Red-Hair. This foolish thing you do. We here scout soldiers. Not make talk-talk. Do not go, my friend."

"If we don't make talk-talk, this fight will go on forever—or until the last Apache dies. I have to go, Running Horse. I have to prove to you and Geronimo that all of you will be safe if you surrender. There's a risk; I won't deny it. But it's no greater than the one I am asking you to take. Watch and listen carefully. I think you'll learn something tonight."

Running Horse lifted his rifle. "I watch," he promised. "I listen. If they raise rifles to kill you, I kill them first."

"Put that gun away, Running Horse. You aren't going to need it. Once I've spoken to them, I'll return as soon as possible. Don't worry if I'm gone for a while."

Running Horse ignored him. "If soldiers raise guns, you crouch and run like jackrabbit. Return here fast. We mount horses and flee in darkness."

Noah bit down on his exasperation. "You just won't trust me, will you? You and my wife seem to have the same problem. You can't accept that I might know what I'm talking about."

Running Horse grunted. "Better listen to wife, Red-Hair. Shaman Woman make good sense."

Knowing he could not win the argument, Noah heaved a sigh and set off. He wanted to enter the soldiers' camp before it got too dark for them to see him coming. If they were caught by surprise or thought he was sneaking up on them, they might just shoot him. Mindful of that possibility, he made no effort to be quiet and halfway there, called out a greeting.

"Ho, there! Blue-coats!"

His greeting caused a commotion in the camp which was neatly laid out military fashion. Cavalry saddles stood lined up in front of the picketed horses, which were enclosed within a parallelogram formation of camp tents and bedrolls. As the soldiers scrambled for weapons, any semblance of order disappeared, and Noah experienced his first misgivings. All over camp, blue-clad figures and Indians wearing the distinctive red headbands identifying them as army scouts raised their rifles. Noah suddenly spotted a familiar figure—White Antelope! The Indian was jabbering something and pointing at him, but Noah was too far away to hear what he was saying.

Slowly, raising his hands to show that he carried no weapons, he walked toward the gathered men. So far so good, he thought, until a movement at the corner of his eye caught his attention. A soldier was sighting down a rifle at him, his finger already wrapped around the trigger. While the rest had apparently noticed that he was unarmed, this one seemed undeterred by the fact. Noah's heart began to pound. Sweat popped out on his brow. Yet he was afraid to duck and run; then his intentions would truly be suspect. . . . No, it was better to keep walking calmly toward them, as if he had nothing to hide.

"Brazen Injun bastard," someone muttered, ". . . comin' in here like he owns the place."

"I'll stop him!" cried the man sighting down the rifle. "I'll drop him right where he stands."

"Wait!" Noah cried.

There was an explosion, followed by a puff of white smoke. Instinctively, Noah ducked. Something whistled by his ear. Another roar of gunfire followed—this time coming from behind. His attacker flew backward, dropping his weapon as a bright crimson flower blossomed in the center of his chest, and he crumpled to the ground.

Noah dared not wait any longer. Dropping to a crouch, he turned and fled in a zigzag pattern as the Indians had taught him. As he ran, he thanked Running Horse for saving his life—and for teaching him the skills necessary to get himself out of this place in one piece. Dashing back to the stand of *mesquite,* he found his friend already astride his little mare.

Holding out Patch's reins, Running Horse cried: "I warn you this would happen—hurry! We must flee."

Noah mounted as Running Horse had taught him— by vaulting over Patch's rump to land in the middle of the saddle. Running Horse had drilled him unceasingly until he could perform the maneuver without hesitation. Assuming that none of the soldiers could mount so quickly or ride bareback, their escape should be easy. But as Noah glanced over his shoulder, he saw that someone *had* mounted a horse in the exact same manner. He rode bareback, guiding the animal with only his knees; even if Noah had not seen his face beneath the red headband, he would have known he was Indian, not white.

"White Antelope!" Running Horse bellowed. "He come after us."

The young brave set his mare to flight and Patch followed. As they raced across the valley, Noah fumbled for his rifle. He doubted the soldiers could catch them, but he was not so certain they could outrun White Antelope. His horse was a fleet-footed stallion of nearly the same size and quality as Patch. The soldiers and scouts had made camp early today, and their horses had been fed and watered. Patch and Running Horse's mare had had no refreshment and were at a disadvantage.

Noah's big paint quickly pulled ahead of Running Horse's game little mare, but White Antelope was slowly gaining on them. A shot rang out. Noah glanced over his shoulder. To his horror, he saw Running Horse slump over his mare's neck. As he watched in dismay, Running Horse tumbled off the mare and crashed to the ground. Noah brought Patch to a skidding halt, wheeled him around, and raised his own rifle. He sighted carefully. Screaming a shrill cry of blood lust, White Antelope bore down upon Running Horse's prostrate form. He did not seem to notice the danger from Noah—or else he doubted that Noah could hit him.

Noah had ample time to line up his shot and calmly crank it off. The Springfield recoiled, jamming him hard in the shoulder, but he was prepared for it and did not flinch. With great satisfaction, he watched White Antelope topple and fall. The Indian's horse veered off and kept galloping, excited by the gunfire, but White Antelope did not stir from the ground. Noah caught Running Horse's mare and quickly rode back to his fallen comrade. He slid off Patch's back in a single smooth motion and knelt in the scrubby grass beside Running Horse. His friend was still alive and managed a weak, white-lipped grin.

"You ride and shoot like Apache, Red-Hair. Must have good teacher."

"I should have guessed you would take all the credit," Noah retorted, trying not to show alarm at the seriousness of his friend's wound.

Twilight was descending, making everything gray and shadowy. But it was not too dark to see the damage done to Running Horse. It was severe. His friend had been hit in the back, on the left side of the spine. The bullet had ploughed through organs and soft tissues and exited the front. Running Horse was bleeding profusely from both back and belly. Noah wondered how he could still talk and joke after such a grievous injury.

"Go, Red-Hair," Running Horse said, pushing at his shoulder with surprising strength. "Leave me. I die soon anyhow. Better you escape and tell Geronimo what happen. If soldiers come, they shoot first, ask questions later. You no have time explain."

"I'm not leaving you." As he spoke, Noah tore a long strip of fabric from his breechcloth so he could wrap it around Running Horse's middle. "I'm taking you back to Shaman Woman. If anyone can save you, she can."

Running Horse's eyes momentarily rolled back into his head. With visible effort, he refocused them. "No, Red-Hair. I never make it. Go now before soldiers come."

Trying not to hurt his friend, Noah nonetheless worked quickly. He rolled Running Horse to one side, maneuvered the cloth under his torso, then rolled him back again and tied it snugly around his belly. Where the bullet had entered showed less damage than where it had exited. The inadequate bandage hardly served to keep Running Horse's entrails from spilling out.

Glancing up, Noah saw a distant flash of red and white on the horizon. It was a cavalry guidon, the distinctive flag the soldiers carried with them into battle, and its appearance meant he did not have much time.

"I'm sorry to hurt you, my friend, but I've got to get you up on your horse. Can you possibly ride?"

"An Apache can ride, no matter what," Running Horse muttered.

Lifting the young man in his arms, Noah rose and set Running Horse on his mare. The Indian took the reins with one hand and clasped his bleeding belly with the other. Blood streamed down his thighs and stained his mare's spotted coat. Noah felt sick; this was all his fault. Running Horse had begged him not to do it, and he had insisted. Now his friend was dying—bleeding to death while he helplessly watched.

"Let's go," he said. "It won't take us long to get away from here. The soldiers will never catch us. We'll hole up somewhere for the night, and I'll tend to your wound."

"What you do, Red-Hair?" Running Horse gasped. "Sew it shut like a squaw mends a tear in garment?"

"If I had an awl and some thread I would. Don't worry. I'll think of something." Having no idea what he could possibly do, Noah swung onto Patch's back. Juliet could help—but Juliet was far away. He had no one to rely upon but himself.

Dawn found Noah hiding in a copse of ponderosa pines in the heart of the Chiricahua mountains. The weird rock formations identified it as the area where he had first found Juliet. Running Horse called it the Land of the Standing-up Rocks. Cradling his dying friend in his arms, Noah gently turned him so the young Apache warrior could watch the sunrise. Throughout the previous night, they had ridden hard and fast, backtracking through *chaparral* and crossing rocky places by the light of a watery moon and distant stars. Remembering all that Running Horse had taught him, Noah had made it as difficult as possible for the soldiers to trail them when daylight came.

When Running Horse could no longer stay upright on his horse, Noah took him up on Patch, stopping only when he was certain he had found a place of safety. On their arrival in the mountains, he had left his friend propped against a tree trunk while he gathered handfuls of softened pine needles and dry leaves to press against Running Horse's stomach to staunch the bleeding. He could think of nothing else to do for him; Running Horse would be lucky to see the morning.

The young Indian's eyes were fastened upon the horizon where a rosy light indicated the approach of the sun. "Ancestors . . . come for me," he whispered. "Tell Half-Moon I wait for her among them."

"I'll tell her," Noah promised, dreading the task of bearing such terrible news to Running Horse's shy little wife.

"Dying better than . . . reservation," Running Horse said. "Much better. This good day . . . good place . . . to die."

Noah chewed his lower lip. It did not seem good to him. Running Horse's death was a terrible waste. Aside from his editor in Boston, Running Horse was the closest male friend Noah had ever had—someone who accepted his weaknesses as well as his strengths and gave unstintingly of himself to help Noah master new skills. Running Horse had never asked asked him how much money he made or who tailored his clothes—had never silently challenged him in the way white men so often goaded each other until a pecking order of success and importance was established.

In Running Horse's world, Noah stood at the very bottom of the Indian pecking order, yet the young Apache had not shunned or belittled him. Instead, he had treated him like a brother, judging him only by his willingness to persevere when at first he failed in whatever he was attempting.

With deep regret and an acute sense of loss, Noah thought of his friend's delightful sense of humor. Like so many of the Apaches, Running Horse enjoyed life far more than outsiders would ever suspect. Once at ease with a person, he laughed, joked, and teased with abandon. He had made Noah laugh at himself and his own stuffy attitudes. Running Horse had opened his eyes to how seriously he took everything and how much he suffered for it.

"Running Horse," Noah said. "I . . . I want to thank you. Because of you, I'm a better man. You've taught me to appreciate things I wouldn't otherwise have noticed or cared about. I see now how much I owe you. I only wish other whites could come to understand how much the Indian has to teach them."

Watching the sun emerge from behind the fantastically-shaped spires and towers, Noah fell silent. As the golden orb rose into the sky, long fingers of dazzling light crawled across the standing-up rocks, awakening

270

vibrant hues of orange, tan, and ochre. The scent of pine filled the air. It *was* a beautiful place to die, but it had taken Running Horse to point that out to Noah. Awe and reverence for the beauty of the moment filled him; he longed for Juliet to share the experience. She would have understood his conflicting emotions and eased his friend's last moments, so that Running Horse would not be watching the sunrise through a blur of pain.

"Yes, I want to thank you before you go, Running Horse," Noah softly repeated.

He glanced down at his friend. Running Horse's eyes were open, as if he, too, watched the rising sun. Suffering no longer twisted his mouth. A slight smile curved his lips. Sunlight bathed his face in a soft mellow light, and he looked contented and at peace. Noah swallowed against the sudden, fierce rush of emotion. . . . Running Horse had already left him.

Three days later, Noah found the new Apache camp located in the southwesternmost range of mountains in the territory of New Mexico. Once, he could not tell one range of mountains from the next. Now it seemed he knew them all—courtesy of the Apaches. he had debated whether or not to bring Running Horse's body home with him and had finally decided against it. He did not know how long it would take him to locate the camp, and he had nothing in which to wrap his friend's remains. Discovering a deep protective crevice in the rocks of the Chiricahuas, he had decided to leave the body there. It had taken him half a day to drag enough large stones to the site to secure it against predators.

By the time he rode into camp early in the evening, he was too exhausted to rejoice over the fact that he had made it entirely on his own, using the skills Running Horse had taught him. Normally, the Apaches would have hooted and hollered at sight of a returning

271

warrior, but they took one look at Running Horse's little mare trotting riderless behind Patch, and they knew something bad had happened. Looking neither to the left nor right, not stopping to talk to anyone, Noah rode straight to Half-Moon's wickiup. He knew precisely where it would be, because the Indians set up camp in nearly the exact same way every time they moved.

He reined in his horse and sat silently waiting while a child dashed inside the dwelling to tell Half-Moon that he had returned. She came out with a joyous look on her face—obviously expecting to see her husband. When she saw only his little mare, she lifted huge, frightened eyes to Noah's face. He did not have to utter a word of explanation. She *knew* that her husband was dead. One slender hand flew to her mouth. Noah expected her to burst out wailing, Apache-fashion, but true to her shy nature, she did not make a sound. She simply ran back into the wickiup.

Noah handed the reins of the mare to the child who stood nearby. Then he turned Patch and headed toward his own wickiup in search of Juliet. He wanted to be the one to tell her about Running Horse's death and how it had happened. Later would be time enough to seek out Geronimo and the other tribal leaders; by now, they had probably already been told of his arrival in camp without Running Horse.

Before he got to his own wickiup, Blue Bandana waylaid him. "Our brother dead?" he inquired, stepping in front of Patch.

Noah nodded. "I will come shortly to report to Geronimo and Naiche. First, I wish to see my wife."

Blue Bandana nodded. "She wait inside." He pointed to the wickiup Noah already knew was his. "Before you see her, Red-Hair should know she have vision while he gone."

"A vision? What sort of vision?"

Noah wondered if she could possibly have foreseen Running Horse's death. Somehow, it would not surprise him if she had. She was Shaman Woman, after all, and it was not uncommon for shamans to have visions. Considering the strange powers she already possessed, he ought to have expected something like this.

"She tell no one, Red-Hair, but Apaches see change in her. She look like Geronimo after he received power. Strange light in eyes, strange smile on lips. Look at people but not see them. She already have power; now have more power."

If she was walking around smiling, she could not have anticipated Running Horse's death; but then what *had* she experienced? Thanking Blue Bandana for the information, Noah rode slowly toward the wickiup.

Chapter Twenty

For reasons Juliet could not have explained, even to herself, she wanted to be alone tonight. All day long she had had a feeling that something special was going to happen. Specifically, Noah would come riding into camp. Or the warriors would find game to fill the empty cookpots. Or word would come that the U.S. Army had stopped searching for the Apaches, and all the soldiers had gone home. . . . Whatever it was, she wanted to be by herself, alone in the wickiup. Instead of joining E-clah-heh or Smiles-A-Lot or shy little Half-Moon for the evening meal, she had decided to build a fire in her own wickiup, cook, and eat alone.

Perhaps her preference for solitude stemmed from the wonderful news she had to give Noah when he finally returned. She wanted to sit by herself and savor it, for it was the answer to all her prayers, hopes, and dreams. Now, there was no reason for Noah to be jealous and angry—no reason for them to argue ever again. They would be closer than ever before; the last barrier to their happiness had been removed. Her memory had not yet returned, but she was certain now that eventually it would. She no longer cared if it did or not. When Noah heard about her latest dream, he would be as happy and relieved as she was!

Gazing into the flames of the little fire, she poked at it with a stick, then hummed a nameless little tune under her breath. She sat down cross-legged and reached for the half-finished water basket she was weaving and would eventually coat with pitch pine to waterproof it. Her work was nowhere near as fine as her teacher's—Half-Moon—but she was satisfied that her technique was steadily improving, and she looked forward to the day when her baskets would be indistinguishable from everyone else's. Well maybe not indistinguishable, but at least they would not stand out as having been woven by an amateur.

Totally engrossed in her work, she suddenly looked up to discover Noah standing in the doorway. A cry of gladness burst from her throat. Dropping the basket, she scrambled to her feet and launched herself into her husband's arms.

"Oh, No-ah! You have come home! You have found us! I am so happy; I have such wonderful news to tell you! You will be so pleased!"

In the midst of her joy, she noticed that he looked tired and sad, but she attributed it to the hardships of the journey. Besides, she knew how to make him smile again and to bring the light back into his eyes.

"What is your news, sweetheart?" He held her at arm's length and warily searched her face. "I saw Blue Bandana outside, and he told me you had a vision while I was gone."

She drew him close to the fire, examining him for any injury as she did so. He looked as strong and handsome as she remembered—except for the deep grooves on either side of his mouth and the frown wrinkling his forehead. His breechcloth was filthy, torn, and stained—probably by the juice Running Horse sometimes gave him to darken his hair and clothing and make him look more Apache.

"It was not a vision. . . . Oh, I should wait to tell you later, after you have rested, eaten, and told me all of *your* news. But I fear I will burst if I must wait much longer! No-ah, the most wonderful thing has happened; I dreamed of Jason again while you were gone.

. . . No, no, do not frown so! 'Twas a *good* dream. You will be delighted when I tell you . . ."

"Tell me what? Don't play games, Juliet. Say it and be done with it."

A little of the joy drained out of her. Faced with the same sarcasm and suspicion that had tarnished their relationship in the past, she could not maintain her enthusiasm. Surely, Noah's attitude would now change! At long last, he would understand he had nothing to fear from Jason.

"No-ah, this time when I woke up from dreaming about Jason, I remembered what he looked like. . . . No-ah, Jason's face was *your* face! *You* are the Jason of my dreams, the one I have loved in the past, the one I shall love forever—past, present, and future!"

Noah just stood there, showing no emotion except disbelief. He did not say a word. Perhaps he was too stunned to say anything and needed time for the truth to sink in. She herself had had several days to get used to the idea and to work it all out in her head, but for Noah, it must come as a shock. She could see she would have to explain it all to him.

"No-ah, do you not understand? You and I . . . we found each other long ago, somewhere in the past—Greece, I think. Somehow—I do not know how or why—we were separated. Fortunately, our love was so strong, so great and enduring, it brought us together again. It gave us back to each other. I first loved you as Jason! What *my* name was I still cannot remember. However, when I realized that *you* were—are—Jason, it all fit together. I finally understood it. . . . Think of it, No-ah! There is no need for you to be jealous ever again. I never loved another man; it was *you* I loved right from the beginning."

She paused to catch her breath. Noah was still staring at her. He looked slightly dazed. She could not help giggling at his dumbfounded expression. It did sound incredible, but once he had a chance to think about it, he would reach the same conclusions she had drawn.

"No-ah, we *must* have lived in Greece the first time. That's how I know about things like *himations* and Zeus and . . . and other things. The places in my dreams look nothing like Arizona or New Mexico. I will tell you sometime what I have seen in my dreams—what I can now remember—and then you must tell me if they resemble the Greece you have read about in your books. I am sure they will. When first you heard it, the name Jason sounded familiar to you, did it not? If you reach back into the farthest corner of your mind, can you not recall people calling you by that name? Can you not remember the sweet kisses and the love we shared in the vineyard of my parents?"

"Juliet," he growled, seizing her by the shoulders. "I was never named Jason."

"Oh, but you were! You said yourself that as a child you wanted everyone to call you Jason, after Jason of the Golden Fleece. The name *was* familiar to you. I did not at first realize the significance of that, but now . . ."

Noah cut her off, his voice rising in agitation. "I was never Jason who kissed and made love to you in another life. I have never lived in ancient Greece. And neither have you, Juliet."

"But I can remember it all so clearly now! . . . Or at least, most of it. We were childhood friends. We met secretly in the vineyards. We thought we were bethrothed, but our parents quarreled, and my father promised me to another . . ."

"Juliet!" His hands gripped more tightly, hurting her shoulders. "This is all nonsense. You are making it up."

"But I am not, No-ah! I have finally remembered. You are Jason, the man of my dreams. Somehow, after years and years . . . after centuries . . . we have found each other again. . . . The gods have restored . . ."

"Stop it!" He shook her—hard. "You're imagining all this. You're losing your sanity!"

"I am telling you the truth! Whether you want to believe it or not, 'tis reality, No-ah. . . . 'Tis not some fantasy!"

Suddenly realizing what he was doing, he released her shoulders and stood glaring at her and breathing hard. "No," he grated after a moment. "Whatever you're spouting, it's *not* reality. Reality is Running Horse bleeding to death in my arms three days ago. Reality is Half-Moon grieving alone in her wickiup. Reality is soldiers bent on hunting down the Apaches as if they were crazed animals instead of people. *That's* reality, Juliet—not this silliness you're babbling."

It took a moment for everything he was saying to penetrate. "Running Horse . . . is dead?" she questioned. Before he could answer, a wailing began outside the wickiup; a chorus of female voices rose in chant to mourn the passing of a tribal member to the spirit world.

Noah nodded. "He died defending me. I walked unarmed into a detachment of soldiers, and one of them tried to shoot me before I could even explain why I had come. Running Horse shot and killed the man. We got away but White Antelope came after us. He shot Running Horse, and I shot him. Running Horse lived until the following morning, then died in my arms somewhere in the Chiricahua mountains as we watched the sun rise."

"No, no, no . . ." Juliet murmured, horrified by this string of tragedies. Her own problems—her argument with Noah—paled in comparison. No wonder Noah did not want to listen or believe; it was not the right time. He was grieving for a dead friend, and she had been too wrapped up in her own good news to even notice his suffering.

"I must go and comfort Half-Moon. The girl will need me. I am so sorry for her."

"What can you or anyone say to her?" Noah's face

was stark with bitterness. "What comfort can you possibly give? Running Horse is dead. He's gone for good."

Juliet straightened her shoulders and dared to confront him eye to eye. "Perhaps . . . perhaps not. If their love is strong enough, they will meet again in another time and place. I will tell her that. Unlike you, she will believe it and be comforted."

"They won't meet anywhere. You'll be telling her lies . . . *lies,* Juliet. It's all a pack of lies."

"The Apaches themselves believe in another life," she gently pointed out, trying to be patient with him. "That's why they put tools, weapons, and food for a long journey alongside their dead."

"But they don't believe that people live life over and over, meeting and falling in love with the same persons!"

"I do not claim that we have lived *many* lives, Noah, although 'tis certainly possible. I claim only that we have loved once before, became separated, and have somehow been reunited. I still do not know where I was before I met you on that ledge."

"Maybe you were in Greece!" he snapped sarcastically. "Maybe you came directly here from there. You were dressed in a nightgown that looked Grecian to me; why would you hesitate to believe that if you can accept all the rest of this nonsense?"

Juliet thought about the possibility for a moment and decided she could not rule it out. "Perhaps I did come from Greece. Something . . . bad had happened. I do remember feeling that. And something—or someone—rescued me."

Noah's eyes darkened. "I won't stand here any longer listening to this foolishness. I won't allow you to dwell on it. Don't mention it again, Juliet. It isn't healthy. It isn't sane. When you talk like this, it makes me wonder if you really have lost your sanity."

"I am as sane as you are, No-ah. And we most

certainly *will* discuss this again. Now, if you will excuse me, I must go and comfort Half-Moon."

He did not try to stop her. He did not even look at her. He stood in the middle of the wickiup, clenching and unclenching his fists. His expression brought a chill to her heart that had nothing to do with her grief for Running Horse or the sorrow she felt for Half-Moon and all the rest of the Apaches. Shivering with grim foreboding, she hurried from the wickiup and walked quickly through the camp.

Noah would not permit Juliet to mention the matter again. He thought that if he refused to discuss her outrageous theories, she would give them up and eventually realize how dangerous they were. Losing one's memory was one thing; inventing wild stories and actually believing them quite another. He hated to admit it, but Juliet was teetering on the brink of madness. The signs were all there. Almost overnight, she became morose and withdrawn, no longer laughed and rarely smiled. . . . This could be attributed to Running Horse's death and the increasing desperation of the Apaches, but it could also be a symptom of withdrawal from reality. Noah was convinced it was the latter.

Several times in the days that followed, he awoke during the night to find Juliet drenched in perspiration and muttering in her sleep. Later, she would deny that she had been dreaming—or else she would try to re-open the discussion of Jason. Once, she followed him out of the wickiup, again insisting that both of them together had somehow been plucked from the past and thrust into the present to save their lives from some threat or danger. He may have forgotten it all, but she had retained these "ancient memories," as she called them, in the form of her dreams, and he should take them seriously.

"No!" he had shouted. "I won't listen to this nonsense. And if you know what's good for you, you'll do your best to forget it, too!"

"I do not wish to forget it! I wish to remember it even better than I do now! I want to remember *all* of it. Oh, please, No-ah, listen to me. We were going to be married. Our parents had finally given their consent. The wedding was all planned . . . but something happened to stop it. Something terrible. There is *still* some threat, some danger . . . I can feel it hovering over us."

In response, he had only walked faster, pushing away her hand as she sought to stop him. He could not deal with this. He was losing her to madness, and it terrified him. Something had to be done, but he could not fathom what—until the fateful evening when once again he quarreled with Geronimo.

More soldiers had been spotted in the foothills. More Indian scouts than ever before were combing the mountains in search of them. The waterholes were all being watched, heliographs were flashing signals back and forth from mountain to mountain, and every Apache in camp sensed that time was running out . . . yet Geronimo would not surrender or even discuss it.

Noah had made it a personal campaign to bring up the subject of surrender at every opportunity, and on this particular night, with the icy chill of autumn in the air and the wind moaning around the wickiups, he joined Geronimo, Naiche, and several others around a campfire in Geronimo's tipi. There, he calmly asked how the Apache chief intended to feed his people through the winter. Geronimo answered, and though it wasn't really necessary, and everyone knew it, Blue Bandana translated—a less than subtle reminder that Noah was white, not Apache.

"We live as we have always lived—we hunt. We raid. If starvation come, we slaughter and eat war ponies."

"That is not how you have lived in the past," Noah disputed. "In the past, you had caches of food hidden away—*mescal* from the *agave* plant, and yucca, dried berry cakes and piñon nuts. You had arrowhead and wild onions, dried elk, antelope, and deer meat. You have none of that now; there has been little time to gather these foods, and with so many people invading the mountains looking for you, the game has gone elsewhere."

"If not find game here, Apaches move. Go other mountains," came the response.

"Your people will not last the winter. You are making a grave mistake, Geronimo. I have told you this before, and I will say it again: Surrender is the only way to protect your people's future. You must think of the young ones. They deserve a chance at life. Remember the children who will suffer the most. Set aside your own disappointments, old man. Surrender and return to the reservation."

While he was speaking, Geronimo sat motionless. His small dark eyes gazed off into space. His round face bore an expression of sadness too deep to articulate. The grooves near his mouth were as deep as canyons. Slowly, he shook his head, then said a few words, which Blue Bandana hastened to translate before Noah could open his mouth.

"If you not happy among Apaches, Red-Hair, it time you leave. Take Shaman Woman and go. This not your battle. Not your fight. Why you stay?"

"I have stayed because I thought I could help you. I wanted to live your life, learn your ways, and write down your history—especially the story of the great Geronimo. When I leave here, I will take back all I have learned and try to convince the whites to listen to me. I will tell them you are a good people who have been treated unfairly and driven to murder and theft. I will do everything I can to persuade them that you, too, want peace."

"Freedom," Geronimo said clearly in English, before Blue Bandana could translate Noah's speech. "Want freedom most."

His voice vibrated with deep passion, surprising Noah not only because he had spoken in English but also because of his simple eloquence. Noah had never known how much English Geronimo understood. He obviously knew many Mexican words, but feigned ignorance of Noah's language. This time, no translations had been needed. In his zeal, Geronimo had abandoned the pretense of ignorance.

"Book," Geronimo then said, looking him straight in the eye. "Where book?" He made writing motions.

Blue Bandana touched Noah's arm. "He want see book you write in."

"I'll fetch it," Noah said, rising. Normally, he carried the journal with him when he sat at the campfire. However, since Running Horse's death, he had not been able to bring himself to describe that event or any others. The passion to record Apache life had abruptly left him. No longer did he even wish to write Geronimo's biography. The old Apache's story could only end in tragedy too painful to recount.

Going into the wickiup, Noah said nothing to Juliet who was seated on a mat diligently working at her weaving. Since their estrangement over the matter of Jason, they had spoken little to each other and slept apart, she on the sleeping rug and he on a mat on the other side of the dwelling. But he was very much aware of her presence; day or night, he knew where she was and what she was doing. He had only to glimpse the pale cloud of hair encircling her head and shoulders, and something leaped in the pit of his belly.

He had only to feel the warmth of her clear-eyed gaze, and he wanted to take her in his arms and beg her forgiveness—promise her she could believe anything she wanted—so long as she did not stop loving him. He averted his gaze as he saw her glance up hopefully and smile when she saw him. The smile would soon fade; it always did when he did not return it. He gave her a covert glance as she resumed working, this time with a slump to her shoulders.

He hated himself for being so cruel, but he could not let her weaken him with her woman's wiles, so that he meekly accepted her convoluted logic for the sake of maintaining peace. Before he would touch her again, she must admit she was confused and in need of help. But it was hard—so hard! Their estrangement was pure torture. Snatching up the leather case containing his journal, he stomped from the lodge.

Walking back to the tipi, the idea came to him: Geronimo was right. This was *not* his battle. He had done all he could, and no one would listen. Did he really want to spend the winter starving in the mountains? Day by day, Juliet was growing thinner, her strength sapped by her inner battles. She was so fragile looking he sometimes feared her bones might suddenly break. Her delicate skin was almost transparent.

If they left now, before winter came, he could reach Tucson and get help for her before the arrival of the cold heavy rains that turned to snow in the highest reaches of the mountain passes. That was what she needed—professional medical help, a *real* doctor to examine her and suggest treatment to stop the deterioration he was presently witnessing. He wondered why he had not thought of it before. There was nothing to hold him here now; Geronimo had no intention of changing his mind about surrendering. It had been a waste of time for him to think he could get the old man to accept the idea.

Entering the tipi, Noah removed the journal from its case and handed it to Geronimo. The old man took the leather-bound volume in his gnarled hands and gently stroked the cover. He opened it and studied the stiff, yellowing pages as if he could actually read them. Noah had tried to keep the book dry and free from mildew, but he had not been able to protect it from the hot desert sun and the dryness. It was not that old, but it looked old. Geronimo fingered the pages almost reverently, as if they contained magic. When he spoke, his voice was low and soft.

285

"He ask if his story told here," Blue Bandana said.

"Some of it. Not all. He would never tell me very much."

"You not true Apache. Your heart not Apache," Blue Bandana accused. "That why he not tell you."

"Very few Indians I know can read and write. It would be hard to find a true Apache who could set down Geronimo's story for posterity," Noah countered. "He should have talked to me while he had the chance. If I leave here, his story will die with him. It will never be told from his point of view."

"Geronimo say maybe one day when he old, old man, he tell story to Red-Hair."

"He is already old. If he insists on continuing to fight white men, he will die before he ever has a chance to tell his story. The soldiers will see to that. They'll shoot him on sight."

Geronimo suddenly shook his head and muttered angrily.

"He say white man's bullets no can kill him. He possess special power. Spirits tell him long ago he not die from white man's bullets. . . . This true, Red-Hair. If not for power, Geronimo be dead many times. Power protect him. Usen watch over him. Guide his footsteps as he leads his people."

Noah had already heard the tale—how Geronimo had seen a vision in his youth and been told he was invincible and could not be killed. In his own way, the old man was as mad as Juliet. Both embraced ridiculous ideas and staunchly refused to accept reality.

"So Geronimo will be the last Apache left alive, is that it? Everyone else will die, and he alone will live. Is that what he wants—to be the last of his race? The rest of you aren't immune to bullets. Like Running Horse, you have no special powers. How many more of your finest young men must die before he will listen? How many more of your women and children must be enslaved by the Mexicans?" Noah reached over and took the journal from Geronimo's hands.

"Tell Geronimo I will write no more of his story in these pages. It is too sad to tell, and I have no wish to witness the tragic ending. If you do not starve this winter, you will die in the spring when the soldiers and scouts return to the mountains. I cannot be a part of this madness any longer. I am done being an Apache and done with coddling insanity. I will leave and take Shaman Woman—Juliet—with me. In the morning, we will go."

"So be it," Blue Bandana grunted. "I tell him."

Chapter Twenty-one

Nothing Noah could have said would have surprised or dismayed Juliet more thoroughly than his greeting that morning as she awakened to find him already up and about: "Juliet, pack our things. We're leaving today for Tucson."

"What?" She sat up and brushed the hair back from her eyes. "What did you say, No-ah?"

She was still grappling with the remnants of her dream—which had *not* been about Jason, this time, but about the Apaches. The Indians had been walking single file up a lonely windswept mountain. She had been calling out to them, asking where they were going, and they would not answer. They would not even look back. They simply ignored her and trudged up the rocky slope. Only Smiles-A-Lot had finally stopped, turned, and waved to her. It was then Juliet saw the tears spilling down her friend's cheeks.

Smiles-A-Lot had mouthed something to her—the Apache word for goodbye.

"I said we're leaving today for Tucson, Juliet. I'm going to get Patch, and I'll return here shortly. I would appreciate it if you were ready by then."

The horror of it struck her full force. He had actually said they were leaving the Apaches and going to Tucson. She scrambled to her feet. "Why, No-ah? Why today? Why must we leave at all? Surely, you do not have the whole of Geronimo's story—and the Apaches do not want us to leave. I am their Shaman Woman. What will they do if someone falls ill?"

"They will do exactly as they have always done—rely on the cures they already know. Geronimo will chant sacred songs over them and give them herbs. They'll survive somehow. It won't be sickness or accidents that kill them anyway. It'll be U.S. soldiers or Arizona ranchers."

He started to leave but she ran after him and grabbed his arm. This time, she would not let him walk away in the middle of an argument; for once, she would stand up to Noah and insist that he respect her feelings.

"No-ah, I do not wish to go! My home is with the Apaches. 'Tis the only home I can remember. These are my people. I will not desert them in their hour of need."

At that, he stopped. His dark eyes burned with a feverish intensity as he regarded her somberly. "And what about me, Juliet? Where do I figure into your list of priorities? Are your feelings for the Apaches stronger than they are for me?"

"No-ah, my feelings for you are strongest of all! You are my husband—the man I love above all others. Would you go off and leave me? Is this the sad end to which we have come?"

"You tell me, Juliet. I'm going to Tucson. Geronimo refuses to listen to me. Therefore, there's no reason to stay. To be truthful, Geronimo's not the only reason I want to go; I think it's time to get out of here. You need help, the kind I'm powerless to give you. You need a real doctor. That's the only way you'll ever regain your memory and realize you haven't been plucked out of antiquity and deposited on a ledge in the Southwest a couple thousand years later."

"No-ah," she said calmly, though her heart was beating like an Apache war drum. "Just because you cannot accept what I have told you does not mean it never happened. All life is a mystery. We poor mortals can rarely understand it. We know not why we live or why we die. Life and death are mysteries. Healing is a mystery. You have witnessed what I can do; therefore, you no longer deny it. In time, you will no longer deny this. Taking me to a doctor will not convince me that my dreams are foolish. . . . I know in my heart that they are *real*. They actually happened. In time, the rest of what I do not know will be revealed. We must be patient and it will happen."

With every word she spoke, Noah's face grew grimer, his eyes colder. He had shut her out and she could not reach him. Neither could she let it rest. "Please, No-ah. Let us remain here. Do not insist that we return to Tucson. If you truly love me, let me stay among my beloved Apaches."

"What about your love for me, Juliet? If you truly love me, you will do as I ask. You will pack our things and accompany me to Tucson. You will let me get help for you." He picked up her hand and thrust it under her nose. "Look at your skin, Juliet. Look at your hair." He grabbed a handful of the flyaway mass and held it out in front of her. "You're a white woman. I'm a white man. We don't belong among the Apaches. We never did. Whatever happens to them will be their choice. It need not be *our* choice. I'm leaving, and I want you to come with me. If you refuse, I'm going anyway. Make up your mind; which is it going to be—me or the Apaches?"

She covered her face with her hands. "No-ah, 'tis too cruel to force me to choose between you! Why can I not have you both?"

"Because I'm not an Apache, damn it, and I refuse to die like one! There's nothing more we can do for them here. We can help them far better in Tucson. In Tucson, we can talk to other whites and try and convince them that imprisoning the Apaches, taking their land, and treating them worse than animals is wrong."

"Do you honestly think people will listen, No-ah?"

In the midst of her despair, Juliet felt the first glimmer of hope. It would not be so bad to leave her friends and go to Tucson if she and Noah could actually change attitudes among the whites and help the Apaches.

"I won't lie to you, Juliet. They probably won't—at least not at first. But we can try. Staying here will accomplish nothing except getting us killed or making certain we starve to death this winter. . . . Look at it this way: If we're gone, there will be fewer mouths to feed and one less horse competing for sparse winter forage. Leaving the Apaches now will be doing them a favor."

She did not want to accept his logic, but Noah was beginning to make sense. Food supplies *were* severely limited. The warriors could not hunt because they were always either scouting the soldiers or fleeing from them. She had heard the women talking about a possible return to the Sierra Madre; if they did return, how would everyone survive the harsh winter of the high country? Her skills could not save the Apaches from starving. She could not call the animals to her to be killed for food. Even if it were possible, it would be a terrible misuse of her powers which were meant only to heal and bring relief from pain.

"All right, No-ah," she finally conceded. "I will pack our things. But then you must give me time to say goodbye."

"A short time," he agreed. "Do it quickly, Juliet. The longer you take, the more it will hurt."

She wondered if he had any idea how much it already hurt. Her home was among the Apaches. With them, she felt safe and comfortable. They were her family. She knew no one in Tucson. Could not even imagine what it would be like there. Noah might as well be taking her to a foreign country—or to the moon. She had agreed to go, but she could not help resenting the fact that he had forced her, making it all but impossible for her to stay.

* * *

They left the camp late that morning, with Blue
Bandana for company. Geronimo had insisted that
Blue Bandana lead them through the immediate area
where the cavalry was most likely to spot them. Blue
Bandana was to accompany them to a place from
which directions to their destination would be easy to
follow. They took Patch and another horse which
Juliet rode, but left most of their belongings behind.
Juliet had decided to return nearly everything she and
Noah had been given. It was easier to say goodbye
that way, and they would be less heavy-laden on their
journey. Besides, as Noah had pointed out, Indian
things would not be needed in Tucson.

Juliet proudly wore her Apache clothing, but Noah
donned white man's garments. His boots had been
returned to him, and also his trousers, but she did not
recognize his yellow shirt. He had also cut his hair and
now more closely resembled the man she had first met
than the Apache warrior he had become.

Juliet, Noah, and Blue Bandana rode silently; it was
too dangerous to speak or make noise. Juliet welcomed the quiet, for she had little to say. Explaining to
E-clah-heh, Smiles-A-Lot, and Half-Moon why she
was leaving had been agony. She feared she might
never see them again. It was the Indian way to show
no emotion at partings, and no one had wept except
Juliet herself. Her resentment against Noah for causing this suffering bloomed in her heart like some insidi-
ous weed. She seriously considered riding all the way
to Tucson without speaking to him—not that he
would notice, preoccupied as he was with his own
thoughts.

They rode all that day and part of the night, keeping
a close watch for soldiers and being careful to obliterate their trail. They spotted soldiers only once; fortunately, the blue-coats were far away and did not see
them. Blue Bandana then backtracked a short distance

and brushed out their hoof tracks, though the surface was so hard and stony that Juliet herself could not see them. When at last they stopped, she was half dozing in the saddle. Noah lifted her down, wrapped her in a blanket, and propped her against a tree trunk. His gentleness was the last thing she remembered.

When she awoke next morning, Blue Bandana was gone.

"When did he leave?" she demanded of Noah who was going through the packs searching for food.

"While we slept, I assume. He explained last night where to go from here so he probably figured he had done his duty and was free to leave."

"I did not get to tell him farewell," Juliet complained, blaming this, too, on Noah. "I would have liked to thank him for all he did for us while we lived among the Apaches."

"I'm sure he knows how you feel, Juliet. It's better he left while it was still dark. We're only a day's ride from Fort Bowie. From here on out, the region will be crawling with soldiers. He'd have been placing himself in great danger by staying with us any longer."

"This fort. . . . We are not going there, are we? I thought our destination was Tucson."

"It is, but I think it best to stop at Fort Bowie. From there, the soldiers will escort us to Tucson. Considering that my last encounter with the ranchers of this area was less than cordial, I'd feel much safer with a military escort, especially when I've got you to look after. Aside from irate ranchers, we could possibly encounter some of the scum who ride these hills hoping to take a few last Apache scalps. In Mexico, bounty hunters can still get a hundred dollars for a warrior's, fifty for a woman's, and twenty-five for a child's. I wouldn't put it past animals like that to kill us both and dye our hair just to get their filthy hands on some of that money—and what they'd do with you before they killed you . . ."

There was no need for him to finish the sentence;

despite the heat of the morning sun, a chill rippled down Juliet's spine. She nervously chewed her lower lip. If Noah himself feared the whites and the Mexicans, they must be far more savage than the Apaches. And she doubted that the soldiers would be any better. They were the very creatures Geronimo's band had spent months outrunning—the ones responsible for so many needless deaths.

"What will you tell them, No-ah? How will you explain where we have been?"

"I'm a reporter, Juliet. Trust me to come up with a good story. When we get to Fort Bowie, all you have to do is close your mouth and let me do the talking."

"But what if they shoot us before we can explain? I am still dressed like an Apache."

He laughed, the first time she had heard him laugh in a long, long time. "Sweetheart, with that cloud of pale hair and those big golden eyes you look more like an angel than an Apache. No one in his right mind could possibly mistake you for an Indian."

Her face grew hot. Of course, she ought to have remembered about her hair and coloring, but she had truly come to think of herself as Apache and forgotten. Only rarely did she concern herself with her appearance anyway; E-clah-heh possessed a mirror—a looking glass, she called it—but Juliet had gazed into it only once. Aside from taking comfort in the fact that her features were familiar, she had paid little heed to how she looked. As long as Noah found her beautiful, that was all that mattered. . . . Unfortunately, he had not seemed to notice or remark upon her beauty for quite some time now.

Her feelings of insecurity compounded, and she began to wonder if he no longer thought her beautiful. She had blamed their recent lack of intimacy on his inability to accept her dreams as truth—had been counting on the fact that his desire would eventually conquer his fears and uncertainties. . . . But what if he no longer desired her? What if his passion had irrevocably cooled? These days, he treated her with polite disdain. All their closeness had evaporated like a rain puddle under the desert sun. The past continued to loom between them like an unbreachable wall, but perhaps it was not the only thing separating them. Noah might be falling out of love with her and regretting his hastily-made promises. Now that he was returning to *his* people, he might be realizing just how different they really were.

How bitterly ironic if their love had survived ages only to die when they were finally reunited!

"Here," Noah said, handing her several strips of dried antelope meat. "Eat, then we'll be on our way."

She took the food but only nibbled at it. She was too nervous to be hungry—and too upset. If Noah had ceased to care for her, she did not know what she would do. Fort Bowie and Tucson were full of strangers, both places alien to her. She had no way of knowing how much—if anything—of the white manner of living she would remember once she got there. Maybe not much. Without Noah, how would she manage? Without his love, how would she survive? Somehow, she must reawaken his faltering passion and remind him of all they meant to each other!

She thought about it all day while they rode through the mountains en route to Fort Bowie. One part of the range looked familiar; they skirted a place of fantastic rock formations that reminded her of the area where she and Noah had met on the ledge. As they proceeded farther north, she ceased to be distracted by the terrain.

All day she agonized over her problems and by nightfall had a possible solution. By then they were almost to the fort, and she realized she would have to wait to see where they would spend the night—and what privacy they would have—before she could put her plan into motion. Amazingly, they had met no soldiers, not even when they entered a long narrow valley called Apache Pass, the main route through the mountains from east to west, which Noah claimed was used by all the settlers and wagon trains headed toward Tucson on their way to California.

A spring issued from a ravine that emptied into a canyon in the pass. It was the only water in the otherwise arid region, so they stopped to drink and water the horses before proceeding to the fort itself, which stood on a steep hillside overlooking the pass.

"Noah, wait!" she called out softly to him, as he started to remount Patch.

He reined in the stallion. "What is it?"

The sun had set, but a full moon was rising. Against the dark purple sky framing the mountains, Noah's broad shoulders were clearly silhouetted.

"No-ah, I am afraid. Please . . . could we not spend the night out here and enter the fort in the morning?"

He rode closer to where she stood holding her horse's reins. Eyeing her impatiently, he answered: "I suppose we could, but what's the point? I was looking forward to the comforts of civilization—a hot meal and something softer than the ground to sleep on tonight."

"I . . . I would prefer to sleep out under the stars one more night," she faltered. "I would like to be alone with you tonight, No-ah."

He sat and studied her for a moment, apparently trying to guess what she was thinking. Then he gave a long sigh. "Juliet, we have had plenty of time to be alone before we got here. Back at the Indian camp, we had our own wickiup and as much privacy as anyone could want or need. Now what's this all about?"

Tears stung her eyes. He was not going to make this easy. Instead, he would pretend he did not know what she wanted—just as he had been pretending it since Running Horse's death. She saw now that he had been avoiding looking at her, talking to her, touching her. . . . Not only had they not made love, they had not *communicated* since then—not since she had told him he was Jason. If she rode into Fort Bowie with him

297

now, she would lose him forever. Among strangers, the distance that separated them would only widen and eventually he would leave her for good.

There was only one way to test his feelings—to see if she could still reach him. Wordlessly, she led her horse toward a sheltered area behind a patch of willows growing alongside the spring.

"Damn it, Juliet, where are you going?"

He followed her on Patch, his tone furious at her defiance. Discounting any concern for her thoughts and feelings, he wanted and expected complete obedience and docility. Obviously, he considered himself her lord and master, and thought he knew what was best for her and what was not. . . . Well, she was tired of having him treat her as if she had no mind or will of her own. She was not ill or insane. She was his wife but not his property. From now on, she would demand that he respect her individuality and stop ordering her about like a lowly slave.

Tethering her horse to a branch, she calmly removed its saddle. "I am passing the night here, No-ah. You may do as you wish. Stay or go."

"Juliet, this is ridiculous and you damn well know it! . . . Dear God, *now* what are you doing?"

Having set the saddle on the ground, she was casually removing her own clothing. She said nothing for a moment while she quickly discarded her skirt, then paused in the act of tugging off her blouse. "I am undressing, No-ah. That is what I am doing."

"Out here?" He maneuvered Patch so that the stallion stood between her and the fort, though it was too far away and too dark for anyone to see them if they did happen to glance in their direction.

"Once you did not object if I removed all my garments beneath the night sky."

"We're right near the fort! Anybody could come along and see you."

Dispensing with her blouse, she kicked off her moccasins. "No one has seen us yet, or some sort of alarm would have been sounded."

Completely nude now, she untied her hair and fluffed it around her shoulders, then glanced boldly up at him. "Do I no longer arouse you, No-ah? Does the sight of my naked body bore you? Is that why you object so strenuously?"

She straightened her back and shoulders, thrusting her breasts forward for his inspection. It had grown quite dark, but she was certain he could see her. Light from the rising moon filtered through the tree branches, and the stars were already shining, silvering the mountains all around them.

"You know damn well you don't bore me. . . . Why are you doing this, Juliet?"

"I am trying to discover if you still love and want me, No-ah. I am not the victim of some terrible disease who will infect you if you come too close. Lately you have rejected me and treated me cruelly. I am your wife. I have needs and hungers only you can satisfy. Yet you seem determined to starve me—to punish me for things I cannot help. I grow weary of it. I want it to be as it was before for us. . . . I want to be loved and kissed beneath the stars, to soar with you and become one. I want that little piece of heaven only you can give me. . . . I will not set foot inside that fort while this distance still separates us, No-ah. This may be our last opportunity to be completely alone. In the fort, we may have no privacy. Come to me, No-ah. . . . Make love to me. Prove to me that nothing—ever—can destroy our love for each other. Our love is all we have. 'Tis all we need. Come to me, and I will make your doubts disappear."

For a moment, she thought he was going to refuse. Then he rode closer, bent down, hooked an arm around her naked waist, and lifted her to sit sideways on the horse in front of him. "Not here, Juliet. I will not take you so close to the fort. We'll ride a bit farther away from it and find a more secluded spot."

He kneed Patch into a rocking canter. Trusting him to watch where they were going, she locked one arm around his waist and laid her head against his chest. He had not refused her. In itself, this was a small victory, but he had not sounded too happy about the invitation either. She would *make* him happy. She would make tonight a night he would always remember.

Chapter Twenty-two

Noah took Juliet up a steep mountain facing away from the location of the fort. The typical *chaparral* of the region covered the hillside: beargrass, *agave,* yucca, *manzanita,* and mountain mahogany. By now, he knew them all. He rode higher still, to the elevations at which oak, piñon pine, and juniper could be found. There, the sandy earth offered softer, barer patches of ground where a blanket could be spread beneath the stars.

When he found a good spot, he reined in, dismounted, and lifted Juliet from the saddle. Gazing up at him, her eyes reflecting the moonlight, she slid provocatively down the front of him. He did not need the blatent invitation; desire had been raging in him from the moment she had first begun to remove her clothing. Having her naked in his arms for the short ride had fueled his lust to dizzying heights.

Desire warred with shame as he realized just how cruel he had been to her and how lonely she must have been to go to such extremes to get his attention. How could he explain his own feelings of fear and anxiety? At times, he felt choked with fear—was sure he had already lost her. His terror had created an enormous gulf between them. Mentally and emotionally, he had been preparing himself to live without her. So many times he had wanted to take her in his arms and simply hold her, but had ruthlessly quelled those feelings and fought down desire as well. His once iron-clad nerves were as fragile as glass, as easily shattered and broken. If he succumbed to his feelings, he suspected that he, too, would shatter and break.

As long as he did not touch Juliet, did not make love to her, did not spend too much time in her company, he could live with the terror and even convince himself that all would be well. All he needed to do was get her to a doctor. A doctor could fix everything. What he had not foreseen was that Juliet would be less than content with the crumbs he could spare her. He had not expected such sweet defiance. Once again, she had found a means to breach his defenses. He could not say no to her. She had stormed his citadel. He *had* to have her, to love her, to tell her with his body what he found so difficult to say with words.

She gave him no time to spread out a blanket. No sooner had her feet touched the ground when she pressed herself against him and wound her arms about his neck.

"No-ah, please love me," she whispered. "I cannot bear this coldness that has grown between us. I will die if you do not love me."

If ever a woman had said that to him in his previous life, he would have thought it amusing, melodramatic, and maudlin; he would have felt contempt for her. But this was Juliet, and he knew precisely how she felt. She was the air he needed to breathe, the water he thirsted to drink, the sun that warmed the cold wastes of his heart and made flowers bloom there. He could well understand how a person could wither and die from a lack of love. He himself had been withering and dying.

"Sweetheart," he murmured, stroking her silky hair. "Forgive me once again for hurting you. I never meant to cause you pain. Somehow I can't seem to avoid it."

She touched his jaw, her fingers soft as rose petals. "Why did you do it, No-ah? Is it that you no longer love me?"

"I *do* love you, Juliet. More than I can say. That's

not the problem. It's your dreams and beliefs . . . the strange theories you insist upon expounding. They're going to destroy us. You've got to give them up. They aren't real. If you cling to them, it will mean the end of us."

Her eyes clouded, and she pushed slightly back from him. "I knew it was that. You have held yourself apart from me ever since I told you that you are the Jason of my dreams."

"I'm *not* Jason. You've got to accept that fact. We've never lived other lives before this. Never loved each other in some ancient past. If we did, why have I forgotten it? Why are you the only one to remember?"

Tears glinted in her beautiful eyes. "I cannot answer your questions, No-ah. I do not think I am supposed to remember the past either, but somehow I do. Perhaps something went wrong, and my transition to the present was not completed. I still feel the threat of some evil hovering over us . . ."

Noah's hands tightened on her shoulders. He had to remind himself not to squeeze too hard. Whenever they discussed this subject, violent impulses swept through him like hurricane winds bent on destroying them both. "The only threat hovering over us is your illness, Juliet. It's not a physical malady but an illness of the mind. That's why I'm taking you to a doctor. You're angry because I made you leave the Apaches, but I'm only doing it for your own good. You've got to believe that and trust me. When we get to Tucson, you may find it easier to remember things. Among our own people, more of the *real* past will surely come back to you. Hell, you might remember how to read and what your name is!"

Slowly, she shook her head. Tears tracked silvery paths down her pale cheeks. "I do not think so, No-ah. I have never lived in Tucson or anywhere else in Arizona. 'Tis not illness or madness that drives me to say these things; 'tis a deep inner knowledge that surfaces only in my dreams. You can force me to go with you to Tucson, but that does not mean I will remember how to read and write your language."

"Not *my* language, it's also *your* language."

"No . . . 'tis not. I was given the ability to speak and understand English when I came here, but English is not my native tongue. That is why I cannot read it."

Fear clawed at his insides; he had to convince her. If he did not, he would lose her. The madness would claim her, leaving only the shell of the woman he loved. "I'll *prove* to you that you're wrong, Juliet. When we get to Tuscon, I'll find something printed in Greek. You won't be able to read Greek either. You won't understand it. Then you'll realize you've made up everything. It's all a product of an overactive imagination. You had to have suffered a head injury, and it's the root of all your problems."

"They are not problems, No-ah—except when they separate us and drive us apart. Will you let your doubts poison your heart against me?" She took his hand and placed it on her breast. Beneath his palm, her skin was soft as satin. "Or will you love me as we were meant to love? Time has not been able to destroy us; we found each other in spite of everything that's happened—things neither of us can remember. Do not let your doubts and fears bring ruination upon us now!"

It wasn't his doubts and fear but her stubborness that would prove their undoing, Noah thought. If she refused to fight her illness, he would. He would battle it with every weapon at his command—but he would not make her miserable in the process. Somehow, he must conquer his own demons while at the same time conquering hers.

"You're right about one thing anyway," he conceded. "It does no good to keep apart from you. I've tried it, and it doesn't work. I can't ignore what I feel for you, Juliet. Ignoring you doesn't make my lot in life any easier; it doesn't banish the fear or pain. I still need you and want you. . . . Oh, God, how I want you!"

He pulled her to him and slanted his mouth over hers. She returned his kiss as if kissing were the only thing in the world that mattered. . . . Perhaps, it was. In their lovemaking, he could forget everything but the burning obsession to make her his and to elicit her soft moaning cries of pleasure. Lovemaking was a journey to another world—a place of safety, joy, and fulfillment. The trip there was as wonderful as the place itself, and he centered all his efforts and concentration on making it exquisitely enjoyable for both of them.

Somehow, the blanket was spread out, his clothing discarded, and Patch had obligingly wandered off a short distance to munch the dry grass. Then there was only himself and Juliet, naked beneath the moon, loving each other as nature and destiny intended. Noah took endless time to awaken Juliet's senses. He kissed and caressed every quivering inch of her. Only when she lay open and welcoming—panting with need—did he succumb to his own frantic desire. Outstretched upon her, heart thundering, he thrust into her, over and over, exploding finally, and pouring his essence, his love, and all that he was, ever had been, and ever would be, into her deepest recesses.

He had no more to give her. Had given all he had. Pray God, it would be enough to save her from the black abyss into which she would surely tumble if he did not stop her!

The stars, the moon, and Noah . . . I fell asleep dreaming of them, but then the dream changed and shifted. The chaparral *dissolved. The piñon pines and juniper disappeared. There were olive trees now, with twisted, gnarled trunks and silvery leaves. A white bull stood motionless among them. Red-eyed and majestic, he snorted, stamped, and swung his silver-tipped horns in my direction.*

You think you have escaped me. Hera has come to your aid. Foolish child. You can never escape; I am all-powerful.

"Who are you?" I cried. "What is your true name?"

I am known by many names. In every time and place, people have found a name for me. The names change. The people change. But I remain the same. Call me whatever you will. I am what you fear—and desire—the most. I am your best instincts gone awry, the temptations which hound you through the ages and across the centuries. I am the fallen archangel, bearer of light and darkness. . . . I am all that is beautiful and all that is ugly.

"There is no beauty in you! You are totally evil and wicked."

Perhaps I am. Primitive creatures would tend to think so. Pure goodness and evil is all you can understand. But I tell you that between the two are many shadings. I am more like you than you might guess. I am both good and evil. Neither all one nor all the other.

"Then there must be someone above you. I thought you were the highest, the most powerful of all."

I am! Of course, I am! I am the greatest, the highest, the grandest—I can hurl thunderbolts. I can change my form into whatever I wish. My powers exceed your imagination . . . and you cannot escape me no matter how hard you try.

I struggled to understand. Could there be someone greater—a being more like Usen of the Apaches, or the God that Noah mentioned when he cursed and swore? If there was someone greater, all was not lost. I could dare to hope that I might yet escape.

I will claim you soon. I will come for you when you least expect it. You cannot deny me. Do not even think of it. When I call you, you will come. And you will come willingly.

"I am Noah's—Jason's! I belong to him. I will never leave him."

We shall see which proves the stronger—your puny love or my great desire. Poor, pitiful human. 'Tis the eternal battle: love against darkness, evil, and pride. Love against lust. You cannot win. You will never win. In the end, I will have you.

"Noah! Noah, help me! Noah, where are you?"

I ran screaming from the olive grove and fled into the mountains. I ran until my sides ached, and my lungs were afire. Tripping and falling among the rocks, I scraped my hands and knees. Worse than the physical pain were the lacerations on my soul. Then someone was shaking me. Lifting and holding me.

"Juliet, honey, wake up. It's only a dream. . . . Juliet, wake up."

Juliet clutched at Noah's solid form and opened her eyes. The sun was shining. Noah bent over her, his hair gilded by the sunlight. The air was already hot, but she began to shake. Unable to stop herself, she trembled and quaked in his embrace. Sobs burst from her throat. Clinging to Noah, she wept on his shoulder.

"It's all right," he crooned. "It was only a dream. You're safe."

"This . . . is still Arizona?"

"You *know* it is, Juliet." Desperation tinged Noah's voice. He sounded almost angry. "Damn it, you know this is Arizona, and we're near Fort Bowie. We're going to go first to the fort and from there to Tucson, where we'll find a doctor or someone who can help you."

"Yes, yes, I remember now. I will be better in Tucson. I will recall how to read. Will I recognize anyone, No-ah? Will they recognize me?"

Tenderly, he wiped the tears from her cheeks with his thumbs, then gently kissed her forehead. "Juliet, I don't know, but I'll move heaven and earth to make you better and find out who you are. I've told you all along there has to be a logical explanation for everything that's happened. We're going to find out what it is. You can trust me. You can depend on me. I swear to you, sweetheart. I won't let you down."

"You love me," she whispered, desperate to reassure herself that it was true. "And I love you. That's all we need—our love. 'Tis very strong. It can overcome anything. Do you believe it, No-ah? Is our love not strong?"

"I believe it, sweetheart. Our love is strong enough to conquer even nightmares and madness. . . . Here now, look at me."

She raised her eyes to his face. He was so solid and substantial. His brown eyes brimmed with love; his sensuous mouth smiled. She touched his beard-stubbled jaw, then ran her fingers through his tousled reddish-gold hair. She stroked his chest where more hair of the same color curled into tight, fuzzy ringlets. He had put on his trousers but not his shirt or boots. He was completely, totally beautiful—all that was good, safe, and wholesome in the world. The horror of her dream faded. Noah was her world now. Her dreams could not touch her. The white bull did not belong here. He would never find her in Arizona. As long as Noah loved her, and she loved him, she was safe. They were both safe.

She smiled and then managed a laugh. "Dreams are so foolish, but they can seem so real."

"Do you want to tell me about it?"

She shook her head. " 'Tis not worth the telling. And I must find my clothes."

"They're already here." He nodded toward a pile of blue fabric lying beneath a bush. "Your horse is here, too. I left you covered with a blanket and went and got them while you slept."

"You take care of me so well, No-ah."

"I'm going to take care of you even better. We'll both take care of each other. Agreed?"

"Agreed."

"Then let's get going and meet the folks at Fort Bowie."

Fort Bowie consisted of a collection of buildings laid out in a square and partially surrounded by stone breastworks. About the same time Noah and Juliet caught sight of the fort, soldiers spotted them. The blue-coats immediately rode down the hillside to meet them and proceeded to accompany them toward the buildings. Noah undertook an animated conversation with a slender young man sporting a fringe of brown hair along his upper lip, but Juliet maintained a cautious silence, preferring to listen rather than speak.

Noah explained that he and Juliet were the unfortunate victims of an Apache attack on a wagon train bound for California. He claimed that the rest of the train had gotten through safely but they had been captured and detained in the mountains, forced to live among the Apaches until ransom or an exchange of prisoners could be arranged. Juliet listened intently as Noah described how they had made good their escape while the warriors were out scouting the soldiers. He sounded most convincing, but she could not help wondering if his concocted story would be accepted.

None of the soldiers remotely resembled the monsters she had pictured before meeting them. This particular one had a pleasant face, a long nose, and piercing blue eyes that seemed to miss very little. However, all he did was nod and ask a few innocent questions that Noah easily answered. Then the young man turned to her and politely tipped his hat.

"Lieutenant Gatewood at your service, Ma'am. I'm real sorry to hear about your recent trials. You were most fortunate to escape them red devils with nary an injury t' remark upon."

Juliet lifted her chin. Ignoring Noah's warning glance, she set the young man straight. "The Apaches were most kind to us, Lieutenant. They gave me these

309

beautiful garments to replace my own clothing which was ruined. They fed and housed us. I do not harbor any ill will against them, for they are only fighting to regain the lands that were stolen from them."

The lieutenant's brows shot up. "Ma'am, your sentiments come as a great surprise to me and will doubtless shock—and anger—most everyone you meet here at the fort. We've seen a different side of the Apaches. In our experience, they rarely spare those whom they attack, with the sole exception of children. These are taken and made into Apaches. If you'd seen as many burned-out homesteads and massacred bodies, and heard as many tales of thievery and murder as I have, you'd be callin' 'em red devils, too."

"But surely you must admit that the Indians have had provocation for their violent behavior, Lieutenant."

"Yes, Ma'am, I guess I can admit to that. I can also admit to havin' a certain respect for ol' Geronimo and the other Apache leaders. But that don't change the necessity of confinin' 'em to a reservation. The raidin' an' killin' has got t' stop—an' it's goin' to stop 'cause the U.S. Army in general and myself in particular are committed to huntin' 'em all down an' capturin' or killin' 'em."

Juliet was about to respond to that when Noah interrupted. "You'll have to excuse my wife, Lieutenant. She suffered a head injury during the attack and lost her memory as a result. She cannot recall the many depredations of which you speak. You mustn't assume that what is common knowledge in these parts is something she would know. She doesn't remember her life before the Apaches entered it."

Lieutenant Gatewood's sharp-eyed glance turned sympathetic. "Pardon me, Ma'am, I didn't realize. Seems you got injuries nobody can see. Well, don't you fret; we got officers' wives and a physician here at the fort who'll look after you and see that you get all you need. With a little rest and care, you'll regain your memory in no time."

"We won't be staying long, Lieutenant," Noah continued. "I'd like to get my wife to Tucson as soon as possible. I was hoping an escort could be provided for us."

"I'll see what can be done, Mr. McCord. We do make it a practice to see folks safely through Apache Pass, so I don't see why we can't arrange for a military escort to Tucson."

"We'd be much obliged," Noah said. "Have you been posted at Fort Bowie for long, Lieutenant?"

"No, sir. I served first at Fort Apache. However, I hope to stay in this area until Geronimo is captured. I'm ready to storm the Sierra Madre, if need be, to do my part in bringing him in. If General Crook sees fit t' send me, I'll be eager to go."

"An admirable attitude." Noah's tone was noncommittal. He then asked several innocuous questions calculated to keep Juliet from saying anything further to Lieutenant Gatewood.

Then and there she decided it was hopeless to try and defend the Apaches to the soldiers; their minds were made up and would not be changed by anything she had to tell them—especially if Noah continued to "explain" her opinions as a consequence of her loss of memory. She ceased listening to the conversation and directed her attention to the fort they were entering. It did not look like anything she had seen in her dreams.

Most of the buildings were constructed of thick, heavy blocks, the same reddish-tan color as the earth itself. Some were trimmed with wood. They rode into the center of the square and stopped in front of a two-level structure. A wide porch ran along the front of it, and the building itself was fancier than the others.

"This here is the commanding officer's quarters, Ma'am. If you wait a moment, I'll fetch someone to take care of you." He swung his lean, lanky frame down from his horse and handed the reins to one of his comrades.

Juliet toyed with her own reins to conceal her nervousness, but Noah sensed it anyway. He leaned over, and his strong brown hand covered hers. "Relax, sweetheart. No one is going to bite you."

"They will when I express my views regarding the Apaches," she answered in a low voice.

The soldiers had quickly dispersed, leaving them waiting in front of the pretty house the lieutenant had just entered. Still, she worried that someone might overhear them.

"Then don't express them," Noah said. "Wait for the proper time and place. You'll get your chance. Just don't make enemies before it's necessary. You have to learn diplomacy, sweetheart."

"Have you learned it?"

He laughed. "Hell, no! That's what always got me into trouble in the past. Now that I have you to protect, I'm going to be more careful. I'll think before I open my big mouth. The last thing we need is a passel of enemies just itching to carve out our livers."

"Oh, here comes someone!" Trembling with nervousness, Juliet studied the dark blue, high-necked gown and piled-up hair of the woman descending the steps ahead of Lieutenant Gatewood.

"Don't be afraid. Just smile and act friendly," Noah whispered.

"Hello," the woman said, marching straight toward them. Her pretty white face glowed with welcome. "I'm Mary Browne, one of the officers' wives. Shading her eyes, she smiled at Juliet. "My, that sun is hot! Come get down and we'll go into the house. I'll fix you some lemonade, and you can tell me all about your ordeal."

"Smile," Noah ordered, gathering up her horse's reins.

Juliet turned to him in rising panic. "You are not leaving me, are you? Where are you going?"

"To stable the horses and find whoever's in charge."
He leaned closer and spoke softly for her ears alone. "I
hope it's no one from Fort Apache who might remember me and dispute our story. I was worried when
Gatewood said he had been stationed there, though I
don't recall ever having met him."

Lieutenant Gatewood nodded when Juliet looked at
him. Fortunately he did not seem to realize they were
discussing him.

"Don't leave me, No-ah!" she pleaded in a whisper.
Before she could say more, Mary Browne advanced
upon her as if she meant to help her down from the
horse.

"Don't be frightened, my dear. I understand you've
had quite an adventure in the mountains. Things may
seem strange to you now, but you mustn't worry.
What you've forgotten will all come back to you. In
the meantime, I would like to be your friend. . . . Come
along now. What you need is refreshment and perhaps
a nice long nap."

"Let me help, Ma'am." Lieutenant Gatewood gallantly stepped forward as Juliet attempted to swing her
leg over the saddle in a discreet manner. Apache
women thought nothing of riding astride, their full,
colorful skirts hiked above their knees, but she knew
instinctively that white women did not ride that way.
Mary Browne's form-fitting gown did not look at all
suitable for riding.

"There you are," Lieutenant Gatewood said as he
lifted her down and set her on her feet. "While you
meet the ladies, I'll show your husband around the
fort."

Noah grinned encouragingly. Juliet realized she had
no choice but to turn and follow Mary Browne up the
steps to the house, while Lieutenant Gatewood set off
with Noah.

Chapter Twenty-three

"Now, my dear, while you drink your lemonade, I'll introduce you to some of the other wives here at Fort Bowie. They'll be coming by to meet you once the word gets round that you've arrived. We're quite a close-knit little group, which is only natural in such an isolated outpost. As you can imagine, we all have to rely upon one another. . . . Ah, here is dear Louise, and she's brought Penelope with her. Ladies, this is Juliet McCord, who just escaped from the Apaches. We won't press her to talk about it yet, but we can be certain it was a terrible experience."

Juliet opened her mouth to protest, then abruptly closed it again. She could not help feeling intimidated by these white women in their somber gowns and carefully arranged hair. Fair-haired Mary seemed friendly enough, round little Louise somewhat less so, and tall, angular Penelope downright formidable as she gave Juliet's bright, loose-fitting Apache garments a thin-lipped perusal.

"We must find you new clothing," Penelope stated, gazing down her nose at Juliet who was seated on an overstuffed chair in what Mary called the front parlor. "What you are wearing simply will not do."

"I rather like what I am wearing," Juliet managed to get out, though she did not feel as brave as she would have liked. "It's . . . comfortable," she finished lamely.

"Oh, I dare say it's preferable to going naked, but

315

we can find something more suitable, I'm sure. We shall each contribute a necessary item of apparel and help you alter it to fit your size," Penelope insisted.

"There may not be time for that," Juliet pointed out. "My husband and I are leaving soon for Tucson."

"Tucson, my dear? Not Fort Lowell?" Mary inquired with a frown. "Why, Tucson is hardly civilized. The town consists mainly of saloons and adobe huts. It's called the Old Pueblo, and there are as many Mexicans and Spaniards there as whites. You should tell your husband you would prefer staying at Fort Lowell until the Apaches are caught, and it's safe to start ranching or farming. Fort Lowell is only seven miles from Tucson, but it's far more secure and has numerous amenities. Why, they've got floors made of California redwood shipped in by rail, sturdy tin roofs, and . . ."

"Concerts, tennis matches, dramatic readings, and croquet games!" Louise eagerly added. "I wish my husband would be transferred to Fort Lowell. It's ever so much nicer than here or in Tucson. Fort Bowie is the worst of cultural backwaters, and Tucson is wild and lawless."

"Complaints! Complaints!" Penelope scolded. "How we do go on—and in front of someone who's recently been living in a wickiup. For shame, ladies."

Juliet did not know what to say. If she talked about the Apaches, she risked alienating these women who did not seem entirely bad—only woefully ignorant. Yet she could hardly discuss the future with them when she had no idea what she and Noah would be doing. The ladies assumed they would be ranching or farming, but Noah had never mentioned such activities. He had come to Arizona to write a book about Geronimo, but now his main concern was getting her to a doctor. None of these topics seemed fit for discussion, so she silently sipped her lemonade, enjoying the tart sweet flavor, then surreptitiously studied her remarkable surroundings.

Mary saw where she was looking and said softly: "It's all quite different from a wickiup, isn't it, my dear?"

Juliet nodded. "I cannot recall ever having seen such furnishings as these."

"Yes, I would imagine that sofas, chairs, mirrors, and these few simple decorations look quite different to you, after living so long with no furniture whatsoever."

"It's . . . overwhelming," Juliet admitted, gazing more openly around the overcrowded room. Not a surface had been left bare. Books and objects she could not identify cluttered every available surface—and even hung upon the walls.

"Why, this is nothing to what you would find in a parlor back East," Penelope sniffed. "There should be plants and potted palms to finish off this room, but they're hard to maintain in the desert heat and dryness. Still, we have done our best to create a gracious atmosphere in the middle of the wilderness."

"What is that?" Juliet pointed to an indentation in one wall, where two black things held some logs.

Louise's eyebrows rose. "A fireplace, of course."

With an apologetic glance at Juliet, Mary hastened to explain. "Ladies, our guest suffers from memory loss—a consequence of injuries sustained when she and her husband were attacked by the Apaches. I hope you don't mind, my dear, but Lieutenant Gatewood did mention that fact to me."

"Why, I'm so sorry," Louise apologized, her light blue eyes brimming with sincerity.

"Dreadful," harumphed Penelope. "No wonder everything seems strange to you."

Juliet saw an opportunity to ward off awkward questions and took it. "I would appreciate it if you would identify some of the objects in this room for me. Perhaps such an exercise might help me remember."

"What a grand idea!" Mary exclaimed. She rose and

317

walked to the fireplace. "Do you recognize this object up here on the mantel? It's called a clock."

Juliet shook her head. "Whatever is its purpose?"

The women glanced from one to another, then launched into explanations for nearly every object in the room—from lamps to doilies to framed pictures from back home in the East. Two more ladies joined the group. Their names were Hortense and Mildred, and they, too, seemed delighted to be of help. The explanations consumed a great deal of time, broken only by more refreshments. Something sweet and delicious called a Jenny Lind cake was served, and before Juliet knew it, Noah was standing in the doorway, watching her with an expression of wry amusement.

"Oh, my dear, here's your husband come to claim you!" Mary cried. "Mr. McCord, we have just been reintroducing your wife to a host of things she has apparently forgotten."

"Why, then, I thank you ladies. I'm in your debt. Had you not undertaken to prod her memory, I should have had to do so myself." Noah bowed from the waist, and Hortense, a plump exuberant woman, giggled.

"Think nothing of it, Mr. McCord," she bubbled. "We love having company here at the fort. We sincerely regret your wife's memory loss, but it has provided us with several hours of worthwhile activity—something to relieve the boredom from which we all suffer here at Fort Bowie. I forsee many more sessions of delightful instruction during your stay here."

"Sorry, but we won't be here long," Noah said. "I had hoped to have the fort physician examine my wife, but it seems he left this morning for Fort Apache. We ourselves are headed for Tucson as soon as we can get an escort."

"Oh, Mr. McCord! You really should take Juliet to Fort Lowell instead," Mary argued. "It's a much better place to wait for Geronimo's capture. Safer. More comfortable. Lord knows you can't begin farming or ranching while the Apaches are still terrorizing the countryside. Why, even some of the ranchers' families have sought safe haven there."

"Sounds like an excellent idea but Tucson has its own attractions," Noah politely pointed out. "There's said to be a fine doctor there—the best in the region. We'll simply board in town until the Apache crisis has ended."

"Why, then," said Hortense. "If you're determined upon Tucson, you might consider staying at my sister's. She and her husband run a mercantile establishment there. Once the Apaches are gone, Tucson will surely grow and prosper. My sister and her husband have great plans for the future. In the meantime, while things are less booming, I'm certain they could use some extra income letting out a room to you. Tucson hasn't much to offer travelers, but I could write a letter of introduction and perhaps they might consider it."

"We'd be pleased to investigate that possibility," Noah said. "Wouldn't we, Juliet?"

"If you wish, No-ah," she agreed without enthusiasm. The session with the ladies of the fort had exhausted her, and she suddenly had a headache. Though fascinating, the parlor was close, stuffy, and airless. She longed to be out of doors again.

"While you're here, you're most welcome to stay in the officer's quarters or one of the other buildings," Mary offered. "Never fear; we'll find comfortable accommodations for you."

"No, ladies, that's not necessary," Noah gracefully refused, much to Juliet's relief. "We're used to sleeping out under the stars. We'll camp outside, unless of course, it rains or gets too cold at night. I've already been to the sutler and purchased all we need on credit. I've also sent a wire back East and requested funds to be forwarded as soon as possible. You don't know how glad I was to learn that you had a telegraph office here."

Positively oozing charm, Noah grinned and held out his hand to Juliet. "Come along, sweetheart, and we'll stroll the grounds and pick a place to bed down."

"But you'll dine with us, won't you?" Mary planted herself determinedly in their path. Tilting back her blond head, she eyed Noah with a worried frown. "You'll take meals with us while you're here, won't you, Mr. McCord? We aren't lacking in hospitality, and we've taken your Juliet straight to our hearts. We intend to help her all we can while we can, don't we, ladies?"

There was a chorus of assent. "Indeed, we do!"

Humbled by their enthusiasm and offers of friendship, Juliet wondered why she had ever doubted that white women could be as kind as Apaches. Women everywhere shared basic traits, she decided. They were all willing to feed and clothe the needy—except when the needy were enemies. Had these kindhearted white women shown such concern for the Apaches, perhaps the Indians would never have fled the reservation.

As Noah steered her out of the large house, Juliet suddenly realized that no matter how nice the women were, not one of them had been open to her thoughts—nor had she attempted to transmit them. In this, the whites differed greatly from the Apaches. They seemed oblivious to internal communication or maybe insensitive was a better word. She had not tried to transmit her thoughts because she had already known they would not be receptive; they would not even realize what she was trying to do.

She thought of E-clah-heh and Smiles-A-Lot, and her heart ached with homesickness. She wished she could put up a wickiup to live in, but she knew Noah would not like it. Sighing to herself, she let him lead her across the square.

They stayed at Fort Bowie for four days. During that time, Juliet learned as much as she could from the helpful women. They taught her how to cook simple dishes, wash laundry, and arrange her hair in the latest fashion, pinned atop her head beneath a bonnet they said she must wear at all times to protect her skin from the sun.

She was tempted to ask them why they did not simply rub a salve made from aloe into their skin to prevent it from burning or drying out, but then decided that her knowledge of the desert and its many plants belonged to her Apache life, not her white one. She must learn to absorb the ways of white people now, even if those ways appeared foolish or incomprehensible. Her ability to adapt to new situations and learn quickly served her well, just as it had served her among the Indians. By the time she rode out of Fort Bowie in a supply wagon surrounded by a dozen soldiers, she considered herself well prepared to cope with the life she would find in Tucson.

The only thing she couldn't do was read the little book of recipes and remedies they had given her—nor could she write to the ladies as she had promised—but she intended to have Noah teach her how to read and write as soon as they had the time and the privacy to do so.

On their journey, they crossed the Southern Pacific Railway, and Juliet gaped in amazement when a train came rattling down the tracks and frightened everyone's horses. She had never dreamed such a thing as a train existed, and she could easily imagine how alarmed the Apaches must have been when first they witnessed the noisy "iron-horse."

The soldiers set a leisurely pace for Tucson, and it took them two and a half days to get there. An Apache warrior riding hard and fast, changing horses as he went, could probably have done it in a single day, but Juliet was content to jolt along in the lumbering wagon provided by the army. Her hard wooden seat gave her an excellent vantage point from which to admire the desert scenery and the various mountains rising in the distance. Tucson lay in a broad triangular-shaped valley surrounded by five different mountain ranges. Lieutenant Gatewood told her and Noah that the name itself came from an Indian translation meaning "At The Foot of the Dark Mountain."

Juliet was disappointed when she first saw the town—a raw-looking assortment of adobe-brick buildings and dusty streets baking in the afternoon sunshine. Noah thanked the soldiers, most of whom parted company when they reached the main track that was clogged with other wagons, men on horseback, and people strolling up and down in front of shops and noisy saloons—places where men went to drink and watch dancing women in scanty costumes. Or so the ladies of Fort Bowie had told her.

"What's the name of your friend's sister?" Noah asked, while the wagon driver, an amiable soldier named Clem, patiently waited.

"It's Prudence. Prudence Lathrop. Her husband's name is Eugene. He owns the largest mercantile."

"I see it," Noah said, riding ahead and leaving her and Clem to follow in the wagon.

Several men stacking barrels outside a building turned to watch as Noah kneed Patch through the street traffic. Juliet was not sure if the onlookers were admiring the stallion or speculating about it's rider. There seemed to be a lot of rough-looking men on the streets or on horseback passing through the town; they all wore guns and cartridge belts.

A boy hopped into Noah's path and waved a paper under Patch's nose, causing him to snort and side step.

"Arizona Star, mister? Get the latest news about Geronimo."

Noah reached down, took the paper, then rode back and handed it to Juliet. "Hold onto this so I can read it later. Don't know what the *Star* knows about Geronimo that we don't know."

"Probably just another editorial about him," the wagon driver, Clem, spoke up. "Tellin' everybody

322

what a demon he is and wonderin' if the army will ever catch him. We will though. Sooner or later. You wait an' see.''

Juliet took the paper and anxiously scanned it, wishing with all her heart that she could read. Since she could not, she folded it and put it into a pocket of the plain gown that Mary at Fort Bowie had given her. Then she waited for Noah to locate the mercantile. He rode part way down the street, dismounted in front of a shop there, looped his reins around a hitching post, and entered the building. A few moments later, a tiny, birdlike woman with Hortense's smile but not her plump figure came bustling out, followed by Noah.

Looking up and down the street, she spotted Juliet, picked up her skirts, and hurried toward the wagon. "I declare! So you're Juliet, a friend of my sister, Hortense. Well, I'm delighted to meet you. My husband Eugene will be equally delighted."

Juliet leaned over the side of the wagon and extended her hand to Prudence Lathrop. The woman's face was a mass of sun-darkened wrinkles beneath a gray-streaked knot of brown hair coming loose from its pins. Nowhere near as perfectly groomed as the ladies at Fort Bowie, Mrs. Lathrop was far less forbidding. Juliet immediately liked her. "I'm pleased to make your acquaintance, Mrs. Lathrop."

"No, no, call me Pru, please. Everyone else does. Welcome to Tucson, Juliet. Climb down from that wagon. I'm a dyin' to show you the mercantile and the house we can put you up in . . ."

"A whole house? Not just a room?" Juliet darted a look at Noah who was grinning from ear to ear. He came and lifted her down from the wagon while Mrs. Lathrop answered the question.

"Oh, it's a small house but plenty adequate. We bought it thinkin' our son might settle here with his new wife, but he moved on to California and left us stuck with the place. We can't live in it ourselves 'cause we got to keep an eye on the mercantile. It's jus' more convenient to live in the same buildin' where we got all our assets. We was gonna sell the house, but now that you've come along, we'll wait 'til you're done with it. Why, you might want to' buy it yourself."

"She says it's close to both the post office and the doctor's office." Noah's hands were still around Juliet's waist, and he gave her a little squeeze. "A prime location."

At the mention of the doctor's office, Juliet stopped smiling. She had no wish to see a doctor and knew it would do no good. But that was why they had come to Tucson, and Noah looked so pleased with himself that she did not have the heart to refuse.

"Your husband says you took a bump on the head and lost your memory when the Apaches captured you," Prudence said, eyeing her with concern. "I'm sorry it happened, but glad you escaped and made it t' Tucson. Not everybody likes the town, but I do. Soon as the Apaches get rounded up and hung, this town's gonna grow an' prosper. You see if it don't."

"Not hung!" Juliet burst out. "Surely the Apaches will not be hung if they're caught."

Prudence Lathrop cocked her head in surprise. "Don't know as folks will settle for anything less. They sure can't go back to the reservation; they'll just escape again first chance they get an' go right on back t' raidin' an' killin'."

"Not hung," Juliet insisted. "They must not be hung."

"Let's go see the house the Lathrops are offering," Noah cut in, offering Juliet his arm. "There's a stable nearby for Patch. Sounds exactly like what we want. . . . Clem, I'd like to thank you for driving that wagon and getting us here safely. Sorry I can't reimburse you for your trouble but I trust the army can use Juliet's horse."

"No trouble, Copper," Clem said, using the name by which all of the soldiers had begun calling Noah. "Tweren't no trouble a-tall, but we do thank you for the horse. We can use all the horses and mules we can get. Come back t' Fort Bowie and see us all again real soon. I get by here regular t' make a few purchases, an' I'd be happy to give your missus a ride back an' forth t' the fort."

"Thanks, I'll remember that."

"Here's the key t' the house, Mr. McCord." Prudence plunged her hand into a pocket and withdrew a heavy gold key. "It's right down the street where I told you. I got t' get back t' the store now. Days when it's busy like this, it takes two of us to wait on customers. You make up a list of what you'll be needin', an' I'll give you credit 'til your money comes."

"Thank you, Mrs. Lathrop. I'll do that."

"Oh, there's already some furniture in the house—a brass bed, a table, a lamp . . . a couple chairs. It ain't like what you're used to back East, but it'll serve. We had it all ready for my boy, you know, before he got ideas about movin' on. Said he didn't want his wife livin' in such a wild town, with Apaches an' all still runnin' free in the countryside. His pa and I think he made a mistake, of course, but there's no reasonin' with the young an' foolish."

"We'll come down to the store later, Mrs. Lathrop," Noah said, leading Juliet away.

The house turned out to be more luxurious and charming than Juliet had expected. She liked its thick walls that offered coolness from the heat and warmth from the night chill, the window openings with shutters that could be closed during bad weather, the walled courtyard in the back of the house that allowed her to be outside but still away from prying eyes, the little hut at the back of the courtyard for relieving oneself in private, and the big *saguaro* cactus that dominated the courtyard itself.

Most of all, she liked the wide brass bed Mrs. Lathrop had mentioned. Set off by itself in the middle of the smallest of the three rooms in the house, the brass bed looked wonderfully comfortable, though Noah said it needed sheets and goose-down pillows to suit his tastes.

Sitting on the edge of it and marveling at the softness of the mattress, Juliet didn't think the beautiful bed needed a thing. "No-ah, this is indeed marvelous. Must we wait until dark to try it out?"

"What did you have in mind?" Noah quizzed from the doorway. His arms were full of blankets and other items he had taken off Patch.

A blush heated her cheeks as she ran her fingertips down the shiny brass frame at the head of the bed. "Can you not guess? It has been a week since we were completely alone," she reminded him. "If this is to be our new home and our new bed, I would like to make it truly ours."

Setting down his armload, Noah entered the room and pulled her upright. "Tonight will be soon enough to test the comforts of this bed, sweetheart. Before we get settled, I'd like to go down the street and see if the doctor is in his office. He should be at this hour."

Juliet's heart skipped a beat. "The doctor? Today?"

He kissed the tip of her nose. "That's why we're here, isn't it? I see no point in waiting."

"But No-ah. . . . We just got here! Surely, it can wait until tomorrow. I . . . I would at least like to freshen myself before I see him."

"Look, I'm going to go get us a water barrel first thing, and you can freshen up right away. It won't take long. I saw one back there in the courtyard, but I don't know if it's full or empty or how long it's been standing. I'd rather get a new one if I can buy it on credit. I imagine I can; so far, people have been most accommodating."

"No-ah, I do not wish to see your doctor today."

"Well, prepare yourself, honey, because if he's in, you're going. I doubt he'll do much during this first visit but ask a few questions. There's nothing to be afraid of. One thing he won't do is make you drink funny herbs, nor will he dance around a fire, chanting."

"No-ah! You are mocking Apache customs!"

"Ooops, sorry. Didn't mean to ruffle your feathers, but you're in your own world now, sweetheart, and it's time you got used to it. You're not an Apache anymore."

"I am not at all certain I am going to like this new world!"

"Oh, you will!" He drew back from her and winked. "You already like brass beds, don't you? Does that bed stir some distant memory? Maybe you slept on one as a child."

She jumped to her feet. "It stirs nothing! I have *never* slept on one before."

"Guess I'm glad to hear that. I'd be crushed if the sight of it reminded you of sleeping with another man."

She balled her fists and glared at him. "Oh, you are impossible!"

"But you love me anyway." He reached out to tweak a strand of her wild, unkempt hair.

She felt like kicking him. Here she was in a strange town in a strange house about to visit a strange man who would poke and prod at her until she was ready to scream, and all Noah could do was make unfunny comments. While she was quaking inside, he was rejoicing. He would rather take her to a doctor than to bed. Well, she had lost her desire to go to bed with him. At the moment, she preferred throttling him with her bare hands.

"Relax," he soothed. "It will be all right. You'll see. You'll be glad we came to Tucson."

He blew her a kiss and headed for the doorway. But she was very, very certain she would *not* be glad they had come to Tucson.

Chapter Twenty-four

"This is taking too damn long. They ought to be done by now."

Noah stood in the empty front room of Dr. J. Harold Bailey's office and stared at the closed door separating him from Juliet. The physical examination had been completed, and the balding, elderly, bespectacled physician had requested that Noah leave the examining room so that he could question Juliet in private. Noah hadn't wanted to go, but realized he had no choice. He had begged the doctor to see Juliet today, even though regular office hours had ended, and it was growing late.

Too nervous to sit on the bench in front of the open window, Noah had been restlessly pacing the floor. If the doctor couldn't help Juliet, he didn't know what he would do. He had no confidence in military physicians. They were usually surgeons, good at removing bullets and arrows from wounded soldiers, but he doubted they had the proper training to deal with complex mental problems. He had not expected to find a psychiatrist here in the sparsely-settled Southwest, but he hoped that Doc Bailey, old saw-bones that he was, knew *something* about the diseases of the human mind and spirit.

On his first visit to Tucson, way back in the spring when he first got off the train in Arizona, Noah had stopped in the pharmacy the doctor maintained in his front room. A woman—perhaps the doctor's wife—had waited on Noah as he purchased a headache remedy. She had been effusive in her praise of Doc Bailey in answer to another customer's questions, and he had not forgotten it. Noah doubted that she would remember him—nor would anyone else in town—for he had not stayed long enough to make any acquaintances. Now, he was glad of that fact, for he hoped to keep using the story he had already concocted regarding himself and Juliet; only with the doctor would he be honest about what had really happened.

In view of the sensitivity of his self-assignment, he had wasted little time in idle conversation with strangers and made the trip to Fort Apache as soon as possible, leaving the next day with the mail coach. He had arrived just in time to hear about Geronimo's escape and then had hooked up with the ranchers. In Tucson, he felt relatively safe from the ranchers, for none of them had lived in the immediate environs. Providing Doc Bailey could help Juliet, he planned to stay here. It was as good a place as any to keep track of the campaign against the Apaches. He could send news stories back East regularly and even resume working on his book, if the notion took him . . . but he wouldn't be doing any of this if Juliet didn't show some improvement.

Hoping to distract himself, he peered more closely at the shelves lining one wall of the long narrow room. There were the usual tools of the medical trade: assorted surgical instruments—some quite gruesome looking—and row upon row of bottles, jars, and crocks. Noah read the labels on some of the containers; there was ether, opium, calomel, chloroform, sassafras, bromide, and a large clay vessel marked LEECHES.

Juliet would probably be fascinated by all this, but Noah was repelled. Spotting several shelves full of books at the back of the room, he walked over to study the titles. *A Manual of Surgery*, a book called *Sick*

330

Call, and a copy of the Holy Bible occupied the most prominent positions. More books jammed the rest of the shelves. Noah discovered that the doctor had a taste for knowledge outside his own field. Several of the volumes were printed in foreign languages, some were classical works, and quite a few were historical.

With rising excitement, he ran a finger down dusty spines that read *The Collected Works of Euripedes, Medicine According to Hippocrates, The Iliad, The Odyssey,* Plato's *Republic,* and *The Tragedies of Sophocles.* Doc Bailey was familiar with the writings of ancient Greece! Noah reached for a book with the best title of all: *A Compendium of Greek Literature, Mythology, and History.*

He had just removed the book from the shelf when the door to the examination room opened, and Doc Bailey himself stuck out his bald head. "Mr. McCord, could you come in here, please, sir?"

Noah jammed the book back into place. "Coming right away."

Pivoting on his heel, he hurried into the small room that was simply furnished with two chairs, an examination table, a smaller side table and a lamp. Juliet sat in one of the chairs, and Doc Bailey motioned him to the other, then fetched a third from the front room.

"Well, now," he said, shutting the door behind himself and taking a seat facing them. He removed his spectacles, retrieved a handkerchief from his breast pocket, and began assiduously wiping his glasses.

Noah could tell nothing from Juliet's expression; she looked cool and remote. He fastened his attention on the doctor. "Well, what? Can you help her? Will she regain her memory?"

Doc Bailey replaced his spectacles on his nose and narrowed his watery blue eyes on Noah. "You didn't tell me about your wife's other problems," he bluntly accused.

Noah was slightly taken aback. "I figured she would tell you."

"Hmmmm," he said. "And so she did."

"She told you she's from ancient Greece?" Noah questioned. "And that she can remember it in her dreams?"

"She did. That's not your interpretation?" Doc Bailey peered at Noah over the rim of his spectacles.

Noah wondered why he had spent so much time cleaning them if he did not intend to look through them. "No, it's not, Doc. I find it difficult to believe that my wife was somehow lifted out of a past life and deposited on a ledge in the present. I believe she must have read a great deal about Greece in her childhood, and the memory of what she read has stayed with her, buried deeply in her brain. I, too, have read the Greek classics and studied Greek history. So have you. The books out there on your shelves indicate a similar fascination."

"So you think that when she lost her memory, either by a blow to the head or some other trauma, only her knowledge of Greek history remained."

"What do *you* think?" Noah demanded. "You're the doctor."

"I think it's a possibility." Doc Bailey ran a pudgy hand through his nonexistent hair. "However, your wife disagrees. She claims she came directly from Greece, but you refuse to accept it."

"I *know* what she claims. That's why I brought her to you."

"Hmmmmm," the doctor repeated, glancing from Noah to Juliet and back again.

Juliet's golden eyes sought Noah's. Her silent message was easy to decipher. *See?* she seemed to be saying. *I knew he could not help me.*

Noah's frustration rose to the boiling point. "Can you treat her condition or not? That's all I want to know."

Doc Bailey did not answer. Instead, he rose ponderously to his feet. He had earlier removed his suit coat, and a patch of wetness showed between his rounded shoulder blades as he turned to leave the room. "Wait here a moment, please."

As he exited the small chamber, Noah took advantage of his absence to assess Juliet's mood. "Are you all right?"

She shrugged her slender shoulders and would not meet his eyes. She looked like a child sitting there in her dark brown dress, which did not suit her half as well as her brightly colored Apache garments. Noah made a mental note to buy fabric for a new dress as soon as he received his money. With her pale hair, Juliet should wear more vivid hues, he decided— bright green or a sunshine yellow. He hoped Lathrop's Mercantile carried such colors.

"You don't look all right," he said, wondering at her mental state. She seemed too quiet, almost defeated. She was deathly pale.

"I would like to leave," she murmured. "This is useless, No-ah."

"We're not leaving until he tells me whether or not he can help you. You can't go on like this, Juliet. You know you can't."

"I'm not ill, No-ah. Aside from my memory loss, I simply have bad dreams occasionally. This man doctors the body, not the mind. I cannot understand why you were so anxious to bring me here."

"Because there's got to be a treatment for you— some pill or elixir to stop the dreams and aid the return of your memory. Hell, he's got shelves full of medicine out there in the other room. I'm even willing to give Lydia Pinkham's Vegetable Compound a try. I can remember when it was a cure-all for all kinds of female ailments. Of course, that was a number of years ago, but it couldn't hurt to try it, if he's got some available."

"Who is Lydia Pinkham?" Juliet asked.

"If you had your memory back, you wouldn't have to ask! You'd remember! There was time when a woman couldn't live without her famous compound."

Exasperated, he stopped and got hold of himself. "Try and cooperate, Juliet. Try and . . . and open your mind to this."

She gave him a level look. "I cannot communicate internally with whites, No-ah. Only with animals and Apaches. Can your Dr. Bailey explain that?"

"Did you tell him what you can do with animals and Indians?"

She shook her head. "No. It did not seem relevant. And I doubted he would understand."

"Perhaps you should have. All of these things are instances of abnormal behavior. He can hardly treat you if he doesn't know the whole story."

"I do not wish to be 'treated' for that particular ability. I would hate to lose it."

Noah rose, knocking over his chair in his agitation. He snatched it upright and set it down with a thud. "Juliet, you're the most impossibly stubborn woman I've ever met!"

Before he could continue, Doc Bailey reentered the room. "Mrs. McCord, I've brought a book I would like you to try and read."

Juliet gazed coolly at the wall. "I have already told you; I cannot read. It seems to be something I have forgotten, if I ever knew."

"Try *this* book, madam. Just as an experiment." He held out a small volume and opened it in the middle. "Pick something at random. Doesn't make any difference what it is."

Noah leaned over Juliet's shoulder to get a better view. He recognized Greek alphabetical symbols on the yellowed page. Juliet took the book in her slender hands and held it up to the light coming through the open window. The sun was setting, but it was still bright enough to read.

Her eyes widened. With a trembling finger, she pointed to the symbols. "I recognize this! 'Tis an alpha. And this is a lambda . . . a delta . . . an epsilon. Over here is an omicron. This is an omega. Noah! I can

334

read these; I know what they are! And they are not so very different from the symbols in your journal, are they? Now that I see them like this, I can recognize the similarities."

Juliet's face was shining, her eyes aglow. Noah felt as if he'd been kicked in the stomach by a mule. "Impossible," he muttered, hardly realizing he had spoken aloud.

"Mrs. McCord," Doc Bailey said, taking the book from her hands. "The Greek alphabet preceded the English alphabet we use today. They are indeed similar. If you can read this, you can read English."

Juliet's eyes filled with denial. "But I cannot. I have tried, and I cannot." She fumbled in her pocket and took out the newspaper Noah had given her earlier. "Not a word written here makes sense to me."

Doctor Bailey pointed to the newspaper. "What about this? It's the letter a, the same as you call an alpha. Don't you see the resemblance?"

"I . . . I suppose." Juliet's lower lip quivered. A look of panic crossed her delicate features. "Can we leave now, No-ah? I should very much like to go."

"Here now, Mrs. McCord. Don't upset yourself." Doc Bailey patted Juliet's arm. "We'll stop for a bit and give you time to compose yourself. Why don't you go into the other room and let me have a word alone with your husband?"

Juliet almost leaped from the chair, her relief painfully evident. "Yes, thank you. I will just wait out there until you are finished. Please hurry, No-ah. I am most anxious to leave. Actually, I . . . I'm hungry. Is it not time to eat? We have no food. We must go and get some from the mercantile."

Noah wasn't fooled. Juliet rarely complained of hunger—or of anything else, except his behavior. She was clearly upset. This session with the doctor had alarmed rather than soothed her. He had not expected that. Indeed, he had naively assumed that everything would be wonderful once they got to Tucson and

335

found help for her. As he watched her flee the room, he had a sick feeling. More than ever, he felt as if a mule had kicked him.

When she had gone, Doc Bailey closed the door, then busied himself lighting the wick of the table lamp. Telegraph wires had reached Arizona but not Thomas Edison's new invention. A rosy glow soon chased the shadows from the little room—but nothing could chase them from Noah's heart. With mounting dread, he watched the doctor.

Harry J. Bailey's round face radiated sympathy. "A lovely young woman, your wife . . ." he began.

"Can you help her?" Noah burst out.

The old man sighed and sat back down. "I must be honest, Mr. McCord. I'm not sure I can. Physically, there's nothing wrong with her. Oh, she could use a bit more meat on her bones, but otherwise, she's perfectly healthy. As for her mental condition . . . well, I just don't know."

"What do you mean you don't know? You're a doctor; you're supposed to know."

Doc Bailey rubbed a fat palm across his knee. "Yes, well, that's certainly true . . . but medicine cannot solve all of the world's problems, Mr. McCord. We've unlocked many mysteries during the last decade—why, we've even found ways to treat tuberculosis! We know how to vaccinate against small pox, and yellow fever is not the threat it once was. However, the mysteries of the mind continue to elude us. We don't really know how the brain works, you know—or why some people can't refrain from baying at the moon or banging their heads against a wall . . ."

"You're not suggesting Juliet is capable of such behavior!"

"No, no . . ." He raised his hand as if to placate Noah. "I'm not suggesting anything of the sort. I'm only trying to find a less alarming way of telling you that I have no idea how to treat your wife. Memory loss is not that uncommon. Some or all of what a person forgets as a result of injury or trauma usually returns. But in your wife's case, I doubt that will happen. Her loss may be permanent."

Noah slammed his fist down on the examining table. "Why?" he grated. "Why do you think that?"

"Because her case strikes me as so unusual. You say she had no lumps on her head when you found her. She had no injuries of any kind."

"No. None."

"Then her loss of memory must be due to emotional trauma. Perhaps she saw her entire family massacred by the Apaches. Or her loved ones deserted her— dropped her off, as it were, in the wilderness, and she cannot face the pain of her abandonment. *Something* happened to cause this debility, and whatever it is, she cannot accept it. She may never be able to accept it."

"But her dreams, her nightmares—her obsession with Greece! How do you account for those?"

"Oh, I think it likely that your explanation is as good as any other. Obviously, she studied the period extensively at one time, derived great satisfaction from her studies, and has substituted childhood fantasies for real life. If she cannot be induced to face reality, she will probably continue with her delusions."

"But there must be something we can do! What if she retreats altogether from reality?"

"That is certainly a possibility, Mr. McCord. I cannot deny it. What I can do is give you medication to induce a deeper state of sleep, so that she is not as likely to experience these disturbing dreams."

"What sort of medication?" Noah eyed the doctor with deep suspicion.

"Laudanum, which is, of course, tincture of opium. I wouldn't recommend it on a daily basis. It's a mind-altering drug and also habit-forming. But on occasion . . ."

"No laudanum. What other treatment can you suggest?"

Doc Bailey rolled his eyes. "Well, were we back

East, you might want to subject her to certain experimental treatments using electricity applied to various body parts to achieve . . ."

"No electricity! What else is there?"

The doctor raised his hands palms upward. "There *is* nothing else, Mr. McCord—unless you would like me to try leeches."

"No leeches."

"Well, then, I suggest you simply let nature take its course. In time, she may recover quite nicely on her own. Or she may never recover. She doesn't seem to be *dangerous,* Mr. McCord. Perhaps all you need do is keep her busy and occupied, so she has no time to dwell on these obsessions. If she doesn't improve, at least she won't get worse. In the event that she does worsen, you may wish to try the laudanum or the leeches. I *can* help you with either of those; only the electricity is out of the question."

Noah went to the window and leaned on the sill. It had grown dark outside. In his heart, it was darker still. He had centered all his hopes on getting medical help for Juliet; now he knew how foolish he had been. Laudanum, leeches, and electricity! He would have done better asking for Geronimo's help. A dance around a fire and a few weird chants made more sense than modern medicine.

"Maybe I should take her back East—where there are *real* doctors," he muttered.

"Maybe you should," Doc Bailey answered without rancor. "There may be many new discoveries. Out here, I've had no opportunity to keep up with them. Then again, maybe you should just give your wife more time. Time has a way of working more miracles than medicine ever could."

Struck by an idea, Noah turned back to the doctor. "Can I borrow some of your books on ancient Greece? I've wired a friend in the East to send me my personal library, but it will be months before anything gets here."

"Feel free to take whatever you'd like. I'm sorry I cannot be more helpful. I would appreciate knowing what else your wife recalls about ancient Greece besides the alphabet. Discounting the tragedy of the situation, hers is a most interesting case."

"I'll keep you informed of any great discoveries I make," Noah dryly offered. "You may want to write her up in some medical treatise."

Doc Bailey smiled. "I may at that. It isn't every day I meet a beautiful young woman who thinks she's been catapulted forward in time from an ancient society—and has found the same lover."

"I wish *I* could remember all that *she* claims to remember—no, forget I said that. I don't wish any such thing. What I really wish is that she would forget all this nonsense and be a normal wife to me. That's all I want—a normal little wife who thinks the sun rises and sets on me."

The doctor chuckled. "That's all any man wants. Good luck to you, Mr. McCord."

"I'll have to wait and pay you for this consultation when my money arrives from the East."

Doc Bailey waved a pudgy hand. "I wasn't able to help you, so there's no charge."

"I'll pay you anyway. In a way, you *have* helped. I'm a little more resigned now to giving time a chance."

"Time can work wonders."

"I sure as hell hope it does." Noah opened the door to the examination room and stuck his head out. "Juliet, are you ready to go?"

The main room was empty, but the front door to the office stood wide open. Noah could hear a couple of drunken cowboys singing a bawdy saloon song as they rode past on their horses. "Oh, I loved a li'l gal down Mexico way . . ."

He bolted out the door and cast a frantic glance down the street. Juliet was nowhere in sight, and Tucson had come alive. Gunshots sounded from around the corner, horses whinnied, and men bellowed and cursed. Five riders galloped down the center of the road, firing pistols left and right into storefronts. Noah ducked as they came abreast of him. Then he set off running, hoping he didn't find Juliet lying dead in the street halfway back to their house.

Chapter Twenty-five

Juliet had no trouble making her way back to the house alone. Ignoring shouted comments from passing men, she ran the whole distance, pulled the key from her pocket, and unlocked the door. Once inside, she raced to the bedroom, threw herself down on the big brass bed, and proceeded to drench the blue and white mattress with her tears and pound it with her fists. . . . Oh, how she wished she had not put her ear to the door to eavesdrop on Noah and the doctor!

Then she would still be blissfully unaware of Noah's desire to have a normal wife who thought the sun rose and set on him. Since she already did think the sun rose and set on him, Noah's disappointment in her had to stem solely from the fact that she wasn't normal. She had known he was worried about her and wanted to help her "get better," but had somehow never realized the depth of his dissatisfaction. How he must regret their marriage!

If indeed they were actually married. In the eyes of the Apaches, they had a binding union, but whites might not consider it so. She had no knowledge of marriage customs among white people. Had never heard of opium or electricity either, though she did have a passing acquaintance with leeches. What had the doctor intended to do with leeches? She could not imagine, but suspected she would not like it, and neither would the leeches.

Not only was she hurt, she was furious! Noah had betrayed her. Had forced her to tell the doctor or had himself revealed things she had told no one but him. How could he have done that to her? How could he have discussed their most intimate, personal problems with a stranger? She supposed she ought to have suspected what he intended, but somehow she had thought that the doctor would simply examine her, pronounce her healthy, and let it go at that.

She had not expected the intrusive questions—the speculation—the raised eyebrows—the look of amazement. They both thought she was mad, but she knew she was not. She was as sane as either of them. She had tried so hard to be patient with Noah, hoping that eventually he would come to understand, but her patience had finally run out. If Noah could not accept her the way she was, she would leave him, go to Mrs. Lathrop, and ask if she could live at the mercantile until she found a way to support herself. She would volunteer to work in exchange for food and shelter.

What she would *not* do was spend the night in this house, in this big fancy bed, with a man who thought she was sick in the head! Let him sleep alone. Let him meditate upon the errors of his logic. Let him pine for her and realize that he needed her as she needed him— sick, well, or somewhere in between. Did he think *he* was so perfect? In looks perhaps he was, but in other areas, he was sorely lacking. A pig had more sensitivity, a horse more compassion. Animals did not brood for days on end—or lecture, preach, and scold. They did not insist that she think like them; only Noah considered himself so free of defects that he never once doubted he was right and she was wrong.

Juliet sat up and wiped the tears from her face. It had grown dark as pitch. There was a lamp on the table in the outer room, but since she was leaving, she saw no need to light it. She smoothed back her hair and straightened her gown. If she wanted to be gone before Noah returned to the house looking for her, she

342

had better hurry. The front door banged open. Too late. He had already arrived.

"Juliet! Damn it, where are you?"

Composing herself, she sat quietly and waited for him to discover her presence. He must not see how upset she was. She had her pride, after all.

He stormed into the bedroom. "Juliet! Are you in here?"

"I am here," she admitted.

"You scared me out of my wits! I was frantic with worry. . . . Wait a minute."

He thundered back into the outer room, made a noisy job of lighting the lamp, and finally returned, holding it in front of him so that its light illuminated his flushed face. "Why didn't you wait for me? Anything could have happened to you out on the streets alone after dark in this town."

She would not defend herself. She was done with defending herself. Noah must be made to realize she was a grown woman, not an incompetant child. She blamed herself that he treated her like a child. In allowing her fear of Tucson and Fort Bowie to get the best of her, she had been acting like one. If she could not make it on her own in Tucson, she could always leave and return to the Apaches. The desert and mountains did not frighten her half as much as the world of the whites; in the mountains, she could survive.

"What have you got to say for yourself, woman?" Noah set the lamp on a small round table beside the bed, then leaned against the doorjamb, folded his arms, and glared at her.

"I have nothing to say, except that I am leaving you, No-ah. You need not concern yourself with my welfare any longer." She stood up and brushed the wrinkles from her gown while Noah gazed at her openmouthed. The silence hung thick between them, and the lamp sputtered, casting eerie shadows on the wall.

"You're walking out on me because I took you to a doctor?" he finally got out.

She straightened and looked him full in the face. "Not because of the doctor, but because of what you said to him."

"What in hell did I say?"

"Think about it, No-ah. Perhaps the answer will come to you. You thought I could not hear you, but I put my ear to the door and listened. I am glad I did for I learned that I do not please you or make you happy. . . . You wish I were not who I am." An errant tear rolled down her cheek. She blinked to forestall a flood.

"You think I wish you were someone else?" Abandoning his casual pose, Noah raked his fingers through his disheveled hair. "Damn it, Juliet, I *love* you. How many times do you need to hear it? Do you think my feelings change from day to day, hour to hour, minute to minute?"

"I think you wish you had married a woman of your own time and place, *this* time and place, which is the only one you can remember. You wish I had not complicated your life or made things difficult for you. You wish I were 'normal', whatever normal means."

A light dawned in his eyes. "So that's it. You misinterpreted everything I said."

"I did not misinterpret. I heard you clearly."

"You *misinterpreted!* I never meant to imply that I don't love you the way you are. I do. I love everything about you."

"You do not love my dreams or the past we shared or the fact that I keep trying to explain what happened to us and how we got here."

"Sweetheart, you don't *know* how we got here. You're only speculating. Well, my theories are as good as yours. Why shouldn't I defend them? I've never in my life heard a tale like yours; it's too incredible to be true. But just because I can't accept it—just because I wish you didn't have these crazy dreams and theo-

344

ries—doesn't mean I don't love you." His hands encircled her shoulders and gripped them tightly. "Honey, I've made my commitment. I'm in this for good. You won't get rid of me that easily. I don't intend to walk out of your life, and I won't let you walk out of mine."

"But . . . what are we going to *do*, No-ah? We came here so the doctor could help me, and it seems he cannot. What happens now?"

"Now we see if we can find your family or anyone who knows you. We set up housekeeping and strive to act like 'normal' married folks. We make love on this big brass bed. We eat, belch, argue, ride out into the desert to watch the sunset, we make babies . . ."

"Babies?"

"Isn't that what normal married folks do? Settle down and have cute, smelly little babies? I thought all women wanted babies."

"Well, I do, but . . ."

He laid a finger across her lips. "But nothing. We *live*, Juliet. We do all the mundane ordinary things people do every day. We don't think about your dreams or worry about them. We don't agonize about the past or future. We enjoy the present. It might work, you know. Given a little time, this whole problem may resolve itself."

"But *how* will we live, No-ah? Will you still write your book about Geronimo and sell it?"

"I don't know about the book, honey. It's not the right time for it. The ending is too uncertain, and people aren't ready to hear good things about Geronimo. What I will do is keep abreast of the day-to-day news about the Apaches and wire stories back home to my boss at the newspaper where I used to work. If he doesn't want them, I'm sure I can find other buyers on the eastern seaboard. In any case, I've got enough money saved to keep us going for a good long while. If I don't feel like it, I don't have to work at all for a couple years. I think we should stay in

345

Tucson at least for the winter. I sure as hell don't want to travel anywhere until spring. When spring comes, we'll reevaluate our situation and decide what to do next."

"Oh, No-ah!" Juliet threw her arms around his neck. "You are right. We will stay in this sweet little house, make our home here, and hope everything will be fine and wonderful! Perhaps it can work out, after all."

He hugged her so tightly her ribs were in danger of cracking. "It can, and it will, sweetheart. I promise."

"You will teach me to read English? So I can read the newspapers and the stories you write?"

He laughed in her ear. "If you want, of course, I will. We'll also borrow books from Doc Bailey and anybody else who'll lend them to us. I think when you read some of the doctor's books, you'll understand how it's possible to have stored all this stuff about Greece in your head, and . . ."

His continued skepticism dulled her euphoria. Drawing back from him, she studied his face. "I am able to read Greek, No-ah. How can I do that if I never spoke it sometime in my past?"

"It's . . . a puzzle, Juliet. That's all I can say. You've forgotten some things and remembered others. Probably no one on earth can explain or fully understand it."

"And the dreams? What about the dreams? Did the doctor say why I have them?"

He gave her a wry smile. "I thought you were listening at the door."

"I was, but I did not hear it all. What did he say about my dreams?"

"He doesn't know any more about them than we do, sweetheart. In time, they may just go away. He thinks you probably suffered some terrible trauma, and your mind doesn't want to remember it. Whatever happened, we can't force the issue. All we can do is live one day at a time and make the most of each one."

346

She melted into his arms again. "I am so tired, No-ah. I do not wish to think about it anymore. Thinking only exhausts me. 'Tis an excellent idea to give ourselves over to the present and cease worrying about the past."

"Well, that's exactly what we're going to do. I'm disappointed that Doc Bailey had no immediate cures, but I'm not sorry we came here—and I'm sure as hell not sorry I fell in love with you. You're the best thing that ever happened to me, Juliet. If I hadn't met you, I'd have died of loneliness and cynicism. Little by little, you're making a new man of me. . . . By the time I become a proud Papa, I'll be ready for it. I just hope we have a pretty little golden-eyed girl with pale frizzy hair that I can love and cherish as much as I love and cherish her beautiful mama."

Somehow he always knew what to say to calm her fears and make things right between them—a baby! Who would have imagined that Noah Copper McCord relished the thought of becoming a father? She pulled his face down and kissed him deeply, falling in love with him all over again. Noah could be arrogant, stubborn and impossible, but he could also be the most wonderful man on earth. She did not know what she would do without him and did not want to ever find out. How fortunate that he had come before she left him!

When he came up for air, he was laughing. "Hey, didn't you say you were hungry?"

"I am not hungry anymore," she whispered. "Later, I will be *very* hungry, but right now I am more in need of . . . bed rest."

Grinning wickedly, he leaned her backward until she collapsed on the big brass bed. "First things first then. Let's go to bed, though I doubt you'll be doing much resting."

They soon lost themselves in the wondrous pursuit of pleasure and unity. But even as they rolled together on the big brass bed, a little part of Juliet hung back,

347

watching and worrying. She had driven the white bull away—banished it to some dark corner of her mind—but she knew it would come charging back again, strong and determined, as menacing as ever. *You cannot escape me.* The threat echoed and reechoed in her heart. Try as she might to pretend that the past did not matter, it did. It very much did.

It did not take them long to get settled in Tucson. Prudence Lathrop took Juliet under her wing as if she were the daughter-in-law the birdlike little woman had always wanted to fuss over. Juliet quickly learned everything she needed to know to survive in Tucson. At Prudence's urging, she spent the afternoons at the mercantile helping to put together orders for customers. This was usually the time when Noah was busy writing his news stories so it gave her something to do while he was busy.

Occasionally, he "free-lanced" as he called it, for the *Arizona Star,* but mostly he wired stories back East and wrote in his journal, taking notes for a book about the Southwest in general rather than Geronimo in particular. News about the Apaches continued to trickle into Tucson, causing a great stir every time an incident occurred. In early November, an Apache named Jolsanny, also known as Ulzana, whom Noah and Juliet remembered as the soft-spoken, gentle-mannered brother of Chihuahua, rode into New Mexico with ten braves and left a trail of bloody havoc, raiding and killing everywhere they went.

For days afterward, all Juliet heard in the mercantile were condemnations of the Apaches. No one seemed to understand that the Indians were raiding because the natural foods they depended upon were scarce this time of year, and they were hungry. Everyone assumed that the Apaches raided out of boredom and bloodlust; to the residents of Tucson, Geronimo's followers were predatory animals who killed for the sheer enjoyment of it.

At the end of the third week of November, Jolsanny and his warriors swooped down upon Fort Apache and murdered some of "their own people." Only Juliet and Noah realized that they were wrecking revenge on Apaches from rival tribes who had joined the army to harass them in the mountains. Recalling White Antelope's defection to the whites, they knew that Jolsanny wouldn't be killing other Apaches without good reason, but the residents of Tucson lumped all Apaches together and did not distinguish between tribes that had long been traditional enemies.

Troops gathered all over the territory, Lt. Gen. Philip H. Sheridan arrived from Washington to confer with General Crook at Fort Bowie, and newspapers across the country clamored for the Apaches to be stopped. Crook was widely quoted as saying that Jolsanny had "traveled not less than one thousand two hundred miles, killed thirty-eight people, and captured and wore out probably two hundred and fifty head of stock." In retaliation, Capt. Emmet Crawford was sent to the Sierra Madre to route out the renegades.

"Why do they never tell the Apache side of the story?" Juliet groused to Noah after painstakingly poring over some of the newspapers Noah had collected. It was several days before Christmas, a holiday which Juliet was eagerly anticipating, for Prudence Lathrop had told her all about it. Now, however, she could think of nothing but the plight of her hounded friends.

"Because white sympathies lie with the ranchers and settlers, not with the Apaches," Noah answered, pushing some of the newspapers aside and pulling Juliet closer to him on the bed where they had been sprawled on their stomachs reading together.

"I showed you how my last story was edited, didn't I?" he continued. "They deleted enough lines and words to slant the piece *against* the Apaches when I started out to try and tell their side of things—diplomatically, of course."

"Tis so unfair!" Juliet cried. "Why does no one even wonder or care how Geronimo must feel—losing his little son at Fort Bowie?"

On a visit to town, Clem had mentioned in passing that one of Geronimo's wives who had been captured by the soldiers and taken to Fort Bowie in August had had to bury her two-year-old son, Little Robe, in the cemetery at Apache Pass. Juliet had not socialized much with Geronimo's wives, but she remembered Little Robe and still mourned him. None of the newspapers had expressed sorrow over the child's loss, but Little Robe was as much a tragedy of this conflict as anyone else. Hunger, fever, and constant running had weakened him, as it always weakened the young and the old. Eventually, it had taken his life. Now even the cold, windswept high country of the Sierra Madre would not be a safe haven for the Apaches.

"How many more will die before this is over?" she wailed, crumpling a newspaper and tossing it across the room. "Oh, No-ah, sometimes I get so angry over this unfair fight that I want to climb atop a barrel in the mercantile and tell everyone exactly what I think of them!"

"Now, now . . ." he soothed, moving closer and wrapping his arms around her. "Remember we agreed not to preach and make enemies. It's all right to say what you think here in this house, but you can't go spouting off in the mercantile. It's simply too dangerous. Besides, the whites have as much to complain about as Geronimo. I interviewed a woman yesterday who lost her husband, son, and brother to the Apaches. Why, she barely managed to escape with her own life."

"How terrible!" Juliet burrowed deeper into Noah's embrace. "Oh, I realize that the Indians are at fault, too, No-ah, but they are the ones who were wronged in the first place. Now, they are sadly outnumbered.

Captain Crawford has hundreds of soldiers while Geronimo can't have more than thirty or forty warriors left."

Noah nosed her neck. "Hmmmm, that's true. And if the army doesn't catch him before spring, they intend to gather up every Indian who can follow a trail and hire him to help track Geronimo. He won't stand a chance against so many."

"Is there nothing we can do to help him, No-ah?"

Noah regarded her somberly. "Nothing, sweetheart. We certainly can't go looking for him in the mountains ourselves at this time of year. Even if we could and we found him, we couldn't persuade him to surrender."

"But now that he's lost his whole family, maybe he would be more inclined to listen."

"I doubt it. Don't forget that he reclaimed one of his wives," Noah reminded her. "And his oldest son, Chappo, is still with the band. More importantly, he's still Geronimo, the proudest, wiliest, most stubborn old Apache alive. He thinks bullets can't kill him. If he was ready to surrender, he would have done so by now."

"I still wish we could speak to him again," Juliet whispered. "This time, I would take *your* side and urge him to surrender just as you did. I realize now that surrender is the only chance the Apaches have of surviving."

"So you've learned a few things since you came to Tucson, have you?" Noah resumed nuzzling her neck. "I knew it would be good for us here, Juliet. Why, you haven't had a bad dream since we got here, have you?"

She stiffened slightly, but did not answer. She hated to lie to Noah but did not want him to know that she had had a half dozen or more dreams since their arrival. Fortunately, she was getting better at concealing them and usually awoke before awakening him.

"Juliet?" He lifted his head to study her face. "*Have* you been dreaming about Jason again?"

351

Vigorously she shook her own head in denial. This much was true. Jason no longer invaded her dreams—but the white bull came more and more often, issuing threats and instilling terror.

"Thank God for that," he breathed softly. "You see? You *are* getting better."

Some small spark of rebellion made her answer, "I was never ill."

"You were too stubborn to admit it—and *still* too stubborn. But I can accept small victories in lieu of major ones. The cessation of your dreams is an excellent sign that tells me you're improving. I'm so glad, Juliet. Now if I can just find out who you are—locate someone who knew you or your family. . . . I've been asking everyone I meet. Sooner or later, we'll discover something."

He hugged her again, but she could not relax and embrace him with equal enthusiasm. She had not lied but she had not told the truth either—how she hated being dishonest with Noah! Every time she dreamed of the white bull and did not tell him, she was being dishonest. Letting him think that he was going to find her family or someone who knew her compounded her dishonesty. Nothing would ever come of his inquiries, but she let him keep hoping—and that was a lie. For the sake of peace between them, she no longer argued. But for how long could she continue such dishonesty? The lies were abominable. She desperately wanted truth between them!

"No-ah, I *do* still dream," she murmured. "And . . . they are not pleasant dreams."

His muscles tensed. Slowly, he pushed back from her and narrowed his eyes on her face. "What do you mean, they are not pleasant?"

"I keep having the same nightmare over and over. A . . . a white bull comes to claim me and take me away from Jason. He wants to prevent me from marrying. He . . . he lusts after me, and in his anger that I will not yield to him, he chases me and hurls thunderbolts into my path. . . . I think he is the god, Zeus, but he may be someone else, someone wicked and evil, not a true god at all. . . . Can gods be evil as well as good? These things confuse me. All I know is that once I escaped him, but he keeps coming after me. He will not give up. He will not leave me alone. He stalks me in my dreams . . ."

She shivered in remembrance of the terror the dreams invoked. She had learned to submerge her fear and hold it at bay, but occasionally, it resurfaced even when she was awake. She wondered if he was simply biding his time, waiting until the proper moment. At times during the day, she could sense his presence . . . feel his red eyes watching her every move.

"Dear God!" Noah breathed. The blood had drained from his face, and he was watching her with an expression of horror. "Juliet, why didn't you tell me all this before now? I thought you were getting better. I had no idea you were still having nightmares—and such terrible ones, at that!"

Immediately, she regretted her confession. How could she have expected him to understand? "I . . . I was afraid to mention it. I wish I had not done so now, but I was trying to be honest with you, No-ah."

He sat upright on the bed, his mouth tight with anger. "Did you lie to me when you said you hadn't had any more dreams about Jason?"

"No. That was not a lie. I dream only of the white bull now."

"The white bull," he repeated, lifting his palm to press it against his forehead. "In Greek mythology, a white bull is Zeus' symbol . . . but in this case, I think he means something more. He symbolizes your withdrawal from reality."

She could almost read his thoughts—his fear, his denial, his outrage that she dared defy his will by having nightmares instead of getting better. "I am not withdrawing from reality, No-ah. The white bull is a . . . a reality on a different level. He may be the reason

353

why we were sent forward into the future. I . . . I have wondered about that. I have considered it. But I am still confused. Was Zeus an evil god? How does he compare to . . . to Usen . . . and to the God you always mention?"

Noah's color went from pale to crimson. He looked as if he wanted to cry but was too angry to do so. Instead, he glared at her. "Go get that book on Greek history that Doc Bailey lent us, Juliet. Fetch all the damn books he said we could look at. I think it's time we read them—a task I've been avoiding because I didn't want to disrupt things when they were going so well. . . . Hah! So well. Little did I dream we were this close to disaster."

"I do not wish to read your books on Greek history, No-ah. Forget that I mentioned my nightmares. I am sorry I did. It has only provoked your anger."

"Not anger—panic. Desperation. Fear. Can't you see that this is going to destroy you, Juliet? It will destroy us both. I don't know who or what you think the white bull is, but it's clear to me that he represents your surrender to madness, your escape from reality. You don't want to recall what really happened to you up in those mountains, so you've made up this incredible tale to explain it all . . . only you didn't quite make it up. Nobody is that inventive. You got it all from your past reading and your fascination with Greek mythology and literature. It's all in those books somewhere, and I'm going to find it and show it to you. *We* are going to find it. Once and for all, I'm going to prove to you that you've made it all up."

"You will be unable to prove it, No-ah. The truth of what happened is not in books—but in here!" She clapped her hand to her heart. "I know what I feel. I know what I know. You have somehow lost that capacity. You cannot even communicate your thoughts. Perhaps you once could, but not anymore."

"Damn it, I *never* could! There's logic behind everything, Juliet. Logic rules the universe. We haven't un-

354

raveled all its mysteries yet, but that's only because we haven't found the logic. It's there—waiting to be discovered. Just like we've discovered how to send messages over a wire and how to illuminate entire cities!"

This gave her pause. "You can make whole cities light up?"

"Go get the books," Noah responded wearily. "I won't be distracted. Later, we can talk about electric lights. Now, we're going to talk about Greek mythology, history, and literature."

"If you insist. But it will do no good, No-ah, for I already know how we both got here and why."

Chapter Twenty-six

They spent the remainder of the day studying Doc Bailey's books, and Noah made a shocking discovery: Juliet could recount Greek history with great authority as far back as the Archaic Period. She knew the Classical Period best, up until the year 401 B.C., but after that, recalled nothing.

Relentlessly, he quizzed her and established that she could discuss Homer's writings about the Trojan War, recall the arrival of democracy in 508 B.C. and relate numerous incidents regarding the Peloponnesian War between Athens and Sparta. She was able to pinpoint when democracy was temporarily lost and when it was reinstated in 403 B.C. Most amazing of all, she could accurately describe the city of Athens during this period.

With a description of the ancient city in front of him, Noah queried his wife about the location of the *agora* or marketplace, the Dipylon Gate or main entrance, the Panathenaic Way or main road to the Acropolis, and other important landmarks. Juliet spoke of them as if she had seen them with her very own eyes. She recalled many details of daily life—what the ancient Greeks wore, what they ate, how they lived, and the gods they worshiped.

All of this required very little prompting. The book furnished brief facts, and from them, Juliet could reconstruct an entire civilization. Noah grew more and

357

more depressed, while Juliet became more and more elated. He could only conclude that prior to losing her memory, she had possessed a phenomenal capacity for storing vast quantities of information. However, Juliet believed that this was proof positive that everything she had been telling him was true.

"Do you not see now, No-ah? The white bull *is* Zeus," she exclaimed as they pored over descriptions of Greek gods and goddesses. "See here? It states that Zeus had many affairs with mortal women and appeared to them in various disguises, such as a bull, a shower of gold coins, and a swan. Is that not what it says?"

"That's what it says, all right." Noah did not believe it for a minute but was willing to forestall further argument until he'd had more time to think. "Too bad he didn't come to you as a shower of gold instead of an ugly old bull."

Juliet peered at him from beneath her lashes. "You do not really mean that, No-ah. You are mocking me again."

"No, no, I'm not. The bull in your dreams is definitely Zeus. Funny, but I don't recall that he was such a wicked fellow. Capricious maybe, but not wicked. Wish I could remember where he came from and how he got that way. Sometimes I think *my* memory is slipping."

Juliet wrinkled her forehead, thinking. "I recall some of his story. According to legend, Mother Earth—Gaea was her name—rose out of chaos and gave birth to a son, Uranos or Sky, who then became the husband of Gaea."

"Weird," Noah snorted, paging through the book until he found a section entitled 'Myths and Legends of the Deities.' "Too weird for me. Don't know why I found this stuff so fascinating as a child."

"Because it *is* fascinating! Uranos and Gaea had many children, but the most important among them were the fourteen Titans. Cronos, one of the Titans, led a rebellion against his father and deposed him. Cronos then married his sister, Rhea. Their youngest son was Zeus. Zeus gathered his brothers and sisters together to fight the Titans, deposed them, defeated Cronos, and became the leader of the new gods. The new gods all retired to Mount Olympus and were called Olympians."

Noah read for several moments, then shut the book with a snap. Everything Juliet had just described was written there—the legend of how Zeus became the leader of the gods and goddesses of ancient Greece. How could Juliet remember all this but not be able to recall her own name, her parents, or where she herself had been born?

As if she could read his mind, Juliet said, "I know all these things, No-ah, because I grew up hearing them in my family."

"Then you *do* remember your family!"

"Not exactly," she hedged. "Not apart from my dreams. But 'tis as I told you, No-ah. I lived back then. I knew all the gods and goddesses as well as you know the story of Jesus, who was born centuries later on Christmas day."

Noah wanted to shake her, wanted to do anything but swallow the incredible tale.

"Juliet, if we were to read the Bible instead of Greek history, maybe you'd remember more about Jesus and less about Zeus. You're just recalling what you've read. For some reason, you can't remember anything that happened after 401 B.C. I can't explain why, but I bet if we chose books at random, other things would come back to you. You must have loved to read; obviously you devoured everything you could get your hands on."

"No, my dearest love. I recall what I do because I lived in that era—and so did you."

Noah leaped from the bed. "Don't *say* that! Don't think it, because it isn't true." He began to pace the floor. "I'm going to take you back East, Juliet. That's what I'm going to do. There are better doctors there, someone who can help you and explain what's happening—what's *happened*—and how you've distorted it all. You've mixed everything up in your head, and you're trying to draw conclusions to explain your unusual situation. But I can't let you go on this way, sweetheart. I've got to make you face reality."

She sat very still on the bed, her beautiful golden-brown eyes filled with sadness. "I *am* facing it, No-ah. You are the one who is not. Zeus will eventually come for me. When he does I know not if I can fight or resist him. He is much stronger than I—far more powerful and persuasive. In one of my dreams, he told me he is the fallen archangel, the bearer of light and darkness, all that is beautiful and all that is ugly. I do not understand what he meant, but . . ."

Noah's breath exited his lungs in a sudden whoosh! He stood rooted to the floor. "A fallen archangel? You mean like Lucifer?"

Juliet frowned. "Who is Lucifer? The name means nothing to me."

"As I recall it, Lucifer was one of God's archangels—the greatest beings He ever created. But Lucifer was proud and ambitious. He thought himself the equal of his maker, and he challenged God. The details of the story elude me, but I do know that God defeated Lucifer and cast him into eternal torment, a place called hell, where he supposedly lives today, spending eternity luring humans to join them."

Juliet's frown deepened. "Lucifer is like one of the Titans created by the Earth Mother?"

"Created by the Father," Noah corrected. "He certainly sounds like them. And you must have known what an archangel was in order to recognize the similarities. You *said* the white bull claims to be an archangel."

"*I* do not claim it; the white bull claims it."

"He says he's an archangel."

"He used that term, yes."

Noah knelt on the floor in front of Juliet and took her hands. "Then don't you see? That's proof that you know something of the present. Like me, you were taught about God and archangels. You had a Christian upbringing. So you *couldn't* have come from the past; your knowledge of the past is derived from books."

Tossing her cloud of hair, Juliet refused to look at him. Her expression was so forlorn that he ached to comfort her. Comfort but not *agree*. He could not afford to agree with her. One little capitulation on his part, and she would think he had bought the whole pack of lies and fabrications.

He tilted up her chin, so she had to meet his eyes. "Honey, we'll wait until the spring to travel, but then I'm taking you back East to find a doctor who can deal with this and cure you. Back East, I'll put notices in all the major newspapers requesting information about your family. We'll solve the mystery of who you really are. I promised that we would, and we will."

Juliet did not say a word. She only gazed at him with great sorrow and hurt, her pain digging deeply into his own heart. Her suffering was his suffering, but he could not ease it by pretending to accept her delusions. He had to keep fighting the madness; the white bull was a good symbol for it. He felt as if he were indeed grappling with a white bull or a fallen archangel or Lucifer himself.

"You do not love me enough to believe me," she whispered in a broken voice that seared his heart. "Oh, No-ah, you do not love me enough!"

He gathered her stiff body into his arms. "I *do* love you—I do! Believe me, Juliet, I love you."

She let him hold and kiss her. Let him caress her and remove her clothing. Let him make love to her. She let him plunge into her, thrusting over and over, spending his passion in her sweet, pliant body. But she did not once gaze into his eyes and give him what he wanted most—her innermost surrender. She did not concede that he might be right or give him any hope that she would abandon her impossible beliefs. He realized then that she could *not* abandon them. She clung to them because she had no choice. They possessed *her,* not the other way around.

Christmas came and went. The year of 1886 arrived, and more news about the Apaches filtered into Tucson. In late January, the army under the command of Captain Crawford located and destroyed the Apache *ranchería* hidden among the towering peaks and yawning gorges of the Sierra Madre. All of the provisions and the Indians' entire herd of horses were confiscated. Geronimo then sent word via a woman of the band that he wanted to talk. Before the meeting could be held, a group of Mexican irregulars, army volunteers serving without pay in the hope of gaining plunder, mistakenly shot and killed the army captain.

The second in command, Lt. Marion P. Maus, held the meeting, at which Geronimo reportedly summarized his fears that he would be executed if he surrendered. Despite these fears, he agreed to send nine hostages back with the lieutenant as a guarantee that he would attend a later meeting to be held in March, at which time he was willing to discuss terms of surrender with General Crook himself.

The hostages were expected to arrive at Fort Bowie any day now, and Juliet was in a fever wondering who among her old friends might be imprisoned at the fort, and whether or not she could convince Noah to allow her to go and visit them. He did not think visitations would be permitted, but had agreed to discuss the matter with Clem, the next time the soldier came to town.

"I hope that bloodthirsty renegade, Geronimo, *is* killed!" Prudence Lathrop declared to Juliet one night, as they were sweeping out the mercantile after it had closed for the day. "I hope every last one of those murderin', thievin' Apaches gets what they've got comin' to 'em."

Juliet clutched her broom and swept with greater vigor. Prudence's viewpoint came as no surprise to her; it echoed the opinions of nearly everyone else in town. Still, she hated to hear it. She could not understand how a woman who was normally the soul of kindness and generosity could be so vindictive when it came to the Apaches.

Prudence quit welding her broom and faced Juliet with a disapproving frown. "What do *you* think, Juliet? Wouldn't you like to see the Apaches who took you prisoner shot or hung? I know you got a soft spot for 'em, but after all that's happened, surely you can admit that the only way to stop 'em is to kill 'em."

Noah had made Juliet promise that she would not rush to the defense of the Apaches every time the topic was mentioned. She had therefore grown adept at avoiding discussions such as this one. Now, however, they were alone in the store. It was closed, and Eugene had gone off somewhere in the company of several of his cronies. Juliet swept more slowly as she debated what to say; surely she and Prudence were good enough friends by now that she could risk telling her the truth.

"No, Pru, I do not wish to see the Apaches executed. They treated me very kindly while I was with them. They were a bit rough on my husband at first, but they finally accepted him, and after that, they treated us both quite well. I made friends among them, and I can well understand why they're fighting. I'd be fighting too, if I'd lost my lands and my way of life like they have."

"You don't say!" Pru exclaimed, looking as if she had been dashed with cold water. "You were actually friends with those heathens?"

"Heathens?" Juliet questioned. "Do you mean people who do not believe in gods?"

"God," Prudence corrected. "I mean people who do

not believe in the true Christian God and may, in fact, worship the devil."

"The devil!" Juliet exclaimed in surprise.

"That's right, Lucifer, the evil one. I bet that's who the Apaches worship and pray to—the devil himself."

"Usen is their God," Juliet explained, confused. "They also recognize many other powerful spirits who may or may not be gods."

"Heathen spirits, the lot of them! You had best not defend Apaches to me or my customers, girl, or I'll have to ask you not to work here in the store anymore."

Hands suddenly trembling, Juliet clutched her broom so tightly that her knuckles turned white. "Are you actually saying that I will not be permitted to work here if I speak kindly of the Apaches?"

"Nor live in my house," snapped Prudence Lathrop. "It's not that I'm intolerant, mind you, but my customers are. They might not patronize the mercantile if they think I'm harborin' an Injun-lover under my roof."

"But I cannot lie about the way the Apaches treated us. They are not vicious animals. If you knew them better, you would probably like them, Prudence."

"I can't ever like an Apache, Juliet—not after all they've done. And if you can't help feelin' sorry for 'em, then you'd better just do what you've been doin'—button your lip when the subject comes up. Some of the hotheads in this town would be only too happy to put a bullet through an Injun-lover just as quick as they'd put one through an Injun. Don't mean they'd shoot *all* Injuns on sight, but they'd shoot Apaches. If the army ever does capture Geronimo, they're gonna have to send him somewhere else just t' keep him alive. He can't stay in Arizona 'cause folks won't allow it."

"Do not tell me the Apaches will not be permitted to return to their reservation!" Juliet was aghast. "That would be too cruel."

"Why, the Injuns oughta be pleased not to have to go back there. From what I hear, it's a terrible place—a furnace in the summer and freezing cold in the winter. Plus, it's full of mosquitoes and disease."

"Then how could anyone have expected them to remain there in the first place?"

" 'Cause they're Injuns an' don't deserve better. Nobody was hardly willin' to let 'em have decent land that settlers wanted. No, it'd save a heap o' trouble if they all up an' died. I didn't think that once, but I do now. Why, way back in the seventies I can remember readin' an editorial in the *Arizona Citizen* that said it all in plain, memorable English. These were the exact words: *'The kind of war needed for the Chiricahua Apaches is steady, unrelenting, hopeless, and indiscriminating. We must slay men, women, and children . . . until every valley, crest, crag, and fastness shall send to high heaven the grateful incense of festering and rotting Chiricahuas.'* Yep. that about sums up how people around here feel, me included."

Juliet just stared at Prudence. She could not imagine such virulent hatred.

"Powerful words, ain't they? Guess that's why I remember 'em so well. . . . No, the Apaches can't stay in Arizona if an' when they finally get caught or surrender."

After this enlightening conversation with Prudence, Juliet had to agree. Silently, she resumed sweeping, wishing she could sweep prejudice out the door as easily as dust and spilled coffee grounds.

Juliet did not get to visit the prisoners at Fort Bowie because Noah managed to convince her that no possible good would be served by making an issue of their pro-Apache sentiments. When Noah himself encountered some ranchers in the street who recognized him and drew their guns, she needed no further proof of the danger of their position. Only the timely appearance of the sheriff and the fact that Noah had quickly drawn his own pistol had averted disaster. After that, Juliet ceased asking.

She found consolation in the knowledge that their beliefs were being aired elsewhere. Several of Noah's articles appeared intact in Eastern newspapers. His publisher friend forwarded the clippings which arrived along with a box of books and a letter from a young woman named Emily who wrote that she had met and married a wonderful young man and hoped Noah would understand and not be too disappointed.

"Are you disappointed?" Juliet asked as they rode out into the desert to exercise Patch and a dainty mare Noah had bought her to replace the horse they had given to the army. There had been a lot of rain and cold lately, and the horses greatly needed exercise, almost as much as she and Noah needed to be out in the bright afternoon sunshine beneath the cloudless blue sky.

"Hell, no, how could I be when I'm happily married to you?"

Juliet basked in the glow of hearing the word "happily". They *were* happy as long as they weren't discussing the past. By mutual silent agreement, they had not discussed it lately, and Juliet was certain that Noah had no idea how often she awoke drenched in perspiration and trembling with terror because she had dreamed of the white bull again. The dreams were occurring two or three times a week now, but at least, she was able to wake herself up almost as soon as the animal appeared standing motionless in his olive grove.

She sensed that some final confrontation was approaching, but preferred not to dwell on it. For as long as possible, she wanted to savor the bliss of living with Noah, making love to him in the wide brass bed, and sharing all the intimate satisfying rituals of daily life. There was no sense spoiling the present by worrying about the future. If she wanted to be worry, she could always brood about Noah's promise to take her back East to the doctors there. Since he hadn't mentioned it since the day they read the history books together, she hoped he considered her so nearly normal now that he didn't think it necessary to take her back east.

Better to talk about this mysterious Emily than introduce more disturbing topics.

"Did you love Emily?" she probed, intrigued by this glimpse into Noah's past which he rarely discussed.

"Not the way I love you." He gave her a sly, sensual appraisal from beneath his dark lashes that made her blood race. "She never made me feel as you do. Therefore, I'm delighted she found someone besides me to love. Emily is a wonderful girl, and she deserves the best. I've already wired my congratulations and explained that I, too, have found a wonderful mate."

Directing her mare around a large clump of prickly pear cactus, Juliet noticed something. "No-ah! The desert is starting to bloom!"

Tiny, tight buds were emerging from the round, flat, needle-studded surfaces of the plant. Studying the landscape, Juliet noticed that other plants and trees of the *chaparral* were also budding. It would not be long before the entire desert bloomed with color. Although she had no memory of past springs in the desert, just by looking at the buds she had an intimation of the grandeur to come.

"No-ah, 'tis going to be beautiful!"

"Yes," he said. "I expect it will be. Spring has finally come."

She glanced at him to see what he was thinking, for his tone held a somber note. He met her gaze with a troubled one, as if remembering something serious and important.

"Juliet, I didn't suggest we ride out here merely to admire the scenery and exercise the horses. There are some things we have to talk about."

She gave her attention to guiding her horse through a maze of thorny obstacles that could lacerate the unwary. "I am much better now than I was when you first suggested returning East, No-ah. I had hoped you had abandoned that idea."

"Well, I haven't. But in deference to how much 'better' you claim to be, I've decided to put off traveling east until after the Apaches surrender."

A reprieve. The Apaches might not agree to surrender for a long time yet. She dared to look at him again. "You think they actually will surrender?"

"The meeting between Geronimo and Crook is set for the middle of March," he said, ". . . and that's coming up fast."

"Yes, I know."

"I've requested and received permission from General Crook to attend. Crook's at Fort Bowie now, awaiting word of Geronimo's arrival at the meeting place."

"Where is that?"

"In northern Sonora in Mexico, about ten miles south of the Arizona line and eighty-odd miles from Fort Bowie."

"I see. . . . When will you be leaving?"

"Tomorrow morning."

"Tomorrow!" Her horse jumped and the hem of her skirt—a special one made for riding—brushed across some *cholla* and came away stuck with a hundred needles.

"That's what I wanted to tell you. I think it best that you stay here with the Lathrops while I go to Fort Bowie and wait for word from Lieutenant Maus that Geronimo has come down from the mountains for the meeting."

"But No-ah, I want to go with you! I would be no trouble. You know how well I get along with horses; my mare and I are already good friends. I can easily keep up with the soldiers."

"You can't go, Juliet. I myself was lucky to get permission. At first, I wasn't going to ask, but as you say, you seem to be 'better' lately, so I thought I'd risk it. You haven't been having any more nightmares, have you?"

"No," she lied. Guilt instantly consumed her, but she knew what he would say if she told him the truth. He would forego this once-in-a-lifetime opportunity to witness history in the making and insist on taking her back East instead.

"Will any other women be going?" she asked. "Any of the officers' wives perhaps?"

He grimaced. "Don't be foolish. You know they won't. The only women who may be going are a couple of the Apache prisoners. I understand that Crook hopes to soften up Geronimo and soothe his fears by letting old Nana's wife provide the latest gossip and describe the good treatment they've been receiving in their imprisonment."

"If the Apache women are going, I do not understand why *I* cannot!"

"You're *white,* Juliet. When are you going to remember that? I'm sorry, but you just can't go."

They rode in silence for a bit, while Juliet tried to think of more arguments why she should be permitted to accompany him. Finally, Noah said, "Juliet, stop pouting. I'd like to take you, but it's impossible. If you make a fuss or try to come along, Crook will probably withdraw his approval of my request . . . and I have to be there. Every other white in attendance will be biased against the Apaches. I'm the only one who can be depended upon to tell the truth of what happens at this meeting and give a fair account of the Apache side of things. My presence alone will help ensure that the Apaches are treated fairly. General Crook is aware of my sentiments. He's even read a few of my articles. Apparently, someone sent him the same clippings we've already seen. He knows who I am and why I came here. I took Clem and young Gatewood into my confidence, and both men have done an excellent job of presenting my case to him."

"Yes, of course, you must go, No-ah. 'Tis only that

369

I shall miss you so much and worry all the while you are gone."

"Nothing's going to happen to me. If a bunch of ranchers had been invited, that would be a different story. I'll be perfectly safe riding along with the army."

"I hope so, No-ah."

He reached across the space separating them and grasped her hand. "Come on, sweetheart, smile. I won't be gone that long. When I come back, we'll make arrangements to return East to see those doctors."

She almost snatched back her hand, then thought better of it. "You mean we will *discuss* returning back East. I really see no need for it, No-ah. I like Tucson. I want to make our home in the vicinity. Leaving the desert and mountains would be most difficult for me."

The look he gave her was measured and speculative. "We'll talk about it when I get back," he agreed.

Juliet found consolation in the thought that if Noah was gone for a while, there was less chance he would discover the extent to which her nightmares had increased. She would have a bit more time to confront her deepest fears and overcome them. The struggle was between her and Zeus—or whoever he was—not between Zeus and Noah. She had to win the battle with the white bull on her own . . . or lose it on her own. Certainly she could make a stronger stand if Noah were not there to witness her struggles.

Chapter Twenty-seven

The meeting between Geronimo and Gen. George Crook took place on March 25 under some large cottonwood and sycamore trees in a place called the Cañon de los Embudos in Mexico. Before it began, Noah walked around taking notes describing the area and everyone in attendance. At least twenty-five Apache warriors were present besides the leaders Geronimo, Naiche, and Chihuahua.

The Apaches had made camp in a lava bed atop a small conical hill surrounded by deep ravines. Noah suspected it would take several armies to route them out of it, if they did not want to leave on their own. The soldiers occupied almost an equally strong position on a nearby mesa. Between the two camps lay several steep, rugged gulches. Careful not to enter the canyon meeting place in a large, vulnerable group, the Indians came in small groups of twos or threes, while their comrades stood back and kept a careful watch. All of the Apaches were well armed, well dressed, and in excellent physical condition, a testimony to their hardiness in the face of adversity. Noah could not help marveling at their recovery, considering that they had lost everything not long ago.

A photographer, C. S. Fly, from Tombstone, Arizona, bustled about trying to get the wary Apaches and the army principals, General Crook and Lieutenant Maus, to pose for pictures—not an easy task in the tense, volatile atmosphere. General Crook was wearing the practical pith helmet he favored and Lieutenant Maus a slouch hat; neither man cut a very dashing figure nor remotely resembled a person of authority, yet everyone knew who they were, and of course, the entire assemblage recognized Geronimo and Naiche.

C. S. Fly exercised great aplomb in persuading his recalcitrant subjects to line up and assume proper poses; Noah had to stifle a grin or two when Mr. Fly requested this or that fierce-looking Apache to tilt his head a certain way or rearrange his posture to facilitate a better photograph. Geronimo nodded to Noah, and Blue Bandana also acknowledged him with a brief grin, but no one else singled him out for conversation. They seemed too impressed by the seriousness of the occasion to make idle small talk.

General Crook had ridden a mule to the meeting—a mule named 'Apache' being his favorite mount—and most of the animals in the army pack train were also mules. The Apaches eyed the mules with slit-eyed interest, but did not comment upon them. The many interpreters available had nothing to do until the actual conference started. Those Apaches not directly involved in the negotiations, Blue Bandana among them, assumed armed positions on the fringes of the area, clearly indicating that any false moves would be met by rifle fire.

General Crook took it all in stride, never so much as blinking an eye in nervousness. He greeted Geronimo cordially, invited him to choose from among the army interpreters, and then offered him the opportunity to state his grievances and explain why he had left the reservation at Fort Apache and embarked on a trail of blood and violence.

Noah was surprised to see that Geronimo had worked up a sweat and was fingering a buckskin thong with uncharacteristic anxiety. He had not expected the old man to show signs of apprehension, but the preceding months since Noah had last seen him had

372

obviously taken their toll. Geronimo's mountain haven had been invaded and his family captured. His little son was dead and his band growing smaller and smaller, while his pursuers continued to multiply. No wonder he was sweating as he stood face to face with an enemy far more powerful than he had ever imagined.

"I wish to talk first of the causes which led me to leave the reservation," Geronimo said, then detailed his growing fear that he would have been hung or jailed if he had stayed at the reservation—this despite the fact that he had done nothing wrong while in captivity.

He cited news stories and editorials calling for his execution and the destruction of all Apaches. Noah himself could verify these stories but hadn't realized that Geronimo knew about them. To Noah's further surprise, Geronimo apologized for his depredations, explaining that they had been necessary to his survival and that of his band.

"There are very few of my men left now," the old man sadly stated. "They have done bad things but I want them all rubbed out. Let us never speak of them again. From now on we want to live in peace."

Yes, Noah thought, Geronimo had come a long way since the last time they had argued over the issue of surrender. The Apache leader demonstrated none of his former bitterness and desire for revenge and freedom. As much as Noah had longed for this moment and done all he could to achieve it, he still found it a tragedy that this proud, fierce man was being forced to give up everything he had known and cherished in his life.

"There is one God looking down on us all," Geronimo reminded his rapt audience. "We are all children of the one God. Usen is listening to us. The sun, the darkness, the winds, are all listening to what we say now. To prove that I am telling the truth, remember that I sent you word I would come from a place far away to speak to you. You see us now. Some have come on horseback, some on foot. If I were thinking bad or had done bad, I would never have come."

Noah had no trouble accepting this as indisputable proof of Geronimo's intention to live in peace. The old man would never have come down out of the mountains unless he meant to stop his warring ways and live peacefully from this day forward. Geronimo might be guilty of many things, but lying wasn't one of them. In the ancient code of the desert, an Apache's word was his bond. Only through association with whites had the Indian discovered the fine art of saying one thing but meaning another. However, General Crook did not share Noah's certainty that Geronimo's impassioned speech constituted proof of his good intentions.

"You're lying," the general boldly stated, his blue eyes hard, his bearded face implacable beneath his pith helmet. "What you're saying is all bosh. No one was going to arrest or hang you while you were on the reservation. You broke your word to live in peace there, and you'll probably break it again the first chance you get."

Geronimo denied that he could not be trusted. He patiently repeated the reasons why he had left, but the afternoon ended in a stalemate, both sides agreeing to think about what the other had said and to meet again the next morning for further discussions. That night, Noah shared a bottle of whiskey with C. S. Fly and slept later than usual in the morning. When he finally awoke, he discovered that he had not missed anything for nothing had occurred.

The Apaches did not return to the canyon to resume negotiations that day. Instead, they spent it in their volcanic stronghold arguing among themselves. Messages were sent back and forth to General Crook who informed the Apaches that their surrender must be unconditional. Noah requested an interview with the general and quizzed him about his instructions from

Brig. General Sheridan. Crook would only say that "the time has passed for easy forgiveness," and "the Apaches will gain little by delaying the inevitable."

"What *is* the inevitable, General?" Noah asked the redoubtable old mule-lover.

"Why, they're all going to be shipped east to Florida, Mr. McCord. They will not be permitted to return to the reservation as they are demanding."

"You can't grant them *any* concessions?"

"Sorry, I can't."

The interview abruptly ended, but as the day wore on and some of the Indians weakened while others refused to budge, Crook softened his position and sent word that the imprisonment would not exceed two years, after which the renegades would be returned to the reservation. He also promised that the warriors could choose who among their families they desired to accompany them into exile.

Chihuahua was the first to accept the new terms, Geronimo the last. At noon on March 27, the Apache leaders again met with General Crook to make formal speeches of surrender and acceptance of terms. Chihuahua's oration was so obsequious that Noah found it difficult to conceal his disgust.

"You must be our God," Chihuahua told Crook. ". . . the one who makes the pastures green, who sends the rain, who commands the winds, who makes the fruits appear every year on the trees. . . . Everything you do is right." He humbly added: "Please send my family with me wherever you send me. I ask you to inquire if they are willing to go or not."

Geronimo, at least, retained his pride in the face of what must have been a bitter defeat. "Once I moved about like the wind. Now I surrender to you, and that is all."

Appropriately solemn, he shook hands with Crook and asked to have his family there to meet him at Fort Bowie when he arrived. Crook readily agreed. When his turn came, tall, handsome Naiche was equally brief and restrained. "When I was free, I gave orders . . . You now order and I obey. Now that I have surrendered, I am glad. I will not have to hide behind rocks and mountains; I will go across the open plain."

Following the formal speeches, the Apaches retired to their camp with the understanding that Crook would depart at once for Fort Bowie to await them, and the Apaches would gather the remaining women and children still hiding in the hills and join Lieutenant Maus and the scouts for a more leisurely journey. Noah was torn between riding back with Crook—whose eagerness to leave stemmed from his desire to telegraph news of his victory to General Sheridan—and staying with the Indians. He missed Juliet terribly, more than he had ever thought possible; he also had a vague premonition that something might be wrong at home. Ignoring his impulse to gallop Patch all the way back to Tucson, he decided it would be best to stay with the Apaches.

Until Geronimo was safely incarcerated at Fort Bowie, Noah dared not leave him. He recalled how Mangas Coloradas, the revered Apache leader of earlier times, had been shot and killed trying to "escape" his guards after voluntarily surrendering. Noah intended to keep a close watch to ensure that nothing similar happened to Geronimo. History must not be permitted to repeat itself.

General Crook departed the next morning, and by that night, Noah found more reason to be fearful. The Apaches obtained *mescal* from a bootlegger named Tribolett whose reputation for selling whiskey to Indians on the Mexican side of the border was well known. On this, their last night of "freedom", the Indians embarked on a raucous drinking spree.

Along with nearly everyone else in the soldiers' camp, Noah lay awake all night long listening to the Indians get drunker and drunker. Shots were fired, voices raised in challenge and argument, and Noah expected at any moment that all hell would break loose. To his credit, Lieutenant Maus did not attempt to stop the debauchery. Apparently realizing he was sitting on a powder keg, he chose to look the other way while the Indians caroused one last time in their impregnable stronghold.

Bunked down in a tent with the doughty little photographer, Noah barely slept that night. When he did chance to doze off, he dreamed that Juliet was calling him—her voice laced with panic as she begged him to come and save her from the white bull. He awoke drenched with sweat and wishing he had gone home after all. His sense that Juliet needed him was so strong that he bolted upright and staggered out of the tent in search of Patch, intent on leaving then and there—and Geronimo be damned!

It was just past daybreak. As Noah approached the string of picketed horses, a familiar figure flew across the no-man's-land separating the two camps. Noah recognized Juliet's friend, E-Clah-heh, the wife of Naiche. She was babbling hysterically. Noah could not make out what she was saying. He reached her at the same time as one of the interpreters.

"What's wrong?" Noah barked, impatient to make sense of the rapid flow of words.

"She say Naiche fall down and cannot get up. She say beware Tribolett. That one make big trouble. He tell Geronimo army intend to hang him soon as they get him across border."

"Damn!" Noah swore. "I'll go help Naiche while you inform the lieutenant."

The interpreter, a young Indian scout of another tribe, nodded and ran off, while Noah followed the frantic E-Clah-heh back to where her husband lay sprawled on his stomach, arms outstretched, one hand curled around a pistol. Naiche's eyes were closed. A pool of foul-smelling vomit lay near his handsome face. As Noah knelt beside the usually quiet, reserved Apache leader, he could have strangled the man called Tribolett.

He had never met him, but he knew exactly the sort of scoundrel he was—one of many troublemakers who profited from the Apache wars and didn't want to see them end. His kind hardly cared that they were contributing to the ruination of an entire people and causing murder and havoc.

Noah gently turned Naiche over on his back, while E-clah-heh stood at his shoulder, moaning and wringing her hands. Hoping he might see someone who would fetch him a bucket of water, Noah glanced about and spotted Lieutenant Maus stalking toward them, accompanied by several soldiers, rifles at the ready. The lieutenant's face was dark as a thundercloud. E-clah-heh started forward to waylay the officer. At that moment, Naiche raised his head, opened his eyes, and witnessed his wife hurrying toward the blue-coated lieutenant.

It all happened quickly. As if his hand had a life of its own, Naiche raised his pistol and fired. E-clah-heh screamed and crumpled to the ground. Too late, Noah grabbed the smoking pistol from Naiche's shaking fingers. The Indian offered no resistance. His dazed eyes stared unseeing into space. He grinned lop-sidedly and with a long sigh, subsided back into unconsciousness.

"They're all drunk as lords," Maus snarled. "Lucky he didn't shoot you instead of his wife." He knelt to examine E-clah-heh who was lying on her side weeping. "The damn fool got her in the leg."

"He didn't know what he was doing," Noah defended. "I'll see that they both get help. You'd better find Geronimo and that fellow Tribolett before there's any more trouble."

"Right," Lieutenant Maus agreed, rising.

The soldiers found Geronimo but not Tribolett. Geronimo was in no better condition than Naiche. Since travel was now out of the question, Lieutenant Maus decreed that they would not leave for Fort Bowie until the following day, the twenty-ninth of

March. That night was quieter, but still a restless one for Noah. A few random shots were fired in the Apache camp, but for the most part, silence reigned. It wasn't until morning that Geronimo was discovered missing. During the night, he and Naiche, along with twenty men, fourteen women, and six children stole two horses and a mule and slipped silently away, leaving not a single trace of their passing.

"Noah! Noah! Noah!" Juliet awoke suddenly to the sound of her own screams bouncing off the adobe walls.

For a long breathless moment, she could not remember where she was. The gray shadows of early morning cloaked the room, and vivid images of her dream still held her in thrall. Thunder continued to boom in her ears. Jagged slashes of lightning stabbed the twisted bed sheets. Her hair crackled with its energy, and a burning odor stung her nostrils.

Struggling to reorient herself, she sat up and covered her face with her hands. After a few moments, her heartbeat returned to normal. Her breathing slowed, but the dread remained. This time, the white bull had almost gotten her. In the midst of the terrible storm, she had heard his panting and felt his hot breath down the back of her neck.

It had been the worst of all her nightmares. If Noah had been home, he would have awakened long before she did. She began to weep unrestrainedly. For some time now, she had feared going to bed and sleeping. Nor were her fears confined to the night hours. Sometimes during the day, she had a sense of something evil—some dire threat—hanging over her head. Lately, nothing was as it should be; she was even losing her special powers.

Yesterday, she had found a scrawny cat slinking about the courtyard. It would not let her catch it, though she had tried to reassure it with her thoughts.

It would not come to her even when she set out food for it. Hissing and swiping whenever she got too close, it had finally clawed its way over the wall. In a panic, she had run to the stables to see if her mare would still accept her thoughts. The horse had whinnied when she entered the shelter, but that might have been its normal welcome for anyone it recognized. She had concentrated with all her might, but none of her messages seemed to be getting through to it.

She felt diminished—not her normal self—and wondered if one day she might simply fade from this world and be thrust back into the past. Perhaps that was how the bull would get her; she would go to sleep one night and never wake up. Once again she would lose the only man she had ever loved. So she wept not only for herself but for Noah, who would never understand. Trapped in the present, Noah would conclude she had died. If her body went with her, he would think she had run away and left him.

Either way, he would be devastated. *She must not let it happen.* Getting to her knees on the bed, she folded her hands and tried to pray to whoever had saved her the first time. Noah and the Apaches had taught her that there were many gods—or perhaps only one God, known by many names. Zeus or the white bull may not even be a god; he might be a fallen angel, someone who had defied God but still possessed great power. If that were indeed the case, only God Himself could defeat him.

"Help me. . . . Tell me what to do," she begged, gripped by despair.

The riddles of the universe were beyond her abilities to understand, but there had to be someone somewhere listening and willing to help. The world was too beautiful a place to have been born out of nothingness, derived from thin air. The smallest flower, the humblest cactus plant, the birds and animals were all evidence of a guiding intellect greater than any human's.

In the mountains, on the ledge where she had first

met Noah, she had gazed across a landscape chiseled by a sculptor to whom centuries meant nothing and eons scarcely mattered. In the mountains, His presence had been overwhelming; she had felt it the strongest of any place. The Apaches had felt it, too—and so, perhaps, had Noah. In Tucson, that elemental awareness and primitive certainty had disappeared entirely. But then Tucson was a creation of men, not God. It could most accurately be described as godless. In the East where the cities were larger than Tucson, the truths she most ardently sought would be even more distant. The power of Usen could not reach her there—could not help her elude the grasp of Zeus.

"Please . . ." she whispered. "Guide me. Help me."

Kneeling on the bed, her hands folded, she strove with her whole being to reach out into the universe and connect with the Holy One—and the answer suddenly came to her, as clearly as if a voice had spoken: *Return to the mountains. There, you will be safe.*

The mountains, the Land of the Standing-Up Rocks . . . the ledge in the Heart of Rock where Noah had found her. . . . Her panic ebbed away. Peace and determination replaced it. Yes, she must go back to the mountains, to that very ledge where it all began. It was her only chance. If she was ever to defeat the white bull and win the right to remain in the present with Noah, it must be done there. Somehow, she must convince him to take her back as soon as possible.

Chapter Twenty-eight

Several days later, Noah entered the house holding the most recent newspapers proclaiming Geronimo's surrender and almost simultaneous escape. Juliet had already seen them and heard the latest news: President Cleveland himself had rejected the conditions Crook had granted the Apaches. The Indians would be sent East with no guarantees of release from imprisonment. Those still on the loose were to be hunted down and either captured or destroyed. Sheridan, Crook's immediate commander, was blaming Crook for Geronimo's escape, and Crook himself, stung by the allegation, was on the verge of resigning. The newspapers predicted that his successor would be Brig. Gen. Nelson A. Miles.

Juliet knew all of this as she ran to greet her husband. Launching herself into his arms, she kissed and hugged him. Neither said a word. Words were unnecessary to convey the extent to which they had missed each other. Noah's emotions revealed themselves in his rib-cracking embrace—and in the way he looked at her when he drew back. Geronimo's escape had been a terrible disappointment, a defeat that Noah took personally.

Wanting to make everything better, convinced that she could fix *some* things at least, she blurted out her desire to return to the mountains, quickly explaining how and why she had reached this conclusion—and how it would solve all their problems. "I had a terrible nightmare—the worst ever. I was weeping and praying, No-ah. And suddenly the answer came to me as clearly as if someone had spoken."

Noah's reaction was anything but what she wanted—or had anticipated. All the pleasure of their reunion drained from his face. "No, Juliet, no. I won't take you back to the mountains."

"But No-ah, you must!" she started to argue, only to be silenced by his upraised hand and embittered exclamation. "Hell, I knew something was wrong! Somehow I sensed it, but I never dreamed it was *this*. Sweetheart, you're ready to snap. I should never have left you; by now, we could be halfway to Boston."

"I will not go to Boston or any other large city in the East." Juliet folded her arms and stepped back from him. She must win this argument or suffer the consequences—which were exactly what Noah feared most. They would lose each other. "With or without you, No-ah, I am going back to the ledge. After that, assuming everything is all right, I intend to search for Geronimo and persuade him to surrender. If he does not do so willingly, the soldiers will kill him on sight. As you can see from the newspapers," she nodded at the table where he had tossed them down in order to take her in his arms, ".... the President himself has ordered it."

Noah studied her in the cynical fashion she had learned to hate. Beard-stubbled, trail-dusty, and tired-looking, he needed a bath and a good night's sleep. She ought to have waited, but she had already waited too long. She had been so impatient for him to come home so she could tell him, and they could leave. The sooner they left, the sooner she would be his entirely, with no threat of Zeus or anyone else to tear them apart.

"President Cleveland," he drawled. "So you do remember him."

"No, but 'tis all in those newspapers, and thanks to

you, I can read now. Enough to understand that. The President has said that all the Chiricahua Apaches must be shipped to a place called Fort Marion in St. Augustine, Florida, a long way from Arizona. They will leave shortly. Geronimo and those who are with him will be the only ones left in the territory, other than some who have been working for the army against their own people."

"You are well informed. You *seem* perfectly sane. But you're not, Juliet. You're teetering on the brink of madness. Taking you back to the mountains will only push you over the edge. I won't risk it. Besides, if thousands of soldiers and a couple hundred Indian scouts haven't been able to find Geronimo, we sure as hell can't. No, we'll leave at once for the East."

"Then you will have to tie me or lock me in chains, No-ah. Unlike the poor Apaches who did surrender, I will not go calmly to meet my fate. I will not place myself at your mercy, trusting you know what is best for me. You do *not* know. No more that the whites know what is best for Geronimo. Somewhere along the way—or perhaps when we get there—I will die or fade away."

"Fade away? What in hell are you talking about?"

She faltered slightly, realizing she could not adequately explain. Still, she must try, though her explanation would probably add to his fear that she was slowly going insane. "I . . . I am losing myself, No-ah. Parts of me are . . . weakening."

His reaction was predictable. He stared at her as if she had sprouted green hair. "What parts?"

"My ability to communicate with animals, for one thing—and perhaps in other ways as well. I am not certain."

"That was never normal anyway! I hope you do lose that ability!"

She bit her lower lip. "For me it was normal. I should think you could admit to that by now. . . . Oh, No-ah! If you will not take me back to the mountains for my own sake, because I ask you, then take me for the sake of the Apaches. I am the only one who may be able to persuade Geronimo to surrender, instead of being killed. He is afraid, No-ah. Afraid and alone. I know exactly how he feels because it is the way *I* feel when you will not listen to me. If I tell him he will come to no harm, maybe he will believe it. You know he trusts me as much as he trusts anyone. I am Shaman Woman. Since he, too, is a shaman, we share a sacred bond."

"You don't share a damn thing except a wild impulse for self destruction! God in heaven," Noah muttered, turning away from her. "How did we ever reach this impasse? Why is it that whenever I go off and leave you, you come up with something new to shock the hell out of me?"

She could not let him wallow in skepticism and disbelief. This time, she *had* to reach him. Had to convince him. Before it was too late.

"No-ah look at me!" she begged. When he pointedly gazed at the wall, his eyes cold and distant, she sank to her knees in front of him. "No-ah, I am pleading with you. Take me back to the mountains. Do not refuse. *Trust* me. Just this one time, listen and believe what I say."

She raised her arms in a gesture of supplication, but it had the opposite effect of what she wanted. He grabbed her arm and hauled her upright. "Don't kneel to me! Don't behave as if I'm some monster! Do you know how it makes me feel to see the woman I love on her knees before me, weeping and pleading? I am not some damn ogre! I'm a normal human being trying to grapple with something I've tried to understand but can't!"

Unflinching, she met his furious gaze. "Just take me back to the mountains, No-ah. 'Tis all I ask. In the mountains, I will be healed—at least, *you* will consider it healing. I will consider it resolution. My transfer to this world will become permanent. No longer will I be threatened with leaving."

"Damn it all, Juliet, you're talking nonsense!" He paced up and down the room. He raked his hair with his fingers. He muttered and swore under his breath. Then he drew to a halt and simply stood there, glowering at her. She knew the precise moment when he relented. Something wavered and shifted in his eyes.

"You're sure of it, Juliet? You're absolutely certain?" After that momentary breakthrough, the old skepticism curled his upper lip. "How can you *possibly* know such things and cling to them so stubbornly?"

She reached for his hand and carried it to her breast. "In my heart, I know them, my love. I can offer you no other explanation. Believe in me, No-ah. For once in your life, set aside cynicism and doubt. Trust as you have never before trusted . . . love as you have never before loved . . ."

His face softened. He lifted his hand to caress her cheek, and tears glinted in his eyes. "You ask too much of me, Juliet. You demand too damn much."

"Only what is necessary, No-ah. I would never ask it otherwise. All love is a leap of faith. 'Tis a journey into the unknown; the outcome can never be ascertained beforehand."

"I have gone farther with you than with anyone." His voice broke, and a tremor ran through him. "To go farther still repudiates everything I am, all I've ever believed."

"That is what love does to a person," she whispered. "It forces you to risk your whole self, all you are, all you have, all you believe. Love me, No-ah. . . . We will take the risks together. Oh, No-ah, I need you so much!"

He nodded—a slight inclination of the head, but she took it for assent. He would take her back to the mountains. Whatever awaited her there, they would face together. They were united now. They stood together against the white bull. She lifted her face for his kiss. His lips claimed hers. They clung together, and desire poured through her like a white-hot river. His touch scalded her. His kisses obliterated all the hurt he had inflicted with his doubts. Lifting her in his arms, he carried her into the bedroom. They sank down on the bed. Arms and legs entwined, they sought and found their own small piece of heaven, the one place where doubts, fears, and hurts never intruded.

They could not leave immediately. Too much was happening, and Noah had to honor his commitments to several newspapers. In early April, seventy-seven of the previously captured Apaches, including wives and relatives of the renegades, were shipped east to Fort Marion in Florida. E-clah-heh, Smiles-A-Lot, and Half-Moon were among them, and Juliet's heart ached for her old friends who did not even have their husbands with them. Noah had told her what Naiche had done in his drunkenness; she had wept for poor E-clah-heh, wishing she could have bade her farewell, at least, but visits to the fort during this time were still discouraged.

On April 12, Brig. Gen. Nelson A. Miles arrived in Arizona to replace General Crook. Miles quickly assembled an army of five thousand regulars, dismissed all but a few of the Indian scouts as unreliable, and set up more heliograph stations throughout the mountains. Lt. Charles B. Gatewood, whom Noah and Juliet had first met at Fort Bowie, was assigned to search the mountains for Geronimo in company with two Apaches who had been among the docile ones remaining on the San Carlos reservation when Geronimo first fled from it. Hearing the news, Juliet expressed doubt that these "old friends of Geronimo" would be very persuasive in convincing him to surrender.

"We ourselves stand a better chance," she informed Noah as they prepared to leave Tucson. "It shouldn't be too difficult to find him. After all, we found him once before."

"No, he found us—rather, Blue Bandana did," Noah reminded her. "I'll take you to the mountains, Juliet, and we'll locate that ledge. But if whatever you hope is going to happen doesn't happen, then we're heading east."

She stopped what she was doing and went to him, lifting a hand to caress his face. "It will happen, Noah. I am certain it will."

His brow dipped downward. "It's a fool's errand, Juliet. I myself must be going mad to let you talk me into this. The army will be out there combing the same mountains we are—along with every other range between here and Mexico. And Gatewood will be searching the Sierra Madre. What if we get caught in the middle of a fight, or die of thirst like we almost did the last time?"

"You worry too much, No-ah," she gently chided. "We learned much among the Apaches. We can survive on the desert and in the mountains. This time, we know where to find water—and we can stay clear of any battles."

His frown deepened. "How can you be so certain—and so damn calm about it all?"

She smiled but did not tell him, for she knew he would not understand. Since they had made the decision to return to the Land of the Standing-Up Rocks, she had not dreamed of the white bull even once. At first, the lack of nightmares had puzzled her, but now she understood. The battle lines had been drawn; in the mountains she would confront the white bull one last time. In the mountains, her future—and Noah's—would be decided. So would the Apaches'. Until then, she need not worry.

"I am calm because I know we are doing the right thing," she soothed. "When you rely upon instinct and your inner voices to guide you, you can only win,

No-ah. Losing is impossible, so you need not be afraid or apprehensive."

He snorted. Instead of reassuring him, she had only provoked more worries. Noah Copper McCord was not accustomed to relying on intangibilities. He had spent his life paying homage to facts, worshiping logic, and searching for dark truths beneath falsely bright exteriors. Accompanying her to the mountains on a whim—merely because she said so—sorely tested his newfound trust. He had restated his objections more than once, but each time, she had reminded him that he had given his word, and she was counting on him to keep his promise.

Hating to lie to her friend, Juliet nonetheless told Prudence Lathrop that she and Noah were traveling to Fort Lowell, ostensibly to visit friends, and then to buy land for a ranch. Prudence's eyes widened at the news that they had bought a pack mule.

"What'll you be needin' a pack mule for? Fort Lowell's not that far away, an' you can get all you need right there."

" 'Tis not my idea," Juliet hastily improvised. " 'Tis my husband's. If we decide to look for land first, we will have plenty of provisions with us."

"Hmmmph!" Prudence snorted. "Best land for ranches is south of here, but only fools would risk lookin' at it while Geronimo is still at large. 'Course, you bein' an Injun lover an' all, you probably think Geronimo wouldn't harm you."

"He wouldn't. You don't know him like I do, Prudence. He's just like you and me—he protects his friends and battles his enemies. He's no monster as everyone claims." Juliet waited for the usual arguments and protestations. Surprisingly, there weren't any.

"Well, if you say so. I ain't never met the man, but you have, so I guess I'll have t' take your word for it. I'm gettin' a little tired of hearin' all the tall tales about 'im anyway. Why, if I was t' believe 'em all, I'd have to believe the man could be in a half dozen places at the exact same time."

Coming from someone whose sentiments had always echoed the very worst of Geronimo's detractors, this small concession pleased Juliet enormously. It gave her hope that other residents of the territory might one day revise their opinions of the Apache leader—or at least be willing to hear his side of things. With genuine sorrow, Juliet bade Prudence Lathrop goodbye.

By the time Noah and Juliet rode out of Tucson, most of the desert plants had finished blooming. Juliet was therefore surprised and delighted when they encountered a stretch of Goldpoppies that reminded her of the rare spendor to be found in unexpected places in this untamed land. Scattered among the poppies were blue lupine and many shades of rich enticing green. It was a good time of year for travel and for harvesting the bounty of the desert. Patch tossed his head and whinnied his satisfaction at being out of the stable, the mare joyously echoed it, and the mule brayed a complaint at his heavy load.

Juliet smiled with pleasure and anticipation. She knew everything was going to be fine. In contrast to her ebullient mood, Noah was grim-lipped and silent. She wished she could ease his mind and enable him to relax and enjoy the beauties of the journey. With the sun shining on the Goldpoppies, the entire world seemed bathed in golden radiance. On such a wonderful morning, fear could gain no foothold. She was going back to the mountains; in the mountains, all her prayers would be answered.

It was relatively easy to find the Chiricahua range; only a fool—or a stranger to the region—could miss it, and Noah was neither fool nor stranger. The Chiricahuas dominated the skyline running roughly north to south from the central part of the Arizona Territory almost to Mexico. By now, he could identify each of the mountain ranges, having come to know all of them in the southeastern portion of the territory. One could hardly ride a day in any direction without being shadowed by distant ridges colored bluish-purple in the evening twilight.

Finding the location of the Land of the Standing-Up Rocks was a bit more difficult. Noah knew it was in the Chiricahua Mountains, but he had never marked the exact place. Riding at a leisurely pace, they followed the old Butterfield Stage Route, which had been abandoned some twenty-odd years before, and soon reached the Sulphur Springs Valley.

Once across the valley, their search began in earnest. Starting early in the morning, they rode up into the foothills hunting for the distinctive rock formations— the spires, towers, and pinnacles—that marked the general area where Noah had found Juliet on the ledge and Running Horse had died and was buried. When they did not find anything, they rode farther north, but the search proved fruitless.

All through the month of May they explored the mountains, taking time out only to hunt, forage for the Apache delicacies Juliet remembered, and locate water. Rain was sparse, and as May drew to a close, the desert became drier, the days hotter. Noah grew discouraged, but Juliet maintained her usual optimism. He had fallen in love with that resilient, resourceful, optimistic girl and cherished this time alone with her, because it reminded him so forcefully of that earlier time. Since they now had plenty of food and water, the interlude was more like a honeymoon than a quest; at night, they made passionate love beneath the stars.

June arrived, and they had still not spotted any sign of Geronimo, though they did evade detachments of soldiers on several occasions. Heliographs, five thousand soldiers, and Apache scouts notwithstanding, the Chiricahua mountains were a wonderful hideout. It was easy to lose oneself in them; the terrain was so rough in places that in order to properly explore it, they often had to dismount and proceed on foot.

Juliet was easily distracted—"No-ah, listen! I hear a wonderful songbird. Let us see if we can find him!"

After several such delays, Noah began to wonder if she was really serious about finding the ledge. Maybe it was enough for her simply to be in or near the mountains. Maybe she had begun to doubt whatever miracle she expected to occur. Or maybe she was avoiding the trip back East. He strove to be more methodical in their search, and at long last located the secret, hidden Land of the Standing-Up Rocks.

On the day they found it, they had ridden into a canyon, skirting an encampment of buffalo soldiers guarding a water hole. The company was composed entirely of black enlistees, members of the Tenth Cavalry, some of whom Noah had befriended at Fort Bowie. Not wanting to explain what he and Juliet were doing there, he led her a good distance out of the way to avoid being seen. Climbing the oak, juniper and pine-studded mountainside, they encountered unexpected traces of snow. As the going became hazardous, Noah dismounted, and leaving Patch with Juliet, who seemed more interested in the snow than in discovering the geological treasures of the area, he hiked to the mountain's rim in hopes of being able to spot the fantastic rock formations that had been eluding them for so long.

His efforts were amply rewarded when he found himself standing atop a crest affording breathtaking views of weird-shaped rocks, pinnacles, and cliff faces. More mountains abutted the stunning formations, and all were flanked by the deserts and valleys in which they had been camping. This was indeed the haunting, unforgettable site where he had first found Juliet. . . . Which precise ledge would mean days, if not weeks of additional search, but he had finally found the general area.

He filled his lungs with the cool, clear air. At this elevation, the air was thin. He could not recall the ledge being up so high, but he did remember the magnificent views in all directions. Nor could he be certain which mountain was his and Juliet's; they would have to take their time exploring until they discovered the right one.

Elated, he turned and hurried back to Juliet. She was not where he had left her. Patch, the mule, and the mare were all grazing contentedly, plucking the sparse greenery from the rocky terrain, but Juliet was nowhere in sight. A momentary panic swept him. Worried, he called her name. She did not immediately answer. Twice more he hollered "Juliet!" and heard his own voice bounce off the rocks. His heart constricted—then he suddenly saw her.

She was standing on a promontory a little above him. From her expression, he knew that she, too, was aware that they had found their destination. He climbed the incline and joined her. The view was as grand as his had been. He slipped his arm around her waist in the vague fear that she might slip on the loose stones and catapult over the edge. Absorbed in the scenery, she jumped when he touched her.

"Oh, No-ah! You startled me." She favored him with the sweetest of smiles. "Is it not beautiful?"

It *was* beautiful. Large rocks balanced precariously atop small rocks. Deep fissures created a grandeur that could only have been designed by a divine hand. They were looking down into an amphitheater of rocks, and across from them, the outline of a mountaintop against the sky suggested the face of an Apache. Superstition mingled with awe. This was a sacred place, a holy place, one in which Noah could easily believe that strange, wonderful—or terrible—things could happen.

"Well, we've found it, sweetheart," he murmured against Juliet's pale hair. "What happens now?"

"Now we must find the ledge," she whispered. " 'Tis somewhere in the Heart of Rocks."

"The Heart of Rocks?"

She motioned with her hand. "Here or perhaps in another spot. Whenever the Apaches spoke of this place, they called it the Land of the Standing-Up Rocks and referred to the Heart of Rocks, a particular part of it. I think that is where our ledge is. We must find it, No-ah."

"We've made it this far, we'll find the ledge," he assured her. "Or something that looks just like it."

She turned to gaze at him with shining eyes. "It must be the exact same one, No-ah. If we do not find it, I . . . I will never be healed."

Again, his chest tightened; he tasted deepest panic. "Are you . . . still fading?" He had witnessed no instance of her ability to communicate with animals on this journey.

She nodded. "Little by little. That is why I have stopped so often. Occasionally, I feel . . . weak."

He pulled her closer, not realizing until this moment that her strength had not been all it should be or had been. He scrutinized her covertly but discovered no sign of ill health. If anything, Juliet was more beautiful than he had ever seen her. Eyes, face, hair—they all glowed. Even her skin glowed. He thought he had never loved her as much as he did now, this very moment. It may have been a fool's errand to have come, but the trip was worth it just to witness her happiness.

"Let's make camp up here," he suggested. "Tomorrow, we'll start hunting for the ledge."

She readily agreed. However, they had to go down lower to find a level spot. It was colder that night than it had been on the plain. Noah didn't mind, since it gave him an excuse to keep Juliet locked in his arms all night. He made love to her beneath the blankets, prolonging the act for as long as he could restrain himself. He sensed that tonight was very special . . . and tomorrow would be special, too. Tomorrow, he suspected, they would find the damn ledge.

Chapter Twenty-nine

Juliet awoke early the next morning and poked Noah in the ribs to make him get up and watch the sunrise with her. It was spectacular, the sky red as fire, the rocks drenched in vivid color, the clouds tinged with scarlet and gold. She had never before observed such a magnificent sunrise—and she enjoyed it immensely until Noah pointed out its deficiencies.

"Wonder if those clouds mean a storm later on today," he grumbled. "On the day I found you on the ledge, there was a brilliant sunrise just like this one, tinting the sky and the clouds all red. Later on, we had that terrible storm. . . . I'll never forget it."

"I . . . I remember the lightning," she said, shivering slightly. Suddenly the sunrise was no longer so beautiful; instead, it seemed ominous.

Noah slipped an arm around her waist. "Don't worry. We'll keep an eye on the sky while we're hunting for the ledge. If it looks like rain, we'll quit searching and take shelter. There are plenty of overhangs and cubbyholes in the rocks around here."

"What about the horses? If they panic and run, they could be badly hurt." She was thinking of the horse she had butchered somewhere in the Heart of Rocks.

"We won't take the horses with us today. We'll lead them farther back down the mountain and let them graze where it's safer. If they panic at the lower elevations, they won't do as much damage to themselves.

Patch will come at my whistle, so I think we can let them loose, and they'll be all right."

" 'Tis a good idea," she agreed. "But we must be careful not to turn them out in an *arroyo* where they might be caught in a flash flood."

"Trust me to know that much, Juliet. I, too, have lived among the Apaches. I've also been in Arizona long enough to know what can happen in a thunderstorm." He tempered the sarcasm in his tone by leaning closer and kissing her cheek. "Did you sleep well last night?" he murmured in her ear.

She knew what he was asking, and it had nothing to do with thunderstorms, nightmares, or white bulls. She lowered her lashes flirtatiously. "Not really. Someone kept me awake most of the night with kisses and caresses I could not ignore."

He chuckled and lightly pinched her bottom through her split skirt. "So you found them . . . distracting."

"I found them delightful, and you know it!" She made a fist and punched his shoulder, but not hard enough to hurt either of them. Noah was wearing the satisfied smirk of a man who had little doubt he had pleased his woman, but still wanted to hear her say it. "What about you?" she challenged. "Did you sleep well?"

His grin turned rueful. "If I slept any better, I'd be too exhausted to search for the ledge this morning. Princess, you do know how to take a man to heaven and back."

Heaven . . . their own private word for the glorious unity and pleasure they found when they made love. She stood on tiptoe to nibble at his ear. "If you are very sweet to me today, I may take you there again tonight."

He laughed. "I hope to hell I have enough energy after a day spent climbing these rocks! Come on, you insatiable little vixen, let's get started."

After seeing to the horses, they spent most of the

day climbing and surveying the landscape in the Heart of Rocks, but without success. They could not seem to find the particular ledge where Noah had first discovered her. By midafternoon, Juliet was getting frustrated. She could close her eyes and picture it exactly—the narrow, rocky little trail, the steep ascent upward, the climb up the rock face using handholds that were no more than chinks in the rock. . . . When she opened her eyes, she could not see it anywhere. Everything looked different, which was hard to understand since it had been only a year ago since they had been here, and it was roughly the same season.

The only difference was that last year had been drier. This year, the soaptree yucca was still in bloom, its branches of white flowers rising erect into the sky or else bending all the way to the ground with their own weight. Nothing had been blooming a year ago. Looking back, she thought it had also been hotter—or else she had grown accustomed to the searing daytime heat.

It was hot now, the air very still. An hour or two earlier, the sun had disappeared behind a huge bank of clouds; their odd color now drew her attention. They were green with grayish black underbellies. She disliked the look of them and thought she scented rain. Noah motioned for her to climb up and join him on a shelf of rock just above her. The climb was steep and arduous, leaving her breathless when she arrived. He grabbed her hand and helped pull her up the last little distance.

"Are you all right? You're pale."

"I am just tired. And worried about those clouds."

"So am I." He tilted back his head to scan the sky. "They're starting to look downright nasty, aren't they? We probably should have quit before this and gone back down to the horses."

A wicked snap of lightning punctuated the comment. Thunder growled in the bowels of the clouds and rolled across the canyon. A second snap—this one stabbing the rock right at their feet—propelled Noah backward, taking Juliet with him. They collided with the wall of the cliff. Its rough surface abraided Juliet's shoulders despite the short, waist-length jacket she was wearing over her split skirt.

"Damn it! We've waited too long, sweetheart. Don't know why I wasn't paying attention. Got too caught up in looking for the ledge, I guess."

Another rumble of thunder drowned out his observation. Juliet wondered why *she* hadn't noticed the proximity of the storm before this. She had been keeping an eye on the sky as Noah had suggested, but the last time she inspected it, the clouds had been distant—hovering near the horizon—and they had not been this ominous color. She felt too vulnerable and exposed pressed against the cliff face.

"No-ah, we must find a safer spot."

"Up or down?" Noah dryly inquired. "Don't think it makes much difference. We'll just have to look for an overhang or indentation that offers more protection than this."

"Down," Juliet said, though they had been heading up. "I prefer to go . . ."

A second bolt of lightning cut her off midsentence. This one cut so close that the air crackled in front of them, and a sulfurous odor stung Juliet's nostrils. Thunder crashed, and the whole mountain seemed to shake at her back.

"Blast it all!" Noah cuddled her close. "Trust me to get us into a bad situation like this. I should have known better. I *do* know better."

No sooner had the thunder died down, when a gust of wind lifted Juliet's hair and flung it stingingly against her face. The coldness of the wind shocked her; she gasped as it flattened her garments against her heat-dampened skin and pressed her against the wall. The clouds were suddenly churning, the entire mass dipping low overhead—so low that she thought she could touch it if she tried.

Noah hooked an arm around her waist and shouted: "Come on!"

She followed as he half pushed, half dragged her down the steep incline. It had grown dark. She could barely see where they were going. The wind buffeted her as the sky exploded into an awesome spectacle of sound and fury that rivaled any nightmare she had ever had. Terror welled up in her. Stopping, she raised a balled fist to her mouth to keep from screaming. This was *worse* than all her nightmares put together. Lightning bounced from mountaintop to mountaintop. Thunder reverberated like a thousand rifles going off all at once in the canyon. She stood transfixed.

Noah tugged on her hand. He said something, but the wind whipped away his words. All she could hear were the horrific booms, one following so closely upon the heels of another that no other sound could compete. Sudden vicious rain slashed at her face and body, and the truth bore inexorably down upon her; the white bull had kept his promise. He had come for her, and there was no escaping him this time. The lightning bolts were his spears, the cold wind his breath, the thunder his ponderous hoofbeats. . . . She did not want to go! Did not want to leave Noah.

Blinded by the rain, she screamed Noah's name. He pointed to something she could not see farther below on the trail, then beckoned for her to follow him, but she was too afraid to move. Her feet were like blocks of wood, heavy and clumsy. Noah returned to her, drew her into his arms, and tried to calm her. She shook her head and wrenched away from him, cowering against the wall of rock. He slapped her face. The shock of it momentarily stunned her, then the impulse to flee boiled up, impossible to be denied. As panic consumed her, she pushed past Noah and began running. She ran blindly, unable to see where she was going, not caring where she went. The only thing that mattered was escape . . .

* * *

In the moment before Juliet broke and ran, the lightning's glare revealed her unreasoning terror. Noah saw it and understood. She associated lightning and thunder with her deepest fears. She was so afraid of the storm that she had even invented a persona for it; the storm and the white bull were one and the same. Somehow he had always known this, yet never with such blinding clarity. The violence of the storm had convinced Juliet that the white bull had come for her.

"Juliet, no! Wait!" he cried. "It's only a storm. It's just a thunderstorm, that's all!"

She did not hear him. Her eyes were the eyes of a hunted creature when it senses the hunter is near, and there is no escape. . . . Foreseeing its own destruction, it cannot help trying. Juliet had rather die in frantic flight than surrender docilely. Like Geronimo, she *had* to flee. She trusted no one—not even him. Not that he deserved her trust, doubting her as he had always done. Finding no safety in his presence, she bolted and fled.

He chased her. Stumbling on the rocky terrain, he sprawled on his hands and knees, and the slight delay gave her the advantage. He scrambled up and followed, but she had a speed born of terror, an agility born of desperation. He could not match either. In the rain, wind, and darkness, he lost sight of her. Still, he ran until his chest was heaving, and his side ached. He ran until he came to the edge of a precipice—revealed in the lightning's glare—and realized that one more step meant a plunge into nothingness.

Falling to his knees, he peered into the yawning void. The lightning illuminated a drop of such great distance that no one could survive the landing on the tumbled boulders below. He could not be certain if Juliet had run off the edge of the precipice or not; he had not seen her fall, but it seemed more than likely—where else could she have gone?

402

He would have to wait until the storm spent itself before he could search for her. Lying on his stomach, fearing the worst, he vented his sorrow and regret. He beat on the rock with his fists and cursed his own stupidity and weakness. He blamed himself for having brought her here. Through it all, the rain pounded him like a thousand pummeling fists. Thunder shook the wierd rock formations that stood like silent sentinels to his anguish. She must be dead—or if not dead, crippled and broken. Undoubtedly, her sanity was gone. She had lost it the moment before she broke and ran.

He could not imagine how he would live without her. The mere act of breathing almost defeated him; how much worse it would be when he finally found her! He recalled the many times he had told her how much he loved her; now he knew just how much that really was. He relished being Juliet's husband, friend, and lover; the thought of being plain Copper McCord, hard-boiled loner and news reporter, revolted him. Juliet had changed him in ways he could appreciate only now that he had lost her.

He wept and cursed and beat on the stone until his fists bled. The pain finally pierced his self-absorption. By then, the worst of the storm had passed, though it continued to rain until long after night claimed the mountains. Sometime during that endless span of darkness, he rose and sought shelter beneath a huge boulder balanced atop a smaller one. There, huddled against the rock, he shook and shivered and prayed, begging the God he had always repudiated to let Juliet be alive when he found her.

Every time he closed his eyes, he saw her body lying crumpled among the rocks. He dreaded finding it—and dreaded more *not* finding it. To never know precisely what had happened to her would be a living hell. In those cold, desolate hours of the night, when no light shone anywhere in all of the heavens, he resolved not to leave the mountains until he *had* found her, or what was left of her. His Juliet. His beautiful, half-mad Juliet whose love was the only sane thing in the entire universe. Yes, he would find her. He would stay in the mountains until he did.

But Noah did not find Juliet's body. He searched the mountains, the canyons, the cliffs, the rock formations . . . and discovered not a single sign of her. He did, however, locate the ledge—only a little farther up the mountain. Had the storm not burst upon them, they might have reached it within the hour. He lived on the ledge for many days—how many he had no idea. He drank where the wild animals drank and ate what the Indians would have eaten. By the time he thought to look for Patch, Juliet's mare, and the pack mule, they were gone. He found only his partially ruined supplies, which he laboriously carried up to the ledge. The supplies enabled him to survive—and to continue his search through the hot dry days and furious thunderstorms of the rest of the summer, every waking moment of which he spent searching for Juliet.

Only dimly aware that he had succumbed to his own sort of madness, he avoided any contact with other human beings. On three separate occasions, he spotted buffalo soldiers in the far distance. He could have walked right into their encampment in the canyon, but he wanted nothing to do with the soldiers. They would have tried to convince him that Juliet must be dead by now—her body stripped of flesh, her bones bleaching in the Arizona sunshine. He did not want to hear that. The only sound he craved—the only human voice— was Juliet's, Juliet calmly expounding on her incredible theories, Juliet patiently agreeing when he occasionally said something that made sense to her, Juliet arguing, scolding, questioning, laughing, challenging . . . whispering words of love and desire . . .

He spent his days in the lonely, solitary grandeur of the Heart of Rocks, but his eyes craved a different beauty—Juliet's golden-brown eyes, her cloud of pale hair, her slim but voluptuous figure, her elegance and grace, her loving smile. Half a loaf would have been better than none, he berated himself. Why had he spoiled their brief time together fighting over the past? Instead of trying to change her, he should have been satisfied with what he had. Mad, sane, or somewhere in between, Juliet in any guise would be better than no Juliet at all.

If indeed there *was* a white bull or a Zeus or a fallen archangel, the deity—or devil—had won. He had come back for Juliet and taken her, exactly as she had feared . . . but Noah still did not want to believe it. The logical side of him insisted that her body or bones were here someplace; he could not free himself from the wretched coil of grief until he found them. This terrible chapter of his life could not be closed until he discovered the truth of what had happened to her.

He did not anticipate anyone finding *him,* but one day, someone did. It was early evening, and he glanced up from his tiny cookfire to discover Blue Bandana silently watching him. The Indian held Patch by an Indian bridle, but neither horse nor rider had made the slightest noise to alert Noah to their arrival. Patch whickered softly in recognition, but Blue Bandana simply stood there—unsmiling, his face haggard, his body thinner than Noah remembered. He was still wearing a blue scrap of cloth tied around his forehead to hold back his long black hair, but his garments were tattered and unfamiliar. They looked Mexican, and war paint streaked his high cheekbones.

"I see Patch running alone on plain, and I know you come to mountains," Blue Bandana said without greeting or preamble. "I look for you, but no find. Soldiers come, and we flee. Now we return. What you doing in Chiricahua mountains, Red-Hair? Last time I see you, you sit among white men at Cañon de los Embudos. Shaman Woman not with you. Not with you now. Where Shaman Woman?"

Noah shrugged. "Somewhere in the mountains. I lost her during a storm. All this time I've been searching for her . . . I don't know . . . for two moons maybe?"

Blue Bandana frowned. "She dead, Red-Hair. Or else you find her—find ashes of campfire, find tracks, find sign the way Apaches teach you."

"I've found nothing," Noah admitted, setting a portion of the rabbit he had snared to roast on a spit over the low flames. "Come and join me, if you wish, but don't try to convince me to abandon the search. I don't intend to quit looking for her until I at least discover her remains."

Blue Bandana shook his head. "Never discover here. Too big land. Too many hiding places. Maybe rocks fall down during storm and cover."

"Maybe," Noah agreed. "But I'm not quitting until I find her. I'll stay here the rest of my life if I have to. I'll live in these damn mountains forever."

"Hunh," Blue Bandana grunted, dropping Patch's reins and joining Noah near the fire. "Red-Hair talk foolish. Once, Apaches think they live in mountains forever, too. Not true. Nothing last forever. Only moutains and rocks. Maybe not even mountains and rocks."

Noah glanced sidelong at his old friend. "Are you finally considering surrendering? Is Geronimo giving up?"

Blue Bandana shrugged. His expression was sad, his eyes grave. "Geronimo weakening. So few left now. What good stay out? Apaches dying, Red-Hair. Better surrender than see whole people die."

For the first time since he had lost Juliet, Noah focused on something other than his own devastating loss. "If you're so tired of running, why don't you stand up to Geronimo and tell him you want to quit before you're all dead? I know he has great influence, but the final decision belongs to you. In the end, each man must decide his fate for himself. Make up your own mind. Do what *you* want to do."

Blue Bandana nodded. "You speak wisely, Red-Hair, but I honor Geronimo too much to abandon him now. Maybe no need abandon. Geronimo send women to Fronteras in Mexico to scout possibility of surrender. Maybe do it finally. Maybe not. Still need convincing."

"I'll come and talk to him," Noah offered without thinking. Then, as he considered the idea, he embraced it with more enthusiasm. For this—and this reason alone—he would postpone his search for Juliet. Juliet would want him to help alleviate the misery of the Apaches. She would never forgive him if he didn't do it.

"Good," Blue Bandana grunted. "Eat first, then travel. I take you to him."

By the time Noah and Blue Bandana reached the Apache camp in the Torres Mountains of Mexico, the two women Geronimo had sent to explore the possibility of surrender with Mexican officials had returned, leading three ponies carrying food supplies and *mescal.* They had been permitted to trade, and Geronimo was jubilant; had he gone himself to explore the possibilities, the Mexicans would have killed him. Instead, the Mexicans hoped to lure him back with the promise of more *mescal,* a lure he was not stupid enough to accept. He had food and whiskey; perhaps that was all he really wanted, Noah decided.

Geronimo was also jubilant to see Noah—until he learned that Juliet was not with him, and that he might never see her again.

"I grieve for your loss," Geronimo solemnly stated as they shared a meal of fresh venison in his wickiup. "Shaman Woman be much missed."

"We came to the Chiricahuas to look for you," Noah told him, stretching the truth a bit. "She wanted to persuade you to surrender. You should have done it at Cañon de los Embudos."

Gernimo shook his head. "They would have killed me. Too many want me dead. That why I run away again. Also because they do not agree I can return to reservation."

"It's true many want you dead, but that's all the more reason why you can't return to the reservation. It would be too easy for your enemies to kill you. I don't know why you want to go there anyway; your family, friends, and relatives have all been shipped by rail to Florida. Only the Indians who never revolted remain there now."

At this, Geronimo's head jerked. Blue Bandana's eyes narrowed. They exchanged troubled glances. Apparently they hadn't known that any members of their tribe had already been sent east.

"If you surrender, you will be well guarded until you reach Fort Bowie," Noah continued. "I know Lieutenant Gatewood. He will do his duty. At Bowie Station, you'll soon board a train and join the rest of your people—Chihuahua and the others—in Florida. You can end it, Geronimo—the running, the killing, the fear, the constant looking back over your shoulder and struggling to find your next meal. . . . You can end it very quickly."

"Gatewood," Geronimo muttered. "He is the man we call Long Nose?"

Noah nodded, recalling that the young lieutenant indeed had a long nose. "Yes, and he's searching for you in company with two Apaches whom you knew at the reservation."

Blue Bandana leaned forward. "This we already know. We scout daily. Watch them search through white man's glasses."

Noah realized he meant field glasses—probably stolen in some raid. "Do you also know that Long Nose is a fair man? He does not love you, but he will not betray you. He is honorable. You can trust him."

"More important we can trust new white chief," Geronimo shrewdly observed.

"Do you mean Brig. Gen. Nelson A. Miles?" Geronimo's knowledge of what was happening in the white man's world surprised Noah. Some things he knew; some he didn't. The Apache evacuation had been a shock, but not Crook's dismissal or Miles's appointment. Geronimo never ceased to amaze him.

"The same," Geronimo grunted. "Red-Hair meet him?"

"No, but Long Nose has. Miles sent Long Nose to talk you into surrendering. He probably thought Long Nose would have more luck approaching you, since you recognize him."

A spark of humor lit Geronimo's dark eyes. "Better he send you, Red-Hair. No man come closer to making Geronimo change mind."

"Then you will at least talk to Gatewood—Long Nose?"

Geronimo stared at him a long moment before answering. "Yes, Red-Hair. I talk to him."

Noah felt a surge of something faintly reminiscent of joy. Then depression set in again. Without Juliet to share his triumphs, he would never feel joy again.

Chapter Thirty

Geronimo met with Lieutenant Gatewood within a week of Noah's arrival. First, a man named Martine, an old friend of Geronimo's, assured the Apache leader that no harm would come to him. Failing to mention that Geronimo's family had been shipped to Florida, Martine glowingly described his wonderful life at the reservation: "I get plenty to eat, go wherever I want, talk to good people. Go to bed whenever I want and get all my sleep. I have nobody to fear. I work my own little patch of corn. I am trying to do what white people want. There's no reason you shouldn't do it, too."

Noah could think of plenty of reasons, but to men who had been sleeping little, eating on the run, and contending with constant fear, it sounded like a better life than what they had been living for well over a year. One by one, the weary Apaches drifted into Gatewood's camp for the meeting. The young lieutenant prudently passed around tobacco, which kept the Indians busy rolling cigarettes in oak leaves, instead of fingering their weapons.

Geronimo opened the council by demanding to hear General Miles's message. Gatewood promptly delivered it. "Surrender and you'll be sent east to join the rest of your friends in Florida. The President will decide your final disposition. Accept these terms or fight it out to the bitter end."

Geronimo paled slightly and requested a drink. Noah knew that all of the Indians had partaken of the *mescal* brought back by the women, and some were still shaky. Gatewood wisely refused, and Geronimo then got down to business. "Take us to reservation or fight," he demanded.

It was Naiche who softened the ultimatum, assuring Gatewood that his small party would not be harmed whether or not the war continued. Gatewood then played his ace, informing the Apaches that the reservation itself no longer existed. *All* of the Indians there had been deported, including those who had not joined Geronimo in his previous escapes.

Noah was shocked. So were the Apaches. Shoulders sagged. Expressions grew grim. Geronimo requested permission to parlay with his warriors. While the Indians discussed this unexpected blow, Noah joined the lieutenant. "Is it true about the reservation?"

Gatewood looked both surprised and pleased to see him. "If it hasn't happened by now, it'll happen soon. All of the hostiles must leave Arizona; the army can't guarantee their safety. . . . By the way, I thank you for whatever part you've played in persuading Geronimo to meet with me. I never expected to see you here. Your lovely wife is well?"

Noah hesitated before answering, then finally blurted: "My wife died a couple months ago."

Mercifully, Lieutenant Gatewood did not pry. When Noah did not elaborate, he simply expressed his condolences. "Sorry to hear that. Guess that explains why you're willin' t' take your life in your hands negotiating a surrender with these red devils."

"I thought I might be able to help," Noah said quietly. "Actually, I think the Apaches were ready to talk surrender again on their own. I'd hate to be living the way they have this past year."

"Guess I do feel kind of sorry for 'em myself," Gatewood sighed, shaking his head. "This whole business is enough t' turn a man's stomach."

412

"And then some," Noah agreed.

That evening, Geronimo again conferred with Gatewood, but it wasn't until the next morning that the Apaches finally reached a decision: They would accompany Gatewood back to the United States, and there surrender to General Miles himself and accept the conditions Gatewood had offered. Their main concern was safety, a guarantee that there would be no treachery. Noah didn't blame them for fearing the army, bands of roving Mexican soldiers, or irate ranchers, all of whom might prefer to see them dead rather than imprisoned. Lieutenant Gatewood promised protection and granted them permission to bear arms all the way to Skeleton Canyon, a rugged, ancient raiding route between Old Mexico and the mountains in Arizona which had been selected as a convenient meeting place.

Convinced that this would be the last chapter of the book he planned to write, the reason he had come to Arizona, Noah accompanied the cavalcade of Indians and soldiers as they set out for Skeleton Canyon. Once again, he was witnessing history in the making—and gaining a respite from grief. Grief had taken him to the very edge of madness; he had gazed into the pit and known he was but a step away from plunging headlong into it. Fortunately, Blue Bandana had come along and given him the excuse he needed to leave the mountains—because Juliet herself would have wanted him to help convince Geronimo to surrender.

On the third day of their journey, a Mexican force of two hundred infantry appeared from the direction of Fronteras and briefly chased them. Noah, Lieutenant Gatewood, and the Apaches eluded the force, leaving Gatewood's second-in-command to deal with the situation. The Mexicans caught up with the main body of soldiers, and Gatewood's junior officer, a man named Lawton, arranged a rendevous for everyone involved. That meeting also proceeded without incident; all the Mexicans really wanted was a guarantee that Geronimo had indeed surrendered and would raid no more in Mexico.

The cavalcade arrived at Skeleton Canyon ahead of General Miles. Then began a waiting game, with Lieutenant Gatewood sending messages back and forth to the general, urging him to hurry before the Apaches changed their minds and bolted. Geronimo set up camp with his usual eye for strategy, choosing a spot high up in the rocks which could easily be defended.

Noah passed the time interviewing Geronimo and Naiche, whom he doubted he would see again once they were taken into custody. He considered applying to President Cleveland for permission to visit Geronimo in Florida—he still wanted to do his biography—but realized it was too soon to start thinking about the future . . . a future without Juliet. As always, Geronimo was reluctant to talk about the past. Intent on living his life in the present, the old man continued to amaze Noah with his pride and dignity, even in this last and final episode of defeat. Noah deeply admired Geronimo's quiet courage, all the more so now that he knew what it was like to lose everything in life that mattered.

General Miles did not arrive until the third of September. As soon as Geronimo spotted him, he mounted his horse, and rode down to meet him. Grabbing Patch, Noah followed. Geronimo went straight to the general, dismounted, and shook his hand. The general introduced his interpreter who immediately began: "General Miles is your friend."

With a sly grin, Geronimo replied: "I never saw him before this, but I have needed friends. Why has he not been with me?"

Needing no interpretation, Noah was the first to burst into laughter. The moment was rare proof that Geronimo had a sense of humor!

General Miles, a flashy-looking man with a carefully curled mustache, slowly looked the old Apache up and down. Noah read admiration as well as amusement in his eyes, and he began to relax. It would be all right. Miles would protect his famous prisoner and see that he arrived unharmed in Florida.

The actual speeches of surrender were delayed until the fourth of September. A stone was then placed on a blanket between Geronimo's warriors and the general's troopers, and the leaders gravely watched each other across it. The stone symbolized their treaty, which was to last until the stone crumbled into dust. Geronimo and Miles then raised their right hands and swore to honor the treaty and "not to do any wrong to each other or scheme against each other."

Watching them, Noah's throat clogged with emotion. How Juliet would have loved witnessing this moment! Only she would have understood the bittersweet mixture of relief and sorrow he felt. What had happened to the Apaches was cruel and unjust, but as a people, they might now survive. Their banishment could not last forever. The two year period agreed upon at Cañon de los Embudos had already been rescinded, but Noah hoped that the U.S. Government would eventually recognize the wrongs done to the Apaches and seek to right them. One day, the Apaches would be allowed to return to Arizona and live on the lands that had once belonged to them.

Early on the morning of September 5, General Miles, in company with Geronimo, Naiche, Blue Bandana, and several other Apaches, set out for Fort Bowie. With only a small military escort, they intended to make the sixty-five mile journey in a single day. The rest of the band would follow at a slower pace. Bidding farewell to Lieutenant Gatewood, Noah rode with them.

As they neared the Chiricahua Mountains, Geronimo gazed toward his old hideout with the saddest expression Noah had ever seen on any man's face. "This is the fourth time I have surrendered," he remarked to no one in particular.

Overhearing the comment and requesting a translation, General Miles responded: "And it is the last time I think."

Noah stayed with the group until he spotted the entrance to the canyon leading to the Heart of Rocks. He found he could not ride past it and kneed Patch closer to Geronimo, Naiche, and Blue Bandana. "I must leave you here," he said. "I want to see the mountains one last time."

He avoided Geronimo's piercing gaze; he could not look him in the eyes when he knew that the Apache leader might never again see his beloved mountains. Blue Bandana saluted him—army style. Naiche nodded. Only Geronimo spoke. "Go in peace, Red-Hair. Something good awaits you in the mountains. I am still shaman, and I know this. You will not regret returning to the Land of the Standing-Up Rocks."

"She's dead," Noah snorted, guessing what the old man meant. "She has to be dead, or I would have found her."

He did not need to explain who *she* was. The old man knew. "She is there," he said softly. "Go to the Heart of Rocks, and you will find her."

It was almost enough to make Noah decide *not* to go. Who could believe an old man's prophecies—even if he was an Apache shaman? Even if he *had* predicted that no white man's bullet would ever kill him—and indeed none had? Noah's whole being rejected the idea that Juliet could still be alive and waiting for him in the Heart of Rocks.

Yet he could not ride past without seeing for himself. Reining Patch around, he broke away from the cavalcade and set off at a gallop for the canyon entrance.

It was early evening when he reached the first spires and pinnacles. The rock formations blazed with fiery color, the legacy of the setting sun. Leaving Patch to graze at the lower elevations, Noah began ascending

416

one of the steep mountains overlooking the Heart of Rocks. He did not have to go far to feel Juliet's presence. He told himself it was impossible that she could be here, but he kept turning around and scanning the landscape, half expecting to see her. He could not quell his wild, thundering hope; it soared upward like an entrapped bird breaking free of its fetters.

As the sun sank out of sight, and purple shadows swallowed the blaze of red, Noah sat down on a boulder. He had spent weeks searching the area; every rock was now familiar to him. He knew exactly where to go to find the ledge. But it would do him no good to look for Juliet. If she was really here, she must come to him. He held his breath, listening, and could almost hear her laughter borne on the evening breeze. He sniffed the wind and fancied he smelled her delicate, feminine, flowery scent.

He closed his eyes and conjured her image—pale hair floating around her head and shoulders, sparkling gold-flecked eyes alight with love, tender pink mouth made for kissing, alabaster skin caressed by the sun. Pain and pleasure mingled as he recreated her in his mind's eye. . . . He missed her so much!

He wondered why he had returned here and why he wanted to torture himself with old memories. But as he watched the stars begin to twinkle in the purple velvet sky, he knew why. . . . He had to let go. Had to admit that she was gone and wasn't coming back; he had lost her for good. He could never find peace again—or love—or the courage to chart his future, unless he could somehow bring himself to release the past. Juliet had made the mistake of clinging to it. He must not do the same. Here in the mountains, he must learn to conquer loneliness and longing, so that when he left the mountains, he could live again . . without Juliet.

Noah camped in the Heart of Rocks that night, and the next morning resolved to give himself two weeks more in the mountains—two weeks in which to build a small stone monument to Juliet's memory. At the end of that time, he would ride out of the Chiricahuas and get on with his life. This was the proper, logical way to deal with grief and loss, he told himself. Since he had no grave on which to plant flowers or place a piece of marble to honor her memory, this would be his memorial, a way of writing "The End", to his and Juliet's story.

He started that very day, hunting through the amphitheater of rock formations to find large boulders for the base of his monument and smaller ones for the very top. As he sorted and discarded, he conceived the idea of dedicating his stone memorial to Running Horse and the Apaches as well as to Juliet. He didn't think she would mind sharing the honors. Both the Apaches and Juliet had loved this place, and neither would be returning to it. . . . Yes, Noah thought, he would build his own lofty spire in honor of the lost freedom of the Apaches and the death of his wife, Juliet.

It took him over two weeks to finish his creation—a tower of rocks, wide at the bottom and narrow at the top. It could not compete with nature's lavish, improbable designs, but Noah was proud of it. Anyone seeing it must surely wonder who had built it and why; it stood out from the other spires and pinnacles because of its perfect symmetry. There was nothing whimsical or haphazard about it. It was tall, solid, and carefully balanced, the rocks all the exact same shade of reddish orange.

Gazing at it critically, Noah felt a satisfaction he could never have explained. His tower would last as long as nature's masterpieces. Years after he was dead and gone, it would still be standing, causing speculation and comment. He debated whether or not to chisel a message onto the largest boulder at the base— explaining why he had built it and to whom it was dedicated. In the end, he decided not to do it. The monument's purpose was his secret; it belonged to him and to the mountains—not to uncaring humans who might pass through here.

On the morning of the day he had designated for his departure, he knelt next to his tower, bowed his head, and whispered the first honest prayer of his life that wasn't fueled by fear or desperation.

"God of the universe—Usen—or Whoever's up there listening, this is for the Apaches . . . and for Juliet. Wherever they are, watch over them, Lord. Keep them safe. Make them happy. Hold them close. . . . Thank you, God, for letting me know them . . . for letting me love them. I didn't get to be with them nearly long enough . . . especially Juliet. I will never forget her. May she rest in peace. Amen."

He blinked to hold back a rush of tears. He had sworn to himself that he wouldn't cry. How some people would laugh if they could see Noah Copper McCord on his knees in a mountain stronghold, praying and blubbering! Quickly, he rose, dashed the tears from his eyes, and strode back to Patch, patiently waiting for him on the trail leading to the canyon which would take him out of the mountains. He swung up into the saddle, took one last look at his monument, and rode away without a backward glance.

A couple hours later, he was nearing the spot where the camp of the buffalo soldiers had been. It did not surprise him that the soldiers were gone. With Geronimo in Florida by now, or well on his way, a military outpost was no longer needed to guard the water hole here. He let Patch have a drink while he looked over the small pile of refuse the soldiers had left. Unless they were on the run and could not take time to cover the signs of their passing, the Apaches never despoiled the countryside. In sharp contrast to the whites, they left everything as they had found it.

As Noah was pondering this difference in cultures, he became aware of a voice speaking loudly in the distance. He lifted his head, listening, and determined that it was a feminine voice—a *familiar* feminine voice.

Signaling Patch for a lope, he rounded a clump of birch trees. The closer he got, the more excited he became. As he neared a clearing in the canyon's woody growth, he reined in among the trees and stared.

A young woman stood dead center in the clearing, her arms lifted, her head thrown back. She wore a long white gown, fastened with gold brooches at the shoulders. A gold ribbon tied back her hair—pale, fine hair, a cloud of hair, the color of moonbeams. It partially concealed a lovely face and slender body.

Noah sat riveted in the saddle. He couldn't move. Couldn't breathe. His heart was pounding in his ears. His palms were sweaty. It *couldn't* be—but it was! The girl was tall and moved with grace and elegance. The clean, delicate line of her throat entranced him. He *knew* that throat . . . that voice . . . that hair . . . that gown. He knew *her,* but didn't trust his eyes or ears.

"Oh, Troy, my beloved city!" the girl called out in a loud carrying voice. "Shall I ever see you again? Or in gaining Paris, have I lost you forever?"

Noah was off Patch and running toward her almost before he knew what he was doing. Like a madman, he charged into the clearing, grabbed the girl's hand, and spun her around. "Juliet! My God, Juliet!"

It was all he could get out. Fury wrestled with exploding joy. Aggravation warred with amazement. The girl was indeed Juliet, but she looked and behaved as if she didn't know him—had never seen him before.

"What are you doing, sir? Let go of me!" Her voice spiraled to a shriek, and terror heightened the gold in her eyes. "Father! Oh, Father, get the gun! A madman is attacking me!"

Noah hauled her into his arms. As he bent to ravish her mouth with kisses, he heard a sharp click.

"Let go of her, young man," said a cultured, educated male voice. "Let go of her this instant. I am armed, and I will not hesitate to shoot."

Turning only his head, Noah noticed a wagon off to one side. A blond-haired boy of no more than ten or twelve was climbing down from it. He held a pistol, which he lifted and aimed at Noah. "I have the pistol, Father, and Annie's getting the other rifle. If you miss him, we won't."

"Just bring it over here, Nathaniel. Tell your sister to be quick with the rifle. If this one misfires, I'll need the other."

The man spoke calmly and precisely, his labored breathing the only sign of alarm. The boy—Nathaniel—stuck his head back inside the wagon which was a high, wooden-sided affair, with posters and paintings decorating the outside walls. "Annie!" he hollered. "Hurry up with the rifle! Father needs it immediately!"

Noah had only a moment to realize that the boy was dressed Grecian-style, like Juliet. The next moment, he felt the prod of a rifle in his lower back. "If you take one false step, sir, I shall blow a hole in you commodious enough to drive my wagon through. I have lost one daughter to Apache marauders. I do not intend to lose another to a scalawag white man. Now, turn around slowly."

Noah obeyed and found himself face to face with a man whose knobby knees showed beneath a white tunic. He, too, wore Greek garments, and his curly, grayish-blond hair was cropped short. His tight-lipped grimace suggested he hoped Noah *would* move, so he could keep his promise and shoot him.

"I don't intend to hurt your daughter," Noah said. "I *know* her. Her name is Juliet. I just want to ask some questions—such as how she found you and when you got here."

"Her name is *not* Juliet. It's Julia, and we arrived here yesterday." The man—he was older than Noah—prodded him in the stomach with the muzzle of his Springfield rifle. "Julia, he says he knows you. Could that possibly be true, Daughter?"

Juliet came up beside the old man, her golden-brown eyes wide and frightened. "Father, I have never laid eyes on this man before in my life. I do take note of all the handsome young men in our audiences, but I do not recall this one."

She's found her memory, Noah thought. She's found her memory and her family, and she's forgotten *me!* "You are my wife, Juliet," he said slowly and succinctly.

"Julia," she corrected, "and whoever you are, sir, you are *not* my husband. If I had ever married you, you may be certain I would have remembered it." The new Juliet—*Julia*—gave Noah a look that was simultaneously innocent and seductive. "I could not have forgotten marrying *you,* sir, especially since my family has been trying to marry me off for several years now."

Her father's chuckle irritated Noah beyond measure.

"Well, you *have* forgotten it, and you *did* marry me," he snarled. "Among the Apaches. It was an unconventional ceremony, I admit, but I considered it binding, and so, my dear Juliet, did you."

Julia's face lit up. For a moment it seemed she might remember after all. "Among the Apaches? You married someone who looked like me among the Apaches? Father! Maybe it was Rhea he married! Oh, where *is* she? Your wife, I mean."

"I didn't marry anybody named Rhea," Noah snapped. "I married *you,* Juliet . . . and not long ago, you died, or I thought you did."

"Your wife died?" Julia's joy abruptly fled.

"Well, obviously you didn't die, did you? . . . Oh, what the hell," Noah sighed, exasperated. "Tell your father to put down that damn rifle, and I'll try to explain."

"You cannot explain this conundrum, I fear." A sudden suspicious sheen filmed the eyes of Julia's father. "Because our dear foolish Rhea is indeed dead. I know it in my bones. We will never see her again. The Apaches killed her. Shortly thereafter, Julia, Nathaniel, and I returned to Texas to wait for Geronimo to be caught before continuing our performance tour of the Southwest and California."

"When and where did all this happen?" Noah demanded, pushing the muzzle of the Springfield away from his stomach. "Did you cross these mountains on your way to California?"

"Yes, we did, and the Apaches attacked us somewhere in this very area." Julia's father reluctantly lowered the rifle. "Well, if we are going to talk instead of do battle, perhaps we should be civilized and have a cup of coffee. Come sit down with us. We will each relate our stories. I am most anxious to hear of your marriage among the Apaches and why you think our Julia is your Juliet."

"Not think—*know*. Your daughter—*this* daughter—is my wife. There could not be two women on this earth with her beautiful hair, her smile, her eyes . . ."

As he listed these attributes, Julia blushed. She lowered her golden-brown eyes, then gazed at him through her long lashes. "Many people think Rhea and I look—looked—much alike. Cosmetics enhance the resemblance. I play her parts now, and hardly anyone notices the difference, even those who knew her well."

"Her parts?" Noah struggled to keep from reaching out to touch Julia's hair or her cheek. He wanted nothing more than to enfold her in his embrace and kiss away her doubts, but he couldn't, not while she was denying the entire relationship.

"In our traveling show. We perform Greek and Shakespearean classics. You see?" She pointed to the side of the wagon, and Noah gave it a closer scrutiny. The posters prolaimed that this was the renowned Edmond Whitaker family, known world-wide for their astonishing theatrical performances.

How astonishing or successful the performances could be, he could not guess, but he did note that the wagon was old and shabby, the posters yellowed and peeling. The Whitakers' two grazing horses appeared in good health but were white-muzzled and slightly sway-backed. The girl, Annie, a miniature version of Juliet, climbed out of the wagon while Noah was reading the showbills and shyly handed her father a second rifle, this one a Winchester. Edmond Whitaker propped both of them against the side of the wagon and motioned Noah around to the opposite side.

A small cookfire burned there, over which hung a blackened coffeepot. "Annie, fetch the cups and the sugar. Julia, get the spoons. Nathaniel, bring some of that skillet bread Julia made this morning. Our guest might be hungry."

The two younger children, both resembling Julia and her father—the family stamp was unmistakable—hurried to do their father's bidding, but Julia moved langorously, as if she had all the time in the world. Her golden-brown eyes never left Noah. "Yes, Father," she trilled softly, giving Noah a tiny fleeting smile that made him want to grab her and tear off all her clothing. Not only did he recognize her garments, but he knew what she looked like without them.

Julia disappeared inside the wagon, emerging several moments later with spoons and something else in hand. She gave Annie the spoons, motioned for Nathaniel to pass out the cups, and slipped a round object into a hidden pocket of her Grecian costume. "I'll pour and serve, Father, while you and Mr.—what is your name, sir?—begin."

"Noah," Noah said. "My name is Noah Copper McCord." He watched her closely to see if she recognized it.

"Copper, because of your hair?" she questioned.

He nodded. Her smile widened. She could claim she didn't know him from a chipmunk, but her eyes and her smile mirrored her feelings—and he *knew* she felt the same vibrations, the same strong pull between them, that he did.

"I believe I recognize the name," her father said. "You write for the newspapers, do you not, sir?"

Noah turned his attention to Edmond Whitaker. "Yes . . . yes, I do. I originally came to Arizona to interview Geronimo. I'd be more than happy to tell you my story—and explain about Juliet—but I'd like to hear your story first, if you don't mind."

"A famous newspaper writer, right here at our little campfire!" Edmond exclaimed. "We are honored, sir. And I would be delighted to tell you our story."

Chapter Thirty-one

A year ago the previous spring, the Whitakers had arrived in the Arizona Territory about the same time as Noah. En route to Tucson and eventually California, they had been looking for Apache Pass, but wound up entering the mountains south of the main trail. Somewhere in the area, they had made camp for the night and rehearsed a play they were going to perform in Tucson. Just before dark, the Apaches attacked. Edmond, Julia, Annie, and Nathaniel had taken shelter behind the wagon. Rhea had wandered off to admire the nearby cliffs and wasn't with them.

The family had successfully fought off the warriors, who seemed less interested in killing them than in stealing their horses, an extra team of mules, and their milk cow.

"It was all over in a few minutes," Edmond recalled, cradling his cup of coffee as if his hands were chilled and he meant to warm them. "Screaming like banshees, the Apaches rode down from the mountains, grabbed the animals, and were gone almost before we realized what had happened. It was only later, when I counted heads, that I realized Rhea was missing."

"Rhea always did have a mind of her own," Julia sadly confided. "Some might call her headstrong. She often wandered off to look at things after Father warned her not to. At the time, we didn't know about Geronimo's escape from the reservation, but we knew we should exercise caution, so none of us would get lost or hurt in this rough country."

Her gaze collided with Noah's. Again, a deep rosy blush crept up her cheeks. Noah did not remember Juliet blushing so much before—but this was a slightly different woman than the one he had known. He still believed she was the same person. She *had* to be. Aside from her appearance, her mannerisms and unconscious gestures all proclaimed it.

"And you never found Rhea again, or any trace of her?"

Edmond grimly shook his head. "Not a thing. We searched the area thoroughly. Stayed for weeks. When the soldiers found us, they helped. Apache trackers were with them, but even the Indians could not find a clue. They took us all to Fort Bowie, where we purchased new horses. Eventually, we decided to cut short our journey and return to a safer place. There was no point continuing. Not only did we fear the Apaches, but Rhea was our star performer; without her, we had to refashion all of our performances and memorize new parts."

" 'Twas grief made us change our minds," Julia interjected. "Without Rhea, it was simply impossible to continue. We had lost our enthusiasm for the adventure."

"I *still* miss her," young Annie piped up, her sweet face filled with sorrow.

"So do I," added Nathaniel, looking woebegone. "Oh, Julia does an excellent job performing her parts, and Annie and I fill in for Julia's old parts, but it just isn't the same. Everyone always came to see Rhea, not *us*. Besides, Rhea made acting fun!"

"Sometimes she made it too much fun," Julia reminisced. "She loved nothing better than to cause one of us to laugh during the most serious, important scenes. Indeed, she hated doing classical works and was always trying to talk Father into abandoning the classics and writing our own plays—something light, naughty, and funny—perhaps with singing and dancing."

"She didn't like Greek tragedies?" Noah leaned forward, his cooling coffee half forgotten. "But I'll bet she studied Greek history—and knew the *Illiad* and the *Odyssey* backward and forward."

"No," scoffed Nathaniel. "Rhea *hated* studying things like that. She could never understand why Father thinks they are necessary to a good education. Julia's the one who likes them. Julia can read and write in Greek. Her favorite story is about someone named Jason who stole a golden fleece."

"I *knew* it," Noah said, studying Julia's face. This was indeed his Juliet—though he could not explain what had happened. Everything he had learned so far suggested that Rhea must be his lost love; the puzzle pieces all fit. Yet the strong connection he felt to Julia, and the physical resemblance—not to mention the obsession with Greece—could not be denied. He knew in the very marrow of his bones that Julia was his Juliet.

"So that is what happened to us, Mr. McCord," Edmond said. "It has been long enough now since our dear Rhea's passing that we thought we should return this way and continue as we had planned. This time, I deliberately avoided Apache Pass and came here, because I wanted to place a stone marker in the canyon in my daughter's honor. It's in the wagon. Perhaps you will help me get it out and find a suitable place to put it."

"I'd be happy to," Noah assured him. "But you haven't told me how old Rhea was or what she looked like."

"She was a year younger than I am," Julia said, "and looked very much like me."

Noah's heart sank into his boots. His Juliet *must* have been Rhea.

"Oh, we weren't as similar as identical twins," she continued. "But people often mistook us for such, until they saw us side by side. Her hair was a lighter shade of blond. Actually, she was almost silver-haired. And her eyes were a lovely deep amber, like Father's, not light-colored like mine. Rhea was—oh, I don't know—more *vivid*, more beautiful altogether, a Grecian goddess. She far outshone me. Next to her, I was a mere humble wren, while she was a peacock in all its glory."

"I find that hard to believe." Noah gulped the rest of his coffee, which was cold and bitter. Rhea *had* to have been the girl he found and fell in love with. *Had to be.* So why did his heart keep telling him differently?

"Here, I have a portrait of her, if you would like to see it." Julia slipped her hand into her pocket and withdrew a small, round miniature in a plain gold frame. "It was painted three years ago, but you should be able to recognize her if she was indeed the girl you met and married among the Apaches."

Noah accepted the miniature with shaking fingers. He gazed long and hard at the smooth, beautiful face of the silver-blond young woman. She wasn't his Juliet—though she was undoubtedly Julia's sister. Any fool could see the family resemblance. Aside from the subtle color differences, the features were different, the expression more haughty. . . . No warmth emmanated from those cool dark eyes. The lips held a hint of cruelty or selfishness. This girl would do precisely what she wanted, when she wanted, and her family could go to hell. Noah knew the type; he had been that way himself until he met Juliet.

His Juliet sat across from him, watching his every move with that odd mixture of shyness, eagerness, stubbornness, and character he had come to treasure. She had not, he knew, a selfish bone in her body.

"You see?" she queried. "She is the peacock, and I am the wren."

"Hush, now," Edmond scolded. "Mr. McCord isn't interested in your childish rivalries with your sister. . . . Well, sir? Is our Rhea the young woman you married? From your expression, I would say not."

Noah handed the miniature back to Julia. "No, she isn't. When I tell you how I met her, you will think she is, but . . . but I'm sure she's not." He cleared his throat, gathering his courage. "It happened like this."

As he began explaining, something burst inside him, and it all poured out—how he had found her on the ledge after the storm, how she had nursed him through injuries and fever, how they had had to fight to survive in the desert and mountains, how they had fallen in love, and been found by the Apaches. . . . Hoping that his tale would strike a chord of familiarity with Julia, he told them nearly everything, withholding only the more incredible details, such as how his wife had insisted that she came from the past, from ancient Greece, and how she had feared she would have to go back there, that Zeus, the white bull, would come and get her.

"An amazing tale," Edmond Whitaker said, when Noah had finished. "You say you lost your wife during a storm very like the one after which you initially discovered her?"

Noah nodded. "Sounds a little crazy, doesn't it? Actually, it sounds insane."

"You must have loved her very much to have returned here to build a monument for her," Julia murmured.

I still do love you! Noah wanted to shout, but he held his tongue. Julia's eyes sought his, and he read compassion, sympathy, and yes, pity, in them—none of which were what he wanted to see. First and foremost, he wanted recognition and then love—the love he had grown accustomed to seeing there and had taken for granted. Indeed, he suddenly realized, he now wanted from Juliet what *she* had always wanted from him: acknowledgement of their shared past. Realization and appreciation of their ancient bonds.

It hit him like a bolt of lightning that he had never given her that, and she would probably never give it to him. Now he knew precisely how she must have felt when he could not provide what she needed most.

"You are absolutely certain that Rhea is not your Juliet," Edmond said. "How disappointing! 'Twould ease my mind so, if I knew what had become of her . . . and it would comfort Julia. Being only a year apart, they were as close as twins. They were nothing alike, but they had a special relationship. Their mother—and Annie's and Nathaniel's—died when Nathaniel was born. So we understand your grief, Mr. McCord. . . . Perhaps you simply want to believe so much that your wife is still alive that you are subconsciously denying the obvious."

"Perhaps," Noah conceded, though he really did not think so.

"I would love to see the monument you built for her," Julia said.

"What could be so special about a pile of rocks?" Nathaniel demanded.

"Nathaniel!" Annie scolded. "A pile of rocks *can* be special. So can a single rock such as we brought to place here for Rhea."

"That's different!" Nathaniel bristled. *"Our* rock is pure marble."

"It's too late in the day to ride to the Heart of Rocks, where I built the monument," Noah said, still watching Julia. "But I could take you there tomorrow."

"I would adore going tomorrow!" Julia touched her father's arm. "You would not mind, would you, Father?"

Edmond smiled and patted her hand. "No, no, dear. . . . I would not mind. I think we can trust Mr. McCord to take good care of you. While you are examining his wife's monument, the children and I will look for a good place to put Rhea's stone."

"Are we still going to have our dress rehearsal this afternoon, Father?" young Annie inquired. "Or did we put on our costumes and get all dressed up for nothing?"

"I suppose we should still have it," her father replied. "We will shortly be performing in Tucson, and we need the practice. If Mr. McCord doesn't mind, he can be our audience."

"I'd be honored," Noah said, not about to go anywhere without Juliet. Now that he had finally found her again, he wasn't going to let her out of his sight—not unless she ordered him to leave, that is, and maybe not even then.

Annie got a wooden bucket for him to sit on, and after a few moments preparation, the performance commenced. It had something to do with Helen of Troy and her lover, Paris, but Noah scarcely heard a word of it nor followed the plot. He did note the ingenious use of various props to distinguish the characters, but otherwise, had eyes only for Juliet—Julia. Logic be damned, he had *found* her! And the fact that she did not remember him was not so very much different from his having "forgotten" her when they first met. This was just one more obstacle—one more challenge—to test their love. He would not give her up without a fight!

Tomorrow he would take her to the Heart of Rocks and show her his memorial—his monument—to her memory. There, perhaps, she *might* remember. But if she didn't, it would make no difference to how he felt about her and what he would do next. He would just have to make her fall in love with him all over again!

In the morning, Noah and Julia packed food and water and began the long ride into the Heart of Rocks. Not trusting the stamina or surefootedness of the Whitakers' old cart horses, Noah put Julia up on Patch. Riding the same horse would give him the opportunity to make the journey with his arms wrapped around her waist. Before they started out, Julia had to pet the stallion and croon to him, making friends, which Noah counted as one more proof of who she really was.

"I love animals!" she informed him as he settled into the saddle behind her.

"I know," he said.

"You do?" Her brows rose in question.

"Do you sometimes talk to them in your thoughts—and understand *their* thoughts?" he asked, taking up the reins.

"Why . . . I did when I was younger," she admitted, looking amazed. "But then I discovered that people found it very odd, and so I stopped. I can't actually read their thoughts, you know—at least not anymore. But when I was a child, I fancied I could."

Noah waved to Annie who was standing near the wagon watching, a wistful expression on her pretty face. He would have taken her along except they only had Patch to ride, and it was too far to walk. Besides, he wanted this time alone with Juliet—*Julia,* he reminded himself for the hundredth time.

"Be careful, Mr. McCord," Edmond called out to them, raising his breakfast coffee cup to salute them. "Don't get lost."

"I won't," Noah promised Julia's father. "Don't worry. I'll take good care of your daughter."

"I know you will, Mr. McCord, or I would never let you ride off alone with her. I'm a good judge of character; any man who writes with such sensitivity and truth as you do, can be trusted with a young woman's safety and reputation. Yesterday, I forgot to mention it, but I've followed your work for years, and I greatly admire your courage. I haven't always agreed with you, but you've made me think even when I didn't."

The praise was unexpected and sweet as honey, but Noah merely nodded. He didn't know what to say. Fortunately, young Nathaniel came running up to them, and he didn't have to say anything. "Mr. McCord, when you come back, would you let me ride

Patch? He's a beautiful animal. I've never seen one colored like that."

"You can ride him," Noah promised. "He's what is called a Paint. An Apache gave him to me—and helped me tame him."

Nathaniel's eyes widened. "I guess the Apaches cannot be all bad then, can they, Mr. McCord?"

"No, they're not, Nathaniel. Whether or not they killed your sister, Rhea, I can't say. Considering that my wife and I never saw her while we lived among the Apaches, they might have. But our people have killed plenty of their people, too. The killings are done now. The Apache Wars are over, and we have to put bitterness behind us."

"Yes, sir. I expect you're right."

As Noah reined Patch around to set off for the Heart of Rocks, Julia twisted in the saddle and whispered: "I am so glad you said that. Nathaniel needs to hear it. So do we all, for we have all been bitter. Rhea was young, vain, and sometimes foolish, but we loved her, and she did not deserve to die."

"She may *not* have died," Noah said. "She may have . . . gone somewhere else. Entered a different plane of life."

Twisting back around, Juliet pondered that a moment. "What do you mean—gone somewhere else? What sort of plane?"

"I mean . . . Oh, hell, forget it. Let's just say that there are many things in life—and in the universe— that we'll never be able to understand, Julia. There are all kinds of possibilities. Things happen that we can never explain, but we have to try and be open to them. Have to let our minds expand . . . let ourselves dream and imagine."

They rode along quietly for a bit, and then Juliet said, "I think I understand a little what you are trying to say. I . . . I have—had—abilities that no one understood, so I quit using them, and then I lost them."

"Your ability to exchange thoughts with animals."

"Yes! And . . . and I sometimes have strange dreams, but they are so foolish that I never mention them to anyone."

"Dreams or nightmares?" Noah demanded.

"Oh, just dreams . . . pleasant ones actually."

"Tell me about them . . ." Noah urged.

She laughed nervously and leaned back against him as he negotiated Patch up the narrow steep trail. "No! You will think they are most foolish! I'm sure I only have them because I've read and studied so much Greek history that it all resurfaces when I sleep."

"I doubt I'll find them foolish at all," Noah said. "Surely, they're no more ridiculous than the playacting we do as children. When I was a little boy, I used to pretend I was Jason, hunting for the golden fleece."

"You didn't!" Again, she twisted to look at him. "That is amazing—utterly amazing! We both loved the exact same legend or fairy tale or whatever you want to call it."

"I can assure you we have far more in common than that." Noah could hardly keep from grinning. "However, I won't attempt to amaze you more than once in a single day."

"But I love to be amazed," she protested, resettling herself in the curve of his body. "I am considered the practical one in the family, but I enjoy letting my imagination run rampant. 'Tis my secret vice. Rhea always wanted *real* adventures, but I find more than enough right inside my head."

"I'll bet you do." Noah pressed a light kiss into the sweet-smelling cloud of hair that tickled his nose whenever she moved. "That doesn't surprise me a bit. . . . Tell me, if you were to leave your family's traveling show and it folded, could they manage without you?"

"Oh, they could manage quite well, I think. Father is always in demand as a professor, teaching literature, history, and foreign languages. He may be lacking in worldly riches, but he is amazingly well educated. We only conceived of the idea of a traveling theatrical

436

group because of Rhea. As I said, she craved adventure. She wanted to see the world. When Father said she couldn't possibly set off on her own, she threatened to run off to California by herself or else find a handsome young man to take her. That scared poor father half to death, for she was only fifteen at the time."

"I imagine it did."

Julia sighed. "She always could twist him around her little finger, and nothing I or anyone said made a difference. Father agreed that when she reached eighteen, we would all travel to California, earning our bread along the way with theatrical performances. We often put on parlor entertainments at home in Philadelphia. He thought the trip west would be educational for all of us, and indeed, it has been. We've been traveling and performing for over two years now, but we are all ready to settle down and do something different. Father is thinking of opening an academy of higher learning; it would be good for Nathaniel and Annie to have a permanent home and a good school to attend."

"Maybe when you get to Tucson, all of you will like it so much you'll want to stay there instead of going on to California," Noah slyly suggested. "Tucson will grow now that Geronimo is no longer a threat. Families will settle there; professors of literature, history, and foreign language will be needed. I'm thinking of settling there myself."

"Maybe. . . . We'll have to see. At the moment, I cannot think of any reason why I would want to leave my family, whatever Father and the others decide to do. Why did you ask that particular question, Mr. McCord?"

"Noah. Please call me, Noah. . . . No reason, just curious."

Because I'm going to marry you again, he thought but didn't say. He might never be able to explain how he had found Juliet again, but he *was* determined to keep her. He'd do whatever he had to—*say* whatever was necessary—to make her his forever. Their love was too precious to let die or be lost now. It had survived challenges of time, distance, and jealous gods and goddesses. Somehow, despite everything, it had survived. The universe had adjusted to let them find each other once more.

The old Noah would *never* have allowed such outrageous thoughts to contaminate his ordered brain; the new Noah toyed with tantalizing possibilities and let himself ponder the idea of reincarnation, rebirth, and miracles. He *did* wonder what had happened to Rhea. If the Apaches hadn't gotten her, she was probably somewhere out there in the galaxy searching for adventure—and love. Yes, he knew her type. He, too, had thought that only adventure mattered; it had taken Juliet to convince him that love mattered more.

As they approached the Heart of Rocks, Noah could detect the change in Julia. She sat up straighter and gazed about in rising excitement and wonder. " 'Tis so beautiful here! 'Tis so wonderful! I never dreamed that mere rocks, cliffs, and boulders could be this magnificent."

The rock formations so awed her that she did not immediately notice the monument. Noah reined in, slipped off Patch, and lifted Julia down while she was still exclaiming over the grandeur of the place. "Oh, No-ah, thank you for bringing me here to see this!"

The way she said his first name delighted Noah. He had expected to have to correct her several times before she remembered to call him Noah, instead of Mr. McCord, and he had hardly dared to hope that she would say it with the same breathy little pause between the two syllables. Perhaps her tongue was already recalling what her brain had forgotten.

"This is the memorial I built for Juliet." He turned her around to face the tower of rocks.

It stood tall and proud in the very center of the huge amphitheater—both part of and separate from the other spires and pinnacles. The noon sun bathed it in dazzling gold sunshine. Overhead, the sky was a pure cobalt blue. As he watched Julia examine the memorial, Noah held his breath, waiting for her reaction. He wanted her to feel something, to sense the connectedness, but perhaps it was too soon. . . . Perhaps she never would. He could live with that, he decided. He could live with anything except total rejection.

For several moments, Julia said nothing, then she turned glowing eyes on him. "No-ah," she whispered. "I feel it! She's here! In the rock, in the tower, in the sky . . . in you and me."

"Yes," he said, sliding his arms around her slender waist. "Yes, she's here, isn't she? You feel it, too."

A look of perplexity crossed her lovely face. "I *know* her," she said in wonder. "But how can that be if she isn't Rhea?"

"Because she *isn't* Rhea. She's *you,* sweetheart. Juliet is you—Julia. Don't ask me to explain, because I can't. I know that Rhea's the one who disappeared, while you remained with your family, but you're the one I found way up on that ledge, which I'll also show you. You had lost your memory and didn't know who you were until your dreams revealed that we were lovers in another lifetime, in ancient Greece. Fool that I was, I didn't believe you. I was more skeptical than you are now."

"None of it makes sense, does it?" she asked, frowning, her golden-brown eyes doubtful. "It all sounds so . . . so impossible."

"No, it doesn't make sense, not sense as we know it. In time, it might. You may even remember it yourself." He tilted up her chin and whispered: "See if you can remember *this.*"

He bent his head and kissed her, rediscovering the sweetness of her mouth moving beneath his own. Deepening the kiss, he clasped her to him, kissing her with all the love and longing he had been forced to deny. After a long, long moment of drowning in her sweetness, he pulled back to gaze into her dazzled dreamy eyes.

"I think I know where this leads," she said. "I . . . I think I remember."

"Where?" he prompted.

Her tender lips curved upwards in a smile. "To heaven."

That was when he knew for certain that it would be all right. He would marry her and take her to bed and kiss her until she remembered everything, and if she never did remember, it would still be all right.

"I'll take you there someday," he said. "To heaven."

Her grin was shy and tremulous. "Promise?"

"Promise." He enfolded her in his arms and hugged her, content for now to simply hold her, knowing that eventually more would follow. There was no hurry; they had a lifetime to enjoy the rest.

"Oh, No-ah!" she suddenly cried. "No-ah, look! There's a . . . a peacock!"

He let go of her and spun around. "A *peacock!* Where?"

She pointed to a spot high up on the side of the cliff, where the ledge was located. "Way up there! Do you see it?"

"The sun . . . the damn sun is so bright! I don't know if I do." He shaded his eyes, thinking he did see a flash of brilliant blue, but he couldn't be sure. "Maybe you're imagining things."

"No, I'm certain I saw it. Imagine a peacock way out here, in the middle of nowhere! . . . Oh, well, it's gone now. No-ah, did you know that a peacock is Hera's symbol? Hera was the wife of Zeus, and she was always very jealous of Zeus' mortal lovers and punished them whenever she could. Some might say she was cruel, but I never thought so. She was only protecting her interests, for she loved him so much. . . . I

440

can understand her anger. I'd be angry, too, if my husband chased other women. Of course, had the women *resisted* or fought him, she might have been more inclined to mercy. She might even have helped them escape."

Noah took her hand. "I would think it very difficult to resist a god, a devil, or any other powerful, supernatural being."

"It probably is, but *I* would resist such a being, especially if I loved another." A spark of determination lit her golden-brown eyes, then she began to laugh. "What must you think of me—prattling about a Greek god and goddess when you brought me here to see your wife's memorial?"

"I think you are adorable, my beautiful Julia. I think you are perfect. The most exquisite creature on God's green earth." He stopped, embarrassed by his own effusiveness. "Have you seen enough?"

She nodded. "We don't want Father to worry if we are gone too long."

"No, we don't. I'll take you back now." He led her towards Patch.

She walked a short distance then stopped. "No-ah, can we return here again one day—to see the rocks?"

The question told him everything he needed to know—and already knew. "We'll come back often," he promised. "And someday we'll bring our children."

Epilogue

"No-ah, the book is wonderful!" Julia crowed, hugging it to her breast as she lay against the plumped pillows of their big brass bed. "You told the story of the Apaches so well. Anyone who reads it will surely have a better understanding of why Geronimo fought so long and so hard to stay free."

Noah set aside the newspaper he hadn't really been reading and gave his full attention to his beautiful, tousled, enthusiastic, desirable wife. "That's not the only reason why I wrote it, sweetheart, but thanks just the same."

"If that's not the reason, then why did you write it?" She was watching him with her wide golden-brown eyes, her pale hair fluffed about her shoulders, her nightgown unbuttoned to reveal the enticing curve of a pink and white breast.

"The second reason is so that the Apaches will be permitted to return to Arizona. Enough bad things have been said about them, enough lies told, enough accusations made, that I wanted to provide a more balanced view in the hope that they can return here to the reservation once they are released from Florida."

"Do you think that will really happen, No-ah? People are still so bitter. They have not forgotten nor forgiven."

"Nor accepted any responsibility for having done anything wrong themselves." Noah shoved the newspaper onto the floor. He had been lying on the bed in nothing more than his britches. Now he got up and began to pace the floor in his bare feet. "I hope it will at least improve the conditions of their imprisonment. Apaches who never broke out of the reservation are confined at Fort Marion—why, some of the scouts who worked for the U.S. Army are being detained there. And family members have been kept apart in complete disregard for the agreement that Miles made with Geronimo. From what I hear, the food is terrible, the Indians are dying like flies from disease, and those who are together are stuffed into tiny quarters that would be considered unacceptable for white prisoners."

Julia set down his black leather-bound book on the coverlet. Pushing back her hair, she sat up. "Calm yourself, No-ah. You have done all you can. No man could do more than the articles you have continued writing—and now, this book."

Noah went to her, knelt on the bed, and gripped her shoulders. "I'm going to do more yet, Julia. I've already petitioned President Cleveland to let me write Geronimo's biography, which means we may have to go to Florida, if that's where they keep him. The President may refuse—he's refused other writers—but I'll keep writing and pushing until conditions improve for the Apaches."

Julia threw her arms around his neck. "I will support you, No-ah!"

"Will you, sweetheart? Even though the Apaches may have had something to do with your sister's disappearance?"

Julia nodded. "Rhea is one of many whites who 'disappeared' during the Apache Wars. But I cannot hate the Apaches because of it. As you say in your book—'*Blood has been shed on both sides; neither is blameless. Arizona belonged to the Indian before it belonged to the white man. The Indian must always have a place there, even the Apache, especially the Apache.*'"

"I knew you of all people would understand."

Noah kissed his wife's forehead and held her close. He did not remind her that she had once been Shaman Woman. She still did not remember that year when they had first lived together; he had made his peace with the realization that she might never remember. This time, her transition into the present was complete. She dreamed no dreams of the ancient past, and he sometimes wondered if he might not have dreamed the whole thing himself.

Perhaps he had, but he didn't think so. And he intended to teach his own children not to be too cynical, too closed-minded, too arrogant to admit that anything was possible if a person had enough love, faith, and determination. . . . A tiny wail interrupted what might have become a delightfully intimate interlude.

"No-ah," Juliet whispered. "The baby's awake."

"He can wait a minute." Noah tightened his embrace, savoring his wife's precious presence, her love, her support . . . her very existence in his life.

"No-ah, he's hungry, and he's getting angry."

"Then he had better learn patience."

"But you do not have patience, No-ah. You are always *im*patient," she murmured from the depths of his arms. "Why, you could hardly wait to rush me into marriage . . . then to get me pregnant, and to write your book. Now you want to bring the Apaches back to Arizona before people are ready to accept them . . ."

As she continued her laundry list of his imperfections, he sighed and released her. "Good God, woman, I can't be perfect, can I? I mean I've learned a lot in the past few years, but I need something to work on for the rest of my life."

She gave him a blinding smile. "As soon as I change and feed him, I will hurry back," she promised. "And then you can work on achieving perfection in some other areas I might mention."

"Such as?"

She coyly lowered her lashes. "Well, my husband, I do so love it when you take me to heaven, but . . ."

"But what?"

She grinned impishly. "You could take me there more often and get me there a little sooner."

"What? Why, you little . . . !" Words failed Noah, and he reached for her, but she flung herself off the bed and ran laughing from the room.

Shortly thereafter, his son's wails ceased, and a cooing sound ensued—the sweetest sound Noah had ever heard. Happiness swelled in his heart. He thought he must be the happiest man alive. For a confirmed cynic, he had certainly grown sentimental. That's what love did to a man. . . . Maybe someday he would write a book about it.

Author's Note

I hope you have enjoyed this unusual mixture of history, romance, and fantasy. I confess I've never written a book like this before—nor read one either. If you ever visit Arizona and see the Land of the Standing-Up Rocks, you will find it easy to imagine that my story could actually have happened. It's a magical, mysterious place, where the impossible seems possible.

In case you are wondering about the Apaches, this is what happened to them. Many died of tuberculosis or other lung ailments during the first years of their captivity in Florida. Wherever they went, they were treated as curiosities—wild people to be gawked at, as if they were subhuman. Many of the children were removed from their parents to be "educated", though the Apache women tried to hide the smallest ones beneath their full skirts.

In 1894, the entire tribe was relocated to Fort Sill in Oklahoma, where they took up farming and ranching. As unaccustomed to the climate there as they had been in Florida, they still sickened and died. In 1904, Geronimo was exhibited at the World's Fair in St. Louis. He appeared in other exhibitions and Wild West shows, drawing huge crowds and always pressing for concessions for his people.

In 1905, a man named Stephen Melvil Barrett finally obtained President Roosevelt's permission to transcribe Geronimo's memoirs. Geronimo died of peneumonia in 1909 and was buried at Fort Sill. Not until 1913 were any of the Apaches permitted to leave the reservation. Because the U.S. Government wanted to enlarge its military installation at Fort Sill, the Apaches were encouraged to move to the Mescalero Apache Reservation in New Mexico, lands similar to what they had known in Arizona. One hundred eighty-seven Chiricahuas chose to go; the rest remained at Fort Sill, and their descendants live there today.

As a people, Geronimo's Apaches never did return to Arizona. Such is the price they paid for loving their lands and their freedom too much to give them up without a fight.